Praise for
Savage Art

"A chilling and suspenseful debut, Danielle Girard's *Savage Art* explores one of the dark places: the soft underbelly of vulnerability. But *Savage Art* isn't just about jeopardy, it's also about hope and resourcefulness and perseverance in the face of terror. Girard writes her compelling tale with the authority of a woman who knows what it takes to survive."
  —Stephen White, *New York Times* bestselling author of *Cold Case*

"*Savage Art* hits you like a shock of ice-cold water and chills you to the bone. The tension is real, the intensity almost ̲ ̲ ̲ ̲bearable at times. Danielle Girard k̲ ̲ ̲ ̲ ̲ ̲ ̲ ̲rivet your attention with the ̲ ̲ ̲ ̲ ̲ ̲ ̲ ̲ ̲ ̲ ̲p you reading all n̲i̲ ̲ ̲ ̲
  ̲ ̲ ̲ ̲ ̲ ̲ ̲ *Times*
  ̲ ̲ ̲ ̲dow Hunter*

"*S̲ ̲ ̲ ̲ ̲ ̲ ̲ ̲ppin̲g first novel that is not for ̲ ̲ ̲ ̲ ̲ ̲ or heart. Vivid characters and a very scary villain kept me reading until the end."
  —Phillip Margolin, *New York Times* bestselling author of *Wild Justice*

"A terrific read, guaranteed to keep you up late at night and make you sleep with the lights on."
  —Lisa Gardner, *New York Times* bestselling author of *The Other Daughter*

SAVAGE ART

DANIELLE GIRARD

AN ONYX BOOK

ONYX
Published by New American Library, a division of
Penguin Putnam Inc., 375 Hudson Street,
New York, New York 10014, U.S.A.
Penguin Books Ltd, 27 Wrights Lane,
London W8 5TZ, England
Penguin Books Australia Ltd, Ringwood,
Victoria, Australia
Penguin Books Canada Ltd, 10 Alcorn Avenue,
Toronto, Ontario, Canada M4V 3B2
Penguin Books (N.Z.) Ltd, 182–190 Wairau Road,
Auckland 10, New Zealand

Penguin Books Ltd, Registered Offices:
Harmondsworth, Middlesex, England

Published by Onyx, an imprint of New American Library,
a division of Penguin Putnam Inc.

First Printing, August 2000
10 9 8 7 6 5 4 3 2 1

 REGISTERED TRADEMARK—MARCA REGISTRADA

Printed in the United States of America

PUBLISHER'S NOTE
This is a work of fiction. Names, characters, places, and incidents either are
the product of the author's imagination or are used fictitiously, and any resemblance to actual persons, living or dead, business establishments, events, or
locales is entirely coincidental.

For Claire.
May life be a long, gentle adventure.

ACKNOWLEDGMENTS

For Mom and Dad, for teaching me to carve my own path. For Nicole, Tom & Steve, for sharing your talents and your friendship. And for Chris, for taking my hand and standing beside me, always.

No man is an island, and the creation of this book is no exception. Thank you to the very talented writers who sent me back to my computer when they knew something wasn't done correctly: Monica McLean, Sonia Rossney, Taylor Chase, Diana Dempsey, Joanne Barnes, Lisa Hughey, Deborah Benoit, Cathy Ensley, Janet Acampora, and Lydia Hester. Thank you to the experts who shared their knowledge with me at the drop of a hat: internist Dr. Donald Girard; forensic scientists George Schiro and Mark Goldman; and electrical expert Tom Warner. If I've excluded anyone, it's due to a weary brain and not a lack of appreciation. Any mistakes that remain mean that I didn't take good enough notes.

Finally, thank you to Helen Breitwieser for her incredible faith, her strong support and her light humor. And to Genny Ostertag, for seeing what we did and for making it into a book.

PROLOGUE

April 1999

Crouched in the closet, he waited for the sounds of her arrival. Sweat pooled beneath the black gloves, but his face and neck were cool. The red light on the bedside clock read 11:47. She was never earlier than 11:36 and never later than 12:04. She would arrive momentarily. Anticipation ran like a blade across his skin, arousing each part of his anatomy.

From his pocket, he found the patch of pink satin he had cut from the first one's panties, and rubbed it across his lips. Nearly three months had passed since that first time. Almost five years since his mother and sister, but he didn't count them with the others.

For nearly five years, he'd been content, working in the morgue. Late at night, when he was there alone, he would do a bit of dissection, practice his skills. He was always sure to work on a victim who was headed out to a closed-casket funeral or to the crematorium so no one would wonder about his handiwork. It had been a satisfying experience.

And then the idiot manager had caught him with one of the cadavers, a young woman, and had fired him. He'd felt himself explode at that moment, the trigger firing. He'd gotten into his car and driven it so fast, he'd gone right off the road. It had been a momentary release, to be free and flying.

The doctors had told him that he was fortunate to be alive, but he knew it was more than that. He was chosen. Once he had healed, with a new face thanks to the accident, he'd found himself hunting for another patient.

That was three months ago. He could still see the first one's body writhing for him, with him, against him. The satin caressed his neck, then his chest. He felt himself grow harder at the thought of her.

Lucy, she had called herself. Lucy was a whore just like his mother. "Lucy," he whispered, pressing the cloth against himself.

He smelled the satin, the scent of his own sweat and her blood and tears. The small triangle was the only thing he had allowed himself to keep. Soon, he would need to be rid of it, too. He gathered himself and returned the satin to his pocket.

He let his body cool, using his mind to control its fierce desire, concentrating on his next work. For the one he'd just finished, he had fixated on the face, the center of pain. She had been a model. The face had seemed appropriate for her.

As long as he could remember, he had dreamt of pulling the body apart, of cutting the skin from the organs, of seeing the body in pieces. Originally, he had also dreamt of putting it back together.

But fixing was his sister Karen's job. *You're not good enough—not smart enough, not motivated, not clever.* He'd heard that often from their mother—the man-hating bitch. Not clever—he had shown them who was the most clever.

Being a doctor was just like being an artist, and he had shown he was a wonderful artist. It took skill, and practice. And each time, he only got better. Soon, he would make the perfect doctor. They wouldn't deny him again.

The metal tink of the key in the lock renewed his arousal. His fingers tingled with the closeness of her. FBI Agent Casey McKinley. No victim would be more enticing than she.

Cincinnati rarely captured such high-profile visitors. She had come because of him. His art had drawn her. How he had longed to share his next work with her. Now he would. McKinley would be the next piece, perhaps his first masterpiece.

The light shifted in the front hall as the rented apartment door swung open. The muscles in his stomach tightened, adrenaline rushing like hot oil in his veins. His ears alert, he waited for the sounds of voices. None came. She was alone. It couldn't be more perfect.

Rising slowly, he watched through the crack of the closet door as she staggered inside. Her shoulders slightly hunched, her step heavier than usual, he could tell she was tired. He would change that. Within moments, she would quicken with energy.

He watched her drop her bag to the floor, knowing that her gun was secured in a holster under her left arm. He would have to wait until she put it down. The gun would ruin his plans. Pressing his back to the wall of the closet, he hid himself behind the clothes. He trained his ear to the door. She might pick up the phone or turn on the TV. But eventually, she would come to bed.

Within minutes, he saw her shadow cast against the bedroom wall. The overhead light went on, and Casey took her jacket off and dropped it on a chair. He was so close. He held himself from leaning forward to watch her. It was too risky. Any movement at all was too risky. He needed to catch her completely by surprise.

Still wearing her gun, Casey passed the closet and went into the bathroom. With slow even breaths, he made no sound. He could hear the water running as he imagined what she was doing. Washing her face, trying to rinse the dirt of a serial killer from under her nails? He was anxious to see her expression when she found out the serial killer she had been out chasing was here, in her own closet. The thought held him silent. He could wait.

It didn't take long. Casey came out of the bathroom. She wore an FBI T-shirt and plaid boxer shorts. Her thin, muscular legs strode across the room. Perhaps he would start with her legs. She was a good runner, strong and fast. He'd watched her many times. Setting her gun on the bedside table, she reached over and started to turn the light off. Halting, she turned toward where he was crouched.

His heart pounded as she approached him without her gun. The gun still sat on the bedside table. Her hands were bunched in fists. She liked to box in her spare time. He had seen her a few times in the local gym. She was quite good. She opened and closed her fists as he had seen her do when she was thinking. No, not her legs. He would have to sculpt her hands.

Within a foot of him, Casey stopped and turned back as though she was looking for something. He felt himself tighten as she moved toward the gun. He couldn't risk letting her reach it. Without pausing, he attacked, pushing through the pant suits hanging in her closet and knocking the door open. With a swift arc, he landed the cattle prod on her shoulder.

She screamed, but the shock dropped her easily, giving him a chance to gag her. He took the first handkerchief and balled it, stuffing it in her mouth.

Her fight returning, she landed an elbow to his midriff.

He had prepared for that. His muscles were tight and strong. He took her hand and twisted it back, pushing her to the floor. She tried to look up at him, but he held her face to the ground. Never let them see your face. It made them too powerful. He drew the needle from the holster on his leg and jammed it into her arm.

She fought against him, but he held her down. Within minutes, she would be silent, complacent. It would give him time to prepare his work. He wouldn't let her go unconscious.

"Hello, Mac," he said as her fight started to weaken. He drew a blindfold from his pocket and tied it across her eyes.

She tried to make a noise but couldn't.

He would give the drug another minute and then he would remove the gag.

Pulling her to her feet, he pushed her toward the chair.

With a quick turn, she swung her leg, connecting with a hard blow to his chin. She reached for the blindfold, but he caught her arm and hit her hard with the cattle prod until he almost felt the burning flesh.

She tried to scream as she fell over, collapsing from the shock. From his medical studies, he knew that the stun gun drove the muscles to work at a pace that outstripped the metabolism, forcing the body to convert sugars to lactic acid and making the muscles nonfunctional. Basically, it caused a transient yet polarizing acidosis. It had worked perfectly.

Rubbing his face, he could feel the tenderness in his jaw. Her kick would leave a mark, he knew.

At the small desk chair, he pushed her down. He drew a roll of duct tape from his pocket and taped her body against the chair, leaving her arms free. Next, he taped each wrist to an arm of the chair.

As he finished, she started to talk again. Pulling down the handkerchief he had made into a gag, he leaned down and whispered in her ear. "I'll let you talk, Agent McKinley, but only if you behave."

"The Cincinnati Butcher."

He cackled. "I'm disappointed in you, Mac. I thought we understood each other. This isn't butchering—this is art."

"Art?" she scoffed, trying to sound strong and brave. But he could hear the vibration of fear in her voice. "You're a basic killer—abused as a child. There's nothing special about you," she added, her voice steadier.

He tightened his jaw, forcing himself to control his anger. She wanted him to react. He was in control here, not her. "Oh, but there is. I'm going to show you how special. The great masters didn't do the kind of work I do. Leonardo da Vinci wasn't as good."

"You're going to compare yourself to da Vinci? And here I hoped you might be one of the brighter ones. But it sounds like you're just crazy."

He tensed his jaw. "I am not crazy."

"Your mother told you that, didn't she? Called you crazy? And stupid, too, I bet. That wasn't very nice of her, was it? Did you become a killer to get back at your mother, Mr. Butcher? That would certainly make sense. Sometimes even parents do hurtful things.

I'd like to hear what she did. I'd like to know how she hurt you."

She took a breath, her spine straightening, and he knew she was stalling. It was all a bluff. She knew nothing about him.

"I'm guessing your father wasn't around much," she continued when he still didn't answer. "He left when you were little, didn't he? Did your mother blame you? Let me guess, you've never had a normal relationship with a woman, have you? Women scare you a little, don't they? Your mother certainly did. She was tough, wasn't she? You thought she didn't love you. So, now you can't relate to anyone, am I right? Pretty much a loner?"

He shook his head, fighting to keep her words from penetrating. "No," he whispered to himself, his hands pressed against his ears. She was trying to fuck with him, just like they were always trying to fuck with him. He wasn't listening.

"Did you light fires to get back at her? How many things did you light on fire? Lots of things? Did you ever burn down anything big?"

He felt his arms shake against his head. "No," he said, more strongly. Keep the words out. "No fire."

"How about animals? How many animals did you kill? Did you chop them up, too? Did you wet your bed, Mr. Butcher?"

"I told you, I am not a butcher," he spat.

"Right, you're da Vinci," she said, her voice skeptical. He noticed her response came more slowly, and he could sense the drug taking control. "Did you wet your bed, Mr. da Vinci?"

"You've said enough. Shut up." He moved the point of his knife to her neck.

Her jaw shook, and he saw her fear in the motion

of her lip. The pendulum of his emotion swung from anger to anticipation as he roped in his control, pulling the brimming fury back inside. He would have plenty of time to be angry later, but he couldn't let it affect his work.

"Oh, Mac, it isn't about killing. It's so much more. But, let's not argue. I'm going to show you."

He watched the panic in her brow and lips as she fought against the constraints. Smiling to himself, he opened his bag and pulled out surgical gloves. With his black gloves off, he put on the surgical gloves and drew his scalpel.

He ran his fingers across the warmth of her skin.

She shivered and squirmed, but there was nowhere to go.

"Did you know the tendons in your hands are like a musical instrument?" He drew the scalpel across the back of her right hand, splitting the skin.

She screamed, and he grabbed her shoulder hard. "I would prefer not to be violent with you, Mac. I'd like to do this with finesse. It's art—not violence. But if you make another sound, I'm going to have to put the gag back and be rough," he warned.

Tears soaked the blindfold as sobs choked her. Still, she remained silent.

He watched for a moment before continuing. Removing the thin skin layer from her hand, he ran his gloved fingers across the structure that lay beneath. "I really wish I could let you see this, Mac. It's quite fascinating."

Casey didn't move.

"Did you know that as the tendons pass under the transverse carpal ligament, they are enclosed in two specialized synovial sacs?" he continued. "The larger of the two holds the tendons for the Flexores digitorum sublimis and profundus—it's called the ulnar bursa. Those are your flexor tendons—the ones that allow you to extend your fingers out, say to shoot a gun perhaps."

Finding the outer edge of the ulnar bursa, he held it between his fingers then slipped his scalpel beneath it. The sound of her screaming in pain was heaven to him.

CHAPTER ONE

March 2000

Inspector Jordan Gray reached for the ringing phone, careful not to wake his wife. Shaking himself awake, he sat up in bed.

"Gray," he mumbled into the receiver. He glanced over at his wife's empty side of the bed and ran a hand over his unshaven face.

Every time he woke up, he expected her to be lying there next to him like nothing had happened. But something had happened. A lot of somethings. She'd left two weeks ago—taken Will and Ryan and gone back to L.A. "Home" she called it. She had even enrolled the boys in school there for the rest of the year. Shit.

"You there, Gray?" repeated the patrol officer.

"I'm here."

"We got another one—a puppet."

Jordan swallowed hard and shook his head, fighting to retain his objectivity. "Caucasian female?"

"This one's black."

Jordan raised an eyebrow. It didn't sound like the same killer. "Age?"

"Same as the white girl—maybe ten or eleven."

"Can you identify her?"

"No, sir. You'd better come down."

Blood flowing hot and angry like lava, Jordan took down the address. "Don't let anyone touch her until I get there."

He dropped the receiver and flipped the bedside light on, staring past the empty side of the bed as he reached for his pants. "When it rains, it fucking pours," he mumbled.

He was out the door in four minutes.

As he pulled his '93 Explorer down Fifty-second and onto 580 toward San Francisco, he glanced at his cellular phone. It was three a.m. His sons, Will and Ryan, were in L.A. They were safe. Still, Jordan couldn't stop his fingers from dialing to make sure.

"Hello," came his mother-in-law's voice, like a snappy crow.

Jordan cringed and started to hang up when he heard Angela on another extension.

"It's Jordan, baby."

His mother-in-law quipped something he didn't hear and dropped the receiver. Bitch.

"You know what time it is?" Angela said, her voice filled with the sleepy tone Jordan loved.

"I know. I'm sorry. I had to check. The boys okay?"

"They're fine. They're asleep, Jordan. We're *all* asleep."

"I know." Why had he called? Because he needed to hear that his sons were okay. Was there something so wrong with that? "You okay?"

She stifled a yawn. "Fine. Are you in the car?"

"Yeah."

She sighed, and Jordan knew she was thinking she'd

been right about him and his job. Damn. What could he do about it?

"You okay?"

He pictured Angela lying in bed. Man, she was beautiful. "I'd be better if you were here."

Angela sighed. "We've been through this, Jordan. I can't live like that. You're crazy all the time. And what's worse is you don't talk to me about it, we don't share things anymore."

Jordan nodded. "I know. Listen, can you guys come up for the weekend? I can get off, and we can go see the Warriors."

"You hate the Warriors."

"But you like 'em."

He could hear her smile through the phone. "You can come down," she said. "Why don't you call later?"

"Okay," he said. "I love you, Angie."

"I know you do. Be careful out there, Jordan."

He heard the click of the phone on her end and set the cell phone on the seat. What the hell was he doing chasing down psychopaths when his marriage was failing and his sons were 500 miles away? To make things worse, his partner was on medical leave, and he hadn't been assigned a new one. So he was working the case alone. His life was shit.

He stopped at the curb of the crime scene in San Francisco's Mission District. The mouth of the alley was littered with cans and bottles and the remainder of some homeless person's cardboard box home. Jordan didn't move. Instead, he scanned the area for stragglers. The body would wait. No one would touch it. The girl was beyond saving. But if the perp were here, he wouldn't stay long. There were too many people looking around to risk staying and being spotted.

"The sickos love to watch the excitement they've created," a seasoned inspector had told him years before. "Look for them at the scene, at the site of the body dump, the fire, the robbery, whatever. Look in the crevices and cracks, in the crowds of bystanders watching. That's where they'll be. And that's the best place to catch them. Because they can't stay away."

At three in the morning, though, this particular scene would be an easy place to spot an outsider. Other than the two local news vans, four cop cars, and an ambulance, the street was deserted.

From the head of the alley, Jordan could tell where the girl's body had been left. The buzz of police surrounded her as dense as vultures around a kill. Thick yellow crime-scene tape blocked off the area, but the reporters constantly pushed forward to test the borders like dogs edging along an invisible fence. Three officers held them at bay. As he passed, the reporters pushed after him.

"Keep 'em back," Jordan commanded as he moved past the shouting voices. But this crowd was nothing in comparison to the numbers that would show up when the story really got out.

Even after fifteen years on the force, Jordan had never once spoken to the press.

Years ago he thought eventually they would realize he wouldn't comment, but they still sidled up to him, throwing questions like darts at the bull's eye. He had become so proficient at ignoring the clamoring voices, he often missed his own men calling him in the process.

As he approached, the officers moved aside and the girl came into view. In size and stature, the victim could easily have been his own son were it a boy. She even had the same smooth black skin and hazel eyes. Her naked body had been propped against a rusting chain-link fence that lined the back of the alley, an old sheet thrown across her middle. The area beneath the body had been swept clean of trash, broken bottles, and debris that was scattered about the rest of the alley.

Like the last girl's, her arms had been tied with fishing line and attached to different levels of the chain-link fence behind her. With her arms suspended in the air, she looked like a life-size puppet. The fishing line cut into the skin, but it could hold a hundred-pound fish so it worked fine on a little girl's arms.

A piece of duct tape attached her forehead to the fence to keep her head from falling to her chest. Her hands hung limp at her wrists. Her right arm was high as though she was waving good-bye, her left hung low and flat against her chest.

Though not identical, the last girl's position had been similar enough to be recognizable. And like the previous victim, this one wore a pointed party hat. The last hat had been orange; this one was yellow. Maybe there was a pattern here—the rainbow or something. But then the killer wouldn't have skipped red.

The last girl had bled to death. The thought made Jordan sick, and he tightened his gut and forced himself forward. From the look of this victim, he would guess the same. Thankfully, though, it wasn't his job to guess. The medical examiner would deal with cause of death.

The girl's cheeks had been bound with heavy white gauze, the tie hidden beneath her hat. Her cheeks were puffy and swollen, and Jordan could only imagine what torture the child had endured. The best Jordan could hope was that the girl had been dead at the time. But from the bruising that had begun to develop under her eyes, Jordan suspected that the injuries had not been postmortem. There was nothing he could do about the terrifying manner in which this child had died. But he could certainly stop the killer from doing it again to someone else.

The prior victim's injuries had been similar, but her face hadn't been the recipient of the damage. Instead, her killer had dissected her feet, the defense wounds on her arms suggesting that she had been alive throughout the process. The ballerina slippers she was wearing had been hung limply around her neck. Jordan clenched his jaw.

His mind created the image of a half-man, half-monster evil enough to engage in this sort of brutality, especially to children. Jordan forced the image away. He knew how dangerous it was to use that sort of reasoning in imagining the killer. More than likely, the killer would be someone who looked more trustworthy than himself. And someone who was likely more clever. Creating disillusions about what the killer should be like would only make it more difficult to find him.

For now, Jordan had work to do. His job on a crime scene was to make sure the evidence was preserved, collected, and documented, and that nothing was overlooked. He glanced up at the graying sky. He would be here four hours, at least. He only hoped it didn't start to rain. He looked back at the girl. Rain or no rain, they were going to catch this son of a bitch.

He took another look at the body and shook his head. It was the same futile gesture he'd seen every cop make when they saw something so revolting. As a new cop, Jordan would have been sick to his stomach, looked away, and then ranted and raved about the perverted fuckers that shared this earth. He remembered reacting that exact way.

But he'd learned that it wouldn't do any good. Nothing would until he had the killer in custody. Then the courts took over. And even then, sometimes it wouldn't do any good. It was suspected anywhere from three hundred and fifty to thousands of serial killers were at large in the United States alone. That didn't even begin to account for those who only killed once and weren't considered serial murderers. At times like this, he wondered if it was worth the sacrifice to even fight the battle.

Two ambulance attendants waited to be dismissed, and Jordan waved them off. They weren't going to be any help.

"Medical examiner's office has been called," Leroy Thomas, one of the newer patrol officers, reported, his back to the girl.

Jordan nodded. "Anyone touch the scene?"

Thomas shook his head. "A woman from the ninth floor called it in. Said she saw 'another drunk kid' in the alley. Said he looked a little young, and she thought he'd freeze to death out here with no clothes on. So she called us. Guess she couldn't tell it was a girl from up there."

Jordan removed a notebook from his coat pocket and patted his pockets for a pen. "Shit."

Leroy handed him one.

Jordan looked up to the ninth floor. "What's the woman's name?"

"Louisa James. Lives here with her daughter."

Jordan wrote. "Has anyone spoken to her?"

"Just on the call. I came to check it out. When I saw the body, I called you."

"Good." Jordan looked up at the surrounding buildings, taking careful count of the potential witnesses. Four buildings had views of the alley—one on each side, one behind and one across the street.

He glanced at his watch and pointed. "Starting at seven a.m., I want guys out to each of these buildings. Talk to everyone you can. If anyone saw so much as a fly, I want to know about it. As for Ms."—he glanced back down to his pad—"James, I'll speak to her myself."

Thomas gave a quick nod and disappeared.

The crime scene team arrived like a small parade, marching in line through the alley in their white lab coats. They carried packs of supplies, vials and bags, cameras, a small vacuum cleaner—everything they needed to capture whatever looked like evidence. Their expressions were varying shades of grim as they surveyed the crime scene. Outside crimes were tougher—the actual scene harder to define than inside a living room or a bar.

Here, dispersed among the trash, might be the one clue that allowed the police to pinpoint the killer. And that same clue may have been swept away by a simple breeze, or carried off by a small animal or even a bum looking for food hours before. Thankfully, it hadn't rained—yet. With the heavy rains of this season, the scene's preservation could have been nil. Jordan should have felt lucky, but nothing about the situation felt lucky.

"Interesting setup," Al Ting, head of the crime scene team, announced as he bent down and pulled a pair of rubber gloves from a box.

Jordan nodded, knowing Ting meant familiar. And familiar in crime scenes was not often coincidence.

As always, Al Ting wore a starched white shirt, buttoned to the collar, and a pair of pressed khakis.

Raised in San Francisco's Chinatown by a couple who ran a local grocery store, Al was meticulous from head to toe. As a young kid, his chore had been to clean his parents' store, and Jordan imagined Ting must have taken the job very seriously. Thin, round, gold wire-frame glasses sat flat to his cheeks.

Each of his lab coats was monogrammed with his initials. It was rumored he did this to prevent the other technicians from picking up his coats. But even without the monogram, it would be easy to tell if they had. Somehow Ting was the only one on the team consistently able to get the bloodstains from messy crime scenes out of his clothes. He always joked that as a Chinaman, it was his heritage to know a good cleaner.

Al had been head of the crime scene investigations group for as long as Jordan had been on the force. While Al didn't seem to have aged a day, the fifteen years made Jordan feel at least thirty years older. Al's meticulous nature and sharp eye made him an invaluable asset. And Jordan was counting on him now more than ever.

Al looked up and started directing. "Let's take it in a grid formation—divide it in sixths, everyone does two and then we rotate. I want each quadrant looked over twice."

Jordan interrupted. "Also, I think we may have a partial print to the right of the body along the fence." He pointed to a small patch of mud and the corner of what looked like a tennis shoe track. "Can we get someone to cast that before we step on it?"

Al nodded to one of the technicians. "Deborah, can you handle that one, please."

The woman nodded and headed back to the van.

Another technician moved around the body, a heavy camera covering his face as he recorded the body's resting spot. Al followed close behind, confirming which shots should be captured.

Normally, it was the supervising inspector's role to direct the evidence technicians and the forensic photographer. But Ting was the best, and Jordan watched him work in silence, adding only a rare request for something Al failed to notice.

"M.E.'s on his way," Jordan said when the photographer was done, knowing there would be nothing else to do until the medical examiner moved the body. Jordan was praying this crime was a copycat, but he wouldn't know until the evidence was documented and analyzed. Still, he sensed the girl's leg would tell him. The party hat and bandaged head could be the work of a copycat, but only the killer would know his signature.

Just then, Jordan saw Ray Zambotti, the medical examiner, pushing through the crowd. Ray was a short, heavyset man with skin so pale it was almost blue like skim milk. He had been given the nickname "Skim" for this reason.

Ray shook his head, the bluish-purple circles beneath his eyes more enlarged than normal.

"Sorry for the late call."

"The dead never sleep," Zambotti said, laughing at his own joke.

"Right."

Impatient, Jordan crossed his arms and waited as Ray strutted around the body, waving his arms. "Bled to death. Look how pale she is. Paler than regular dead. Just like the other one.''

"We're not making any assumptions," Jordan said. He didn't want anyone getting the idea that they could or couldn't link the murders until he had evidence. Despite the bodies, that was. Damn if this wasn't getting frustrating.

"We can assume there are some sick fucks, can't we?" Ray said, wearing a full grin.

"Sure."

They returned their attention to the body.

"She was moved, too," Ray continued. He stood and moved closer to Jordan and added in a hushed whisper, "Just like the other."

Jordan nodded.

"Hard to say how long she's been dead. Rigor is slowed with the temperature. But, I'd guess less than twelve hours. Smell's still fine."

That meant she had been killed in the middle of the afternoon. If that was the case, the killer had moved the dead body—just like Ray said. There was no way a little girl had been sitting dead in an alley all afternoon and evening without being noticed. "I'm going to need something more specific."

Ray put his hands on his hips. "Of course. I'll work with the entomologist and see what the bugs say."

Jordan pictured the tiny creatures that were already feasting on the girl's tissues.

With gloved hands, Ray lifted the girl's eyelids wider and studied the eyes. Bringing a mini tape recorder to his lips, he spoke into it. "You've got petechial hemorrhage in the conjunctiva," he said, pointing to the inner eyelids. "Also I can see slight traces of petechiae in the cheeks, confirming strangulation during the process. However, coloring suggests blood loss as means of death."

He turned the recorder off and pointed to the white gauze wrapped around the girl's head. "And the bandages—looks like more surgical work. Boy, you got a wacko here, Gray."

"Thanks for the input, Doc. I want the body moved so we can do a thorough search of the area, but let's check the thigh first."

"Yeah, yeah, yeah. Whatever happened to 'patience is a virtue'?"

Jordan sighed. "It's late, Ray."

"Technically, Gray, it's early."

Jordan exhaled.

Ray laughed, leaning back with his face to the sky. "The thing I love most about working with the dead is they don't always rush you—rush, rush, rush."

Ray's assistant squatted beside the body. His sleeves were rolled up, exposing thick, blond curls and strong arms.

Jordan figured Ray had hired someone strong enough to move the bodies. With his gut, Ray could hardly lift a leg.

"Ready?" the assistant interrupted, though his tone wasn't at all impatient.

Ray raised his hands like he was about to conduct an orchestra. "Ready," he replied. "Let the fun begin."

Jordan shook his head, wondering if one day Ray Zambotti wouldn't end up on one of his suspect lists. As long as the city kept providing the bodies, maybe not. But he sure seemed to have a penchant for what the killers left behind.

"Here we go."

Jordan leaned forward, resting his hands on his knees and holding his breath.

Ray started to pull the sheet off the girl's leg, while others around him carefully swept for evidence around his every move. The thin leg was the same size as Will's. The sight reminded Jordan of teaching his son to slide into home plate. Will had slid so hard, he'd come home with bruises all up and down his left side. His little leg black-and-blue, just like this girl's.

Clenching his teeth, Jordan swore to catch this monster if it killed him. And when it was over, he was going to take a long look and try to figure out what the hell he was doing with his life.

Ray turned the body into the light, a thin gasp escaping from his lips as he did.

Jordan shined his flashlight and cringed at the sight. The same as the other's, the mark looked like an uppercase *L* with touching lowercase *O*s on either side of the *L*. Cut with something sharp like a small scalpel, the mark still oozed blood. Pre-mortem, just like the others.

Zambotti pulled a tape measure from his pocket and pulled one end out against the skin. "The middle mark is one and one-eighth inches; each of these ovals on the sides an eighth of an inch high, a quarter inch wide," Zambotti measured out loud. "I'll check for consistency with the last ones to try again for the type of blade." His gaze met Jordan's. "Looks like the same thing, though—some sort of signature."

Jordan raised his head and looked away. "Damn."

CHAPTER TWO

Without lifting her head from the pillow, Casey Mc-
Kinley snapped up the ringing phone after the machine had picked up twice. "What?" she groaned.

"It's Billy," came the soft male voice that had been
her only contact to the outside world for the six
months since her husband and daughter returned to
Virginia.

Propping herself on her elbows, she pushed her
overgrown bangs off her forehead and looked around
the dark room, blinking. "Where are you?"

Billy sighed heavily, and Casey could picture his
hand nailed dramatically to one hip. "I'm outside."

"Well, why the hell don't you use your key?"

"You didn't answer the door. I didn't know if you
were dead or something." He paused and tapped on
the phone. "I didn't want to walk in on a dead body."

"So you called?"

"Well," he snipped back. "It seemed like a better
idea than just barging in."

"Hardly. Let yourself in, already," she said, hanging
up on him and rolling over in the bed. It was nearly
eleven a.m., and she'd been in bed at least twelve
hours. Still, Casey was sure that without Billy's visit,

she'd have spent all day in bed. Since her release from
the hospital, nearly a year ago, zombie had been her
role of choice. Hiding under the covers had been her
favored pastime. Michael and Amy had fought with
her for nearly five months to get off her duff and start
living again. She'd refused until she had driven them
away. After they left, the job became Billy's.

She looked down at her hands, as though by some
miracle she might have regained the use of them during the night. Instead, her fists stared motionless back
at her.

Using the forefinger on her left hand, Casey pulled
open the drawer in the bedside table and lifted out
the picture of her daughter. The image was several
years old—Amy holding a soccer ball, posing for a
photo at the end of the season.

The picture's edges were tattered and bent. Casey
ran a finger over her daughter's face and then closed
her eyes, holding the picture to her. What was Amy
doing now? What did she look like? Casey heard the
front door unlock and returned the photo to the
drawer, the ache of guilt sharp in her chest as she
rolled herself into a tight ball.

She stared at her lifeless hands. In his savage beat-
ing, the killer she called Leonardo had broken nearly
every bone in her right hand and almost as many in
her left. Over twenty in all. He had also severed a
half-dozen tendons and ligaments in her right knee,
plus he'd cut into her thigh. She had spent six full
days in and out of surgery. And still she couldn't write
with her right hand or drive. She was lucky she could
feel her hands at all, the doctors had told her. Lucky
was the last thing she felt.

She struggled to move the fingers on her right hand.
They formed a loose fist as she fought to clench them

into a ball. Her hand refused to close. Frustrated, she kicked and flailed at the bedsheets and then collapsed.

"Hello!" Billy called, his voice growing closer.

"I'm not getting up," Casey yelled.

Billy stopped in the doorway and shook his head. "Oh, so you tell me to let myself in for nothing. Geesh, you can be such a bitch."

She glanced over, and he caught her eye.

He clicked his tongue to shame her and shook his head again. He wore black jeans, a black turtleneck, and cowboy boots. But today, his short dark hair had been carefully gelled to the side, exposing his bright blue eyes, full of mischief.

Casey pulled herself up onto her elbows, ignoring the difficulty of moving around with useless hands. "You have a date!" she accused.

Without responding, Billy moved past the bed and pulled the shades open. "It's like a cave in here. You need light, woman."

Casey moaned at the bright light as Billy opened the window. Billy's hair had caught her attention, and the undesirable stream of sunlight became less important. "Who's the lucky guy?"

He ignored her, picking up the discarded clothing and throwing it over his arm as her mother had always done when she was avoiding an issue. "Have you eaten?"

"Not hungry. Tell me about him."

"You've got five minutes to get dressed and meet me in the kitchen. I'll start coffee." Billy set the clothes over a chair and then started out the door. "I'll tell you about him while you're eating breakfast."

Casey smiled, victorious. "Deal." With the door closed, she sat up and pulled her pajama bottoms off. Finding her jeans, she dropped them to the floor and

pushed her feet into the legs. Her hands in fists, she
worked the jeans up around her knees, using her fists
to move the fabric up over her legs. With the jeans
around her knees, she lay on her back to let them
shake down around her hips.

Halfway, her teeth clenched, she paused for a
breath. Then, with a deep groan, she continued. It was
getting easier, but the feeling of helplessness had once
come close to drowning her.

Using the pinky of her left hand, she grabbed a belt
loop and pulled the left side of the jeans over her hip.
The jeans had fit her at one time, but they were much
looser now.

Reaching around, she grabbed the belt loop on the
other side and heaved it over her other hip. Using a
hook and line her husband had made for her right
after she'd come home from the hospital, Casey
looped the hook through the zipper's hole and tugged
the line up with her pinky. Now, just the button remained. Casey sank down on the bed, wishing she had
her sweatpants. Michael had bought her sweat suits in
four colors to make dressing eaiser.

But Billy had taken them away, saying they were
too close to pajamas and made her lazy. He had also
told her that she looked like shit in them. It hadn't
been their smoothest day together. But all her husband's love and affection had failed to have even a
fraction of the impact Billy did.

Casey glared at the button hole, remembering the
first time she'd fastened one after the attack. Concentrating, she set to maneuvering the button through the
hole with the knuckle of her index finger.

"What's taking so long?" Billy called from the
other room.

Casey snarled at the door. "If it takes too long, bring back my sweats."

"No chance," he snapped back.

Another minute passed and she heard two quick knocks. "Your eggs are ready." The click of Billy unlatching the door was followed by the sound of him padding back to the kitchen.

Casey smiled at the gesture. On one of Billy's first days, right after her husband and daughter had moved back to Virginia, the door had been latched and Casey had been unable to open it. Sobbing, she'd waited nearly an hour before Billy had come to check on her. "What the fuck is wrong with you? Couldn't you hear me?" she'd shouted.

He'd shaken his head slowly.

In response, she had shoved her crippled fists in his face. "I can't open a goddamn door, I can't tie a shoe, or cut a tomato, or brush my teeth, or fasten a belt, or shoot a gun. I can't do anything."

Billy had been quiet the rest of that day. But afterward he'd never let the door remain latched for long. He also never expressed an ounce of pity for her. Perhaps that was the reason he had been able to motivate her as her husband had been unable to do. She had driven her husband away, unable to cope with his pity.

Looking down at her fists now, Casey opened and closed them in the same slow methodical way Billy had worked with her to do. The left one was better. While she still had trouble controlling the individual fingers, she could spread her palm almost wide enough to hold a large grapefruit. But the right one was still stiff and worthless. Her shooting hand. He'd been sure to destroy that one completely.

"Stop your self-pity," he said.

She turned to see Billy standing in the doorway. "Lay off," she snapped.

"Don't give me that bitchy tone. Get in here and eat these eggs."

Casey shot him a dirty look and pushed past him toward the kitchen. As always, Billy kept it immaculate. Like the rest of her house, the kitchen was sparsely decorated in light pines and whites. Sterile was how some would describe it. No pictures, diplomas, or awards hung on the walls of the living room or den. When Billy had started, she'd had no wall hangings at all. But slowly he had convinced her to buy a couple of Ansel Adams prints. Even those kept the tone of the place cold in their black and white.

She sat hard in the pine chair and stared at her eggs, then raised an eyebrow. "Cheese?"

"Just a little," Billy replied sharply.

She smiled broadly and stood up. Crossing the kitchen to where Billy stood, she planted a kiss on his cheek.

Billy rolled his eyes. "Don't think that's going to get you more cheese next time."

Casey smiled and sat back down. Fastidious about what went in his body, Billy thought cheese was like hardened orange gelato. And cheese was the least of it. One of the first things he had done was to empty the house of alcohol, sweets, and most of the cigarettes.

At least Casey had a small stash of cigs hidden away to steal a smoke when Billy wasn't around. But Billy could always tell when she'd been smoking them. He had also refused to buy anything other than skim milk. Now that she was shopping with him, they compromised on 1 percent.

Coffee had been Billy's next intended victim, but she'd threatened to fire him. They had fought on and off for a few days, but in the end she had won. Though he had successfully weeded most of the vices from her life, Casey knew he had accepted that coffee was one he would be powerless to stop.

She drank her coffee slowly now, knowing Billy would make only one cup. Leaning forward on the table, she said, "Tell me about this man."

Billy stared into his cup, swirling his spoon in the ginseng tea.

"You promised," she reminded him.

He nodded. "I met him at the hospital. He was visiting a friend with AIDS when I was visiting Mrs. Levinski. She fell in the shower and broke her hip."

Casey smiled. "Go on."

"That's it. That's how we met. His name's Kevin. He's incredible. He reads palms—it's so sexy."

"That's his job?"

Billy shook his head. "That's his art. For work, he's a tax accountant."

"An accountant who reads palms?" He sounded like a freak.

"You're so closed-minded, Casey."

"I am not." Casey wondered what his last name was. She'd have liked to have someone check him out. "You met this guy at the hospital? What do you know about him?"

Billy crossed his arms. "I know plenty."

"Have you been to his house?"

"No."

"Have you met any of his friends?"

Billy scowled. "Don't you dare turn Kevin into one of your suspects. Not everyone is a killer, for God's sake. I really like him, so pretend like you do, too. You've got your head screwed on so tight that you can't even see the good in people anymore. I'm amazed you let me come work for you. Or did you do a background check on me, too?"

Casey shook her head. She *had* done a background check on Billy—actually, she'd had the FBI do it. And no one was more thorough than the FBI. But he was right. Leonardo was always her first thought. "I'm sorry," she said. "You're right."

"I want you to meet him." Billy broke into a crooked smile. "I like him." He stared into the distance and then waved her off, ending the conversation. "Go on. Go do something. I'll finish this up, and we'll do your exercises."

In the months Billy had taken care of her, he had never mentioned dating anyone. As much as she hated the idea of sharing him, she knew it was good that he had found someone. Casey sat at the table and looked around. "Did you bring the paper?"

Billy turned and raised an eyebrow at her.

She shrugged and looked away. "Just curious."

He returned to the dishes. "I didn't think you'd like today's paper."

"Why?"

He shrugged.

"Why didn't you think I'd like it?" she asked again.

He didn't meet her gaze. "I just didn't."

"No, Billy. You had a reason. What was it?"

Billy cringed. "Some crazy guy killed another kid."

"A serial killer?" she asked.

He eyed her again.

"Do they think it's a serial killer?" she pressed.

He gave a curt nod and turned his back, flipping on the radio to end her questions. He tuned to his favorite jazz station and hummed along.

Casey paged through the *GQ* Billy had brought, using her knuckles to turn the pages. Since she'd left the Bureau, Casey hadn't been interested in the outside world. While Amy and Michael had been living there, they'd tried to entice her with the evening news or the paper.

But everything about it reminded her of what she'd had—and what she'd lost. She pushed Amy from her mind. Having her daughter grow up without her was one thing she forbade herself to think about. She could handle memories of that night, Leonardo's voice, even the pain, but she couldn't think about the way she had pushed Amy and Michael from her life.

Billy's methods of drawing Casey back into reality had been much more successful. Though she knew they were ploys, she had to respect his ingenuity. At first, he brought the paper and kept it sticking out of his bag. Every few days, he'd watch the news while he folded laundry. But he only did it when Casey wasn't in the room. If she came in, he turned it off. Not abruptly as though it were forbidden, but always with some comment about the "crazies," or "stupid show," or "don't we have problems enough."

When he was on the phone, she would catch snippets of news from his conversations or from the radio while he cooked. Eventually, she lost interest in the novels she'd been devouring, growing hungry for real news.

Now she couldn't help but wonder what this local killer was doing. For years, she'd been enthralled with multiple serial offenders, studied them. It had been her life. The attack had killed that. But recently she felt the tentacles of her old life begin to puncture her fear and wrap around her again.

Billy leaned against the sink and dried his hands.

"Tell me about it," she said.

He glanced down at the magazine and furrowed his brow. "What?"

"This crazy fuck killing kids."

He shook his head, waving her off.

She pulled a piece of paper from a notepad on the counter. "I'm serious."

His eyes widened.

"Tell me, damn it," she snapped, smacking her pen on the table. She gripped it in her left hand, the way she had practiced, and poised to write.

Billy pulled a chair back and sat, crossing his foot over one knee. For more than a month, he had been trying to get her to tell him about her work for the Bureau. But she hadn't wanted to. It hadn't interested her. Suddenly, now, it was starting to.

"What do you want to know?"

"Start with the criminal act—everything you can remember."

"The criminal act?"

"Seven steps to profiling," she explained, shoving aside her own excited reaction at having an opportunity to explain what she had done as a profiler. She had loved it. "First step is evaluation of the criminal act—he killed children—how? What weapon did he use? That sort of thing."

"Okay, let's see."

She looked at the paper. "But not too fast. This left-hand shit is a royal pain in the ass."

"Nicely put."

"I was putting it politely. Do you want to hear the bad version?"

"That's not necessary." He crossed his hands in his lap and nodded. "Okay, let's see. He's killed two kids so far."

"Male or female?"

"Two girls."

"Race?"

"One was white, one was black."

Casey wrote as quickly as she could move the pen. "Doesn't sound like the same guy."

Billy looked down at her notepad. "Why not?"

"Not usual to have different races, especially not in child killings." She rolled her hand. "Keep going."

"Well, maybe the papers are wrong."

"How old were they?"

"The kids?"

She glared.

"Oh, let me think. About the same age, I guess. Ten or eleven."

"And the abduction?"

Billy nodded, remembering something. "Both from shopping areas."

"Malls, grocery stores, what?" she asked, feeling herself fall into the rhythm of a witness interrogation. She watched his body language, read his crossed leg, and remembered how a person's body language often told more than his words.

Billy glanced at the ceiling. "The first girl was in the Galleria Shopping Center on Sutter, I think. The second was taken from near Union Square."

"Where were the kids from?"

He furrowed his brow. "One was a tourist, I think—visiting from someplace like Michigan or Wisconsin—somewhere in the middle. I'm pretty sure the other grew up in the East Bay."

Casey continued writing. "How were they killed?"

Billy scrunched his nose. "Bled to death."

"Same M.O."

"What's an M.O.?"

"Don't you watch TV?"

Billy's eyes widened. "Not with violence."

"M.O. is modus operandi—how they kill. It tells you a lot about the killer's purpose. For instance, shooting someone is less common in sex crimes because it's not intimate. Drowning is very personal, especially if you have to hold them under versus throwing them off a boat with bricks tied to their feet. That's more execution-style. Regular drowning tends to be the result of personalized rage. Bleeding to death could be from stabbing wounds or gunshot wounds. It's not very specific."

Billy leaned forward, looking both enthralled and revolted. "Personalized?"

Casey nodded, smiling inside. People's response to her work had always run the spectrum from awe to fear and disgust. "Personalized means the killer's anger was directed at someone in particular, and he took his anger out on that person. Most killers attempt to depersonalize their victims by mutilating them. Allows them to avoid seeing them as people and treat them as objects instead."

"Oh, this guy did that, too."

She looked up from her notes. "Did what?"

He waved his hand. "Depersonalized them."

"Really? How?"

He raised his eyebrows and shook his head. "Some really strange stuff."

"Tell me."

"I don't remember the details. The kids were found wearing party hats."

Casey wrote down the words "party hats." "That's not depersonalizing them. The party hats are more of a signature, something the killer does to stimulate his own satisfaction that isn't necessary for the crime. Both kids had party hats?"

He nodded. "So what do you think?"

"There's not enough to go on."

"Have you ever had a case like this before?"

She thought about Leonardo and his penchant for cutting people up. His victims had bled to death as well. She shook her head, pushing the thought away. "It doesn't work that way. This type of killer doesn't work by normal motives and reason. We can't base one case on a previous one that looked or felt similar."

"How do you do it, then?"

"You start with what this killer did. I'd get the specifics on the crime scene, the victim, police reports, and the medical examiner's report, and work through them in that order. Once I'd pieced it together, I could start developing a profile."

"Can you take a guess?"

She frowned. "Not really. I'm sure I'm missing too much information, but it doesn't seem to fit. His whole thing with the hats. That's clearly organized." Just like Leonardo had been. She suppressed the thought like nausea.

"What do you mean 'organized'?"

"An organized killer plans his captures and killings very carefully. Probably brings his own tools for the kidnapping, stages the bodies," she continued, looking at the few notes she had scribbled.

"And?"

She looked up to see Billy staring at her, wide-eyed. She shrugged and shook off the strange sensation that something wasn't right. "It's weird is all. It doesn't make sense for an organized killer to risk taking a child in a crowded place. Normally those sort of abductions are committed by someone who knows the child."

"You think he could know both children?"

She shrugged, downplaying the fact that Billy had just told her one was a tourist. If that bit of information was correct, it seemed virtually impossible that he could have known both children. "I'm sure the police are looking into it."

She looked back down at her notepad, frustrated at how little information she had. She wondered what the detective on the case was doing, how he or she was attacking the evidence. Suddenly, a tiny part of her ached to be back in the game.

Studying her notes again, she puzzled. Something wasn't adding up. The sensation reminded her of the Cincinnati case. The killer's methodology had been so mixed. It had taken them nearly three weeks to confirm all four killings had been the same killer. A chill jetted across her shoulders, leaving a tiny wake of shivers. She shook them off and pushed the paper away.

Dropping the pen, she began to stretch her already cramped fingers. It was a waste of time. She wasn't an FBI agent anymore. She would never be an agent again.

"Glad it's not my case," she said, sensing it was something less than the truth.

CHAPTER THREE

"Aaron, I said stay with me," Elizabeth Weisman snapped, grabbing her son's hand and yanking him away from the Tommy's Toys window.

"But, Mom," he whined, resisting her pull.

Elizabeth spun around, Emily propped on one hip. "Aaron." She gave him a hard stare, hoping he wouldn't put up a fuss. Emily started to whimper and Elizabeth bounced on her toes as she turned and started to walk away. "Enough, Aaron. We have to go."

"Mom, I just want to look. Mom, *pleeeaaase*."

Elizabeth felt her body numb in anger. Why was he doing this? She spun back to Aaron and crouched over, sticking her finger in his face. "Stop your whining. We're not shopping for toys today."

Aaron looked back at the toy store window, ignoring her.

She grabbed his arm and shook him. "We need to get a present for Daddy's secretary. That's it. Then, we have to get home. Emily needs to be fed, and Mommy needs to start dinner."

Elizabeth wondered if James was with his secretary now. He certainly hadn't made much of an effort

lately to be home before his daughter went to bed.
His secretary got more of her husband's damn attention than she did. Now Elizabeth was buying her a
present for her birthday. Ironic.

Dragging Aaron by the arm, she pushed through
the crowd toward Nordstrom. What did she get a
woman she suspected was sleeping with her husband?
She pictured her hands wrapped around the woman's
neck. That was it, she'd buy her a scarf.

Aaron pouted as she pulled him onto the escalator.
Putting her free arm around him, she gave him a hug
and pointed to the lights strung from the ceiling
high above.

Her son's eyes grew wide as he took in the bright
lights. "How do they get the lights way up there,
Mom?"

She smiled. "Maybe really tall ladders. What do
you think?"

Aaron nodded slowly. "Really, really tall ladders."

She smiled and rubbed his curly blond hair. "Or
maybe they fly."

Aaron looked back, wide-eyed and serious.

She grinned and raised her eyebrows.

He shook his head and laughed. "No, Mom. They
can't fly."

"How come?" she countered as she led him off the
escalator. Emily's head rested on her shoulder, and
Elizabeth could feel the wetness of the drool that had
soaked through her blouse. Thankfully, it wasn't silk.
She had given up silk when she'd stopped working.
Had it already been six years?

Aaron took her hand and stopped at the banister
at the top of the escalator, his grip tight in hers as he
peered over the edge. "What would happen if you
fell, Mom?"

She clenched his hand tighter. "You'd be in trouble."

He nodded slowly.

With Aaron's hand in hers, Elizabeth backed away from the banister. Before she could focus, she was knocked forward. A strong hand grabbed her arm and helped her balance. She shook her head and regained her step.

"I'm so sorry," a man's voice said.

Elizabeth looked around and found Aaron. She pulled him against her leg as she righted Emily on her hip.

"I wasn't even looking where I was going," the man continued.

Elizabeth eyed the man before her and took a step back, smoothing her blond hair and wishing she'd taken more time getting dressed today. "It's no problem, Officer."

The man's gray eyes flickered as he smiled. "Not like me to be so clumsy." He tucked his forefinger under Emily's chin. "What a doll."

Elizabeth smiled at Emily, sleeping like an angel on her shoulder. She was thankful the officer hadn't caught Emily during one of her tantrums. "Thank you." Her eyes found his badge as she settled on his name. A. Obsgarten. She pointed to the badge. "How crazy. That's my maiden name."

The man looked down at his badge. "Obsgarten, really?" He pronounced it Aub-sgarten.

She nodded. "Only we say O-bsgarten."

"Hmm." He nodded. "Well, I ought to be going. Got to get this little one back to Mom."

Taking Aaron's hand again, Elizabeth thanked him. She gathered herself and thought about the coincidence. Obsgarten was such an uncommon name; she would have liked to find out where he was from.

Only then did Elizabeth notice he held the hand of a girl about Aaron's age. Glancing back, she watched him walk away. The girl looked over her shoulder. "Wave good-bye, Aaron."

Aaron hesitated.

"Wave, sweetie."

Aaron frowned and waved slowly, but the little girl wasn't looking back anymore.

Elizabeth rubbed his head and took his hand. "Let's run our errand and get home. I'm making your favorite tonight—yellow chicken." Since he could talk, Aaron had called her curry chicken "yellow chicken."

But Aaron didn't answer. He was still looking back at the little girl.

CHAPTER FOUR

"I think you'd better take this," one of the patrolmen said, handing Jordan a phone.

"Inspector Gray," he announced, despising San Francisco's antiquated title. Couldn't he just be a detective like everybody else?

"Inspector, this is Sheriff Fletcher over in Marin County."

"Hi, Sheriff. What can I do for you?" Jordan hated being interrupted at a crime scene. He stood in the mouth of the alley. The girl's body had been taken to the morgue two days ago, but Jordan's men were still working the scene. The litter in the area had made sweeping the scene for evidence a much larger task than they were used to. With the body count up to two, Jordan was determined to stay until they came up with something.

"Well, I thought you might want to hear about a case I had over here."

Jordan stared at the ground, concentrating. "I'm listening."

"Little girl, ten, burned inside her father's tool-shed," the nervous sheriff continued.

Jordan shook his head. "And?"

"We ruled it accidental. Didn't do much in the way of an investigation at the scene."

"Okay?" Jordan prodded.

"Well, this happened about two weeks ago. Her father cleaned up the debris and found a partially burned remnant that reminded me of your case."

"What is it, Sheriff?"

"It's a party hat, Inspector."

Jordan's breath caught. Damn. "What color is it?"

"Appears it was red."

Jordan stormed into the station, moving as quickly as he could to avoid comment. Everyone knew about this case. The entire station whispered behind his back like thirteen-year-olds in a coed locker room. Jordan had gotten the bomb case. No case put more pressure on a police force than a child murder. And he had multiple child murders. If he didn't solve the case soon, it was going to explode in his face. He straightened his tie and strode toward the captain's office.

Captain Tapp was a burly man with a thick neck and arms and legs to match. He had the appearance of a lumberjack. Only his height of five-nine suggested he wasn't a forest giant. It was as though he had been destined for six-five or six-six when he had stopped growing upward but continued to thicken.

Jordan had known the captain for ten years, and in that time he had discovered little more about the man than he had learned at their first meeting. Tapp hadn't taken vacation in seven years, and he was never sick. There were rumors of a wife and children, but no evidence that Jordan could see. Tapp's finger bore no ring, his desk, no pictures.

And in the ten years they had worked together, Tapp had never been heard taking a personal phone call. He spoke rarely, and never about anything personal. His once curly reddish hair now covered only a third as much of his head as it had back then. And the gray had taken over like a killer vine.

Tapp motioned Jordan in and pointed to a chair.

Jordan sat, leaned back, and waited.

Tapp refused to be rushed. Even in the most high-pressured cases, the captain managed to keep his cool.

After another beat of pause, Tapp turned to Jordan and smiled. "Heard you got a rough one."

Jordan nodded. "Pretty bad. And I got a call from the Marin County Sheriff's office that links another death—that's three now."

Tapp nodded. "I heard."

Jordan frowned, but Tapp offered no explanation.

Instead of asking, Jordan leaned forward, ready to make his pitch. "I've got three victims—two Caucasians, one black. All female. All done up with party hats like the killer's mother missed his tenth birthday and he's making up for it now." He paused.

Tapp didn't blink.

"I'd like to send it to Quantico. I think they could profile it for us, help us narrow down what we're looking for."

Tapp steepled his fingers and rested his chin on their points. His thick, hairy hands bulged from his shirt cuffs like two partially inflated balloons. "I'll think about it."

Jordan sat forward on his chair, prepared to push as hard as it took. "Captain, I've got three dead children. The media has the scent, and they're tracking us like bloodhounds. I need to give them something."

Tapp nodded. "Mixed races, though. Maybe it's not one killer."

"The dissection of each one, the puppetlike staging,

the party hats, the same M.O.—it's got to be the same guy."

Tapp shrugged. "Stuff leaks."

"Maybe some stuff. But what about the strange signature on the legs—they're identical from case to case. That wasn't given to the press."

"Stuff still gets out."

Jordan frowned. "Are you suggesting a cop was involved?"

"Not necessarily."

Jordan waited. He needed to do something. He tapped his toes inside his shoe, fighting off impatience.

Tapp swiveled in his chair, his hands still steepled at his chin. "I'm still not convinced you've got one killer, but I'll think about the idea."

Jordan tightened his jaw to keep it from hitting the floor. He knew he shouldn't push. Tapp was as stubborn as he was reserved. When he spoke, his mind was made up as sure as if his words were cast in gold.

Jordan shouldn't need to explain the merits of the FBI to a captain. The FBI had the most sophisticated profiling ability in the world. Jordan couldn't help himself. "Captain, I need help here. I'm working this one alone, and the scenes aren't telling me a goddamned—"

Tapp raised his hand and halted Jordan mid-sentence. "I told you I'd think about it. In the meantime, put together a task force."

Jordan started to speak again when Tapp picked up his phone and turned his back.

"Bye, Gray," he said before punching a few numbers and speaking to someone. "I need the records on the Great Western robbery/homicide, please."

Jordan clenched his fists and removed himself from the office. As he shut the captain's door behind him, he couldn't help feeling like he'd had the air punched from his lungs. What the hell was going on? Sending the file to Quantico should have been the next step.

His head lowered, Jordan moved toward the exit.

"Rough meeting?"

Jordan looked up to see his old patrol partner, Harry McClerkin, walk up beside him. Harry was built almost exactly like Jordan—six-four and slender. People used to joke about them being brothers. Apart from the fact that Jordan was black and Harry Irish, it was an easy enough mistake to make. The two men had been inseparable for six years. They'd been split up since, Jordan moving into the homicide department of the inspector division, Harry working narcotics and some white-collar stuff. But they still got together to exchange ideas or discuss station politics, and Harry was a member of the five-man card game on Thursday nights.

Unlike most partners, Harry and Jordan saw eye-to-eye on almost everything. Besides saving each other's lives on more than one occasion, their first children were born within three months of each other, their second within a year. And Harry and his wife had separated only two months before Angie went back to L.A.

"Rough isn't the word," Jordan commented.

Harry slapped his back. "Let's go to Sal's. I'm buying."

Jordan shook his head. "Shit. I don't even know if I could eat."

Harry shook his head and motioned for the door. "Nothing's that bad. Remember the ice robber?"

Jordan nodded. When he and Harry had first started out as inspectors, there had been a string of six armed robberies in Pacific Heights. Before leaving each residence, the perp had removed all the ice from the freezer, placed it in bowls, and ordered his victims to stick their hands and feet in it without moving for forty minutes. The perp had claimed he could tell if they moved and would come back and shoot them.

One older woman had done as he told her and was hospitalized for frostbite. She ended up with gangrene and one foot had to be amputated. Eventually, the gangrene had killed her.

"You ate through that one," Harry added.

"We had living witnesses for that one."

Harry opened the door and headed out into the street. McClerkin and Gray had done some of their best work at Sal's, sitting at a booth in the back corner, thinking through cases without the distraction of phone calls or other officers. Sal had treated them like family, eventually putting up a "reserved" sign on the corner table on the days he expected them. Seven months ago, though, Sal had dropped dead of a heart attack. Jordan guessed he'd eaten too much of his own food.

Since then, the place had lost most of its charm. The yellow walls seemed pasty and sick colored. The new owner, Sal's son, Tony, dressed like a pimp and had a series of nasty-looking characters around the place. All of the old staff except one cook had left. And Tony didn't seem to appreciate his cop clientele like Sal had.

Jordan suspected pissing off Tony was the single reason Harry still ate there. It certainly wasn't because the food was good. And the once bad coffee now tasted like caffeinated swamp water.

At ten-thirty in the morning, the place was almost empty. Tony was nowhere to be seen, and Jordan suspected he was still sleeping off whatever nighttime activities he was partaking of these days. Harry led them to the back table and sat down, hailing the waitress for two coffees.

The woman showed up with two mugs and a pot of coffee, pouring without the slightest pause. "You want to look at the menu?"

Jordan hadn't looked at Sal's menu in years. "Two eggs over easy and a side of toast—wheat, no butter."

Harry held up two fingers. "Make it two."

The waitress nodded and walked away, mumbling something under her breath.

Jordan stared after her.

"So what's going on?"

Jordan looked over at his friend and shook his head. "This kid killing case is a nightmare. I want to send the files to Quantico."

Harry narrowed his eyes. "And Tapp said no." It was less a question than a statement.

Jordan took a long sip of coffee, eyeing his friend. Jordan knew when Harry was holding something back. "What the hell's going on?"

Harry cast a glance over his shoulder and leaned forward. The gesture was so familiar, Jordan could have smiled. Instead, he leaned forward and listened.

"Way I heard it, Chief Jackson had some kind of fight with the director after the way the Mail Killer went."

"Which director?"

"FBI."

"Purcell?"

Harry nodded. "You remember how fucked up things got when they brought the FBI in. Jackson went ape. FBI criticized the way the department handled the evidence and the investigation, but Jackson's convinced they were the ones that screwed things up. Made us look like morons."

"It's been almost two years."

"Department still gets hammered over that one."

"We got hammered over Stinson, too, and we didn't have the FBI on that one."

McClerkin shrugged.

Jordan shook his head. "I can't get help from FBI because Jackson's afraid they'll screw something up and we'll take the rap?"

Harry took another glance over his shoulder. "That's what it looks like."

"What the hell am I supposed to do?"

Harry shrugged. "You're fucked, basically."

"Thanks, asshole."

McClerkin grinned. "My pleasure."

"You have any bright ideas?" Jordan asked.

He shrugged. "Not much of one."

"I'm listening."

They paused as the waitress brought their plates. She set one down in front of each man and then said, "Hmm. I hope I got those right. Well, you can always switch them." She chortled and sauntered off.

"Smart ass," Harry called after her.

She grinned back at him.

Jordan smiled, then looked back at his friend. "You were saying?"

"I figure when the case gets bad, Tapp will get desperate enough to go to Jackson."

"And I'm supposed to sit on my ass until then."

"There's one more thing."

Jordan swallowed a bite of eggs and washed it down with coffee. "What?"

"Remember that lecture series we went to a year ago February?"

Jordan shrugged. "Vaguely."

"You'll remember this one. The hot woman who gave the lecture on FBI profiling—McKinley?"

"Yeah, I remember her."

"Well, she was attacked."

"Attacked? Like mugged?"

McClerkin took another bite and shook his head. "No, like the killer she was profiling found her."

"Holy shit. She dead?"

"No. He cut her up pretty good, but her partner happened into the hall of the apartment bulding and heard something strange from her place. He broke in and saved her—lost the perp, though."

"Jesus. So, how's that going to help me?"

"She's here."

"Where?"

"Living in the Oakland Hills. On permanent disability."

Jordan pushed his plate away as an image of Casey McKinley cut apart like the little black girl entered his brain and ruined his appetite. "How bad is she?"

"Mentally fine, I hear. Physically not as good. It's been a year, and she still can't use her hands for shit."

"How do you know about this?"

"Her husband worked in legal at Drehman Securities with my sister while he was out here."

"Where's he now?"

"McKinley sent him back to Virginia about six months ago."

Jordan clenched his jaw. Women didn't make anything easy, he'd learned that much. At least he had sons. Didn't know what he would have done with daughters. "What makes you think she can help?"

"You remember her. She knew what she was doing."

"Fine, what makes you think she *will* help?"

McClerkin scraped up the rest of his eggs and swallowed without chewing. "That, I don't know."

"They catch the guy?"

Harry shook his head. "Nope."

"What kind of killer?"

Harry's gaze met his. "Guy into some sick shit, from what I got through the grapevine."

Jordan watched his old partner, thankful to have the man on his side. Harry had always gathered information like a squirrel gathered nuts. Even when they had worked together, Jordan had been unable to figure out where the information came from. Every time they were stuck on a case, though, Harry seemed to draw a shell full of information from his pocket to move them forward. "Sick? Like what, children?"

Harry shook his head. "No."

"Then, what?"

"His victims were all lower-class women—a model working as a waitress, a prostitute, a stripper, and one more—I can't remember."

Jordan didn't move. "So?"

Harry grinned like a child caught eating candy before dinner. "So, before this guy, McKinley's record was perfect. Thirty-seven cases, thirty-seven arrests, all within something like three months of being called in. Some kind of FBI record."

"Wow," Jordan mumbled. Only the police realized how truly remarkable a record like that was. Murder cases rarely got solved as fast as the public believed they should. Witnesses took time to interview, subjects to interrogate, not to mention evidence to gather. And DNA processing took at least six weeks.

"Told you she was great." Harry loved to draw out his information, like a man telling a great story, savoring each tidbit.

"There's more?" Jordan was growing impatient.

"His signature."

Jordan motioned for more coffee, knowing that his lack of attention would push McClerkin toward the punch line faster than anything else.

"A guy fixated with the scalpel."

Jordan glanced back at Harry. "What do you mean?"

"I mean, this last guy cut his victims apart, just like they were on an autopsy table—only they weren't. They were alive."

The waitress arrived with more coffee and poured.

Jordan thought about the bandages wrapped around the heads of his victims. "My victims are children. It doesn't fit."

McClerkin shrugged and raised one eyebrow. "Still, your guy is right up her alley. And I've got her address for you."

CHAPTER FIVE

Billy pulled the car into the driveway and heaved a dramatic sigh. "I'm not kidding, Casey. I refuse to take you shopping when you act like that."

"Enough, Billy. You've already said it ten times since we left the store."

"But you nearly killed that woman. I swear, I thought she was going to have a heart attack."

Ignoring Billy's ranting, Casey trained her eyes on the foreign black Ford Explorer parked across the street. Dark eyes peered back. Her internal alarms sounding, Casey scanned the license plate. "2EXP479," she said out loud, committing it to memory.

"What on earth are you talking about?"

Casey ignored Billy and opened the car door. Pushing herself up with her fists, she stood and moved toward the house.

"What's the rush?" Billy called after her.

Without answering him, she let herself into the house and followed the emergency directions. Phone in hand, she punched number one and listened impatiently to the programmed dial.

"Rick Swain," came the computerized voice.

"Casey McKinley at 1421 Canyon Drive. Black Ford

Explorer, California, number 2EXP479." She hung up and turned around.

With a terrified glance over his shoulder, Billy shuffled inside and locked the door, dropping the bags in the kitchen. "Who's out there? I told you, you should just get a good alarm—like normal people."

She shook her head, waiting for the phone to ring. "Come on, Rick."

"We could be dead by now," Billy snapped.

She shook her head. This is what the agency left her with—no use of her hands, one good leg, a meager allowance to cover her rented house and expenditures, and a phone number which was supposed to be twenty-four seven. "Damn it. Ring."

As though responding, the phone rang.

Billy jumped backward and lay his fluttering hand to his chest. "Jesus, Mary, and Joseph."

"None of them are going to be much help," Casey grabbed the phone. "Hello."

"Swain here."

"Who is it?"

"Registered to Jordan Gray of Oakland, California. Not reported stolen."

"Who is he?"

"Inspector, San Francisco Police Department."

"Shit." These days, there was nothing about law enforcement Casey liked.

"You have a good one, too, Agent McKinley," Swain said with exaggerated politeness.

Casey hung up the phone. Every patrol car, every street cop, even the meter maids made her uncomfortable now. What a long way down she'd fallen. As a kid, she'd worshiped the police. Her father had been a police officer in Philadelphia.

He patrolled the same beat for twenty-seven years,

practically a record there. After Casey's younger sister died in a car accident caused by a drunk driver, her father had worked overtime to man the roads for drunks.

At the time Casey thought nothing mattered to him like the job. Then her mother had started to suffer from Alzheimer's, and he'd buried himself in the job even more. Four years later, right after her mother had died, Casey had been attacked. She remembered the one time her father had come to visit her, she'd been heavily drugged and half asleep.

But, ingrained in her mind, clear as crystal was the image of her father turning to the attending nurse. "What's the world coming to?" he had asked her. Then, turning back to Casey, he said, "I've lost all three of my girls to different monsters." It was as if he were speaking to Casey's corpse. He had died four weeks later.

"Casey," Billy called.

She blinked hard and looked at him.

He stared from the door to her and back again. "Well?"

"Well, what?"

"Is it safe to open the door?"

She shrugged. "It's some inspector."

"This is not normal, Casey. You need a good alarm system, not a long-distance guard dog."

She glared. "Answer the door and tell him to go away. I'm going to my room."

"Don't you move," Billy commanded, his voice harsh. His mean voice, she called this one; it was a good octave below his usual. Billy opened the door and started.

Casey struggled to suppress a smile, and Billy shot her a glare.

"I'm Inspector Gray with the San Francisco Police Department." The man at the door was black and trim, easily six-foot-four, two-ten. His deep eyes fixed on her, an air of law-enforcement authority exuding from his every pore. Still, she had learned a hard lesson. With her hands the way they were, she didn't have a chance in hell of taking him. And God knew Billy wouldn't help much. He'd practically been blown over by the wind in the doorway.

Casey scolded herself, knowing Billy's size had more to do with the disease that was killing him than his inborn fragility. She looked at the cop at the door and hoped Swain was right.

Casey glanced down, relieved to see his feet were way too big. She'd known he probably wouldn't be the killer she had tracked, but somehow seeing his shoes made her feel better. Leonardo had a man's size ten shoe. This guy's were easily twelves or thirteens.

For months after the attack, whenever she spoke to anyone, from doctors to psychiatrists to attorneys and law officials, she'd been unable to keep her eyes from drifting to their feet. Perhaps it was another reason she liked Billy so much. His were men's size seven, hardly larger than her own size-eight women's. She thought about what Billy had said earlier. Maybe he was right. She needed to learn to trust people—at least some people. She didn't trust law enforcement—that came with knowing the inspector wanted something. But Billy's friend the tax accountant—she could trust a tax accountant.

At least the detective guy was using the right name. "I thought they only had inspectors in England," Casey mumbled, holding her ground.

"You behave," Billy commanded.

Casey glanced over in time to see the cop's jaw drop and his deep brown eyes widen.

"I want to see ID," Casey demanded.

Billy gasped.

"That's quite all right," the inspector said, opening his coat and showing them his pocket before slowly removing his badge and handing it to her.

Casey rubbed her knuckles across the badge, studying it carefully before giving it back. As he returned the badge to his pocket, Casey watched him.

Billy turned back to the man and waved him in. "Come on in, Inspector."

"Thank you. Please call me Jordan." After wiping his feet on the mat, Jordan ducked his head and entered.

Standing in her foyer next to pale, thin Billy, the inspector looked like an African god in height and stature.

Her hands fidgeting, Casey made her way to a drawer and pulled out a cigarette. Gripping the butt in her hand, she lit it and took a long drag.

"Put that out." Billy came rushing at her, his arms in the air. "Good, God. Are you trying to kill us all?"

She lifted the cigarette out of his reach and put her other hand out. "Touch this cigarette, and I'll start with you."

"I certainly didn't mean to interrupt," Jordan interjected, looking awkward standing in the low doorway.

Casey took another drag on her cigarette. "Of course you did. The question is why." She met his gaze and held it. "You here to see the freak show?"

Billy winced.

The inspector looked around. "You got a man in a cage or something?"

She eyed him carefully, but so far he hadn't so much as glanced at her hands.

"Please, come sit." Billy motioned to the couch. "I'll open this window for a little fresh air."

Jordan nodded. "Thanks." He sat on the couch across from Casey.

Casey finished her cigarette and dropped it into a glass on the table.

"Thank God," Billy said, carrying the glass to the kitchen at arm's length as though the smell were something he might catch.

"I'm sure you didn't come here to see me smoke," Casey said to the inspector.

He shook his head. "No." He straightened his jacket and sat forward. His knees reached halfway up his chest as he struggled to get comfortable on her couch. "I heard you speak at Berkeley about a year ago. You discussed the merits of profiling. I was quite impressed with your speech. I've come here for your help, Ms. McKinley." He met her gaze. "With a case," he added.

With some effort, Casey pushed herself to her feet. "Then, I won't waste your time or mine, Inspector. I don't work for the Bureau anymore."

He didn't move. "I think you'll want to hear what I have to say."

"Why would I?"

"Listen to the man," Billy snapped.

Casey glanced up, surprised she hadn't noticed Billy's return to the room.

She shook her head. "I have enough problems, Inspector. I don't need yours."

Jordan stood, looking relieved to be able to stretch his legs again.

Casey backed away from him, his sheer size making her even more skittish.

"I've heard about your work," he said.

She stared at him without responding.

Billy moved to her side, putting his arm through hers and holding on. The gesture made Casey wonder who was supporting whom.

"I've heard you were the best."

"That about sums it up, Inspector. I *was* the best."

"Please. Let me finish."

She restrained herself from speaking, wondering why it was taking him so long to spit it out. What the hell did he really want? Why was he here? But somehow, she was afraid to ask—afraid he would give her answers she didn't want to hear.

"I need your help," he continued.

"For a profile?" Billy asked.

Her eyes closed, Casey wished he had kept quiet.

Jordan nodded. "Sort of."

The air was thick around the inspector's words. He was holding something back. The thought of what he had left out filled Casey with dread. She thought about Leonardo. It couldn't be him. He wasn't back. It was impossible.

Billy patted her arm as though that would relieve the terror that streamed through her veins like glacier ice. Why was she reacting this way? What did she expect him to say? What was she was afraid of? No. She knew what she was afraid of.

The inspector looked at Billy as though Casey weren't even in the room. "We have a perp who has killed three children. Cut them up—different parts on each one."

His words hit her like a bullet. She struggled for

breath, then straightened her back. Her teeth tight, Casey fought her fear.

"I read about that case in the paper," Billy said. "Remember, Casey? I was telling you about it." He turned back to the inspector. "Casey was profiling it for me."

"Enough," she spit, pulling away from Billy and looking at the detective. "You need to leave."

Jordan didn't move.

"Now," she said.

Billy made no move to contradict her.

"May I call you Casey?"

She gave a wicked chortle at his attempt to befriend her. "You mean as you leave? I don't see any harm."

Jordan smiled and shook his head. "I'm afraid I can't leave just yet. I need to ask you some questions."

"I don't think you heard me. I've got nothing to say."

"Casey, this is a matter of police business," he pressed. But his eyes wavered, and she knew he was caught.

She shook her head and raised a lame hand. "Don't play that fucking game with me."

Billy stepped in front of her as though he could shield her from the words the inspector was about to speak.

She ignored him and continued, "I'm not some naive witness you can intimidate. You and I both know that you have no right to demand my assistance. And I'm certainly not offering it. I was absolved of that duty almost a year ago, Inspector." She spoke the title as though it were a curse.

"And as for any other police business, I've got an alibi. And I'm all paid up on my parking tickets." She

raised her hands to him. "Come to think of it, I don't
even drive anymore."

He didn't so much as flinch at the sight of her crippled hands. The same hands she used to shoot with,
box with, tie her shoes with, and write her name.

His imperturbability only made her angrier. "But.
If you want to press it, I do have a very good lawyer."
She turned her back and moved toward her bedroom,
her heart pounding as it had constantly in her
thoughts, her dreams, and her memories of that night.
She fought the wave of nausea that followed.

"I understand you're going through a rough time,
Casey."

She turned back and put her hand up to stop him,
a bitter laugh escaping her lips. "I had a psychiatrist,
thanks. He was a fucking useless asshole, but he was
a hell of a lot better than you."

The inspector's expression remained unruffled. "I'm
not here to counsel you. I'm here because I'm an inspector. And I've got what I believe is a serial killer."

"Great. Congratulations. You want a fucking medal?
You're in the wrong place."

"I want your help."

She just laughed. "Good-bye."

"Normally I'd let it go, Casey. But I don't want to
lose another kid on my patrol."

"Then, call the fucking Bureau and have them send
out a rent-a-brain, okay?"

She could hear Billy's quick intake of breath, even
from the edge of her bedroom. Shaking her head, she
forced herself to make the words form on her lips.

"Call Quantico," she whispered, then cleared her
throat. "Someone there took over my cases. Like I
said, Inspector, I don't work there anymore."

Jordan sighed and took a step closer and pressed

on. "I can't. I don't have the authority to go to the Bureau. That's why I'm here." He lowered his voice. "You're better than the rent-a-brains, anyway."

She shook her head. Fumbling for her stance on shaky legs, she pushed herself into her bedroom. Slamming the door, she looked around the room as though it was the first time she'd seen it. For the first time, it felt confined and dark. She felt Leonardo's presence. Like in her nightmares, he was suddenly everywhere.

The flimsy glass window caught her attention, and she moved toward it. Dark bars shielded someone from merely breaking the glass, but how easy it would be to simply saw through them. All alone in the middle of the night, she would be helpless.

Billy had pleaded with her to get a better alarm system, but she'd refused. It wasn't about whether she thought Leonardo would come back—or whether she thought she could take him if he did. She simply couldn't bring herself to care what happened to her. She was no use alive—why not dead? But suddenly being faced with that as an option was terrifying. Casey took a deep breath and focused her energy out the window.

Across the street, a gardener stopped and removed his hat, wiping his forehead with his sleeve. His curly dark hair was wet and matted to his head. A thick mustache covered his lip. He glanced in her direction and without thinking, she ducked. Sitting on the floor, she actually wondered what size shoes the man wore. "Stop it," she commanded herself.

Pushing to her feet, she turned and closed the curtains, fighting to close the shades with her two knob-like fists.

With the shades drawn, she forced the inspector's

words from her head. What she needed was a project, something to distract her. She wasn't going back to work, but she couldn't sit on her ass for the rest of her life, either. If she did that, she would be better off dead.

She took mental inventory of the things in the house that still needed repair. The locks on the kitchen window were bad. The back door had only one bolt. The alarm system was fidgety.

Gasping, she stared at her hands. What would she do if Leonardo got in? How could she defend herself? Without the use of her hands, she was a sitting duck. Undoubtedly, that was exactly as he wanted it. Why, after so many months of silence, were the alarms suddenly going off in her head? Was it the inspector's visit, the memories of working cases? Or was Leonardo really here? Could she actually feel him like thick smoke, burning in the air?

If so, she was as good as dead.

CHAPTER SIX

She was as good as dead. He turned off the leaf blower and lifted the worn baseball cap to wipe his brow. From across the street he watched Agent Mc-Kinley move in the bedroom, then quickly draw her shades. He smiled. So she knew. He could see it in her face—the sheer terror of knowing how close he was. And he *was* that close. No, he was closer. She could never imagine how close he was.

He sat on the step and put his cap back on, pretending to bask in the sun that sliced between the tall eucalyptus like a machete. It was an act, of course. He hated the sun, had always hated it. His rage, like molten lava, burned inside him. He had succeeded. He'd waited almost a year for her, hidden out, worked menial jobs, but his time had come. She thought she was so much better than he. Everyone undervalued him.

Even as a child, the kids had made of fun of his pasty skin and scrawny physique—as they had made fun of his drawings. He had practiced sketching, just like his uncle said he should. "Medicine is art. You must be able to draw a perfect line—first with the pen and later with the scalpel."

He had always been good. But they denied it, told him he was a sissy. What did they know? His uncle had recognized his talent and tried to teach him, but his man-hating mother wouldn't hear of it.

He remembered the old copy of *Gray's Anatomy* his uncle had brought for him. He had overheard his mother talking with his uncle at the door. It was his eleventh birthday. Closing his eyes, he could envision it now. He'd only seen his uncle one more time before he died. But his mother hadn't given him the book— she gave it to his sister instead. He'd gotten only a hat, a stupid red birthday hat that had been his sister's only months before.

He didn't care. He had proven himself. He'd studied *Gray's Anatomy* in secret and learned all the parts— every single one. He'd practiced on neighborhood cats, squirrels, and birds, even a dog once, although it was big and bulky and hadn't required nearly so much skill as the smaller animals. The scratches from the dog still marked his arms, war wounds of his own personal battles. He could have been a doctor like his uncle.

But then he had been denied entrance into medical school. He should be a doctor—he was good enough. No, he was better. His mother and sister had mocked him, continued to do so up until five years ago. But that was the last time. His sister's birthday, too. What a perfect final present for them both.

Now he was his own doctor, he performed his own surgery, and created his own art. Each piece was a puppet to his power. Let his coworkers at this latest joke of a job think what they want. Stupid, worthless. That's how they thought of him. He had lied to them about his background in security, about his name. Even his appearance had been a lie—the dark brown hair, the brown contacts. He held the deceits like carrots in front of them, and they had bitten. With each new lie, they moved closer, more trusting. How he would love to show them how stupid they were, how careless and naive. But they wouldn't know. They would never know.

He toyed with the idea of letting them find out one day. The image of their horrified faces filled his head. He felt the warm rush of glee. When they learned that the man they had trusted with their security and then belittled had so much power, they would be terrified. He wanted to haunt them.

But they weren't enough. They were easy targets, worthless worker bees in the intricate hive of his power. He could play them like puppets, but there wouldn't be the same joy. The job had never been enough. A resting place, a time to build his power again, to watch and wait. Now he needed more.

Now he needed Casey. She had caught his attention—and made him think of his mother. Casey had disapproved of him, doubted him, but he had shown her who was in control. And he would again. She was responsible for his new direction as an artist, made him realize he could do even better.

He had always sculpted around a focal point—everyone had one. Casey McKinley's had been her hands—her ability to shoot a gun. The stripper's was her chest, the runner's her legs, the model's her face. It was all about finding their core—that was his art. He was still doing it. He hadn't realized that children had a core, too, but they did. And the children's rawness was a whole new level of excitement that he hadn't expected. He'd taken apart the little ballerina's feet and the face of the girl so self-conscious about her braces.

But now his art gave him an even greater thrill, thanks to Casey. He recalled the day in the mall when he'd seen a mother walking with her child—the woman had looked so much like Casey—and he knew she would congratulate his cleverness in using the children to get to the mothers. What better way to relive the joy of watching his mother suffer as he killed his sister? At first, he'd worried the smaller prey would be duller, but he'd never felt more empowered. He remembered his mother's pleas to let his sister live— she never cared about him, but she had cared more for her daughter than for herself.

Now he sought out children in the malls, each time waiting for the right one. It was perfect. Casey would see the true artistry in it. Her power, her itelligence, had made her the perfect adversary. The fact that he hadn't finished with her made the hunt all the more exciting. Soon she would be forced to give him his due. He felt himself rising in his pants and forced his mind away.

Pulling his gloves off, he looked at his nails. When he'd found a fraying piece of skin, he tugged at it indiscreetly. The layers were red and sore. Still, he dug deeper until he struck blood.

All these months, it had reminded him that he needed to wait. Blood would be evidence. Their blood was joy. His own blood would be damning. He knew when to wait. That was what made him so good.

He rubbed the sore with his finger, feeling the burning of the exposed flesh against the acids in his skin. How wonderful that pain was. In his mind, he could hear them screaming. The pain contorted their faces and made them beg for their lives.

There were the women before—four of them. They had been his mother's puppets, too, but without the same power as her or Casey. His sister had always been the way to pierce his mother's heart. Now he realized. The children were the center of it all. Since Cincinnati, he'd had to wait until Casey was ready to come back to him. There had been only three new pieces of art, but each work was better than the last. The next would be his best yet. The masterpiece was close at hand.

He rubbed his darkened hands across his face, pleased at the new color of his skin. The tan had come from a bottle. With a little help and his own ingenuity, he could be anything he wanted.

Casey's front door opened, and he looked back down at his hands. He found his gardening gloves and pulled them back on, pushing himself to his feet like someone weary from physical labor. The tall black man stepped out of the house and closed the door, easing his way back to the Ford Explorer. The man had the air of a police officer; but without a uniform, a detective might be more likely.

Standing, he turned his back, though he could feel the detective's strong gaze on his shoulder. Excitement and anticipation brewed in his stomach like a wicked ale. He inhaled and soaked it in before hoisting the leaf blower over his shoulder and turning it on again.

He blew the three stairs above where he stood and then moved toward the street. Beneath the bill of his cap, he peeked out at the detective.

The detective was copying down the license plate of the gardening truck in a notebook.

Smiling, he turned his back to the detective again, loving the rush the detective's attention brought to his groin.

He was too good. He had taken care of every detail, worked out every glitch. He'd found the perfect road into Casey's home, the perfect key. He would not be discovered, certainly not so easily as this. Let the detective check the license plate.

It was starting. The game he had waited so long to play was starting again. The police had nothing, but he had planned his next move. Already the score was in his favor.

CHAPTER SEVEN

Rick Swain stood and took a deep drag on his cigarette, then dropped it to the floor and smashed it out with the toe of his cowboy boot. He glanced at his watch and shook his head. It was already five-thirty. By the time he hit the surface, it would be dark. Another day without light. He was going to go fucking nuts down here.

When he'd trained as a FBI agent, Swain had pictured high-adventure trips into foreign countries and forbidden lands. He would crack the codes of the enemy, break through their barriers and find whatever the Bureau needed. That was supposed to be his job. At least, that was what the Bureau had told him seven years ago.

Not anymore. These days, the best hackers were younger than his last haircut. They say he'd screwed up with McKinley in Cincinnati. They'd investigated it. He'd never seen the results of the investigation, never been given a full report. But he was to blame. He still didn't buy it. He'd installed the microphones himself. There had been no mistakes.

Damn if he knew what the hell had happened, but somehow that killer had gotten into her apartment and attacked Agent McKinley. Thankfully, her partner had come down the hall, heard something strange and gone to investigate. But not before the killer had done permanent damage. Swain had been blamed—he'd been the one who was supposed to hear everything that happened in McKinley's room.

Maybe the killer had deactivated the mikes. No one seemed to care enough to tell Swain. He wondered if McKinley knew. He had tried to contact her, to talk to her, but she'd told him to fuck off. Not that he blamed her. God knows it wasn't her fault. He'd just wished he'd had a chance to apologize—and explain. What good would it have done her? She'd been through hell, and he was trying to nurse a broken ego.

Still, even almost a year later, Swain couldn't let go. He needed a look at the case file, but he'd probably never get to see it. Instead, he'd be stuck in this hole forever. He just couldn't give up without knowing for sure.

The door burst open, and Dan Jamison entered. He coughed twice and waved his hand in front of his face. "Are you crazy?" he whined in his nasal pitch. "You can't smoke down here."

Rick turned his back and rolled his eyes.

"I'm not kidding, Rick. You know the rules."

Swain reached the edge of the room and propped one foot against the wall. He could picture himself out on the open land. He needed an assignment. He couldn't handle this desk work anymore. Why didn't something big happen in Alaska or Wyoming?

"Are you listening?"

Rick nodded his head and dipped a pretend hat.

"Oh no, you're channeling Wild Bill again. Are you going to tell me about the call or what?"

Rick shrugged. "What about it?"

"Play Cowboys and Indians on your own time, Swain. Mueller wants details."

Rick pitched himself upright at his boss's name. Mueller was the only one who might get Rick transferred out of the dungeon, if only Rick could get some time with him. "I've been trying to talk to—"

Jamison nodded. "He knows, Rick. It's a hectic time. Tell me about the call."

Rick sat at his desk and rested his folded hands on top. "Came in to my beeper at 15:32 today. Requested ID on a license plate."

"Why?"

"She said the car was parked in front of her house. Made her nervous, I guess."

He sat down and nodded for Swain to continue.

"I checked the plate."

He made a gesture of impatience. "And?"

"Owner's name is Jordan Gray. He's an inspector."

Jamison narrowed his gaze. "What kind of inspector?"

Why the hell did he care? Casey McKinley wanted nothing to do with the Bureau. If the Bureau worried about the people they still had working for them . . .

"What kind of inspector?" Jamison repeated, his voice raised. His skin had taken on a pink tone that accented his fleshy cheeks and neck.

"SFPD."

Jamison didn't move. His gaze attached to the wall behind Rick. His small fists locked into tight balls.

Though tempted to follow his gaze, Rick kept his eyes on Jamison. Why did it matter what Casey McKinley was doing? Rick knew better than to ask. From day one, everything Rick had learned at the Bureau was on a need-to-know basis. And generally, Rick didn't need to know.

"Should I do anything if she calls again?"

Jamison snapped his gaze back into place and popped from his chair like the cork from a champagne bottle.

Rick tried to ask another question, but Jamison wasn't listening. Leaning back in his chair, Rick lit another cigarette. Jamison mumbled something about Mueller as the door clicked shut.

CHAPTER EIGHT

Jordan slammed into the precinct parking lot and jumped from the car. The trip to the East Bay yesterday had been a total waste, and he didn't have time to waste. He'd spent the morning in Marin, checking into the death there with his investigators. The day had passed too quickly. It was going to be dark soon. Another day and not an inch closer to a suspect.

He had tried to push Agent McKinley from his mind, but he'd been so damned excited about the possibility of getting help from a profiler. Even if she had offered, McKinley was in no state of mind to help them. And the last thing he needed on this case was a self-pitying prima donna.

Now he was two hours behind. He needed to set up his task force and get a tips line going before something else happened. The commissioner was going to have to address the media. Jordan greeted a couple of inspectors, heading out through the parking lot.

"Shit's hitting the fan," Sandy Polito said, laughing. His thinning blond hair looked like a wreath of wispy feathers on his shiny head. Despite skinny legs, Polito had a gut that spilled out the front of his pants, making him look strangely top-heavy.

Jordan returned a thin smile. "Probably won't be like Cortez shit, though, huh?"

Polito glared at him as his companion said, "He's got you there."

"Fuck off," Polito snapped.

Jordan pressed forward, hoping this case wouldn't turn into the disaster Sandy Polito's had. Cortez was a heavy Mexican dealer. His ring spanned from Seattle all the way south to the border. He flowed heroin in and money out like water. Polito had been the supervising inspector on the case, and had handled it well. By the end, Polito was armed with enough evidence to put Cortez and almost a dozen of his cohorts away for life.

But in a moment of panic, Cortez had tried to skip town. Forced to make a fast decision, Polito had his men pull Cortez over for speeding and then proceeded to search his car without probable cause. After a huge departmental battle, involving the D.A.'s office, Cortez got off on a technicality that stemmed from Polito's mistake. The case was a classic and an ill-humored joke among the inspectors in the department. Jordan wasn't looking forward to the possibility of being the next Polito.

The thought of how much he had to do shook the fear from his mind as he hurried through the department toward his office. Renee met him at the door, a stack of files in her arms. "I can just tell it wasn't good. So let's move on, shall we?"

All Jordan had to do was nod. Renee was nearly fifty-five, a thick black woman with solid white hair, who protected Jordan's business like a guard dog. From seven a.m. to five p.m., no one, not even the chief, entered Jordan's office without her permission. Despite the comfort her protection brought, it wasn't what Jordan treasured most about his longtime assistant.

Like his mother, Renee refused to dwell on anything negative. Her determination was often enough to keep anyone in her orbit motivated, and Jordan depended on her more than either of them acknowledged. "It's going to be a late one, Renee. We've got a task force and tips line to worry about."

She nodded, propping her notebook on her files and scribbling notes. "What's the task force look like?"

"I don't know. I need a couple of people to go over to Marin and interview the victim's family about the fire and get a statement from the sheriff there. I've been out there, but it doesn't look like we're going to get much.

"Also, we need to know about the body." He swallowed and shook his head. "It was probably cremated." In his experience, most burn victims were. "Burial would mean we'll need the remains exhumed. Carrera will have suggestions on who you can get to go over there."

"I'll get with her and find out. Also, D.A.'s office called."

Jordan winced. "Who are they sending?"

Renee smiled. "They were going to send Willard."

He groaned. Ben Willard was a third, the son of Bernard Willard, II, managing partner of Willard Associates. All three Willards were attorneys; all three had started in the D.A.'s office. For them, the current gig was to gain a little street experience before climbing to the top of the ivory tower and negotiating sentences for the rich and famous. Willard acted like a prissy schoolgirl, carrying around a starched white handkerchief that he used to open doors in the station. Perhaps he was concerned that he might chip a nail on the heavy handles. Whatever the reason, he and Jordan did not see eye to eye—on anything.

"But—" Renee interjected.

"But what?"

"I mentioned the case Strioski is working on?"

Jordan narrowed his gaze. "Which case?"

"The black kid kicked out of the movie theater by some big white bouncer guy. Kid claims he was brutalized because he's black."

"I know that one. It's not a case. It's some punk kid trying to get a free ride at the movies."

Renee grinned. "Willard thinks it's a history maker—battle of the races in San Francisco. Even gave his spot on the serial killer case to Mary Riggs."

Jordan cracked a smile. "Renee, you're dangerous, you hear me?"

She snapped her fingers. "You better believe it. Mary will be by in about an hour." Renee made a note and looked back up with a wink.

"What's next?"

"Becky called, and the chief wants a list of facts for the evening news."

Jordan had anticipated that one of the heads would speak to the public. It was his job to determine what they would be told. Too little, and the tips line would be worthless in helping them. Too much, and they wouldn't be able to weed out the good leads from the bad. "Who's addressing?"

"The mayor or maybe the chief. I don't think they've decided yet."

"Either's fine. We need to have a tips line ready by tonight. Will you call in Monica Pradahn? I'd like her to lead up the group and handle the press." Monica, pronounced Mo-Nee-ka, was a petite, trim, energetic Indian woman who embodied the meticulous organizational and managerial qualities that were invaluable for a successful tips line. Beyond that, she invoked humor and calm at the craziest of times.

When Monica joined the force seven years earlier, from the Los Angeles department, Jordan had continually mispronounced her name. Despite constant criticism from colleagues about his insensitivity and more embarrassment than he cared to recall, Monica never once lost her cool. Instead, she responded to each butchering by simply smiling and correcting him. Again.

"I'll get her on the phone right now. Anything else?"

The truck he had seen in front of Agent McKinley's house came to mind, and he pulled his notebook from his breast pocket. Tearing the page from the spiral, he handed it to Renee. "Will you have someone run a check on this license for me?"

"Rush?"

He nodded. "And I need to have you check with local departments about similar cases."

"Who do you want to try?"

"L.A. Try Detective Sherman there. I saved his ass two months ago. Maybe he'll return the favor. And try Portland—what's his name—"

"Del Negro is there, isn't he?" she said, writing on her notepad.

"Exactly. And Jimmy Atkinson in Seattle." He paused. "That's enough to start. Get anything they can think of. If they've got something—anything—I want to talk to them. And I want as much as you can get on what happened to FBI Agent Casey McKinley in Cincinnati."

"Got it." She shifted the stack of files against her

hip and stared him down. "You talked to Angie, Jordan?"

The name felt like an uppercut to his gut. He stared at his feet. "Yep. And it still doesn't sound like she wants anything to do with me."

Renee shook her head. "Don't be stupid, Jordan. The woman loves you. She'll come around. Now, don't go forgetting your father-in-law's birthday is in three days. I'll pick up a card."

"Thanks, Renee."

"And Will's birthday is in less than two weeks, Jordan. You don't want to be away from that boy on his birthday."

He nodded. "I asked Angie to bring the boys up this weekend. Told me she wanted me to come to her. But I don't want to go stay with my in-laws."

Renee waved her hand at him, dismissing his comment. "Of course not. She'll come up here. She just wants you to work for it. You should send those flowers."

"It won't do any good."

"Won't know till you try."

Jordan eyed her, then shook his head. "I don't know . . . "

"Oh, forget you. You men don't know a good thing till it's gone." She handed him a couple of files and pushed him toward his office. "Now, you get in there and dial up some shop and send your wife flowers. Write something real sweet, now, you hear me? I'll get on the horn and see about getting Warrior tickets. Between the flowers and the tickets, Angie couldn't say no."

"Thanks, Renee."

"Yeah, yeah. Now, git." She waved him off.

Jordan sat at his desk and debated the merits of

sending flowers. Somehow it felt like an admission of guilt. He hadn't done anything wrong, but that wasn't how his mother-in-law would see it. Damn, but he did want Angie and the boys back. It was getting lonely in the house.

Finding a number in the phone book, he dialed a florist and asked the high-pitched male voice on the other end to send something bright and cheery with a card that read, "Come up here before I explode."

"Oh my. Isn't that visual?" the salesman exclaimed.

Jordan thanked him and hung up, a little uncomfortable at the florist's enthusiasm.

With that done, he concentrated on making notes for the press conference later. Ray Zambotti's autopsy report on the black girl found in the alley described what few clues Jordan had. The facts were eerily familiar as he thought over the first victim's autopsy report.

The girl's mouth was a regular sewing project. Her upper lip had been completely detached from her face and, from what the medical examiner could guess by some strange marks on the head, attached to her scalp.

The medical examiner had called to confirm that the signature on the black girl's leg had been compared to that on the white girl, and were nearly identical. He was still working on matching the marks to a style of blade or weapon, though. Scalpel was everyone's best guess.

Jordan told the M.E. to call in whatever resources he needed to determine what instrument created those marks. Maybe it could be used to track the SOB down. Jordan pressed the intercom on his desk. "Renee, could you come in here?"

Less than ten seconds later, Renee entered, notebook in hand.

"You still talk to that woman in records at Quantico?" Jordan asked.

"Betty? Every Monday like clockwork."

"Good. Call the M.E.'s office and request a copy of the photos of the killer's signature. Then, get a copy of it to Quantico and have them run it through their records. I'm hoping to hell they'll find a match."

Renee nodded, writing.

"And, Renee?"

She looked up.

"This one's a JBU." Just Between Us was a term Jordan and Renee had been using since their second day together. Renee used it almost as much as Jordan, and neither had ever let a secret out.

"No problem. Betty'll take care of us. Anything else?"

Jordan shook his head.

"You want a report on that license plate you gave me earlier?"

"Go ahead."

"Registered to a landscaping company—Tim Ramirez is the listed owner. You want me to find out more about him?"

Jordan frowned. He used to have such a keen sense about when things weren't quite right. Why had he felt that way about the gardener?

He ran a hand over his stubble. He hadn't even showered today, and he'd been up since four a.m. That was why.

"Jordan?"

He shook himself from his thoughts. "No, Renee. That's it."

"Monica's on her way."

Back at his desk, Jordan made notes for the news release. His handwriting was atrocious, but he and

Monica would go over it. Words had never been his strong suit.

There was a light rap at his door, and Monica popped her head in. "Is this a good time?"

He nodded and motioned her to the chair.

She wore a navy pinstriped pantsuit over her thin, straight figure. Her hair was cut in a chin-length bob, its black color a sharp contrast to her complexion. Crossing her legs, she sat forward on the chair and propped a small device that looked like a calculator in her hand. She always used it, and Jordan could never remember what it was called. That sort of technology was unheard of in the police station. "You still using that—"

"Palm Pilot? Don't go anywhere without it. You really should get one."

He waved her off. "No way. I can't even program the VCR without help."

She shook her head in a mocking gesture.

"You got that thing up and ready?" he asked.

"Anytime."

"Let's start with the press release. We can release location and identity of all three children," Jordan began.

"It should concentrate on the places where the children were last seen—perhaps we can create a map of the areas," Monica suggested.

"Perfect. Do it."

Monica made notes on her little computer. Pausing, she looked up, the small gray stylus poised in the air. "What's the reward look like?"

"I don't know."

She nodded. "I'll check with Jackson's office."

"Ask Sharon there. She also has the pictures of the kids to provide to the stations."

"Anything else you need to tell me?"

"I want Walter Jones to be given some key responsibilities," Jordan added.

"The rookie who pulled over the guy with his wife in the trunk? I've heard he's good."

"He is." Walter Jones was a rookie patrol cop, but he had the makings and drive to be a great inspector. In a recent case, he'd pulled over a car for running a red light. While requesting the driver's ID, Walter had noticed the suspect was shaking and perspiring heavily.

On closer inspection, he noticed a large defense-type scratch on the man's neck, and that he reeked of booze. Without alarming the man, Jones called for backup. He and another officer searched the car under probable cause and discovered the man's wife in the trunk. She was unconscious and bleeding from wounds inflicted with a gardening tool.

Thankfully, the paramedics on the scene had successfully stabilized the woman, and the man eventually was convicted of attempted murder and sentenced to twenty-to-life.

"I think that's it," Jordan said. "We need to get something to the chief before nine tonight." He glanced at his watch. "That's less than two hours."

Monica put her Palm Pilot away. "I'll write it up and have it there in an hour."

"Then we need to get cracking on a tips line before he gets the word out."

"I think you're going to need a dozen officers handling calls on this one. A multi-race killer. You've got a lot of scared moms and dads out there."

Jordan wrote "twelve" in his notebook and circled it. Monica had an uncanny way of sensing how much feedback they would get.

"Can I ask you something, Jordan?"

He nodded.

"How come no FBI?"

Jordan crossed his arms and leaned back, frowning. She raised her eyes at his expression. "That bad, huh?"

"Worse."

"Political?"

"You guessed it."

"How about consultants? Anyone locally who can help?"

Jordan had already considered some of the crime specialists in the area. "Not yet. I thought I had something." He paused and focused on Monica again. "But it didn't work out." He wished again that he had never heard of Casey McKinley.

Monica nodded and rose from her chair. "I'll get started on this."

Before Monica could reach the door, Renee opened it, her expression a tight frown. "We've got another body, Jordan."

Jordan exhaled. "Damn."

CHAPTER NINE

The darkness made his plan much simpler. Pulling down the ski hat, he moved into the shadows of the tall trees and down the slope of Casey's yard. He peered into her bedroom window, hoping to catch a glimpse of her sleeping. But the shades were carefully drawn.

Disappointment stirred in his chest, but he cast it aside. A wasted emotion. He would see her soon—and so much closer. Billy had made that all possible. The attraction, the hospital meeting, perfectly choreographed, perfectly planned. He could play the part of the lover, the palm reader. And his disguises were the best—even his "lover" wouldn't know him if he saw him now. He had always had a sense of people's destinies, especially those close to him. And no one knew Casey's hands like he did. He paused to savor the richness of the excitement stirring his blood at the thought of touching Casey's hands again—the hands he had sculpted himself. So soon. It was coming so soon. He rubbed himself against the hard surface of Casey's house and then pushed himself back to the task at hand.

Gripping the wire cutters in his gloved hand, he

moved silently down the hillside, keeping his body pressed against the house. Taking every precaution, he had parked the van on the next block hours before, sitting and waiting until night before making his move.

He had dropped off his latest artwork in a secluded area in a park in Pacific Heights only three hours earlier. He'd been sloppy in Cincinnati, leaving the evidence of his pleasure at the scene. Now he was careful to enjoy the kill privately. Nothing would lead them to him until he was ready.

Every step had been planned to perfection, even an escape path down the slope below Casey's house. They would never catch him because he could not be caught.

At the bottom of the slope, he pulled a penlight from his pocket and quickly surveyed the area. If the city building records were right, the outside circuit breaker would be at the far corner.

Switching off the light, he crept along the side of the house until he found the small metal box. With the hook unlatched, he opened the box and found the switch. The inside of the house was still dark. He flipped the switch and waited, his ears honed for movement from above.

It was silent. Placing the two-pronged current detector on the exposed wires, he waited. When no red light appeared, he knew the electricity was no longer running into the house. Wire cutters in hand, he traced the wires in and out of the box to assure he had the ones that led into the house, the ones without electricity.

Clipping the wrong wire would mean electrocuting himself. He found the correct wire and clipped it, noting the steadiness of his pulse as he risked death. Even he could not believe his own power.

With the wire cutters in his pocket, he moved back into the shadows. Pride at his own ingenuity welled as he returned to the nondescript white van parked down the street. He sat back to wait.

CHAPTER TEN

Still slow with her bad knee, Casey hit the top of the hill and headed toward her house, the newspaper under her arm. It was almost seven-thirty, but the storm clouds made it seem like five a.m. Either way, she hadn't been up this early in nearly a year. Michael used to love the mornings. They would rise early, before Amy was awake, and have coffee and lie in bed, strategizing life. Michael had always had the clearest vision and the quickest responses.

"I don't date lawyers," she had responded to his date proposal.

"Good thing I'm only a law student," he had replied.

"I don't date law students," she clarified, making a move from the conversation.

Michael hadn't even blinked. "So if I were in law school to get advanced training in criminal law to apply it to my Ph.D. in criminal psychology you still wouldn't go out with me?"

That stopped her. "You have a Ph.D. in criminal psych?"

He grinned, and it was the corners of his mouth, the small dimple on one side, the light in his green eyes that kept her from walking away. "But I'm a law student."

She hadn't been able to say no after that.

No matter what life threw at them, Michael had an answer. It was the reason Casey had fallen for him. When the doctor told them Amy would be their only child, he'd been there, reminding her how perfect Amy was. What did they need with another child?

Whatever life doled out, Michael could always make the negative positive. Whatever life had doled out until this.

She looked down at his faded Yale sweatshirt and rubbed the worn cotton over her face. "Happy anniversary," she whispered to herself.

Of all mornings, *this* was the one where she had lost electricity to her house. Her anniversary, thoughts of Michael and Amy, all of it made her suddenly restless. Needing an excuse to get outside, the dark house had served plenty. Darkness had become her least favorite thing.

A familiar stirring of panic had moved her more quickly than she thought possible when she realized the power outage could have been intentional rather than accidental. She'd called PG&E, but their service hours didn't start until eight. To be safe, she'd tucked a can of mace into her jeans, but she hadn't seen a sign of electricity all the way down the hill. The strange feeling yesterday, the lights out this morning, there was something.

But it had to be the inspector's visit that was setting off her imagination: the reminder of the fact that Leonardo was still out there. She'd spent a year having panic attacks like this one. She should be used to them. Instead, her lungs still burned and the fresh air only partially subdued her racing heart.

As she rounded the corner, she saw Billy's car parked out front. She frowned, wondering why he was there so early. She wasn't expecting him until ten. Hurrying home, she let herself in and called his name.

"Oh, thank God." He grabbed her by the shoulders and nearly hugged her, his face flushed with worry.

She glanced over his shoulder for signs of a fire or burglary. "Thank God, what? Why are you here so early?"

"I called you."

She shook her head. "I wasn't here. Has something happened?"

He rolled his eyes and sighed, still gripping her shoulders. "No. Nothing's happened, but when I didn't get an answer, I was worried. Plus, there's no power. What's going on with the electricity?"

Detaching herself from his grasp, she dropped the paper nonchalantly on the chair. "Why did you call? You see me every day."

"I'll explain in a minute. Why isn't there power?"

She rubbed her shoulders. "I don't know. It's been off since I got up. I don't think anyone else has power, either. I'll call again."

He eyed the paper then turned back to her, his brow furrowed. "You were out this morning?"

She nodded.

"Where did you go?"

"For a walk," she replied curtly. Her husband had been like that when she was first out of the hospital, wanting to know every single thing she did. It made her marriage feel more like a cage than the hospital bed had. She thought of Michael now, sensing an emptiness that was different from the one she had felt since her attack. Michael's smile, his touch. She pushed them away, unprepared to confront all that was gone.

Billy stared. "A walk?"

She understood his surprise. She hadn't been out on her own since he'd known her.

"Why?"

She shrugged. "For air. Why did you call?"

Billy dropped his question about her walk, but she knew he would bring it up again later. "Kevin called me this morning."

Casey rolled her eyes. "The palm reader?"

"He has psychic powers, Casey."

"Is that why you're here? Because of Kevin?"

He nodded. "Listen, he—"

"Billy, please," she interjected. "I'm fine. I just went for a walk. Tell Kevin his signals are crossed or something. Now, since you're here, would you mind making a call about the electricity? I want to take a shower."

Billy propped his hands on his hips. "Are we going to discuss this?"

"The power outage?" She turned and started toward the bedroom, feeling the stiffness in her bad knee from the walk. Exercising was supposed to be good for her. Well, it didn't feel good.

"Not the electricity, Casey. Kevin says you're in danger."

Casey waved him off. "He's about a year late."

"It's not a joke. You should listen to him. I've invited him here. He has an appointment this morning, but he agreed to come by afterward. He knew you'd be skeptical."

"Wow, he really is psychic."

He glared at her. "It was generous of him to offer to come over. He lives all the way in the Haight."

"Yeah, great," Casey mumbled, though she was curious to meet this Kevin person. Billy was clearly smitten, and Casey was protective of Billy, especially when it came to Kevin and his "powers." It always seemed to her that Billy was naive about people's manipulations, too trusting.

"He's a wonderful person and very gifted. I want you to promise to listen to what he has to say."

Casey didn't answer. But she'd listen all right.

"Did you hear me?"

"I promise," she muttered back, turning toward where she thought the bedroom door was. It was so dark in the house. Damn power outage. There had to be a few candles around someplace. Clumsily, she opened and closed drawers. Before the attack, she had loved candles. The biggest treat in the world was George Winston, a roomful of candles, and a hot bubble bath.

Michael had proposed in the bathtub. They were barely twenty-five at the time, just kids. She had just graduated as a mechanical engineer from Cornell and was getting her master's in Criminology from the University of New Haven, and Michael was in law school at Yale. It hadn't even been fifteen years ago, but it felt like fifty.

As she gathered candles from around the house, she could hear Billy talking to the PG&E people.

"They're going to send someone," he said as he hung up.

She turned back, holding all the candles she could find. "How long will that take?"

"Who knows."

Billy followed her into the bathroom and helped her set up candles. With every candle lit, there was just enough light to see around the room. It reminded her of Michael.

Casey frowned, wishing she could push thoughts of him aside. But, today, he seemed to be everywhere. Michael and Casey had spent their honeymoon in San Francisco, and since then they'd both dreamt of a sabbatical here. Michael even went so far as to take the California bar six months after the Virginia one. After Casey's accident, Michael had convinced her that the San Francisco-Bay Area would be the perfect place to heal. Instead, the move had managed to put a two-thousand-mile distance between Michael and Amy, and Casey.

"It would help if there were some sunshine in this place. I thought this was supposed to be the sunshine state."

"Weather's been weird ever since that El Niño thing. That's probably what happened to the power, too." He looked around. "You don't have many candles."

"I haven't done a lot of entertaining."

Billy pursed his lips. "We'll have to get some more." He disappeared, returning with a giant flashlight. He propped it up and turned it on, shining the light to the ceiling. Spreading his arms victoriously, he said, "I'll leave you to your shower."

"You'll be here if the PG&E guy arrives?"

He nodded. "I'll stay."

"Thanks."

Casey stepped into the steaming water, letting the heat run over her sore muscles. It had been nearly a year since she'd walked even as short a distance as the mile to the bottom of the hill.

Since the attack, she'd had no exercise at all, save what it took to go from the bathroom to the bedroom to the kitchen and back, or to walk down the aisles in the grocery store. She was weak and easily winded.

But this morning's walk rekindled a feeling from beneath the dust and ashes of her past. She felt good—alive and invigorated. The fresh air, the wind, the thin mist had reminded her of what she used to love—the outdoors, the exhilaration of exercise, the excitement of her heart pumping blood to her lungs and muscles. She used to run marathons. Now she could barely walk a single mile.

Pulling her hands to her face, she opened and closed her fists, feeling the muscles fight against their own weakness. Her left was much better. He had been careful to damage the right one first. Had he intended to kill her? She thought so. But he had taken so much time breaking every bone in her right hand, it seemed a waste if his intent was death.

The pain had been his main motivation, she knew. But during the attack, even the pain had faded eventually. She had found a small compartment in her own mind, and she had hidden in there, closing everything else out. Even though the torture continued, she had felt it as though from a distance.

She was sure he had sensed her withdrawal and had started in on her knee, perhaps thinking he could reawaken her pain receptors with an untouched portion of her nerves. He had been unsuccessful there, too, at least in arousing a response, though he had managed to sever the cruciate tendons from her patella.

After six days in surgery and more than thirty hours under the knife, she had only a fraction of her original dexterity. Destruction was always so much easier than repair. Leonardo hadn't been her first experience with the ease of destruction. As a profiler, Casey's home life had been an easy target.

Despite the warnings to keep her personal life separate from her cases, Casey had been unable to forget the violence when she came home. It became as routine as coffee and toast each morning. Her sympathy and patience for the aches and pains of an aging parent and a clumsy child had waned. Didn't they know people were being tortured and chopped into pieces while they were complaining about arthritis and skinned knees?

She shook her head at her own thoughts. When had it started? Certainly by the time her mother was dying. And even before that, when Amy sliced open her finger. While Amy stood in the kitchen bleeding and screaming, Casey had found herself analyzing the pattern of the blood spatter as Amy swung her hand in terror. It hadn't been a dangerous wound. But from the look in her child's eyes when Casey made light of the bleeding, it had been fatal in other ways. Now months had passed since Casey had seen her only child.

Struggling with the awkwardness of her fingers, Casey shaved her legs and massaged shampoo into her hair. Then she stood beneath the hot water until her skin wrinkled and the room around her completely filled with steam. She closed her eyes and completed her daily hand exercises. Noting the slightest improvements, she worked harder than usual.

As she reached to turn the water off, a breeze swept across her, arousing goose bumps on her skin. The flames on the candles danced. "Billy?" she called, unable to see the door from inside the shower stall.

No one answered. Casey turned the water off and stood in silence, listening for signs that she was not alone. In her early years with the Bureau, she'd perfected the ability to stand completely still. Water ran over her eyes now as rain had at other times. Like then, she blinked but did not move. The candles formed patterns of light and dark across her walls, creating a fantasy of movement. She was imagining things. The only sound she heard was the drip, drip of the water off her skin.

Wrapping herself in her towel, she stepped out of the shower and surveyed the room. In her robe, she ran the towel through her wet hair and opened the door to the bedroom. "Billy?"

He appeared at the door.

"Any word from PG&E?"

"The guy was already here. He took a quick look around and then went to check something outside."

She dropped the towel on the bed where Billy quickly grabbed it and hung it up. Tightening the belt on her thick, terry-cloth robe, she put her feet in her slippers and moved into the living room. The morning's walk had changed her. For the first time in almost a year, she wanted to read the newspaper. But she wasn't sure how Billy would react. She didn't want someone gauging her every expression as she read. And she wasn't sure she was prepared to explain herself just yet.

"You want me to brush your hair?"

She looked up at Billy and nodded.

"Is your brush in the bathroom?"

"I think so."

Closing her eyes, Casey pulled a blanket up around her waist and sank back against the cushions. Several minutes passed and she sensed Billy's presence in the room before he spoke. She turned back and saw a strange expression on his face.

Billy held up a triangular patch of hot pink satin. "I found this in the bathroom."

Starting, Casey moved off the couch. Images flashed through her mind like snippets from a horror film—

the prostitute's mutilated body, her cutoff breasts. The bloodstained panties, a triangular piece cut from the front. This was the missing piece, the piece Leonardo had taken for a macabre souvenir. She stood and stumbled on her bad knee, catching herself on the table and falling backward. Frantic, she surveyed the room. He was here.

She looked back at Billy, her legs quaking beneath her in terror. Billy still held up the fabric, his eyes widening as though he sensed what was happening. She stared at the pink satin, the words focusing as her vision blurred. "Gray needs your help, Mac. Come out and play," the black letters read against the pink fabric.

Casey tightened the muscles in her legs and grabbed the back of the couch. She thought momentarily of calling the Bureau, but decided against it. "Call the police." She paused and shook her head. "No, not the police. Call Inspector Gray."

"What is it?"

Pointing to the phone, she glared at him. "Don't ask questions. Do it."

Billy dropped the cloth and picked up the phone.

Casey crouched by the table and reached beneath it. Her fingers found the familiar small wooden box, and she dragged it into view. Opening the lid, she pulled out the subsonic RWS pistol and checked to make sure it was loaded. She hadn't held the gun since the attack.

Her hands were weak and shaky. The gun required only two pounds of pressure, she reminded herself. Surely she could manage that. She was out of practice and knew with her worthless hands, she would be a bad shot. Even without her injuries, she couldn't imagine hitting a target after so long without practice. She only hoped her aim would be at least close enough to scare him off.

If he was armed, she'd be dead before she could pull the trigger. "Think positive," she whispered to herself.

Opening the front door, Casey saw the workman's van was still parked in front. Was Leonardo actually working for PG&E? It didn't seem likely. He could be traced that way. Then how had he gotten a company van? She sensed she was about to find out.

"Don't go out there. Are you crazy?" Billy screamed in the background.

Halting, Casey didn't look back. Agents were taught never to yell at one another. One false look and an agent could easily be blind-sided by a bullet coming from another direction. All her concentration had to stay on her surroundings.

The gun positioned in front of her, Casey moved across the yard, feeling the gravel through her thin slippers. Slowly and out of practice, she surveyed her surroundings before approaching the van. Her heart trampled inside her chest, the rush she had once thrived on now terrifying her.

With a deep breath, she moved on. When she reached the van, she lay her hand on the handle. Was he inside, waiting to shoot her? Her gut said no. He had been in her bathroom as she showered. He'd had plenty of opportunity to kill her then. And he hadn't. She shoved the dread from her mind and concentrated on the van.

Stepping out of the path of whatever might spring from inside, she tightened her fingers and tried to pull the door open. Her fingers cramped, and she couldn't get a grip on the handle. Frustration caught in her throat.

On the back side of the van, she found the door partially unlatched. She pulled the latch up, and the door fell open. Casey groaned as a man's weight toppled her, throwing both of them backward.

The gun fell out of her hand, her grip too clumsy and weak to hold on. She landed hard on her back, knocking her head on the pavement. She flailed to escape. Fighting with the dead-weight, she rolled out from under the body, and pushed herself away.

Standing, her legs collapsed and she fell again, crawling away on her lumpy fists. She wiped her hand against her face and felt the warm stickiness of blood. Startled, she realized it was his blood, not hers. She looked back at the victim. A single bullet shot to the head. A low caliber, judging from the small exit wound. Leonardo had stripped the electrician of his uniform before the kill. Blood soaked his undershirt and shorts.

Casey backed around, peering at the surrounding houses and cars. Where was Leonardo? He had found her. He had been in her house. She was certain he was watching her now.

CHAPTER ELEVEN

Michael McKinley straightened his tie and took a last glance in the mirror. Today, looking sharp was as important as being sharp. Closing arguments in the biggest case of his career—he had primed the jury to believe that his client's technology had been stolen. Already the dealings suggested the settlement would be the largest in the history of his firm—in the order of two hundred and twelve million.

And they would take fifteen percent—thirty-nine million dollars, twenty percent of it his. He wished he were more excited about the money. It was enough to retire on. Still, he found himself longing for something more. Even if he won, there wouldn't be time to get away for more than a few days with Amy. He had to be in Silicon Valley for another case in less than two weeks.

He pulled on the dark suit coat and picked the brief off the bedside table, frowning as he headed downstairs. Silicon Valley was damn close to Casey. Anger welled against his desire. He wanted to see her. She'd become a distant wife and mother, then nearly gotten herself killed, pushed them away, and he still wanted to see her. He needed therapy as badly as she did. He wondered if she'd gotten any. Probably not, knowing Casey. If he still knew her, that is.

Mary handed him a cup of coffee as he entered the kitchen. Her gray hair in one long braid down her back suddenly reminded him of the way Casey had braided Amy's hair when she was little. He glanced at Amy, with her shoulder-length hair styled straight on her shoulders.

Amy sat at the table, drowning a stack of dollar pancakes in syrup.

"You going to have any pancakes with that syrup?" he asked, sitting beside Amy.

Amy laughed and rolled her eyes. "Dad. Syrup's good for you."

"Really?"

She looked at him earnestly. "Gives you energy."

"Who told you that?"

"Mom."

"Mom knows best," he said, then quieted at the reference to Casey. His eyes met Mary's, but she looked away then said, "Would you like some pancakes? I've made enough for both of you."

"Just toast would be great."

Mary nodded and set to the task. "I'm going to go to the store and pick up your shirts today."

He nodded and pulled money from his wallet.

"I'll bring the change."

He knew she would. Mary had come to him after running the household of an older partner in his firm until the children were grown enough not to need her. Now, at least someone in his life was dependable.

Mary set jam and butter on the table and then brought his toast. "Mr. McKinley, there's something I'd like to ask."

Michael looked up at her.

"You're not leaving, are you, Mary?" Amy voiced his own fears.

Mary smiled and shook her head. "Goodness, no. Not until you're fully grown, child."

Michael exhaled. "What is it, Mary?"

"My sister called last night. My mom's a little sick, and I'd like to go to Durham for a few days to visit her."

"Of course. When are you going?"

"I was hoping to leave in a week and stay for perhaps five or six days."

"A week?" Michael frowned. "But I'll be in California. Who will take care of—"

"California?" Amy squealed. "Are you going to see Mom?"

Michael snapped his mouth closed, realizing what a mistake he'd made.

Mary turned quickly to avoid the scene.

Amy dropped her fork and turned to him, her purple-stockinged legs dangling off the chair. "Dad? Are you going to see Mom? I want to come."

He started buttering his toast. "You can't come this time, honey. I'm going for work. What would you do while I was working?"

"Stay with Mom."

He pursed his lips. "You can't stay with Mom." He took a bite of his toast, but he'd lost his appetite.

"Dad, I want to go. I want to see Mom. Take me with you. Please."

He didn't meet her gaze, though he could feel those soft green eyes begging. "You can't miss school."

"Yes, I can. I'm way ahead, Dad. Mrs. Turner won't mind. And I'll make up all my work."

Frustrated, Michael dropped his toast and stood up. "Amy, no. That's enough."

Amy jumped up, knocking her chair to the floor. "I hate you. You don't want me to see Mom because you're jealous. I'm going to run away and go to California. You can't keep me here."

"Amy, please." Michael reached for her, but she'd already run from the table. "Damn it." He sank back into his chair and raked his hands through his hair.

"It might do her some good to see her mother, Mr. McKinley. I think it's rough on a little girl."

Michael didn't respond. Pulling himself from his chair, he climbed the stairs toward his daughter's room.

CHAPTER TWELVE

Jordan revved the engine as he raced up the hill to McKinley's house, taking the corners with screeching tires. Her house would mark the first scene where Jordan knew his killer had spent any amount of time—if this was his killer, as Casey claimed. Another Caucasian female, age eleven, had been found in Golden Gate Park last night, wearing a green party hat. The white girl's body had been dumped just like the black girl in the alley. Just like the other ones—not a single witness, not one piece of concrete evidence.

Jordan would know; he'd been at the last scene until nearly three a.m. The rain, which had so kindly held off for the last crime scene, had soaked them, washing away most of the potential evidence and making it impossible to find and collect anything that might have been left, including any hair.

To make matters worse, the girl's body had been left staged under a tree, her thin body naked in the deep grass. Finding evidence was like searching for a pin in a wet haystack. He still had men working in Marin County on the scene of the victim whose body had been burned in what was supposed to look like an accidental fire. But Jordan wasn't expecting any miracles. He was beginning to think this killer might be invisible.

Fatigue dragged Jordan down like ankle weights. He wasn't going to get anywhere on this case if he didn't get some sleep. He accelerated around the last corner and slowed in front of McKinley's house.

An ambulance and two cop cars met him at the scene. He took a quick survey of the people in the area, but no one looked out of place. Still, he knew his man wasn't far.

Casey was standing in the doorway in a bathrobe, waving her hands as she talked to her caregiver. Besides looking tired and scared, the man seemed as frustrated with Casey as Jordan had been yesterday.

Agent McKinley wasn't going to be easy to handle, he knew. But even as he parked, he could see the shift in her expression. Yesterday, he'd seen only anger and frustration. Now he saw something new. He wasn't certain he would call it fear, but it wasn't the same bitterness. Something in her expression had softened.

He jumped out of his car and crossed the street, shifting through the familiar throng of people. Greeting the crime scene investigative team, Jordan stopped at the back of the PG&E van and took a glove from a box on the ground.

Al Ting worked without looking up. Another investigator was air drying the rain from the surface of the van with a cordless hair dryer so they could dust for prints. Jordan figured they had to get lucky some time.

Lifting the black plastic tarp covering the body, he glanced at the electrical worker.

Officer Nancy Skaggs flipped open a notepad and turned dark eyes up to her boss. "PG&E sent the guy out at seven-forty in response to the call."

"Are those normal service hours?"

She shook her head. "They don't normally service until eight-thirty."

He frowned as she continued, "This was listed as an emergency, possible fire danger."

Given the recent history of the Oakland Hills, PG&E wouldn't risk a fire starting because they hadn't opened up shop. "Who called it a fire danger?"

"According to the guy inside the house"—she glanced back at her notepad—"Billy Glass, it wasn't him. PG&E has a record of two calls. One at seven twenty-two a.m. that came in as an emergency call because their offices weren't open. The service agent told Mr. Glass that they would send someone out during normal business hours.

"PG&E then received a second phone call twelve minutes later at seven thirty-four, again from a male, who stated he was concerned the outage might be a fire danger. Their man then left the center at seven-forty. When he arrived, it looks like someone was waiting for him."

His killer. "PG&E tape the call?"

"No such luck."

Jordan exhaled. Damn. "You check for bugs in the house?"

"There's one on the main phone line into the house; it's out back." Nancy pointed to the side of the house.

"Since when?"

Her expression tightened. "We put a call into Arnie with tech to confirm, but according to Winslow's best guess, it's been there a while."

Jordan tensed his jaw. Had the killer been watching Casey? His first visit to the house flashed through his mind. Surely the killer had known why Jordan had come. Was that what prompted him to break into Casey's home? Was he frustrated by Jordan's appearance on his turf? If anything had happened to Casey, the blame would fall on Jordan's shoulders.

He remembered the gardener he had seen that day and ground his teeth. Something had seemed off. Had that been his man? Had the killer been standing only feet from him, laughing as Jordan wrote down the license plate number? Clenching his fists, Jordan made a mental note to pursue the license plate number he'd seen.

"Oh, Winslow also said he thought it looked like fed equipment."

"FBI?"

Nancy shrugged.

He'd heard that something had gone wrong with the surveillance equipment in Cincinnati the night Casey was attacked. It was the reason Casey had suffered at the killer's hand without anyone realizing. Had the killer disabled the system and kept pieces to use here? He tightened his jaw. Or was the Bureau still keeping tabs on her?

Jordan focused on Nancy. "Check the inside phones, too. He might've bugged something while he was in there. Don't remove anything. And keep it quiet. Has anyone removed the outside tap?"

Nancy shook her head. "Winslow only got close enough to look."

If the bug had an outside microphone, the killer would have heard them talking. "He wasn't alone, right?"

She shook her head. "Lumley was with him."

"Remove that bug. Whoever planted it knows we've found it. Get it to the lab. Maybe we can figure out where it was made and track it that way."

Nancy nodded and made notes.

"But I want Winslow checking inside, and no one

says a word while he's doing it. Don't touch anything that's in place. I want a thorough check of the house—inside and out for anything that looks off."

If Jordan got McKinley to help him, he was going to have to warn his officers to tread carefully. Police didn't like to be told where they could and couldn't go. And he was quickly learning the same was true of Casey.

"Boss," Nancy said, dragging him from his thoughts. "There's more."

He nodded.

"The electricity cable in back's been cut."

"Has anyone talked to either of the residents?"

"The caregiver, Glass, is pretty shaken. That woman McKinley is a piece of work. She wouldn't talk to anyone until you got here. What's up her ass, anyway?"

Jordan shot her a hard stare. "I believe our same killer used a small tool to break all the bones in her hands when he attacked her."

Nancy whistled as Jordan moved past her toward the house. "I'd be bitchy, too."

"Damn straight," Jordan agreed.

Winslow stood, notepad open, trying to obtain a straight answer as Jordan approached the porch where they stood. Casey appeared to be blocking entrance into the house. A third officer, Lumley, stood behind him, trying to keep everyone calm. From what Jordan could see, he was barely successful.

"Ms. McKinley," Winslow pressed. "I'm going to need to ask these questions."

"I'll handle this, Winslow," Jordan interrupted.

Winslow nodded to the inspector and backed up, mumbling under his breath as he headed back to the street.

Casey frowned. "I told them I didn't want anyone in here until you arrived," she blurted before he could speak. "You'd think they were deaf."

"We need to let these guys check for wires inside," Jordan said. "Let's go out to my car to talk. You come, too, Billy."

Casey folded her arms and nodded, following Jordan toward the street.

As he passed, one of the cops rolled his eyes at Jordan and he nodded, motioning the man into the house.

"She's pretty shaken," Billy whispered as he followed Jordan.

Jordan nodded. "Sounds like she has good reason."

"That piece of fabric scared her," he said.

"Where's the fabric?"

"Inside on the floor beside the couch."

"I'll be right back," Jordan said, jogging back inside. He spotted the fabric on the floor and stooped to study it. The triangular-shaped piece of pink fabric was shiny like satin, the edges frayed as though it had been cut from a larger garment. Using his pen, Jordan turned the fabric over without touching it. Frowning, he read the black block letters that spelled out, "Gray needs your help, Mac. Come out and play." He looked up at Lumley. "Bag this, will you?"

Lumley pulled out a plastic bag and his tweezers, and lifted the fabric from the floor.

When Jordan got back outside, Casey and Billy were standing beside his car.

"Did you see it?" Billy asked.

Jordan nodded.

"I still don't understand where it came from, but she won't talk to me."

Casey rubbed her hands over her arms.

"Anyone touch it?"

Billy nodded. "I did. Does it mean anything to you, Inspector?"

"I imagine Agent McKinley recognizes the fabric," Jordan said without looking at Casey. He knew the fabric's presence was gnawing at her. Eventually she would tell them what it was. Speculating might draw her answers more quickly. "Maybe it was missing from evidence she saw in a previous case." Jordan spoke slowly, projecting his voice so Casey couldn't ignore him.

"Stop talking about me as though I'm not here," she snapped. Then she sat down on the runner of his car and hid her hands in her face. She looked exhausted, almost as though she'd been physically beaten. "Damn, I hate this guy."

"Can I do something? Make some coffee or something?" Billy offered.

Jordan nodded. "Thanks. That would be great."

"Me, too, Billy."

Billy looked at her and hesitated.

Casey took the opportunity to pounce. "Jesus Christ, Billy, I was almost killed. I want some damn coffee, okay?"

"Agent McKinley." Jordan put his hand up to stop her then turned back to Billy, his gaze encouraging him to go. "Billy, thank you for the coffee."

Billy took off toward the house.

Jordan looked back at Casey. "You always let your temper go like this? In your lecture series, you told us how important it was to keep cool, not to show frustration at a case or a killer. 'That's what he wants,' you said." He wished he could rein her in. Jordan needed Casey, but he also needed a steady, calm thinker, not the emotional remains of a great agent.

Casey put her head down again. "I'm not an agent anymore, remember? I'm just a victim."

Jordan heard her stumble on the word "victim." Inside, he knew she was struggling with her own label. "You don't have to be," he said, hoping she would muster enough fight to want this guy as badly as he did.

She glanced at her hands. "Yes, I do."

Jordan sat beside her on the runner. "You can fight him. You can help me get him. No one wants him as much as I do—no one but you."

She looked up, and he could see pain well in her eyes. Anyone else would have suspected Agent Mc-Kinley was going to cry, but he had already learned better. This woman was not a crier.

"I knew this could happen, that he might come after me."

"You think it's the same guy?"

"I know it's him."

Jordan nodded, wanting to move past what had already happened. The way this killer was working, they could have another victim by nightfall. "I'll have to talk to the captain. If you're right, this case is in the Bureau's jurisdiction. If not, then at least now we know who we're dealing with. He'll make a mistake eventually."

She kept her eyes to the floor. "Normally I would agree, Inspector. But I know this guy."

"So you can share what you learned."

She shook her head. "I'll tell you what I learned. I learned you'd better pray he makes a mistake before you do." She lifted her hands and then dropped them back into her lap.

Jordan could only imagine what terror Casey had gone through at the killer's hands before her partner had rescued her. He had heard victims tell the tales of their attacks, of the torture. He heard the ones who said they just wished they were dead. Months, even years after an attack, the victim couldn't shake the horror. The point of no return had passed. People who had never tasted such pain and fear thought the victims should be feel lucky to be alive. But the glimpse Jordan had into Agent McKinley's eyes painted a different picture.

As though reading his thoughts, Casey straightened her back and smoothed her hair with rounded fists. Despite his curiosity, he didn't allow his gaze to rest on the killer's damage. He had asked Renee to find out from her contact with the FBI what had happened with Casey's last case, and he had read the police file. He had learned that the killer had severed tendons in both Casey's hands—eighteen places in the right, eleven in the left. And he'd painstakingly broken nearly a dozen bones in each hand. Then he'd turned his attention to her right knee when he had severed another six tendons and ligaments before Casey let out a moan that her partner heard from the hall.

When the doctor got to her, Casey couldn't feel or move either hand. Eventually Jordan would want to hear her story, in all its agonizing detail, but it wasn't hard to understand why she didn't want to talk about it.

Right now, though, he needed Casey to trust him. He would need Casey's help to solve the case. No one knew this guy better than she did—if it was her killer.

Billy appeared and brought them coffee. He seemed thinner and frailer than he had the other day. His skin was peaked, almost blue in hue, as though the fear had cast the new color to permanence in his cheeks.

He set the cups on the ground in front of them and stood, awkward as a servant, waiting to be dismissed.

"Sit down," Casey commanded him, her voice softer, though it still held complete authority.

Billy appeared in no state to argue. He sat on the far side of Casey along the runner, and she moved to him, putting her arm around him protectively. "Drink it."

"It's caffeinated. With sugar," he said, his voice stony and distant.

"It'll be good for you," she told him.

She helped him lift the cup to his lips, and he took a short sip. Taking the cup from his hands, she balanced it precariously in her fists and returned it to the ground. Both arms around Billy, she whispered things Jordan couldn't hear. But the tone reminded him of the way Angie whispered to their younger son, Ryan, when he was afraid of the dark.

She turned back to Jordan and regarded him as a protective mother would a bully child. "What do you need to do?"

Jordan sat forward. "You know the drill. I want to bring some men in to dust. Then I'll need complete statements from both of you. And I've got a composite artist downtown."

"He'll have changed his appearance twenty times in the last three days," she countered.

"He can only change so much."

She glanced at the ground and nodded. "It won't help."

"I have to give it a try. Will you come down and talk to the police artist?"

She shook her head.

He slapped his leg. "Damn it, Casey. Help me."

Her eyes narrowed, she spoke calmly. "I'll do whatever I can, Inspector. But I never saw him."

"He was in your house."

She nodded and stroked Billy's hair. "Billy answered the door."

"Where were you?"

An involuntary shudder seemed to sting her. "In the shower," she responded. Then, as though shaking off whatever sensation had bothered her, she sat erect, her hand held in Billy's. To Jordan, it wasn't entirely clear who was comforting whom.

"I will come to the station to look at the case files if you like," Casey agreed. "But I would prefer you send the sketch artist here."

Jordan didn't argue. "You want to tell me about the fabric?"

Casey closed her eyes, and when she reopened them, they were more focused, harder. "Billy, would you leave us for a few minutes?"

Without a word, Billy stood up and headed for the house.

Casey settled into her spot.

Jordan respected the change he witnessed. FBI Agent McKinley was resurfacing.

She met his gaze, her hands together on her lap as she began. "The fabric was cut from a pair of underwear—a prostitute's. In October '98, Cincinnati saw the beginning of a spree of murders. The first three were all in Butler County on the east side of town. The next one was in Boone County.

"If you're familiar with the geography, Cincinnati is on the border of Kentucky and Ohio. Boone County is actually in Kentucky. The first three victims were a prostitute, a stripper, and a convenience store worker, all killed in Butler County. Then, a waitress was attacked heading to work one night. It happened between eight-fifteen and eight-thirty, so it was barely dark.

"Her body was found tied to a fence, arms raised like a puppet's. She, like the others, had been sodomized, this one with an umbrella the killer had found in her car. Her breasts had been removed with a serrated knife, one stuffed in her mouth, the other placed on her head like a hat."

Jordan made mental notes of the things that reminded him of his own case—the use of a hat, the fact that the body had been tied to a fence. So far, they were hardly enough to take to the bank let alone to the captain. Sealing his lips, he hoped she had more to offer.

"But we'd seen this sort of thing before. Typical disorganized: uses weapons from the scene—the umbrella, the stripper was tied with a bungee chord that came from her car, jumper cables left attached to her labia for shock value—" She shook her head. "Pardon the pun."

Jordan raised an eyebrow, amazed to see the fervor with which Casey spoke about her job.

She glanced up at him, her gaze surprisingly clinical. "But there was a whole other side to the crimes that suggested a much more organized offender. Each of the victims had suffered crude exploratory surgery. When he attacked the waitress, he dissected her face—she was an aspiring model. The prostitute, he dissected her genitalia. The convenience store worker was also a runner. When we found her, he had cut all the way to the bone on her legs, slicing away the skin, tendons, and muscles, all pre-mortem. In the final case, the offender even restitched a wound. And according to the M.E. on the case, the stitches looked professional."

Casey met his eyes for the first time, her strong clinical manner slipping away. "All the injuries appeared to be pre-mortem."

"He made the dissection specific to the victim?"

Casey nodded.

Jordan exhaled. He remembered the kid with braces who had her mouth cut up. The little girl with the ballerina slippers had her feet operated on. Damn, it *was* the same killer. He could sense it. "The surgery sounds like my cases, too."

She nodded and stood, pacing a small circle. He noticed the slight limp in her right leg despite her attempt to hide it. He knew that it, too, had been the killer's work. "It's the same guy all right. Thinks he's da Vinci."

"Da Vinci?"

"Leonardo da Vinci."

"I know who he is."

"Da Vinci dissected bodies as a way of understanding the human body for his work."

"Dead bodies, I assume."

She nodded. "This guy thinks he's creating art by carving up live ones. He thrills in it. He compared himself to da Vinci that night." She shuddered.

Jordan stood. "I'll get someone posted to you full-time."

Without looking at him, she shook her head. "If he wanted me dead, I'd be six feet under by now."

"If this is the same killer, it's Bureau jurisdiction," Jordan said.

"There's no way to confirm it's the same killer. I can tell you I think it is, but you're not going to sell the story far. Most killers don't progress from killing prostitutes and strippers to killing kids. The M.O. is all wrong."

"But you think it's the same killer?"

"I do."

"Then, why the change from adults to children?"

Casey shook her head. "Leonardo's got a game plan. Somehow kids are his focus now. He's got something in mind—the signature is there, the M.O. is the same, but the victims are different."

Jordan contemplated his options.

"I also want to warn you that if you bring in the Bureau, you risk scaring him off. And that means he shows up ten months from now, living across the street from my next house." She shook her head. "He's here for me. He got what he wanted."

"What do you mean 'what he wanted'?"

She looked up at him, her green eyes dark and fierce. "He wanted me back in the game. And he got it."

CHAPTER THIRTEEN

Casey watched the water as Jordan drove them across the Bay Bridge toward San Francisco. Fog covered the tops of the distant buildings like thick cotton. Still, in the water, Casey could make out scattered sailboats and an occasional ferry. The ridges on the bridge's surface ticked a steady beat under the tires as she ticked off items on a long list of things she could no longer do—swim, sail, windsurf.

Not that she'd ever windsurfed, but she might have, someday. Instead, now she was confined to doing things that required less than five pounds of pressure. And that was with her strong hand.

"You seem nervous."

Casey shook her head. "I'm okay."

Jordan shrugged, and Casey turned away from him. Drive, her list continued, although she might possibly add that back to the list someday. Play tennis, ride a bike, eat at a fancy restaurant, hold a wineglass with two fingers.

"It's not as bad as you think," Jordan said without looking over.

"What?"

"Your hands. You seem to be working around it pretty well."

Casey crossed her arms, shoving her hands out of sight, wishing she didn't feel so damn uncomfortable, wishing she could forget about them. "Working around what?"

"Your dis—" Jordan stopped himself.

"My disability. I'm disabled. Was that what you were going to say?"

Jordan sighed. "I was, but it wasn't what I meant. I told you it wasn't noticeable."

"Right, people just overlook it—just like people don't notice you're black."

Jordan met her gaze, his eyes hard. "You got a problem with black people?"

Casey shook her head. "No. I'm stating the obvious, Inspector. Saying people don't notice my hands is like saying that our society is color blind, that it's even a possible notion. Well, it's not. Especially not in law enforcement. It's opened its doors to women and minorities, but you don't see crippled FBI agents. That's what I'm saying."

"Are you saying I got my job because I'm black?" His tone was tight.

Casey shook her head and let out a frustrated laugh. "Jesus, you think like a man. This isn't about you, Inspector. I was using race as an example. I don't know anything about you or how you got your job. All I'm saying is that you have one, and I don't."

"And you think you don't have a job because of your hands?"

"Now you're getting it."

Jordan shook his head. "That's a lousy excuse."

Casey felt her mouth drop. "Excuse me?"

His stare met hers. "I said, that's a lousy—"

"I heard what you said. You think I wouldn't still be at my job if the Bureau would have me?" The words came out before she realized what they meant. The Bureau hadn't fired her. She'd quit.

"I think you left because you were scared. You have a right to be. Shit, I'd be scared, too."

Casey raised her hand. "I don't want to talk about this. I'm going to solve this damned case or die trying. I'm not here to confide my problems, and I'm certainly not here for your advice."

Jordan's jaw tightened.

She paused and shook her head. "I'm sorry. I didn't mean to snap. It's the sympathy routine—I can't stand it." She turned to face the water as her thoughts swept to her resignation from the Bureau. She could work in a different department, her special agent in charge had told her. There was the technical support squad, but she didn't want to sit in front of a computer all day. Of course, she also could no longer type.

Administration was another possibility that she wouldn't like. Then her special agent in charge suggested she could investigate issues for the Office of Professional Responsibility. It was like suggesting she police her own fellow agents. She had told her SAC to fuck himself.

Criminal profiling was what she'd done, what she'd wanted. Eventually, her SAC told her he thought she could go back to profiling. He wanted her to have time to adjust, to overcome the psychological trauma. Bullshit excuses, every one of them.

The psychologists reported her anger and aggression, her refusal to discuss the attack. As if she was going to tell her story to some shrink. She wasn't some weakling that needed to be coaxed and coddled. And all the sympathy had driven her nuts—the cards, the flowers from the agents and their wives. Her partner was walking around like a fucking hero for saving her, and she was a victim. She balled her fists and held herself from spitting.

She wasn't going to be the victim again. Turning toward Jordan, she said, "In return for helping you on this case, I need a favor."

One eyebrow raised, Jordan glanced over at her. "What kind of favor?"

"Three actually."

"Three favors?"

"I want a boxing coach. I don't expect you to pay for him, but I want you to find me one. And not some sissy. I want someone who works with cops."

Jordan didn't respond.

"Next, I want access to the precinct's target range."

Again, no response.

"And finally, I want in on every detail of this case. If you hear a rumor about where our guy took a shit, I want it. It's all or nothing."

"That's a pretty heavy list."

She shrugged. "Take it or leave it."

"You ever boxed before?"

She nodded.

"I know someone."

Anxious energy had stewed inside too long. Suddenly, it was like a dam bursting. "I'd like to start tomorrow."

Jordan let out a long, low whistle. "All right, then."

The San Francisco Hall of Justice on Bryant Street was a typical fifties-style building—a mammoth square box painted industrial white. It reminded Casey of the FBI headquarters in D.C. Only in D.C., a small courtyard honoring J. Edgar Hoover stood to mask the building's dull, boxlike structure.

Sticking out like a strange growth on the far end of the building was a new structure that looked like a space station. Casey read the sign on the glass as they passed—San Francisco Sheriff's Department.

Jordan pulled into the parking lot across from the one filled with little meter maid carts and found a spot.

"As far as anyone here knows, you're a witness in this case, not a participant in the task force. The captain strictly said no FBI. He's not going to be happy if he finds out I ignored his order."

"I'm not with the FBI."

He nodded. "It won't matter to him. You were, and so you are. I'll make sure you see everything you need, but for the most part, your presence is going to be explained by the fact that you got a look at this guy. And maybe you offered to help—doing your civic duty or something. Got it?"

Casey nodded. She didn't need recognition. This case had gone way beyond pumping her ego. She just wanted this guy put away—blown away would be even better.

The inside of the precinct belied its dowdy exterior. Walls were decorated with pictures of chiefs from as early as the 1890s. The light linoleum floors were kept carefully cleaned, the walls painted white. Beyond the front desk, Casey could see a series of long corridors leading back to the inner offices. Signs pointed to the records office downstairs, the bailiff down to the right, and holding cells to the left. Jordan led her past the bailiff and through a door marked "Inspector Division."

"My office is back this way. I'll introduce you to a

few key people before we take a look at the task
force setup."

Casey nodded, taking in the smells of dust and
sweat and gunpowder so reminiscent of her first days
at the Bureau's New York field office. No one wanted
to be located in New York—the cost of living was the
highest, they had the most crime, and it was known
for being all attitude.

Besides the cost of living, the reasons others
avoided New York were the exact ones why Casey
had wanted to go. She was intrigued with the criminal
mind. With Michael at Yale law school, it had been
easy to work from the New York field office while she
was finishing up her masters in criminology.

After her transfer to Quantico, Casey still made it
a point to get to New York for one reason or another
every few months, to keep in contact with the agents
and cases there. She slowly returned her focus to the
room in front of her.

Jordan opened a door and let her pass.

Inside a small outer office, an older black woman
sat at a desk, nodding at someone on the phone. She
glanced up and saw Casey, her brow raised as she did
a quick once-over and then looked to Jordan.

"Absolutely, Marian," she said into the receiver.
"I'll let him know. I expect him back any time." The
woman hung up the phone and stood.

"Renee, this is Casey McKinley."

Renee nodded, and the recognition in her eyes
made it clear that Renee knew exactly who Casey was.

"Casey, Renee Goodard—my right hand." Jordan's
voice cracked as he finished his sentence, and Casey
tucked her hands under her arms.

"Nice to meet you, Casey," Renee said.

Casey nodded, watching as Jordan mumbled something to himself under his breath.

He gathered materials and spoke to Renee about who had called and for what. All the familiar counterparts from when Casey was in the Bureau came back to her—discussions and negotiations with district attorneys, officers, medical examiners, lab technicians, and crime scene analysts.

Casey paced a small circle in the office, feeling the constant weight of Renee's gaze on her shoulders.

Amazed at her own behavior, Casey sensed the spark of excitement renewed. Sitting still, sleeping through the days, the draw of fiction—had all begun to lose their appeal the moment Jordan had shown up at her door two days ago.

More honestly, it had probably begun even sooner than that. Whether she had sensed Leonardo's presence or merely finally surfaced from her emotional coma, Casey wanted back in. And she wanted in now. There were all sorts of records to review—autopsies, videotapes, crime scene notes, lab results.

"You ready to see the task force setup?"

Eager, Casey followed Jordan out of the office again. Though her knee was stiff from so much activity, Jordan's steady pace suddenly felt sluggish.

Rounding the corner, Casey knew they were getting close. Phones rang in the distance. The steady clicking of fingers typing underscored the hum of voices. One of the fluorescent lights overhead flicked off and on in a steady stream of flashes, giving the hallway the sensation of a governmental discotheque.

Halfway down the corridor Jordan stopped at an open doorway, and Casey peered in. Twelve desks, each equipped with an officer, phone, and computer had been set up to man the tips line. The desks were

lined in three rows of four facing the front. Casey
watched as the officers spoke to callers. It appeared
the calls were steady for the moment. Good news,
she hoped.

The FBI didn't have much experience in tips lines.
Since the creation of the TV show, *America's Most
Wanted,* though, they had learned the value of show-
ing the viewing public pictures of fugitives.

At the front of the room, an additional desk, like
the teacher's in a classroom, faced the other desks. A
petite East Indian woman made notes on the white
board that covered the front wall.

Using red, black, blue, and brown—all colors Casey
thought appropriate for the dead—the woman had
created a column for each of the victims. Each list
included cause of death, location taken, location discovered, age, race, and evidence found at the scene.

Above each was a blown-up picture of the child.
Casey moved across the room and studied the pictures, taking in a case as she always did. The last thing
she wanted to hear was what anyone else thought the
answer was.

Start with the facts. From those, she would draw
her own conclusions. Then, if they agreed with someone else's, they would probably be on the right track.
More likely, the results wouldn't match. Casey preferred it this way. It would force her to test her own
logic against someone else's.

The pictures surprised her, but she knew this killer
would be unusual. Two blond girls, a brunette, and a
black girl, not the usual serial killer résumé. Most serial offenders chose their victims in a consistent way.
Disorganized killers preyed on victims in secluded
areas at night or in locations without witnesses—the
wrong place, wrong time methodology.

From what Casey had heard, none of these kids had been left alone in a secluded area. They had been taken from crowded places, which meant they were dealing with an organized killer. If this was Leonardo, then he was choosing his victims as an organized offender. He selected them for a specific reason—to fulfill a particular fantasy, ones who lived or attended school in a certain area, or fit a certain description. She wondered what the police knew about these kids.

"Casey, I'd like you to meet Monica Pradahn."

Casey turned to the woman she had seen at the front of the room.

Monica outstretched her hand, and Casey looked down at her own fingers. This was the reason she had avoided people. Why did she belong to a society that insisted upon the handshake? Why not bow like in Japan?

Instead of seeming awkward, though, Monica took Casey's hand in both of hers and slipped her tiny fingers into Casey's. "It's wonderful to meet you, Agent McKinley. I read the book you wrote on profiling and was quite impressed."

Blinking, Casey stared. The book she'd written had hardly been a best-seller. It had gone to a group of trainees in the Bureau's Investigative Support Unit. Almost no one else had even heard about it.

"I didn't realize you'd written a book," Jordan said.

Monica smiled. "After hearing her lecture last year, I called Quantico to see if they had more information on profiling. The public-relations person I spoke to told me Agent McKinley had a book out."

Casey shrugged. "It was a pamphlet more than a book."

Monica shook her head. "It was very powerful. I hope you know how glad we are to have you here."

Jordan nodded. "Why don't we take a look at the press conference first, and then we'll go from there."

"I'd prefer we didn't."

Monica and Jordan exchanged looks.

"It's important not to let anything or anyone plant ideas in my head before I've seen the evidence. If you want my help, I need to work this like any other profiling case."

Jordan nodded.

"I start with the crime scene reports. Then the autopsy. Did you video the scenes?"

"Stills, too."

"Good. I'll take everything you have." Casey looked around. "Do you have a room I can use to study?"

"There's a small conference room through here," Monica suggested.

The three of them moved into a small room without windows. The floor was carpeted with thin slate-blue carpet—too gray to be blue, too blue to be gray. In Bureau terms, it was effectively noncommittal.

Only a small table and three chairs occupied the room. A rectangular mirror covered a third of one wall of the room, giving people on the far side the ability to listen and see what was happening when someone was being interrogated. As she passed, she noticed the small closet-like viewing room was empty. To give them some space to work, Casey moved into the interrogation room and chose the seat farthest from the mirror.

She was used to FBI interrogation rooms with high-tech recording equipment—sophisticated cameras, which caught even the smallest change in a suspect's expression, recording devices that measured the subtle changes in voice. Tapes that would be studied later to try to determine whether a suspect was lying.

"I'll take the photos first, if you have them."

Jordan handed Casey a stack of files.

She laid the files across the table and opened the first one. What she saw reminded her instantly of Leonardo. A young black girl's face was wrapped in gauze, her puffy cheeks indicative of some sort of ritual pre-mortem surgery.

Casey flipped to the next picture and then the next. The autopsy photos showed that the skin over her jaw had been removed, the muscles connecting the mandible to the skull the apparent point of interest. Leonardo had dissected the girl before death, pinpointing a single area to explore. She felt the intense pain in her hands, the memory of his scalpel like fresh blood.

"You okay?" Jordan asked.

Casey forced herself to nod. She skimmed through all the files, slowly memorizing details as she found them. When she was done, she closed the last one and looked up at him. She couldn't look at these photos now. "I'll need more time with these files later."

Jordan nodded.

"For now, I have an idea."

He frowned. "What sort of an idea?"

"An idea that just may bring our killer out into the open."

"That's an idea I'm ready to hear," Monica said.

Jordan sank into the seat next to her. "What's this idea?"

"If we're dealing with the same killer, he's a mixed profile—organized and disorganized. His fascination with mutilation, he might call it surgery, makes him disorganized; his planning and forethought make him organized."

"So how do you propose to draw him out?" he pressed her.

"I'm getting there."

Jordan exhaled.

"He'll follow the case."

"And?"

"Jordan," Monica said, her tone stern without being sharp.

Casey sat up in her chair and faced him. "The only thing I know about his physical description is his shoe size."

Silent, Jordan shrugged.

"What if we ask for volunteers, relating to the case?"

"What sort of volunteers?" Monica asked.

"Perhaps hold a vigil for the children at a local amphitheater. Publicly ask for security volunteers. They'll be fitted for uniforms. You're looking for a white male, between the ages of thirty and thirty-five, above-average intelligence, men's size ten shoe. Our man will show up to volunteer."

Jordan's eyebrows rose as he digested the idea.

The idea wasn't a new one. She had read about it in a case in Atlanta once, and Casey knew there was a decent chance that Leonardo would recognize it as a trick. But there was also a chance they would catch him. And for that, she would take the risk.

"How do you know he'll volunteer?" Monica asked.

Casey met her gaze, remembering how a serial killer's mind usually worked—the power struggle, the need for dominance and control. It was all about the same things. "Because he's playing a game, and he wants to win," she explained. "We're his opponents, not the victims. He wants to outsmart us. In fact, I think outmaneuvering my efforts to stop him is his central goal now. He must know this is personal for me, and he thrives on the idea that he has lured back his chief opponent.

"He'd probably think—even hope—that we'd be at the vigil. And he couldn't wait to see the crowd, the mourners. The way he'd see it, we'd all be there because of him. He'd probably think of it as his first public art exhibit. It would give him an opportunity to see, firsthand, the destruction he's caused."

Casey clenched her jaw and looked away, feeling anger reverberate against her chest like a bullet in a tin can. "Frankly," she said after pausing to cool her fury, "I can't imagine he could stay away."

CHAPTER FOURTEEN

Jordan leaned forward and watched the Lakers foul out the Warriors. "Yes!"

Angie slapped his thigh. "You're rooting for the wrong team, Jordan Paul."

He leaned over and kissed her. "Maybe here, but later tonight I won't be."

Angie raised her eyebrows. "Don't you go making any assumptions about what's going down after this."

"Me? I'm not assuming." He leaned into her ear and whispered. "I plan on earning my keep every step of the way."

Angie slapped him again, playfully.

Jordan watched as his wife looked around the new coliseum. "The coliseum still isn't doing too well, is it?"

She shook her head.

"They need a better team, get some money pumped into this place."

"The Warriors will come around."

He didn't think it was likely. At the rate they were going, the Warriors would be lucky not to finish last in the Pacific division again.

The Warriors called time-out, and a guy dressed as

a lightning bolt came into the court, followed by three guys in overalls carrying boxes of pizza.

"Dad, it's Thunder." Ryan pointed to the court.

"He's giving out pizzas," Will added, standing and waving his arms.

Ryan jumped up beside him, the two boys waving their arms and jumping up and down, screaming.

Jordan sat back and whistled to draw attention. Supposedly, the loudest fans would get the pizzas.

One of the guys came toward them, and Jordan whistled and whooped louder. The guy came running up the stairs but stopped a few rows short of Will and Ryan.

"Shoot," Ryan said, slumping into his seat.

"We'll get it next time," Jordan said, putting his arm around Ryan.

The game started up again, and Jordan leaned forward, watching the play.

"Dad? How come that guy is so short? I thought basketball players had to be tall," Ryan said, pointing to a player who was under six feet.

"Not all of them, stupid," his older brother chastised him.

"Don't you call your brother 'stupid,' " Jordan said, plucking Will's shirtsleeve. "You apologize."

"Sorry," Will murmured.

"That's okay, Dad. He calls me 'stupid' all the time," Ryan said.

He didn't like to hear Will's mouth getting bad. Angie's father swore too much around the boys. It was rubbing off on Will. They should be here, with him, not down in L.A. Damn if he hadn't missed his kids. Jordan pulled Ryan onto his lap and squeezed him.

Ryan squirmed, and Jordan tickled him. "Dad, stop!"

Jordan kissed his head and let him down.

Ryan jumped back into his seat, straightened his shirt, and then crossed his arms. "Dad, you can't be doing that. I'm too big."

Jordan laughed. "You're not too big until you're bigger than me."

Ryan looked up at his dad, his eyes wide at the thought. "When do you think I'll be bigger than you?"

Jordan looked at his six-year-old son and rubbed his head. "Hopefully not for a couple more years."

"The way they're growing out of their clothes, feels more like tomorrow," Angie said.

Jordan turned back and put his arm around his wife. "I wish you'd come back up here, baby."

"Jordan, I told you," Angie said, dropping her voice. "You've got to do something about that job. Will and Ry need a father. At least in L.A., they've got my dad. He plays ball with them, helps them with their homework."

"Angie, don't talk like that. I don't ignore my kids. I'm just trying to make a name for myself as a cop. It's long hours."

Angie nodded, her arms crossed in the stance that told him this was not a point she would negotiate.

"I agree. I work too much. But, I promise I'll spend more time with the family."

"You could start by cutting out the damn card games."

Thursday night cards with the boys was practically his church. It was the only time he got to talk about cases and the stresses of the job. He needed that.

Angie clucked her tongue at him. "You talk about

wanting us back, but you aren't even willing to make the smallest sacrifice."

Jordan sighed, his eyes on the game but his mind on everything but. "Of course I want you back. If you want me to quit the card game, I'll quit it. Hell, I'll quit the force if that's what you want."

She laid her hand on his thigh. "I don't want that."

Jordan met her gaze. "Well, I would."

Angie smiled. "Come on, baby, let's enjoy the weekend."

He wondered if that was possible. Forcing his thoughts from meandering to the job, he wrapped his arm around Ryan and leaned over him to touch Will's shoulder. "What do you think, Will?"

"I think that guy is a gangster."

Jordan nodded, focusing on the player with the braids. "Probably."

"Why does he need to be a gangster, Dad?" Ryan asked. "Doesn't he make enough money playing basketball?"

Will scoffed. "Millions of dollars."

Ryan turned to his brother in awe. "Really?"

"Yep. All of them make that much," Will added.

"Is that true, Dad?"

Jordan nodded. "Probably."

"Then, how come he's a gangster?"

"I don't think he's really a gangster, Ry. I just think he likes to dress and act that way."

"There's a kid like that in school," Will said. "Got the braids and everything. Thinks he's so fucking tough."

Jordan grabbed Will's arm. "Watch your tongue."

Will shrugged him off. "He does."

Jordan tossed a look at Angie.

"Some kid's been giving him a hard time at school," she explained.

"What do you mean, a hard time?" he pressed, thinking of his own childhood.

"Just regular kid stuff, Jordan," Angie said.

"You talked to the teacher?"

She nodded. "It's just the class bully."

"Sounds like more than just a bully to me."

Angie shook her head. "He's at the best school in the area."

Jordan looked at his wife. "No school's one hundred percent these days."

Angie stared straight ahead. "This one is."

Jordan remembered being in the fifth grade. That was about the time his second oldest brother was killed.

"What's going on at school, Will?"

Will swung his right hand out and down like the cult figures in recent movies. "He's all over my shit."

Steaming, Jordan stood this time and took Will by the arm. "Let's go."

Will tried to shake his father off, but Jordan just gripped tighter, dragging the boy toward the aisle.

"You and I are going to talk."

"I have to go to the bathroom," Ryan called after them.

"Take Ry, too," Angie said, pushing their younger son after them.

Jordan grabbed Ryan's hand with his free one and led both boys toward the lobby.

People milled through the halls, stopping for food and beers or heading into the bathrooms. Jordan remembered Lakers games as a kid. No one would leave in the middle of a play for food, or anything else.

Looking down the hall, he spotted the sign for the

men's rest room and walked to it, still holding on to both boys.

"You want me to go with you?" he asked Ryan.

Ryan shook his head and went into the bathroom.

"We'll be right here, Ry," Jordan said, wondering if he shouldn't go in there with Ryan. There was no way for Ryan to come out except past him. He'd be fine. Jordan took Will's arm and pulled him to the side.

Will shook him off and stared at the people passing.

"You listen here, Will. I won't have you talking like some punk."

"All the kids talk like that," Will refuted without looking at his father.

Jordan shook him, forcing Will's gaze to meet his own. "Do I talk like that?"

Will shook his head.

"That's right. Does your mom?"

"No."

"Then you won't, either."

"It's different, Dad. You don't understand." Will started to walk away.

Jordan took two steps and grabbed his son, spinning him around. Wasn't Will too young for this? He'd only been living in L.A. for a month, but already it felt like he'd been away for a year. "How's it different? Because they're doing it, means you gotta? You gonna follow the other kids, do what they do?"

Will shrugged.

"One kid decides to smoke, you gonna smoke, too?"

Will rolled his eyes. "No."

"Some kid decides to steal something, you gonna steal something?"

"I don't mean like that."

"You're talking like you do. You've got to talk like the other kids. Pretty soon you'll be smoking like they do, drinking if they do, stealing things. I'll tell you what happens to the kids that follow other kids, Will. They end up in jail or dead 'cause they can't think for themselves. Is that what you want?"

"No one's going to kill me. And I'm not going to go to jail because I haven't done anything bad. Dad, you're a cop. You aren't supposed to understand."

Jordan felt his fear harden into anger. He grabbed his son's arm and pulled him close. "I'll tell you something, Will, and then maybe you'll understand. You know your Mema?"

"Grandma Grays?"

He nodded.

"What about her?"

"She had six children. Six, you hear me?"

Will nodded, looking confused.

"I had four older brothers," Jordan continued.

"What happened?"

"I'm getting there. When I was in fifth grade—just about your age, my brother was shot in the head. You know why?"

Will's eyes widened as he shook his head.

"Tyler was in the tenth grade, running with the rough kids. Almost all the kids were rough in Compton, where I grew up. But Tyler had been running with the worst of them, the ones who settled their disagreements with guns." Jordan remembered the gun problems were just starting then—in the 60s. He could only imagine how much worse it was now. "And they disagreed a lot," he continued, "over girls, over drugs, over turf.

"Tyler had started a fight and ended up with a bullet to the head. He was killed because he followed the other kids. He did what he thought was cool. He smoked and stole things and carried a gun. And he got shot in the head."

Will stood perfectly still.

"And six months later, another brother was killed. He was shot, too." Jordan remembered it like it was yesterday. Another bullet, this one to the heart. That had been enough for Jordan's parents to finally get out of L.A. County. Damn if he was going to let something like that happen to his kids.

Will blinked twice, his eyes suddenly glassy. "How come you didn't tell me?"

"Because I didn't want you to know about the bad things that happened to kids. I wanted you to grow up different from how I did. You understand?"

Will nodded, and Jordan pulled him close. "You don't go following those other kids around. They egg you on, call you a sissy or whatever, you ignore them, you hear me?" He could feel Will nod against his shoulder. "I won't let anything happen to you, Will."

"I miss you, Dad."

Jordan tightened his arms around Will, squeezing his eyes closed. "I miss you, too, Will. Man, I miss you so much it hurts."

Will pulled away and wiped his eyes with the back of his hand. "I don't like living in L.A. I want to come back to school here. I like it better."

Jordan ran his hands over Will's cheeks. "I know. We'll get you back up here, I promise."

"Why are you and Mom fighting?"

Jordan sighed, wishing he had an easy answer for that one. All he wanted was to have Angie, Will, and Ryan back home. Ryan. Jordan stood up and looked around. "Where's your brother?"

"Probably still in the bathroom. He takes forever,"
Will said.

Jordan took Will's hand and entered the bathroom.
"Ryan?" he called, looking down the row of stalls.

No one answered.

"Ryan?" he repeated, a little louder.

"Ryan!" Will yelled.

The ache of fear gripped Jordan's stomach in a tight
fist. "Ryan!" he called again, looking under stalls for
a pair of short legs.

The doors opened one by one, and Jordan watched
for Ryan to appear. Jordan started to push the unoc-
cupied doors open, checking for his son. "Check the
open ones, Will."

"I don't see him, Dad," Will said, his voice shaking.

"Keep looking." Jordan checked all the stalls twice
and spun around the room. How could he have missed
Ryan? The boys knew better than to walk away from
him. He'd told them about the dangers. Jesus Christ,
where had he gone?

"Where's Ryan, Dad?" Will's eyes were wide with
fear. It was exactly how Jordan felt.

"I don't know, Will. We're going to find him. Come
on." Holding tightly to Will's fist, Jordan ran out of
the bathroom and looked down the corridor in both
directions. "Ryan!" he called.

"Ryan!" Will called, too.

Jordan started to run to his left, searching over the
heads for Ryan. Jordan couldn't even remember what
his own son was wearing. What was wrong with him?
"What's he wearing, Will?"

"He's got jeans on and my old gray Bulls
sweatshirt—the one with the red bull on it."

"Okay, good. Keep your eyes open for the red
bull."

"Is that him?" Will pointed through the crowd, and Jordan's heart shifted in his chest. Please let it be Ryan, he thought.

They chased through the crowd, and Jordan saw a little boy in a gray sweatshirt and jeans. "Ryan!" he screamed.

The little boy looked back, and his face was like a blow to the gut.

"That's not him."

Jordan shook his head. "Come on, Ryan. Where the hell are you?"

Will started to cry, and Jordan picked him up. "Come on. Be strong, Will. We're going to find him. It's going to be okay." But dread weighed on his shoulders like wet cement. Someone had taken his child. Someone had stolen Ryan because he wasn't paying close enough attention. He'd told Angie that the boys would be better off with their father. But he'd been wrong. He'd lost Ryan.

Jordan hugged Will to him and swung around, looking back in the other direction. He spotted a security guard and raced toward him. Flashing his badge, Jordan said, "I'm an inspector with the San Francisco Police Department. I'm looking for my son. His name's Ryan Gray. He's six, dressed in a gray Chicago Bulls sweatshirt and jeans." He spoke in the calmest voice possible, knowing from experience that a hysterical parent did nothing to assist in the search of a missing child.

The security guard nodded and pulled a radio from his belt. "We have a missing child—name's—"

"Ryan Gray," Jordan repeated, the sound like a bullet ricocheting in his gut.

"Ryan Gray," the guard continued. "Subject's a six-year-old, African-American boy, last seen wearing a gray sweatshirt and jeans."

Jordan squeezed his eyes closed, still holding Will tight to his chest. The words "last seen" bounced around in his head. He didn't want Ryan to be "last seen." He investigated children that were last seen.

"Dad?"

Jordan whirled around and saw Ryan.

Will let out a choking sob and jumped free of his father's arms, grabbing his younger brother.

Jordan dropped to his knees, staring at his son. The thrill of having him back was halted momentarily by the sight of a blue birthday hat strapped on his head. Fear rumbled through him like an earthquake.

"Looks like he just joined someone's birthday party," the guard commented.

Jordan pulled the hat off and dropped it beside Ryan, afraid to look at it. He touched the boy's face, looking him over to be sure he wasn't hurt. "Are you okay?"

Ryan nodded in silence.

His hands still holding both of his sons, Jordan looked down at the hat. From the outside, it looked just like the others except the color. There had been red, orange, yellow, green, and now blue . . . on his own son. Was it just his imagination or was it really the same hat that the killer had been putting on his victims? Looking inside, he cringed at the words scrawled in black marker.

"Not the gangsters you should fear."

Jordan leapt to his feet and searched the corridor. He turned to Ryan and motioned to the hat. "Who gave this to you?"

"A man."

Jordan inhaled quickly. "What did he look like, Ry? Was he black or white?"

"White."

"Short or tall?"

The boy furrowed his brow. "Tall."

"What color hair?"

Ryan's face crumpled as he started to cry. "I don't know, Dad. He just took my arm and told me he was your boss. He looked like a policeman. He even had a badge. He said if I didn't listen, you'd be in big trouble. I was scared, Dad. He was scary. Big and scary." The boy started to cry.

Will was crying, too.

Jordan held both boys and soon, he was crying, too. He was failing. He'd let the madman touch Ryan, touch his own child. Ryan was safe now, but Jordan had let him down. The killer could have taken him, could have killed him. Jordan knew he should try to find the killer, but he couldn't. Right now he couldn't bear to let go of his children.

CHAPTER FIFTEEN

Jamie looked over at Aaron. "You do not know her," he said, firing the last rubber band on his wooden gun at the girl on the TV.

"Do, too," Aaron said, pulling rubber bands over the trigger of his own gun.

Jamie stood and gathered the shot bands from the floor beneath the TV, and then returned to his spot beside Aaron.

"I saw her," Aaron continued.

Jamie looked up at the girl on the screen. She looked a little like Cindy, a girl in his class. Only Cindy had a bigger nose, and this girl was cuter. It was probably the nose. "Where?"

Aaron shot the gun, and the rubber band hit the girl on TV square in the forehead. "Bull's eye," he screamed.

"Try two at once," Jamie said, strapping two rubber bands onto one peg and then pulling the trigger and watching them both release. The two bands snapped against the girl's eyes on the TV. "She's blind!"

Aaron laughed.

Jamie looked back at the girl. She didn't look familiar to him. "You really know her? Is she famous or something?"

Aaron shrugged. "I never seen her on TV before. She was in the mall when I was there."

"When did you go there?"

He shrugged. "Last week or something."

Jamie looked at the girl again. "You think she's cute?"

"No!" Aaron said, his eyes wide. He made a disgusted face.

"Then, why do you remember her?"

Aaron glanced at the TV. " 'Cause her dad was a policeman."

"Really?" Jamie looked at her, too. "That's cool."

"Yeah. I wish my dad was a policeman."

"Me, too. Then, you could ride in the cars and stuff."

Aaron nodded. "And they'd let you turn on the sirens and drive really fast."

"The police drive really fast." Jamie looked over at Aaron. "Why was the policeman in the mall? Was he arresting someone?"

Aaron shot the TV with his rubber-band gun. "I don't know."

"Did you see any bad guys?"

Aaron shook his head.

Jamie looked back at his gun. "I want to see some bad guys. Think they look different?"

"Of course."

"How?" Jamie asked.

Aaron shrugged. "Bad."

Jamie nodded. "Did you go the toy store? There's a new Lego set. It's a spaceship, and the guys have the real suits and helmets that come off. I played with it at Ricky's house. Ricky has all of them."

Aaron looked down. "My mom wouldn't let me look."

"I'm going to get it for my birthday," Jamie announced. His mom had told him his birthday was less than a hundred days away. That sounded like a lot, but she said it wasn't that far.

"Yeah?"

"Yeah. You can come over and play with it."

"Really?" Aaron smiled. "Thanks."

"Sure." Jamie aimed at the TV again, but the picture had changed to a man standing, waving his arms to a crowd of people. He snapped up the remote control and flipped the channels. A woman in a bathing suit was running on the beach.

Aaron snapped his gun and hit the woman in the breast. "I got her boob."

They both laughed and rolled over.

"Her boob," Jamie repeated, laughing so hard snot flew out of his nose. He wiped it with the back of his hand.

The door opened, and his mom came in. "Do you boys want a snack?"

"Yeah," Jamie and Aaron said in unison and headed for the kitchen.

CHAPTER SIXTEEN

Pulling his knees close to his chest, he studied the flickering light from the old television, straining to hear the mayor's voice over the crackle of static.

"It is with incredible anger and outrage that I stand before you today. Four of our children have been brutally murdered."

He smiled and leaned closer, the mayor's sense of drama increasing his excitement.

"These children were not out walking alone. Nor were they grabbed in the darkness. These children were stolen in the middle of the day . . ." He gave a profound pause. "Stolen from the centers of our community, under the watchful eyes of their parents while at crowded shopping malls." The mayor shook his head, playing up the intense emotion. The reporters were silent but for the occasional click of a camera.

Moving his chair closer to the TV, he wished he could be there, to watch in person.

"This monster has invaded the security of our community. But he will not be allowed to continue."

Smiling, he rocked lightly in his chair, a delighted charge singing his awareness. They were talking about him. The same man that Indiana University had dared to reject from its premed program. He crumpled his fists and remembered his mother's smile as he told her. He and his sister and his mother had all gathered at the house that night—but they had not come to comfort him. They'd been together to celebrate his sister's birthday. They had offered no condolences for his rejection. Instead, they had mocked him—made fun at his lowest hour. That had been their gravest error.

He could still picture his mother's face as he had showed her what a skilled surgeon he was—showed her on her own daughter. If Indiana could see his work now, what a master surgeon he had become. He would apply again. He would finish his work here and go back. They would not deny him again. He unclenched his fists and let out his breath, commanding his muscles to unwind and his anger to drain.

"I am here to urge us all, as a community, to come together to fight this predator," the mayor continued. "The families will be holding a vigil this Sunday evening at dusk. We will announce the location as soon as it is known. I hope to see the aid and attendance of the community to support the families of the deceased. By attending, each of us is making the public announcement that we will fight violence, and especially violence against children.

"I assure you—" the mayor shouted, raising his arms like a preacher. "I assure you that the San Francisco Police Department is using all available resources to find the man responsible for this." The mayor looked over his shoulder. "But the department needs your help. I would like to introduce the chief of the San Francisco Police Department, Bill Jackson."

Calmer, he wrapped his arms around his knees and

leaned forward, his nose only inches from the set.
"Bill Jackson," he muttered.

"What do you think you're doing, Joe?"

He straightened his back and turned to the desk,
his face flushing red with fury. Joe Tharpe was his
name at work, and he hated how plain it was.

His boss Dwayne leaned over the desk, his gut like
a thick balloon begging to be popped. Stroking his
graying mustache with his short, cork-like fingers,
Dwayne raised his brow and waited for him to respond. Dwayne's brown eyes sagged into his face, and
he imagined his face without any eyes.

"I was listening about the kids that were killed," he
answered, furious at his own feeling of helplessness.
He hated Dwayne's bullying. He was suddenly a kid
again, helpless.

"You ain't paid to watch the TV, moron. I ain't
having someone fuck up things on my shift."

He clenched his teeth, unable to find a quick reply.

Dwayne leaned forward until his face was inches
away. "You're paid to watch those monitors. You
hear?"

He forced himself to nod.

"You a mute?" Dwayne asked, breathing foul cigarette breath in his face.

"I heard you," he answered, boring his gaze into
Dwayne's forehead and commanding Dwayne's head
to explode.

"Get up, then."

He stood, and Dwayne put out his foot as he moved
to pass, tripping him.

He landed on all fours, feeling the hard marble floor
against his knees. Eccymosis from that fall, for sure.
He'd always bruised easily.

"One more time, and I'll have you fired, Joe. And

I don't know where a screw-up like you's going to find another job."

He picked himself off the floor and stared after Dwayne as he laughed and headed back down the empty corridor. Anger seethed like acid, etching holes in his control. He lifted the two-way radio from the desk, gripping it tight in his fist as he counted to five and then followed Dwayne.

It was time to leave this job, anyway. His plan was coming to a head, and there wouldn't be time to waste here. Tomorrow he would see Casey. He would touch her. Billy had already planned it. Imagining his hands on her filled him with power. Control. Dwayne had tried to strip him of control. But it had been a fatal mistake.

The senior guard waddled down the hallway like a penguin, his belly obstructing the motion of his legs.

Halting at the far end, he paused until Dwayne had turned the corner, knowing where he was headed. Thankfully, it was after ten o'clock, and the building was quiet. Still, people came and went at all hours, especially from the investment-banking firm on the thirty-sixth floor. He would have to be swift.

He paused at the door to the small utility room and listened. The familiar sounds of TV leaked under the door. Dwayne considered the closet his office, and he had somehow managed to rig it with cable TV. As far as he could tell, Dwayne spent his nights watching porn movies and jacking off. And Dwayne had the nerve to call him a moron.

Easing the door open, he saw Dwayne sitting with his back to the door. He crept through the small opening and quietly shut the door behind him.

A woman with huge breasts that filled the screen was bobbing up and down, panting and moaning. The camera zoomed to her crotch. The bobbing motion grew faster as her moans grew louder. Dwayne began to rock in his chair, his hand out of sight.

TV sex or violence had never been much of a turn-on. It was all so much better live. He moved up behind Dwayne and raised the radio above his head. As the woman climaxed with a piercing scream, he slammed the radio down on Dwayne's head. The senior guard fell forward out of his chair and onto the floor.

Adrenaline's acid burned through him as he stepped forward and flipped the body over and pressed his hand to Dwayne's neck. His boss's pulse was clear, and he was pleased. He had plans for Dwayne, clear plans for his death. He shut off the TV, the sounds of moaning distracting from his own excitement. Dwayne would provide the sound effects for pleasure.

Reaching into his pocket, he pulled out his penknife and snapped it open. He spotted Dwayne's overcoat and cut slices from it. He tied Dwayne's hands and feet and then bunched a small piece of fabric into his mouth, careful not to press it back too far. In an unconscious victim, it would be easy to push a gag back too far and suffocate him by forcing his epiglottis or tongue to occlude the airway. That would be far too pleasant a way to go for Dwayne.

Dwayne moaned, and his eyes shuttered open and closed again. He straddled him, poised to strike him when he was awake enough to process what was about to happen and to be afraid. Excited and empowered, he couldn't wait to see the fear in the other man's eyes.

CHAPTER SEVENTEEN

"Again," he shouted, the South African accent adding a spicy flavor to his scratchy voice. "Same sequence."

Sweat dripped across her eyes as Casey pumped her arms.

"Talk to me," Frank yelled. "Got to make sure you're still breathing." He paused as she finished the sequence. "Again."

"Jab, jab, head shot, head shot, hook, hook, under-cut, undercut." Casey snapped her gloved hands out, landing the punches with muffled slaps against the bag. Her shoulders ached, but she didn't slouch.

For four straight mornings, Frank had watched her like a hawk. As soon as he saw her weaken, he made her stop. She was getting stronger, but not nearly fast enough.

"One more time," Frank shouted.

"Jab, jab, head shot, head shot, hook, hook, under-cut, undercut," she said, panting.

"That's it. Let's go to the mat and do sit-ups."

Breathing heavily, Casey would have liked to continue, but she was too exhausted to argue. For four days, she had worked daily on regaining her strength. Starting in the morning, she sat with a foam squeeze toy in each hand, forcing her fingers open and shut, fighting to close her grip. Though her left hand seemed to be slowly regaining some power, her right hand still felt helpless. The hand's dexterity had improved only slightly more than the strength. She still couldn't maneuver a button without a ten-minute struggle.

Her knee, on the other hand, felt much improved. Wearing the brace that the orthopedic surgeon had made for her after the accident, she'd jogged up the hills near her house and then walked down them backward.

She'd also changed some things around the house. She'd had a full, fancy alarm system installed over the old one, changed the locks on all the doors, added bolts, and strengthened the window locks. She'd also had a lock added to the main electricity panel, and the alarm system now ran a five-foot perimeter around the house as well as to all doors and windows.

The alarm system itself had done nothing to ease Casey or her checkbook, but she knew the killer had seen it was there and that made her feel better. She had also pulled out the old case files she'd hidden away in a suitcase when they'd moved out to California. She had reviewed her old notes and added new thoughts as things occurred to her, sharing them with Jordan when they spoke.

She had a full profile on Leonardo again, most of it matching what she'd had originally—loner, above-average intelligence, thirty to thirty-five, well kept, college educated. She thought about the language he had used in her attack. Look for a medical job history—nurse or ambulance technician, maybe a coroner's assistant. Every time she boxed, she pictured him in a bit fuller detail, adding each new clue to her list until she knew him as well as she knew herself.

"Too hard today, McKinley."

"I'm okay," she argued.

Frank shook his head, laying his hand on her shoulder. His dark eyes scolded her. "Too hard."

She started to lower herself to the mat. "I need to get stronger." She leaned back and raised herself up with the first sit-up. The muscles in her abdomen seemed to tear from her rib cage. She felt bruised and beaten. For some reason, the sensation was almost comforting.

Frank knelt beside her and caught her on her next sit-up. He gripped her hands. "I know you're impatient, but rushing, it's not going to help. You need to build endurance, and that takes time."

"I don't have time."

He shook his head lightly. "You got time."

Casey freed her hands and continued her sit-ups. Shaking his head, Frank walked away.

Casey felt her legs begin to shake as she reached forty-three. Teeth clenched, she pushed herself. Only seven more. Forty-four, forty-five, forty-six.

"One thousand, four hundred and sixteen . . . "

Casey looked up and caught Jordan Gray's face upside down, staring at her. Forcing herself to make it to fifty, she laid back and put her arms up over her head to catch her breath.

"You wonder what I'm doing here?"

She shrugged, too breathless to respond.

"Frank said you might need a ride home. And I've got news."

Despite the ache in her belly, Casey sat up, imagining what the news might be. The pain in her stomach tightened and sank like a heavy weight into her gut. This pain didn't come from the sit-ups, and somehow it wasn't one she could fight off like she used to. "Another child?"

Jordan shook his head, lowering his eyes to the floor.

Watching his face, though, she could tell that something had happened. His eyes were bloodshot, the skin around them dark and puffy. It almost looked as though he'd been crying.

"Your family?"

His gaze snapped back to hers, and she knew she was right.

Jordan put out his hand, and she took it, letting him pull her up. On her feet, she touched his arm. "Are they all right?"

The muscle in his jaw tightened and loosened. Finally, he looked up and said, "Fine. No thanks to me."

"What happened? Was he at your house?"

"Get your stuff. I'll tell you on the way home."

Casey watched Jordan pull out of the gym parking lot and head down Broadway toward Piedmont Avenue. Broadway was quieter now than it had been when she'd cabbed down this morning at six. At six o'clock on a Saturday morning, people were still emerging from Biff's all-night diner. Casey watched a tall black man emerge with a woman on either arm. His dark glasses at the early hour indicated it had been a long night. The length of his companions' skirts indicated the women were used to long nights.

Casey focused on Jordan, waiting for him to share his news. His fists were tight on the steering wheel. She studied the lighter skin around his knuckles and envied his ability to grip so fiercely.

Her own hands were still wrapped, a soft foam grip in each one to be sure she didn't break the bones again. The doctor had refused to give his okay to box. She didn't care. At least he was helpful enough to give her suggestions on ways to protect her hands. She pulled off the wraps and struggled to spread her fingers.

"I took them to the Warriors game last night."

Casey looked up at Jordan. His eyes, though blurry and distant, were focused through the windshield. "The boys?"

He nodded. "And, Angie." He paused for a few moments and then blinked hard twice before continuing. "Will was talking trash, and I got so damn mad."

"That's normal, Gray. I get angry with Amy all the time." She caught herself. She didn't get angry with Amy anymore. She never even saw her daughter anymore. She thought of the picture stowed in her bedside table, and the familiar ache took hold.

"He should be with both of his parents, you know?" He glanced over, and then, as though realizing who he was talking to, redirected the conversation. "I took him out of the game to talk to him."

Though thoughts of her own child continued to drift in her mind, Casey remained focused on the story.

"Ryan, my younger son, had to go to the bathroom. So I took them both out." He paused and glanced over his shoulder to change lanes.

Though Jordan didn't shed tears, Casey watched his face crumple when he described the fear first of losing Ryan, and then the absolute terror of knowing Ryan had been in Leonardo's hands. Once, she, too, would have understood it on a deeper level, on the level of a mother. But she couldn't even remember what that was like, the experiences between now and motherhood had so totally destroyed her ability to empathize. "Did you see him?" was all she could think to say.

Jordan shook his head. "I don't get this. I grew up in one of the most violent areas of the country. I lost two older brothers to gang warfare. It was greed and lust and turf. Reputation was everything. I understand that.

"Sometimes, I can even relate to it. The danger of bullet spray and drive-by shootings is almost comforting in comparison to this. This guy makes me crazy. I don't understand him—I can't."

Casey shook her head, her gaze returning to her hands. "I don't think you could."

"But you do."

She nodded slowly. "I don't think it's healthy."

"None of it's healthy. If I wanted healthy, I'd have sold insurance."

She watched his eyes, but he wasn't joking.

"What drives someone to do this? How does he deal with remorse?"

She scoffed. "There's no remorse."

"Come on. He chops up a little kid, and he doesn't feel bad about it later?"

She shook her head. "No. In fact, I think he feels good about it. It makes him feel strong, dominant. Power is very important to him. Wearing the uniform ties in with that. Being seen as an authority figure, especially a trusted one, is very appealing."

"Why is someone like this?"

"He was probably abused as a kid—most of them are, one way or another. In his case, I think he grew up without a father. Probably bailed on the mother when he was young. She felt strapped, took her anger at her situation out on him." Casey reviewed her original profile. Most of it still fit.

"I'd guess a domineering mother," she continued. "Probably had another sibling, one he felt competitive with. Maybe a sister who the mother liked more." She stopped. "The change of victim group is confusing—children from adults. It's unusual. I suspect it relates back to his family, though. A sister who got all the attention. I'm only guessing.

"Leonardo did not grow up with any strong male figures, though. His anger is based almost entirely at females. The children are taken when they're with their mothers, and they've all been female. You're looking for someone who's never had a normal sexual relationship—he'd be very immature sexually. He may even be a virgin. Sex is anger to him. He has no idea how it should function."

Casey thought about all the hours she'd spent profiling Leonardo. "The inability to function in sex carries over into all his personal relationships—he's a loner. He may be nice-looking, though. Remember, he's luring children away in broad daylight and from under the noses of their mothers, so he doesn't look like a monster. That's what makes him so dangerous."

"You think he is taking out his anger on women. What about the PG&E guy?"

"The PG&E guy was in the way. He wouldn't consider that kill part of his portfolio. It might make him feel empowered or dominant, but mostly it's a means of getting to me. He would kill others that way as well—maybe he already has. The ones that matter are the ones he can control, the ones he kidnaps and takes his time with." Casey paused, trying to fit the puzzle together. "I'd like to find out more about the families. Have you asked any of them if it would be all right to speak with them?"

He shook his head. "If this vigil works, we won't need to talk to them."

"There's a good chance it won't."

Jordan didn't meet her gaze.

"It's a crap shoot, Gray. I don't want you to get your hopes up."

He didn't respond immediately. "I told the captain about what happened in Cincinnati, about the fabric, and you . . ."

Casey studied his face.

"He doesn't think it's enough to prove the cases are related. He thinks the case is still in our jurisdiction— no Bureau."

She nodded. It didn't surprise her. She had enough experience with local law-enforcement agencies to know how they worked. "Do you?"

"Do I what?"

"Believe that it's the same killer."

Jordan looked at her and nodded. "After the note at your house, I do."

She looked out the windows, watching the people mill about the streets.

"Tell me more about him," Jordan said after a few minutes.

She frowned.

"Leonardo."

Nodding, she sorted through what she knew. "I expect he was a late bloomer, introverted, maybe perceived as a weakling."

"Small in stature?" Jordan's voice carried a tinge of excitement.

She shook her head. "I didn't say small."

"You said 'weak.' "

"Not the same thing."

Jordan nodded.

"Gray, there's no way to describe the physical elements of a serial killer. Ed Kemper was a big guy— probably six-two, two-ten, looked like a football player. He killed about ten, they think, including his mother. The Atlanta Child Murderer was a black man, though the press and many of the authorities at the time were sure the killings were the act of the Klan. Robert Hansen was a small white man, probably only five-eight and one-fifty or so, worked as a baker. Ted Bundy and Jeffrey Dahmer were both described as handsome. I could go on and on. If I could draw a picture of this guy, I would."

"You think he might be black?"

Casey caught his eye and shook her head. "I know he's white. I knew it even before Billy saw him at the house."

"Why?" Jordan countered.

"I could tell you I think so because of the victims he's chosen and from the evidence we found." She paused. "But that's not why."

"Why, then?"

She shivered and wrapped her arms around herself. Jordan adjusted the heat.

"I think he's white from the sound of his voice. That's the only thing I can still imagine when I close my eyes."

"You never saw his face?" Jordan's voice was barely a whisper, but it crawled up her arms like a poisonous spider.

Shaking it off, she shook her head. "Never saw anything. He injected me with something before I realized what was happening. I struggled, but he blindfolded me almost immediately." Casey could feel the initial incision of the knife into her hand, the electric-like pain of his scalpel cutting the skin.

"Do you think you'd still know his voice?"

She looked up at him. "Half the time I swear I would. The other half, I'm not sure. I hear it in the grocery store or at the doctor's office. Sometimes just a word does it." She shook her head.

"Did your partner see him?"

"He made a ruckus at the door. By the time he got inside, Leonardo had made it out the window."

"Ryan confirmed he was white, too."

"Have you gotten Ryan to talk to a police artist?" Jordan didn't meet her gaze. "He's so scared."

"It will help him work through the fear, you know that."

"I don't know. You didn't see his face. He came walking back, wearing that blue party hat. He was so scared. I swear I felt my insides rip apart."

She nodded, deciding not to press it. Even with a description, she was confident that Leonardo could disguise himself well enough to make the sighting basically worthless. They were going to have to catch him at his own game to catch him at all. If he was confident enough to remove children from a mall in broad daylight or to take Ryan from under Jordan's nose, then he wasn't walking around dressed as himself. A uniform, like Ryan had seen, made sense, but he had to be disguising his face, too.

They pulled up to Casey's house, and she saw Billy's car parked in front.

"He work weekends, too?"

Casey smiled. "I guess, if you call it work. I think he's decided I can't take care of myself, so he's declared himself my mother."

"It's nice to have someone to take care of you."

She nodded.

The front door opened, and Billy emerged as Casey was getting out of the car.

"Nice work with the sketch, Billy," Jordan said.

Billy nodded. "You think it will help?"

"I do."

Jordan pulled the police sketch from a folder in his backseat and handed it to Casey. "What do you think?"

The man in the picture had a wide nose and small-ish, dark eyes with big, dark-rimmed glasses. "The nose is probably a fake."

"And the glasses," Jordan added.

"He could also be light-eyed."

Jordan nodded. "What about the lips?"

Casey glanced at the picture again. It surprised her that the picture didn't show more facial hair. If she were a man looking to disguise himself, facial hair would be the best way. "Hard to fake the lips, but he could have a mouth guard, make them look fuller, or a piece he wears to spread his mouth out and thin the lips. There are some subtle things, too, but the basics are here."

"I thought about facial hair, too. How come no 'stache?"

"It's more power. He's saying he's good enough to trick us without the easy gimmicks, like a beard or mustache. It's a way of telling us he's better than we are," Casey said.

"You really think that's not his real nose?" Billy asked.

"I'd bet on it."

Billy stared at the picture, shaking his head in astonishment. "Would you like to come in for some coffee, Inspector?"

Jordan glanced at Casey. "May as well, Gray. It's hard enough to get coffee out of this guy. When he offers, you'd better snatch it up."

Jordan smiled, but Casey could tell he was still deeply upset by what had happened at the game. He had good reason to be. "I'd like to, but I should be getting back to the kids. I'll swing by Sunday and pick you up—say three-thirty."

"Perfect." The vigil was to begin at eight. It would take them at least three hours to infiltrate their volunteer staff and locate their man, if he was there. And they needed to be sure to do it without scaring him off. She wondered now if it could be done.

Jordan turned toward his car when another drove up. "It's a regular circus around here." He closed his door again, and stood protectively at Casey's side like a rottweiler.

Billy moved to the other car, stealing a glance back at them with a wide grin. "It's Kevin."

"Who's Kevin?" Jordan asked in low tones.

"Billy's new friend."

He nodded.

"You don't need to stick around, Gray. We're okay."

But instead of moving, the inspector merely shrugged. "I'd like to meet him. What's he do?"

"Tax accountant."

"Sounds interesting."

"He also reads palms."

Jordan didn't respond. Instead, he watched as Kevin stepped out of the car.

"Remember, Casey," Billy whispered. "You swore you'd be nice."

She nodded. Casey knew that, just like her, Jordan was bound to be suspicious of everyone who entered her life after the events of late. Kevin was taller than Billy by several inches, but still small. He had curly, blondish hair and an angular jaw with light hazel eyes. Casey studied his feet—they were small, like Billy's— a man's size eight, maybe nine, but too small for Leonardo. Casey glanced back down at the police sketch Jordan held. Jordan's gaze was already there.

"I'm not seeing it," Jordan said, glancing up from the picture to Kevin.

Smiling, she patted him on the arm. "I think it's safe."

Jordan dropped the picture to his side as the man approached.

"Casey, this is Kevin. Kevin, Casey."

Kevin reached his hand out to shake, but Casey kept her hands at her sides.

"Jordan Gray," Jordan said, catching Kevin's hand to prevent further awkwardness.

The two men shook, and Billy gave Casey a warning look. She shook her head. She was at least glad to hear that Billy hadn't told Kevin all about her injuries. "Nice to meet you," she offered.

"Billy said you might be interested in having your palm read," Kevin said, glancing at Casey's hands.

Casey listened to his voice, registering it in her memory and coming up blank. It was too high, too feminine, and even when she adjusted it higher or lower, the pitch felt wrong.

Billy grimaced.

"I think that's my cue to leave," Jordan announced, getting in his car. "See you tomorrow."

Casey nodded, and they watched as he pulled away. "I really need to shower. Do you two have plans today? You really don't need to stick around here on my account."

Kevin looked at his watch. "I can only stay about a half hour. I'm meeting with a client in Berkeley at ten." Kevin touched Billy's shoulder. "Actually, the reason I came by is that I have tickets for Beach Blan-

ket Babylon for tomorrow night and was hoping you
might be able to come."

Billy glanced at Casey.

"I'm going to pop in the shower," Casey said, excusing herself. "Make yourselves at home."

"I'd love to go to the show, but I think tomorrow
night I'm going to the vigil for the kids in Golden
Gate Park," Billy said as she moved out of earshot.

Casey stepped out of the shower, playing Kevin's
voice through her head. It wasn't familiar, but she felt
unease. She shook her head, scolding herself. It wasn't
Leonardo that was causing this particular unease. Billy
deserved to be happy. He was pulling his life together
after learning about his disease. She needed to pull
her life together, too.

And despite her constant suspicion of everyone who
came near her, Kevin appeared to really like Billy. As
much as she would like to blame the tightness in her
gut on something else, she knew her main concern
was losing Billy's attention. In the past year, she had
become so dependent on him. What would she do if
he didn't have time for her anymore?

It was silly, she knew. She was his job. But she
didn't want it to be that way. She and Billy were closer
than employee/employer. She just didn't want to share
him. And that wasn't fair to him.

As she emerged from the shower and toweled off,
she heard the voices from the other room. Dressing
quickly, she joined the men in the living room, forcing
herself to put on a good face. She had promised Billy
she would behave. Plus, Kevin had said it would be a
short visit.

"I made tea," Billy said. "Do you want some?"

Casey nodded. "Thanks."

Billy got up and headed to the kitchen.

Kevin sat on the couch with his legs crossed. He wore khakis and a light-green-and-white-striped button-down. His shoes were Timberland, and she could just see a stripe of his khaki socks beneath them. His hands were clean, his nails carefully manicured. His blond hair was cut short, the curls soft across his forehead. He had simple features and a strong jaw. His cologne was subtle and musky. In comparison, Casey looked like she'd been run over by a garbage truck.

He was a bit timid, and it surprised Casey that Billy would go for the quiet type, but it was hard to find anything disagreeable about him. Soft hazel eyes smiled as he spoke. "Billy tells me you're a little skeptical about palm reading," Kevin said in his soft voice.

She nodded. "More than a little."

"You should give it a try."

"I'm just not so sure I want to hear about my future."

Kevin nodded in agreement. "I understand. A lot of people feel that way. How about your past?"

She shook her head. "Not too fond of that, either."

Billy returned, carrying a steaming cup. "Come on, Casey. Let him try. He can do your personal characteristics."

Casey shook her head, trying to seem like a good sport and failing. "God, that's the worst of the three."

"It's fun," Billy pressed, staring her down.

"I'm really not interested," she said more firmly.

"Show her what you told me about the lines," Billy said.

Kevin gave her a quick glance as though testing her frustration. "It's no big deal if she doesn't want to do it, Billy. Really."

"She's just being shy. Show us on my hand," Billy said.

She nodded, keeping her hands in her lap.

Billy plopped down next to Kevin and put his hands out, palms up. Shifting his body closer to Billy, Kevin took Billy's right hand and displayed it to Casey. "The three main lines that cut across your palm are head, love, and life from top to bottom," he said, focusing on Billy's palm. His voice was so low that Casey had to lean forward to hear. "Billy's most extraordinary line is his love line. It's really thick and clear on the far ends, implying he had a strong love early in his life and will have strong love later in life. His head line is very steady, shows he's not so sentimental that he doesn't think things through." Kevin nodded with approval. "And his life line is stable."

Casey watched his expression as he spoke. He didn't seem to know about Billy's condition. Billy focused on Kevin, clearly smitten. The two of them appeared to be in their own world. She wondered why they were sharing their morning with her.

Billy ran his fingers across Kevin's cheek playfully and then Kevin blushed and continued. "The destiny line is usually less clear than the main lines. Most often, it runs vertically through the middle of the hand. If it starts under the thumb, it means you're firstborn."

Casey glanced at her own hand, trying to make sense of the grid-like lines in between all the scars. As far as she could see, all they told anyone was that she was old and getting older.

Looking over, Kevin pointed to the center of her palm without touching it. "You're a firstborn." She felt a ripple run up her shoulders, and she pulled away. Her stomach tightened, and she rubbed her hands together to stop the tingly sensation.

"That's right, isn't it?" Billy said.

She nodded, unmoved by the coincidence as she closed her hands. Oftentimes she had strange reactions in her hands when there was really nothing there. That was how she felt now—like a thousand tiny spiders were crawling over her skin.

Kevin returned his attention to Billy's palm. "Billy's destiny line starts under his life line and stretches up toward his middle finger. Means he's reliable and works to improve his life through effort and will." Kevin opened his own palm and pointed. "Mine has branches from the destiny line toward the ring finger, which implies good luck in life." He smiled.

"You believe that?" Casey asked.

Kevin nodded. "So far. And hopefully more luck is coming."

Billy laughed. "Try that other line—the sun one."

"The sun line is a smaller line. I don't have one."

Billy took Casey's hand and laid her hand in Kevin's. The touch gave her a strange shock, and she found herself wanting to close her fist. But Billy held it open, seeming oblivious to her discomfort. "You do, though," Kevin said, running his finger across her palm.

The sensation made Casey shiver. What was wrong with her? Was she so far gone that she couldn't even stand another human's touch? How was she ever going to have a life again?

"See how it begins in the center of the palm and then veers toward the middle finger?" Kevin ran his finger over her skin again, and the sensation was too much, too eerie. No one had touched her hands this way since the accident except doctors and physical therapists.

She pulled her hands away. "I really don't want—"

"It's good for you, Casey," Billy argued.

She shot him a look. "I really don't like to have my hands touched."

Kevin glanced over at Billy and then looked at the floor, shaking his head. "It's really no big deal. I understand."

Shaking his head, Billy stood up and knelt in front of Casey. "If you don't work with your hands, Casey, they'll never get better. You need this. I know it's uncomfortable, but it'll get better." Billy pulled her hands out in front of her and turned them upright. "It's therapy, Casey."

Casey fought with the cold nausea that swept over her. Her hands were her biggest weakness. She wanted to hide them, not put them on display. Closing her eyes, she took a deep breath and nodded. "Okay, show me one line."

Billy smiled and turned to Kevin. "Pick up where you left off."

Kevin hesitated, and Casey put her palms out, anxious to get this over with.

After getting a nod from Billy, Kevin pointed to a small crease in her palm without touching her hand. "As I explained, the sun line begins in the middle of the palm and then angles toward the middle finger."

She nodded, commanding her hands not to shake. She swallowed and ignored the tightness in her belly. To please Billy she didn't move. She was hardly even listening to what Kevin was saying. She was bathed in hot and cold rushes and she could feel herself sweating beneath her shirt.

"That's usually indicative of someone who will overcome misfortune." Kevin pointed to another line. "You also have a long marriage line. That means long-lasting love."

Casey thought of Michael and Amy and fought the desire to pull her hand from Kevin's grasp. Everlasting love was hardly what she and Michael had. She needed to lie down or throw up. She forced the sensations away with slow, deep breaths, the way she used to fight the adrenaline in high-pressure situations. Now palm reading was a high-pressure situation.

"I also noticed some loops on your head line."

Billy hunched over her palm. "Where?"

Kevin ran his finger over the line just below her knuckles, and Casey thought she might be sick. She needed to go. Two more minutes. She would endure it two more minutes, and then she would leave.

"See how that line is connected by interlinking loops?" Kevin said. "The loops indicate an over-whelming level of stress."

"She's had that," Billy nodded.

"The loops seem to stop, though. There's only a short period of them. So, whatever the stress is, it's somehow resolved."

"Soon?" Billy asked.

Casey felt her head bob, her stomach tight. Her throat felt closed, and saliva collected in the back of her mouth. She felt fingers across her hand again, and her stomach cramped in a tight knot. She never real-ized how bad the reaction was. She couldn't handle it. She pressed her hands to her gut. "I think that's enough," she said. "Thank you."

Billy started to speak, but she stood and went to her room before he could finish.

Lying back on her bed, Casey held her hands to her stomach, fighting the knot in her gut. She took deep breaths until the nausea subsided. Then, slowly, she worked through the exercises. Open. Closed. Open. Closed.

Holding her hand open, she stared at the small loops on her left palm. Kevin was right. The loops did seem to stop. She thought about the vigil the following night and wondered if that would be the end of her stress.

The very thought that it might ever end, that they might catch their killer seemed impossible to imagine. She shivered at the thought of Leonardo, at maybe seeing him again in less than twenty-four hours.

CHAPTER EIGHTEEN

Jordan pulled up to the curb at the Oakland airport and got out of the car to open the back of the Explorer. Under different circumstances, he would have been crushed to send Angie and the boys back to her parents' house in L.A.

But after the incident at the Warriors game, he had been terrified to let them go anywhere. Even the one time he'd left them to go see Casey, he had been soothed only by the fact that they were going to visit Angie's aunt in El Cerrito.

Negotiations with Angie had gone downhill over the weekend, too. How could he argue that she should move back up north when there was a killer on the loose who knew his children? He couldn't.

Right now, he wanted nothing more than to kiss his children and send them as far from him as possible.

Jordan pulled the two suitcases out of the back of the car and carried them to the curbside check-in.

Will carried a smaller bag and set it beside the others. "I wish you were coming with us, Dad."

Jordan ruffled his son's hair. "I wish I was, too."

"When are you coming?" Ry asked.

Jordan met Angie's gaze. "How about next weekend?"

"Yeah!" the boys said.

"Don't make promises unless you plan—"

Jordan put a finger over his wife's mouth. "I promise. I'll call you tonight to make plans."

He gave Angie a deep kiss and felt himself stir as he pulled away from her and reached down to adjust his pants in the front. "You'd better go."

Angie grinned.

Will tugged on his father's arm. "I swear I'm going to ignore those kids at school, Dad."

Wrapping his arms around his son, he said, "You watch over your brother, too."

"I will."

"I'm proud of you."

Ryan wrestled between them, and Will and Jordan extended the circle to include him. Jordan thought he could have stood there all day.

"Going to have to move this vehicle," someone yelled from behind.

Kissing Angie again on the cheek, Jordan waved his family into the airport. They waved for a moment, and then the boys started tugging at each other and their mother. "Cut it out," Angie scolded playfully.

The dark sliding doors closed, and Jordan turned back to his car, rubbing the heel of his hand over the lump in his chest.

"Sir, this your car?"

Jordan frowned at the skinny cop who pointed to his Explorer. "Yep."

"Nearly wrote you a ticket," he said as though Jordan had nearly gotten himself killed. "Best move it."

Mumbling, Jordan got in and revved the engine. When he found a break in traffic, he pulled out of his spot and headed back toward the freeway. He'd better swing a trip to L.A. next weekend, or Angie would have his butt.

Jordan would have liked to get a run in—sweat out his excess energy and the nervous feeling that crawled over his skin like an army of red ants. But there wasn't time. It was already past two o'clock, and he had to go pick up Casey. At the back of his mind, too, Jordan knew that even a long, fast run wasn't going to shake the anxiety he felt tonight.

The drive to the city with Casey was quiet, and Jordan sensed she was at least as anxious as he was. Like every weekend, Stanyan Street at the edge of Golden Gate Park was closed off for bikers, hikers, runners, and roller bladers. It made having the vigil easier to control. Only people on foot would have access to the area tonight. Jordan pulled into the De-Young Museum's parking area and found a spot.

Casey looked around. "Is this it? I thought it was in the park."

"The road's closed, and I don't want to have to flash a badge to get past the patrol car. It's not far. Can you walk okay?"

Casey turned and narrowed her eyes. "I can probably run it faster than you can."

"Sorry."

Casey didn't respond, and Jordan cursed himself for opening his mouth. He had seen her in the gym just yesterday, and Frank had told him how hard she was trying. As they walked the three hundred yards to a small courtyard where the vigil would be held, Jordan noticed that Casey no longer limped.

Her strides were longer and more confident, and he wondered whether someone shouldn't have brought her back to a case months ago. At the risk of offending her, he kept the thought to himself.

A small courtyard emerged at the end of their path, the DeYoung still in sight behind them. The area around the vigil site was bustling with activity. Four men were building a small stage where the families could sit during the ceremony. A truck was backed up to the area, and from it, people were unloading folding chairs.

A table on one side seemed to serve as the focal point. Behind it, Monica Pradhan was pointing at things, issuing directives. Dressed in jeans and a large ski jacket, she had the appearance of a bird, with her thin legs emerging from the bulky jacket.

Large, studio-like film lights had been set up along the perimeter of the area. The bulbs, faced toward the sky, were still off in the darkening day.

Casey paused to take it all in and then motioned to the lights. "It's a lot of light."

"It'll be dark before the thing even gets started." He glanced at her. "You think it's too much?"

She frowned and walked up to one. Shrugging, she tucked her hands under her arms. "Hard to tell now. Where'd the lights come from?"

"One of the kid's uncles is a photographer at a downtown studio. He brought them out."

Casey shivered and zipped her jacket up.

Jordan watched her reaction and wondered whether anyone would show up. "It's going to be cold."

She nodded. "Most of them will be numb to the cold. We can't do it inside. He won't come." Her eyes narrowed as she watched the commotion.

"You're doubting he's going to come at all."

She looked up at him and shrugged. "I guess a little."

"Let's go take a look at the volunteer list. Monica said she'd bring it with her."

As they approached, Monica asked a woman to set up a folding card table and put the boxes of candles and holders there.

Though she appeared busy, Monica looked in her element. "I'm glad you guys are here. Renee's on her way down with the updated list of volunteers. I expect her any minute." She pulled a folded list from the inside pocket of her coat. "Here's the last one. I think Renee has a few additions."

Jordan took the list out of Monica's hand and opened it. The volunteers, all male, were listed one to twenty-four. Included on the list was name, address, occupation, phone, height, estimated weight, and estimated shoe size. Unfortunately, they hadn't found a company to provide shoes for the uniforms, so the process of searching for a size ten shoe became increasingly difficult.

Instead of asking, which might arouse suspicion, Jordan had the two women who measured the men work together to sneak in a shoe measurement as well. While one was measuring the man's sleeve length, the other dropped to one knee and measured the length of his shoe.

The two women, both dispatchers for the county, were chosen because they had looked harmless. "He'll bolt if they seem like cops," Casey had warned. Winnie and Mary seemed like anything but cops. They also tried to estimate the man's weight, but from the list he held, it appeared that their opinions had differed, and the weight ranges were often as much as twenty or thirty pounds.

Jordan motioned Casey to a small bench outside the vigil area and pulled the list open so they could both look at it. He started to run his finger down the column that listed shoe sizes.

"Not yet," Casey said, taking the page and folding that portion of it over.

"Why?"

"Look at occupations," she said, pointing to the column. "I would expect a police-related occupation."

"Fireman, plumber, security guard, security personnel, personal trainer, security, security—hell, half of them are police-related."

She nodded, continuing down the list. "He isn't going to just pop off the page. I want to think it through. If I were him, I wouldn't give my real address or phone. That would be the first place to check."

Jordan focused on the page.

"We need to know if these are real addresses and phone numbers. Names, too."

Jordan spotted Renee and stood up. "I'll be right back." Crossing the grass, he waved at Renee.

"How was the weekend with the kids?" she asked.

"Good. Listen, Renee, I need a favor."

Turning her ear toward him, she said, "Shoot."

"Call someone at the station and have them tap into the computer. I need you to confirm the names, addresses, and phone numbers on this list. Anything that doesn't match, I want to hear about it."

Renee handed the list to him and took the one he'd been holding. "Here's an updated list. These guys should be arriving at seven for instructions. That gives me plenty of time to check them out."

Jordan touched her shoulder. "Thanks."

"No problem."

Jordan returned to Casey with the updated list. She glanced at it and handed it back to him. "Next to each name, you should write down which parts look suspect. Then, when we get a chance to see the shoe sizes, maybe something will click. Someone's checking the information?"

Jordan nodded. "Renee." Then, turning to the list, he made a notation next to each of the security guards.

"There's one, too." Casey pointed to one he'd missed. "It's quite an assortment of people, isn't it?"

She nodded.

He watched her in frustration. "Walk me through your thought process. I want to understand it."

Looking up at him, she nodded. "Besides the obvious security-type position, we have to think that he might choose an occupation for the opposite reason."

"Something that would seem completely unlike police work?"

She nodded. "Or he might pretend to be someone else, someone maybe who knew the kids."

"Like a teacher?"

Nodding, she pointed to a teacher on the list. "Or maybe an innocent-sounding job."

"Such as?"

"Plumber, gardener . . ."

Jordan remembered the gardener he had seen at Casey's house. Ramirez. "Where's the gardener?"

She pointed to a name on the list. "Carlos Santa Cruz. What made you think of a gardener?"

Without meeting her gaze, he shrugged. "Nothing."

Casey touched his arm. "Tell me."

Jordan felt his shoulders slump. "That first time I came to your house, there was a gardener across the street." He shook his head. "Something about him struck me."

"And?"

"And nothing. Renee checked the plates. He checked out—name was something Ramirez."

"Weird, the same thing occurred to me."

Jordan paused. "Should I call this guy?"

She shook her head without commenting. "If it was him, he's dumped that getup by now." Casey turned back to the list, moving her finger to the address section.

Jordan leaned over the list. "Anyone live near you?"

"Most of them have San Francisco addresses."

"There's a Walnut Creek—Ronald Mendelsen."

Casey made a mark next to the name. "Long way to travel."

"Jordan!" someone called.

He looked up and saw Renee hurrying toward them. Both he and Casey stood.

"Five of them aren't real." Renee held out her list. "And you two need to come see something."

"Let's look at the names first." Jordan took it from her and looked down at the marks. "James Pietrich, Walt Warner, Andy Cole, Kevin Hosilyk, and Tom Henrickson." He looked up at Renee.

"What's not real, Renee?" Casey asked. "The name or the address?"

"The *a* means the address doesn't exist."

Jordan found the marks. "That's Pietrich, Warner, and Cole. What about the others?"

"The others are names found in the system, but not at that address."

Casey frowned. "There could be more than one Tom Henrickson."

"But what about Kevin Hosilyk?" Jordan asked.

"Seems less likely."

Jordan met Casey's gaze. "You thinking of another Kevin we know?"

"Maybe, but it seems too obvious. If this is our guy, then he knows about Billy's Kevin, and this is his way of telling us he knows."

Jordan grimaced, realizing that would mean Leonardo had been close to Casey again.

"What size shoes, Renee?"

"Kevin Hosilyk, security guard, size nine and a half."

"Our Kevin has smaller feet than that. I checked them out when he was over."

Jordan nodded. "Good thinking."

Casey flipped her list over. "I think it's time to check shoe sizes on the others."

"I really think you two should take a look over at the minivan," Renee said again.

Jordan frowned. "What's there?"

"Pictures of the victims' families."

"Let's finish this up quickly, and then we'll go."

Renee nodded, but Jordan could tell she was impatient. She studied her list while Casey and Jordan looked over the other. "James Pietrich, attorney, size nine shoe."

Casey shook her head. "I don't think so."

"But why would an attorney lie about his address?" Jordan puzzled.

Casey shrugged. "We'll keep an eye on them all. Who's next?"

"Walt Warner, electrician, size ten."

"Put a star by that one," Casey said.

Jordan nodded. "Especially because of the electrician who came to the house."

"I thought of that, too."

"Next is Andy Cole, fireman, size twelve shoe."

"Shoes are way too big. Who's next?"

"Finally, we have Tom Henrickson, security guard. Size ten shoe."

Casey nodded. "Star him, too."

Renee made a mark. "What about the others?"

Casey touched Renee's sleeve. "See if you can

speak to the families as they arrive. See if they recognize any of the names on the list."

Jordan looked at her. "You're thinking it still might be someone they know?"

Casey shrugged. "That, or it's a good way to cross people off the suspect list."

Renee made a note to herself. "Are we done? You ought to come look at the family pictures," she said to Casey.

Casey nodded.

"Why?" Jordan asked. "What's wrong?"

Renee tightened her lips and gave a quick shake of her head. It was a look Jordan knew meant something was bothering her.

"Renee, what's wrong?"

She raised her eyebrows. "You two need to come look."

Casey and Jordan followed Renee across the courtyard and stopped beside a minivan with a photo logo on the side. Inside, a teenage boy was unloading poster-size photographs. The first ones were pictures of the children. Jordan recognized them because they were identical to the ones that the families had turned in to the tips line headquarters.

"Show them the family ones, Ray," Renee said.

The kid nodded and pulled out a second set of posters. Straightening out the drop cloth that covered the moist ground, the boy began to spread the pictures out along the side of the van.

Jordan glanced at each of the family shots. The photo of the first victim's family had been taken at a beach somewhere. The three kids looked a bit cold to be enjoying the weather as the parents huddled over them from behind. Jordan studied the little girl briefly and then looked at the next picture.

The little black girl's family picture was more formal. Two boys were dressed in shirts and ties, their sister between them, and Jordan couldn't help but think of Will and Ryan. As he studied the parents, though, he noticed the mom was white.

He leaned in and looked at her blondish brown hair and light eyes. Actually, she looked a lot like Casey. Her face was fuller, less angular than Casey's, but their coloring was very similar. The father was a dark man, creating a strong contrast between the two of them.

Jordan looked at the third family. They, too, were dressed up. This time it appeared to be for the christening of the youngest child. A long white dress flowed out of the mother's arms, and the little girl whose body he'd discovered in the park stood proudly beside her mother. Her mother—Jordan halted, leaning in again.

"You see it, don't you?" Renee said from behind him.

He spun around and looked at Casey.

"What?"

"I knew you'd see it, too," Renee said.

"See what?" Casey said, leaning in to look at the pictures.

"The mothers—"

Jordan watched as Casey studied the pictures. "What about the mothers?"

"They all look like you," Renee blurted out, pointing at Casey.

Jordan blinked hard and looked again, knowing Renee was right. The children's mothers were all dead ringers for Casey.

CHAPTER NINETEEN

Michael slammed the phone down and slumped onto the bed. "Damn her." Where the hell was Casey? In the last week, he'd dialed her number thirty times at least. He couldn't imagine her going out of town. Hell, last time they'd spoken, she wasn't even leaving the house. How could anyone live without an answering machine? Didn't she even care about her daughter?

He gritted his teeth and unfastened the top button of his shirt, tugging his tie loose. The thing was strangling him. He glanced around the room and remembered the last time he'd seen Casey there. He was leaving for California in thirty-six hours. What on earth was he going to do with Amy while he was working?

He left for Chicago in the morning. The case there was going to take too much out of him to be worrying about reaching Casey. At least he had the five days in California that he'd set aside to take Amy to Disneyland. But the week after that, he had work to do. He had assumed he would be able to get in touch with his wife. But what if she didn't answer the phone—ever?

What was worse than worrying about who would

take care of Amy was that Michael couldn't shake his fear that something had happened to Casey. Had she isolated herself completely? And damn him for not keeping better track. He'd scoured his files, and he couldn't even find the name of her physical therapist. Billy something.

What if she had fired him? Would there be anyone out there who would worry about her if she wasn't in touch? Lord knows he had tried, but Casey had done nothing but push her family away. He ran his hand through his hair. And now, here he was, worried about her. "Damn her," he said again.

There was a knock at the door.

Michael forced himself off the bed. "Yes?"

"It's me, Mr. McKinley."

"Come in, Mary."

The housekeeper opened the door and entered his bedroom with a laundry basket. "I've done up the last of the laundry. Is there anything you'd like left out for your trip?"

"If you wouldn't mind putting it all away, Mary. I'll pack later."

Mary nodded and set the basket down, loading the clothes in perfect piles into the dresser.

Michael sat back down and watched her, remembering how particular Casey was about the way her shirts were folded. Michael always folded shirts down the center and then again in the middle.

"It leaves a crease down the middle of the shirt," Casey would complain, unfolding the shirt and redoing it by folding the sleeves over first and then folding it in half. Mary did it the same way as Casey.

When Mary was done, she lifted the empty basket and propped it under one arm. "Amy has insisted on packing by herself."

Michael nodded. She was just like her mother. "Can you pull out a few nice outfits? You can pack them with my things."

"She's done quite a good job, actually. Except that turquoise sweatshirt she likes so much. It has more stains on it than the rags."

Michael smiled. When he'd met Casey, she had one outfit she wore on her days off: a pair of worn jeans and a green FBI sweatshirt that had faded to a dull grayish color. "Let her bring it. As long as she has other things to wear."

"Oh, she does."

"Thanks, Mary."

Mary nodded and headed to the door. "I'll call you for dinner in about an hour."

Michael opened his case and pulled his briefs out. Opening the first file on the bed, he made stacks of the issues he needed to work on. The stack of papers to be reviewed was more than a little daunting. He took the one off the top and carried it to the table and chair that sat in a small alcove of the room. The table used to be Casey's spot for her latest case—all her notes and papers would be piled there. But Michael had returned her case files to the Bureau months ago.

Opening his own file, he read over the motions of the opposition and started to make notes on a yellow legal pad. He paused and slapped his pen against the pad, his thoughts wandering back to his wife. She was probably still lying around in her sweatpants and sleeping all day.

He shook his head. That wasn't fair. As much as he had tried, he couldn't even imagine what she'd gone through at the hands of that sicko. The fact that he was still out there made Michael want to punch something. His wife had been through hell and back. And where had he been?

He reached for the phone and dialed her number again. His heart skittered as he listened to the first ring and then the second. The excitement slowly melted into disappointment when no one answered on the fifth ring and then the sixth. He wished he knew where she was.

It wasn't just about Amy anymore. This was about him, too. He wanted to see Casey. He wanted to see his wife. He hoped he hadn't let too long pass.

It hit him then how much he had missed her. "I hope you're okay, Casey," he said as he set the phone down.

CHAPTER TWENTY

Walter Jones leaned back against the tree and let his eyes wander through the crowd as the group of cops chatted around him. If anyone was watching them, he couldn't tell.

"Warriors are coming back," Lumley said, his voice low enough not to interrupt the ceremony going on less than twenty yards away.

"Warriors aren't ever coming back," Nancy Skaggs responded.

Two other cops commented, and a debate ensued. Walter watched them talk. They'd never had trouble shooting the shit on breaks at the station, but Walter thought this discussion felt forced. He wondered if anyone else thought so, too.

He gazed at the masses attending the vigil. Onstage, a minister spoke about one of the children he had known. Around him, the occasional sounds of sobs rose above the hushed whispers of the murdered children.

Walter shifted his weight, the forty-pound belt settling into his back. He hated just standing around. Some killer might be out there, and he'd been instructed to keep his men all in one place. Hell, they looked like they were goofing off.

That was the point, Inspector Gray had told him. Let the killer think all the cops were just hanging out. Then he would walk comfortably at the vigil, perhaps even make his presence known. Walter knew there were another fifteen cops at the vigil, all of them undercover as mourners. Still, he wished he was with them. He didn't do well on the fringe.

"How long do we have to keep this up?" Winslow asked.

Walter glanced around and then shrugged.

The men stopped their conversation and glanced around. "You really think he's out there?" Skaggs asked.

"If I was some psycho killer, I wouldn't show up," Winslow muttered.

Lumley laughed. "You ain't smart enough to be a psycho killer."

"Shit. I think I'm going to thank you on that one," Winslow said.

"Who's here undercover?" Lumley asked.

Walter shook his head. "Don't talk about it."

The men glanced at their feet and shuffled in small circles. Walter knew they all felt as useless as he did. "We gonna set up a pool for the Final Four this year?"

"Definitely."

"I'm in."

"How much?"

"At least ten bucks," Winslow said. "I want the pool to be nice and big when I take it home."

"You haven't got a shot in hell," Lumley refuted.

Walter nodded. "Ten bucks it is."

"How many people you think we'll get?"

"At least thirty from the station," Walter guessed.

"Sounds good," Skaggs agreed. "Who do you think it'll be?"

"Kentucky," Winslow said.

"I think Kentucky has a chance this year," Lumley added.

"Kentucky? They haven't got a shot," Skaggs countered.

Walter leaned back against the tree and gazed over the crowd again, thankful that he'd gotten the guys to resume talking. He wanted to look at his watch, but he didn't want to be too obvious. Lumley's watch was in view, but it was digital. Shit, he was bored.

"Excuse me." A male voice came from behind him.

Walter turned around to meet the gaze of an older man dressed in a suit. "I'm sorry, sir. Were we disturbing you?"

The man tugged his tie loose around his neck and ran a hand through his graying hair. "Disturbing me?" he hissed.

Walter straightened at the angry voice. His hand moved to his holster as though it had a mind of its own. The others straightened behind him, and he could sense their internal alarms going off.

"There might be a killer out there, and you guys are standing around, talking basketball."

Walter exhaled.

The man moved closer to Walter and stuck his finger out. "This is the sort of bullshit police work that gets people killed. I want you guys to get out there and find that guy."

The man's brown eyes seemed to sag in his cheeks, and his shoulders were slumped like someone who'd been through hell. Walter wondered if he had lost a child to this madman. "Sir, I understand you're upset—"

"Upset!" he screamed.

Walter could feel people begin to turn around and look at him.

"Sir," Winslow interjected. "Could you please lower your voice?"

The man scoffed and threw Winslow a disgusted look. "You want me to shut up? You come make me."

Winslow took a step forward, but Walter held him back. "I know what this looks like, sir. But I promise you that we are doing our jobs." It was the best he could offer.

The man laughed, but he was nowhere near amused. "This is what the police consider doing their jobs? My child is dead because of some psycho, and you're doing your job?"

The man had lowered his voice, but the hate in his voice made Walter shiver. He couldn't explain to the man what they were doing, but he hated to have him think they weren't working. Damn it.

"You sit out here, and you think you'll scare him off just because you're in uniform?"

Walter started to speak. "Sir, please—"

"Did it occur to you that this killer doesn't seem to be scared off by a few lazy cops? He walked into a public mall and stole a child from her mother, for God's sake. And you people were probably sitting in the closest donut shop."

Walter put his hand up. "Stop it. Now, listen and listen carefully," he lowered his voice, but his tone made the man stop cold. "I've got fifteen undercover cops, working this crowd, just waiting for that killer to make himself known. We're hoping if he sees us jerking off, he'll think exactly like you do."

The man's eyes widened, and he looked over at the crowd of people.

"That's right. Fifteen undercover cops. Now, I know this is upsetting. Man, it isn't easy for us, either. I've got kids. You think I don't want to run into that crowd and find that psycho. Well, I do. But, I'm doing my job right here."

The man ran his hands across his face, and Walter thought he saw a flicker of amusement. "I'm sorry. I don't know what got into me. I haven't slept. I—"

"We understand, Mr.—"

"Jordan—Jordan McKinley."

Walter shook the man's hand. "We understand, Mr. McKinley."

The man shook his head and turned to walk away. "I'm so sorry."

Walter looked back at the vigil. Something in his gut felt tight. He straightened the belt around his hips and looked up at the pictures of the families. He had studied them earlier, thinking about how they each reminded him of his own family. It could have been Mike or Brad that had been killed.

"That McKinley guy isn't in any of the pictures," Winslow said.

Walter felt the tightness in his stomach solidify.

"Didn't he say he had a kid that had been killed?"

Lumley touched Walter's arm. "You don't think—"

Walter spun around, searching the crowd for Mr. McKinley. "That was our man." He snapped the radio off his belt, holding it so tight he thought it might burst in his fist. "All units respond. Looking for a male suspect—graying hair, appears forty-five to fifty, medium build, height: six-one, weight: one ninety, dressed in a gray pinstriped suit and tie. Suspect identified self as Mr. Jordan McKinley."

CHAPTER TWENTY-ONE

Casey felt her knees weaken at the crackle of the name "Jordan McKinley" on Jordan's radio. That combination of first and last name could only mean one thing.

Jordan ripped the radio from his belt and scanned the crowd. "What's your location?"

"Northwest corner of the crowd," the officer's voice came back. "He headed east into the park."

Without waiting for instruction, Casey bolted for the northwest corner. Her heart drilled against her ribs as it hadn't since she'd worked for the Bureau. The familiar heat of adrenaline pumped through her muscles. She pushed through the people, meeting irritated, even angry gazes. She wondered if she would recognize him, if his evil would show in his eyes. She couldn't let him get away this time.

A crowd of uniforms caught her attention. The bunch looked around, restless and uncomfortable, and Casey knew from their faces that they had spoken with Leonardo. She rushed toward them. "Where is he?" she demanded.

A tall black police officer raked his hands through his hair. "Who are you?"

"Agent McKinley. FBI," she lied without blinking. "Who are you?"

"Walter Jones," the officer answered, his brow creased deep between his eyes.

"Where is he?"

"He was right here, talking to us. I told him—I told him about the cops in the crowd. Shit, I told him how many of us there were."

Casey took hold of the man's sleeve and jerked his attention back to her. "Where did he go?"

The man pointed toward the park. "In there, somewhere. I wasn't really watching."

Jordan jogged up. "We need police cars to surround the park at all ends. And I want a dozen men on foot. Not a word of this to anyone. The media gets this, and our chances of catching him are nil."

The officer nodded quickly.

Casey scanned the crowd. "Dogs, too."

"We've got nothing to track his scent."

"We will." She turned her back to Jordan. "I need a flashlight."

The lanky officer gave her his.

Casey tried to grip the flashlight in her fist, but her fingers wouldn't close around it. Cursing, she used both hands to guide the flashlight into her pocket and then started off in the direction the officer had indicated. Jordan could worry about getting the park surrounded. She needed to find out where Leonardo had dumped his disguise.

"Where the hell are you going?" Jordan asked, breathing heavily as he caught up.

"He won't go far without changing his appearance. He might leave something behind that will help us find him."

"How are you going to find the stuff? There's a hundred acres in here."

"I'll find it." She picked up her pace and moved toward the darkness of the inner park.

"You're not going in there alone."

"I'd rather not."

"Glad to hear you've got some sense left." Jordan stopped and stooped over his shoe, pulling his pant leg up. From an ankle holster, he pulled a .22 and handed it to her. "Just in case."

She shook her head. "I can't shoot."

He pushed it at her, jabbing the butt into her shoulder. "Like hell you can't. That guy pops out of the bushes, you'll be shooting."

"I can't hold it, Gray, remember?"

"We're posting units at every corner along Fulton, Lincoln, and Stanyan," an officer announced over the radio before Jordan could respond.

Meeting her gaze, he nodded and tucked the gun in his belt, touching her shoulder in a gesture of apology.

Casey returned her focus to the park. A sign ahead pointed to the Japanese Tea Garden.

"Great Highway is covered, too," another officer announced over the radio.

As they pushed forward, the noise of the cars on the closest streets faded into a distant fanlike sound. The moon provided only a shadow of light, and Casey felt herself wanting to use the flashlight, yet knew she wouldn't be able to grip it. Anger seethed in her gut like oil in a hot pan. Besides the complication of holding a light, she realized they were safer without it. It would only draw attention.

Casey glanced around in the dark. "He can hear all of it."

Jordan followed her gaze. "You think he's got a radio."

"I'd bet on it." She turned to him and lowered her voice. "He knew about those undercover cops, too, even before that officer accidentally told him."

"Impossible," Jordan said. "We kept that off the radios completely."

Her mind tried to sift through the evidence. "He got it another way, then. He knows human nature. He could've figured it out just by watching. I'm not sure he's here, Jordan. It doesn't feel right to me. He wouldn't corner himself." She thought about the nerve it had taken him to steal little Ryan from the Warriors game. "If he is here, you can bet he's got a good backup plan."

"Forget it. He's here, and I'm going to find him now—tonight. I don't want this pervert out there another minute." Jordan snapped his radio off his belt. "What about the streets coming out of the park? He might be in a car." He clicked off.

"Roadblocks are established at each of the exits to the park as well," an officer responded.

"He's surrounded."

She thought about the radio and looked around, getting an idea. "Make him think one area isn't covered. We'll lead him out the way we want to and catch him there."

Jordan picked up the radio again. "It's Officer Goodard here," he said in a voice that sounded slightly younger than his normal one. "No coverage on Fulton between Fortieth and Thirty-sixth."

"Officer Goodard?" someone asked through the radio.

Casey held her breath, waiting for one of the officers to screw this up.

"This is Inspector Gray," Jordan patched back in, using his regular voice. "Officer Goodard, continue to patrol the area between Fortieth and Thirty-sixth. We'll send backup as soon as it's available."

Casey and Jordan waited, listening for any responses. It was a weak attempt, and Casey didn't think it would work. But she was praying harder than she had since the last time she'd been with this killer.

"Send a car through to the Japanese Tea Garden," Jordan said into the radio. He turned to Casey. "He's not this dumb, is he?"

Without meeting his gaze, Casey shrugged.

He cursed and started walking again. "We'll follow this road to the Japanese Tea Garden. Then we can drive through the park and come out on Thirty-sixth."

Casey started after him, and they pressed on in silence. She imagined Leonardo's voice as she'd heard it a thousand times in her nightmares. It had become so familiar that she even heard it when she was awake, taunting her. She shivered. Sometimes, though, she doubted the accuracy of her memory. She'd heard the statistics about victims' memories and the effects of trauma. Would she really recognize his voice if she heard it again? Or had she altered it into something more terrifying from her memories? Maybe she'd even already heard it and dismissed it. Leonardo would certainly take pleasure in that.

"Inspector Gray," the radio crackled, and Casey jolted.

"This is Gray."

"We've got a black duffel at the east edge of Stow Lake."

"Don't touch the bag. I'm on my way." Jordan started to run. "It's about a half mile this way."

"I'm right behind you," Casey said.

In the dark, she stumbled along the uneven pavement. The muscles in her shoulders ached from the tension that wound through her neck and back.

Casey twisted her ankle and cursed, ignoring the pain as she pushed herself forward.

"You okay?"

"Fine. Just can't see shit."

"Use the flashlight."

Avoiding a discussion about her hands, Casey didn't answer and instead scanned the area as they passed the Japanese Tea Garden and headed deeper into the darkness. She pushed herself forward, trying to keep up with Jordan's long legs.

The hum of excited voices was the first clue that they were getting close. Through the thick bushes, the light from flashlights became visible only when they were nearly on top of the group. Down a short hill, Jordan and Casey crossed over a small road and stopped at the edge of the water. Casey found herself watching the shadows, expecting to see movement in the distance. He would want to watch this.

"You see something?" Jordan asked.

She shook her head and turned her attention back to the crowd of people on the scene. Many of them appeared to be cops, but in the street clothes they had worn for undercover, it was impossible to tell. "Make sure you know everyone here," she said.

Jordan paused and looked around. "I know them all." Then, with another glance, he added, "You think he'd come here."

She nodded. "It would fit his profile."

He surveyed the area and then turned to the bag. "Any chance it's a bomb?" he asked.

She shook her head. "Not his style." Casey knelt beside the bag and looked at the zipper. The end had a smooth surface large enough for at least a partial print. She didn't want to touch it in case he'd left one there. "Anyone have a pen?"

A burly man with a mustache and full beard held a pen out to her. Taking it clumsily, she turned back to the bag.

Jordan knelt beside her. "Can I help?"

"Use the pen to push the zipper open. I don't want to touch it."

He opened the bag and used the end of the pen to lift out a man's suit jacket. "Anyone confirm this is the coat he had on?"

"That's it, Inspector," one man said.

"Thanks, Lumley."

Casey watched as Jordan emptied the bag, one item at a time. When he was done, she peered inside for something he might have missed.

"Pockets are empty," Jordan said.

"Not surprising." Casey swept her hand around the inside of the bag and felt something like a piece of thread brush her fingers. Something was caught on the inside of the zipper. Pausing, she tried to take hold of it but couldn't. "There's something in the zipper."

Jordan reached in and pulled out several strands of long blond hair.

"Shit, another victim," the burly officer said from over her shoulder.

Ignoring the man, Casey ran her fingers across the hair in Jordan's palm and shook her head. "Can I get some light?"

A flashlight shone on the hairs, and Casey looked more closely.

"What do you think?" he asked.

She looked up at him. "I think it's wig hair."

"Another disguise."

Casey nodded. "Or maybe a way of leading us on a wrong path."

Jordan picked up the radio. "If I call this over the radio, I'm telling him we know."

Casey nodded. "But if you don't, would your officers let a woman pass by?"

Pressing a button on the radio, he raised it to his lips. "Suspect may be dressed as a woman. In addition to current description, also look out for a blond shoulder-length wig."

The radio was silent, and Casey wondered how close Leonardo was. Would he risk watching them?

"I need an evidence bag for this stuff," Jordan said. "Jones, escort this directly to the lab. Tell them we need a full report immediately."

The tall, thin officer nodded. "Right away."

Jordan took a shirt from the bag and handed it to another officer. "Use this for the dogs. Get them on his scent ASAP. I don't want this SOB to get out of the park."

The officer took the shirt and headed for the car with the dogs.

There was a moment of silence before the radio at Jordan's side began to crackle.

"Wilkinson here," the officer said over the radio. "Suspect sighted. Blond hair, emerging at West end of Martin Luther King Drive in a light blue Chevy, CA plate two-alpha-tango-bravo-one-four-seven. Requesting backup."

Casey held her breath.

"Three Frank ten responding," the officer said, identifying himself from San Francisco's F District, the one closest to the park. "At the corner of Lincoln and Forty-eighth headed west. Suspect in view."

"We've got him," Jordan said.

Officers cheered behind her, but Casey waited, listening. It didn't feel right. It was too easy.

Several minutes passed, and Casey felt her body tighten as though she were suspended in some strenuous position.

The radio crackled. "Suspect is Valerie Sween, California license Kite-784-8649. License checks out," the officer announced.

"It's not him," Casey said.

"It has to be," Jordan countered.

Casey glanced up at him, waiting for the crackle of his radio. Despite the desire mirrored in his gaze, she could tell he had doubts, too.

"Plates check out—car's licensed to James and Valerie Sween at 1107 Irving," the dispatcher responded over the radio.

"Shit," someone cursed behind her.

Casey stood and stretched her back, the weight of the evening pressing like bricks into the muscles there. They had missed him. By now, she was sure he was safe, laughing at them. Anger rushed across her skin like scalding water, and she recoiled. They would catch him—they had to. She wouldn't sleep until they did.

"This is three Frank sixteen," a voice crackled over the radio. "We have a suspect running south from the Senior Citizen's Center on Fulton toward the buffalo enclosure. Male, five-ten to six feet, thirty to thirty-five. Suspect was wearing a blond wig. He dropped it about ten yards back."

"That's him," Jordan announced.

"This is three Frank four. We are moving east on John F. Kennedy Drive. Suspect is in sight."

Casey could hear the blare of the sirens.

The radio crackled, and Casey heard the clapping

of shoes against the pavement. "Freeze," someone yelled.

The clapping sped up, and she could hear an officer swearing.

"Do you have the suspect?" Jordan asked into his radio.

"Suspect in sight fifty yards ahead," came the breathy response.

The clapping continued for another thirty seconds, Casey's pulse matching its quick stride. Finally there was a shuffle on the radio, and two voices in the background. A loud slap sounded followed by a moan. Casey closed her eyes, cringing as she waited for the sounds of gunshot. None came. The radio was quiet.

Jordan stood and ran toward the police car parked on the road behind them.

Casey stood and ran after him as much to keep close to his radio as to find out where he was going.

"Suspect is in custody," an officer announced over the radio.

The group let out a whoop as though they were sitting in someone's living room, drinking beer and watching the Super Bowl.

Casey got into the car and stared into the darkness, her mind full of questions, her stomach tight with knots.

Jordan started the car and turned it around, heading out in the opposite direction. "You think it's him?"

Casey didn't answer. Gripping the dash, she felt the pain in her hands as though at that very instant Leonardo were severing her tendons with his knife.

Anger flashed like lightning in her chest, igniting a blaze of emotion. If she met him eye to eye, she'd want to kill him. Could she pull the trigger?

CHAPTER TWENTY-TWO

Jordan stared at the scrawny teenager seated across from him. "I want you to tell me everything from the second this man approached you."

"Well, I was walking through the park." The kid fumbled with a button on his faded surfer shirt and avoided looking Jordan in the eye.

"Be more specific."

The boy practically jumped at the sound of Jordan's angry voice. "I was walking along JFK, just thinking, you know. You see, my girlfriend dumped me—her old man thinks all surfers are punks." The kid shook his head.

"Keep it focused."

The kid glanced up and nodded quickly, shifting in his seat. "I was walking past the Buffalo Enclosure toward North Lake. I live on Cabrillo at Forty-fifth, so I cut through the park all the time," he added.

"And the guy?"

"He jogged up to me, wearing running clothes. Looked like a good runner, you know. Lean and athletic. My brother's like that—runs marathons. You'd think he was skinny until you see him in shorts. He has really strong legs."

"The guy's a runner," Jordan said, redirecting. The muscles cramped as he tried to loosen his clenched jaw. He couldn't believe they had the wrong guy. But the kid he was looking at now couldn't possibly be the killer. He was too young, too clueless.

Still, Jordan was running his license through the system and then calling his parents. He wasn't going to chance it. But everything in his gut said no.

"He came running up and pulled out this wig. He said he was playing a joke on his brother, wanted me to wear it."

"What sort of joke did he say he was playing?"

The kid squirmed slightly and shook his head. "He didn't say."

Jordan exhaled. "What did he say?"

"He offered me a hundred bucks to wear this wig out of the park. Told me to head to the corner of Fulton and Fortieth. His brother would see me there."

"Did he tell you why his brother would think this was funny?"

The kid stared at the button on his shirt.

"I said did he tell you—"

"I asked," the kid responded, meeting Jordan's gaze for the first time. "He said it was a family joke, that if I wanted the cash I had to go right then."

"So you took the cash?"

The kid nodded. "I didn't see the harm. Shit, man, I thought it was a joke. Then, I get up to the senior center and some cop turns right toward me with his lights on. Told me to stop. Scared the hell out of me, and I took off."

"Why'd you run?"

"I panicked."

"Why would you panic unless you knew you were in trouble?"

The kid didn't respond.

Jordan leaned forward, tired and losing his patience. "What had you done wrong?"

"Nothing. I didn't do anything. I just got scared."

"Why were you scared?"

"I don't know. For a second, I thought maybe part of the joke involved the police. But there were so many cops. I didn't want anything to do with that. I got in trouble a couple times in junior high and high school. I've seen juvie. That was enough for me. I'm straight now, I swear."

"What kind of trouble?"

"Smoking reefer mostly. My friend and I sold a little, but mostly to friends. I swear it. I haven't smoked in months."

Jordan stood from the table, pushing the chair screeching back against the linoleum floor as he moved.

"Can I go?"

"I'm not done with you yet."

"I told you everything," the kid said, his voice rising in panic. "Where are you going?"

"I'll be back."

"When?" he asked, his voice an octave higher than it had been.

Jordan slammed the door and turned to see Casey watching through the two-sided mirror.

"It's not him, Gray."

Jordan slammed his fist against the wall.

"This guy's good," Casey said. "I should've known he wouldn't make a mistake like this. He was setting us up. After that first false alarm, I got excited about this one. It's my fault. He wasn't one of the security volunteers. He probably suspected what we were doing and decided to play his own part in the game.

Pretending to be one of the victims' parents was an even better way to be in the middle of the action."

"It's not your fault," Jordan said, his tone as tight as his throat.

Casey put her hand on his shoulder. "We'll get him."

Jordan raked a hand across the stubble on his chin, trying to remember when he'd last shaved, or what day it was, for that matter. Had Angie and the boys left only this morning? It felt like weeks ago. He glanced at his watch. He couldn't let this guy go. What if he was wrong? Could the stupid kid in there be masking a monster? "Where are the lab results on the last scenes?"

"Came in late last night," Officer Ellis said in a husky voice. Her petite size and frame were a contradiction to her deep voice. Ellis handed him a file and waited as he opened it. "The crime tape isn't traceable."

Duct tape was so common at crime scenes, officers had started to call it crime tape. He knew it couldn't be traced. "Can we confirm if the pieces came from the same roll?"

Ellis nodded. "We were hoping to prove that the pieces of tape used in the third murder were sequential to the pieces used in the fourth crime. But the ends don't match. He must've used the tape somewhere else."

"Or he threw a piece away or someone else had access to it. There are a thousand possibilities," Jordan said, too tired to pretend to be patient. "Can they confirm that the pieces come from the same roll?"

"The report says the lab can confirm that the pieces were produced within the same hour. For anything closer, we need additional tests from the FBI lab."

Jordan shook his head. "That's close enough. What about something that will help us find this guy: prints, hair, fibers, DNA?"

Ellis's mouth shrank into a thin line, and Jordan knew the news was not good.

"No prints, no hair. Fibers are consistent with car carpeting—"

"Color?"

Ellis frowned. "Black."

"That's half the cars in this city."

"Only thirty percent, actually. These fibers are less than a year old. That reduced the number to six percent or five thousand vehicles if we limit the search to San Francisco proper."

"Shit," Jordan said. "I suppose it would be too much to ask for body fluid."

"No semen, no body fluid, sir. No sign of sexual penetration, so we don't expect to find much there. We did find blood on the sheet with the black girl's body that isn't consistent with her blood type." Ellis turned the page on the report Jordan was holding and pointed midway down the page. "The girl's blood type is B. The blood found on the sheet is O."

"What about the other victims?"

"Both white girls were O as well."

"So it could be blood from a previous murder."

"Possibly. The lab is running tests to compare."

Jordan nodded and handed the file back to Ellis.

"I have some thoughts," Casey said, coming up behind Jordan when Ellis was out of earshot.

He raised an eyebrow. "Oh?"

"We can talk about it tomorrow," Casey suggested. "But we should print the bag and everything in it. Maybe he was careless there. Hair, too—especially on that jacket."

"It's being done," Jordan mumbled, thinking about what a wild-goose chase the vigil had been. Maybe it had been a mistake to bring McKinley into this. Maybe she was too emotionally involved in this case. He was beginning to lose sight of things, too. He hadn't slept or eaten.

"I also think we should take this kid and get an artist with him. We can use the sketch from Billy and see what things are similar. If he was dressed as a runner tonight, he didn't have room for much of a disguise. Maybe we can learn something new."

"This isn't *your* case," he finally said.

Casey stopped and stared at him. "Excuse me?"

"I mean, this is my case. I need to decide—"

Casey scowled, contempt flashing in her eyes like flames. "You came to me for help. I didn't seek you out. Now you want to tell me this is your case?"

"I'm in charge. I have to decide where—"

"Jordan," Renee called. "Angie's on line two."

Jordan wished he could tell Renee that he'd call Angie back, but it was already late. "I'll be right there."

Casey glared as he walked away. He never had figured out how to say the right thing to women. "Hi, baby," he said to his wife.

"How's your day been?"

"Not too bad," he lied. "How was the flight home?"

"Ryan had a terrible earache; he cried the whole way home. Will was a doll, though—told him jokes and tried to help him clear his ears. I think he has an ear infection. You know, it's a lot colder up there than you'd think. The change in temperature can make you sick, I'm convinced.

"So I have to take him to the doctor tomorrow

morning. Mom says he'll be fine. She says I'm being overly protective. What do you think?"

Jordan rubbed his temples. What did he know? "I'm sure Ryan'll be fine."

"You don't think I should take him to the doctor?"

Jordan shook his head. "I don't know, Angie." He tried to think of something helpful to say. Instead, he found himself aggravated to be wasting time talking about an earache when he had a child killer on the loose. With a deep breath, he gathered his thoughts and said, "Is he feverish?"

"No."

"Then, he'll be fine."

"I think he should go to the doctor. Ear infections can be serious. He could lose his hearing."

"Then, take him to the doctor."

"Don't you take that tone, Jordan. You're his father. I thought you might be concerned about his health."

"Of course I'm concerned, but you're with him. If you think he should go to the doctor, then take him."

"Mom says that if the boys were living with their father, they wouldn't be sick at all."

Jordan shook the cobwebs from his head. "Your mother thinks I'm responsible for Ryan's earache?"

"Well . . ."

"That's a crock, Angie," Jordan exploded. "I don't have time for this tonight."

"You never have time for your family, Jordan."

"That's not fair, Angie. You're picking a fight."

Angie gasped as though he'd struck her. "I am not. I'm trying to have a normal conversation with my husband. God forbid, you find some space in your day for us."

Renee tapped him on the shoulder. "Alta Bates hospital is on line three, asking for you."

"Angie, I'm going to have to call you back later."

"Don't bother, Inspector. I can take care of my sons alone."

"Angie," Jordan said, but the phone was already dead.

He looked up to see McKinley still glaring at him from across the room as he snatched up the other line. "Inspector Gray."

"This is Nurse James in the emergency room," a woman said. "We have a William Glass here. His friend said he asked for you before he went unconscious."

Jordan shook his head. "William Glass?"

"Billy?" Casey said, coming to the phone.

"What's happened?" Jordan managed to ask the nurse before Casey grabbed at the phone. Jordan put the call on speakerphone.

"A man named Kevin Wrigley brought him in. According to Mr. Wrigley, Mr. Glass was complaining of a headache when he collapsed at a coffee shop in Berkeley. He's suffering from a high fever and pneumonia-like symptoms."

Casey slumped, her expression grim. "Is he going to be all right?"

"It's too soon to tell."

"He's going to be fine," Jordan said, after debating a number of ways to comfort Casey.

She shook her head.

"People don't just up and die of pneumonia."

Casey sent him a scalding look and quickly turned away again.

"What? Modern medicine is wonderful. Antibiotics

will knock this out of his system no problem. I had pneumonia as a kid and look at me."

Casey shook her head. "You weren't HIV positive."

"What?" As soon as the word had escaped from his lips, Jordan knew it was a mistake.

"Billy has AIDS, Gray. Full-blown AIDS. He's HIV positive."

Jordan stared, not knowing what to say.

"The same thing Magic has," she added with a nasty tone.

"I know what AIDS is."

"Don't look so shocked, then. Billy's gay, in San Francisco. He's been HIV positive for three years." Casey glanced at her hands. "He's probably been getting sick for months. I haven't even paid attention." She wiped her face, and Jordan stared through the windshield, trying to think of something to say.

"He'll be fine," Jordan repeated, unable to find anything better to add. He searched for words, remembering how protective Casey was of Billy. Nothing came to him. Billy was going to die. It was God's punishment for the homosexuals, his mother used to say. It had seemed like such an easy explanation when Jordan was in high school. Now, looking around at the people Jordan saw killed each year, he wondered how his mother would explain their deaths. What had the little black girl done at ten years old to deserve such a cruel punishment?

"I'm sure there's something the doctors can do," he offered lamely.

She sent him a tired stare. "Do me a favor—don't say another word. Please."

He nodded and held his tongue. He couldn't seem to do anything right tonight.

Jordan was thankful when they reached the entrance to the hospital. He pulled in front and stopped the car. "Go on in. I'll park."

Casey nodded and hurried from the car.

Jordan arrived in the emergency waiting area to find Casey poised at the admissions desk like a bulldog, shouting out orders.

An Asian woman stood with her hands nailed to her hips, shaking her head. "I'm sorry. We cannot release information at this time."

"I'm the only family he has," Casey rebutted.

Jordan approached the desk, keeping a safe distance from Casey's flying arms.

"I'm Inspector Jordan Gray of the San Francisco Police Department," he said, drawing his badge out of his pocket and laying it on the counter. "This is a matter of police business. I would like to speak to the doctor treating William Glass."

The nurse squinted suspiciously and glanced from Jordan to Casey and back again. Muttering something in an Asian language that Jordan, of course, couldn't understand, the nurse nodded and turned her back to them.

"Can you believe this place?" Casey said without looking at him. "We have to be family." She snickered. "As if his family cared more than I do. Bullshit, all of it."

Jordan didn't say anything. Instead he found himself rubbing his sweating palms together, his gut tight as he waited for the doctor.

Jordan hated hospitals, always had. The smell of plastic and anesthetic and blood and rubbing alcohol always reminded him of the night his brother Tyler was shot. He could still hear his mother's shrill sobs, still see his father sitting with his hands on his head, moaning about God's injustice.

It had continued for what felt like hours. His mother would almost settle down when something would happen and her screaming would start again, pulling on the strings of Jordan's young heart.

Kids weren't supposed to know death so intimately—especially not a death like Tyler's. When the doctor came out and told the family Tyler hadn't made it, Jordan didn't understand what that meant. His mother collapsed on the floor, his father had let out a deep choking sound of grief. Jordan had wanted to ask what was wrong, but hadn't. Instead he cried, realizing from his parents' reactions that something terrible had happened.

In hindsight, he was glad he hadn't asked his parents why Tyler was dead. Now he knew there was no why. Why was a child's question. Adults knew there was rarely a good answer.

"Inspector Gray," a woman's voice said.

Jordan turned to meet the gaze of a tall, thin black woman. "I'm Inspector Gray," he answered.

"Dr. Larson," she announced.

"How is he?" Casey asked without giving the doctor a chance to speak.

The doctor didn't seem at all bothered by Casey's abrupt tone. "He's not well."

Casey took a step backward as though she'd been struck.

"Why don't we sit?" the doctor suggested, moving to a cluster of blue plastic chairs in the waiting room.

"I don't want to—" Casey started.

"Hush," Jordan said, taking her arm and leading her to a chair.

Casey frowned without comment.

Dr. Larson sat and held her hands in her lap. "Mr. Glass has developed an opportunistic infection, common to people suffering from AIDS."

"Opportunistic?" Casey said.

The doctor nodded and put her hand up to slow Casey down. "He has pneumocystis carinii pneumonia. It's a fungal infection of the lungs that usually comes on gradually. Though in Billy's case, it appears to have come on fast.

"But he wasn't even sick," Casey argued.

"It's possible he didn't show symptoms. Or perhaps he kept them from you."

Jordan could sense Casey shaking beside him. Not knowing how to react, he took her hand in his. "What happens now?"

"Pneumocystis carinii pneumonia is treatable—actually quite easily when it's caught early on. But Billy's infection is advanced. We'll treat him with pentamidine. It will wear him down considerably, but it's the best hope for fighting off the infection."

"Will it work?"

Jordan squeezed Casey's hand as they waited for the doctor's response.

Before speaking, the doctor glanced at her hands. "Most times it does. I had a patient last month who recovered wonderfully. It's a difficult process. We'll do everything we can to make sure he's comfortable. There are some side effects to pentamidine."

"What sort of side effects?"

"It's been known to cause arrhythmia."

"He could have a heart attack?" Casey asked.

The doctor nodded.

"Is there another medication he can take?"

The doctor's expression was grim. "At this stage, pentamidine is his best chance."

Jordan looked at Casey.

Shock had frozen her face. Jordan couldn't even imagine what she was feeling. Billy was her closest friend. The thought made him ache for Angie and the boys.

"What are his chances?" Casey said, her voice almost a whisper.

The doctor glanced at Jordan and then back at Casey. "The infection is very advanced. And the AIDS itself is constantly debilitating his immune system, making it tougher for the medication to fight off the current infection."

Casey pulled her hand from Jordan's. "What percent chance?"

"I don't like to give percentages. It will depend on his ability to fight. Support from you will help. Talk to him, read to him. He can hear you. Encourage him to fight. I personally believe that will help."

Casey shook her head. "How many patients have you seen with this sort of infection?"

The doctor shrugged. "Maybe thirty or forty."

"How many survived?" Casey asked.

The doctor paused and looked down. "When the infection was caught early on, almost all survived."

"And when it was caught later?" Casey pressed.

When the doctor looked back up, her eyes were distant. "It's much harder to quantify."

Casey shook her head, looking like she was holding her breath. "Try. Please."

The doctor said, "Maybe twenty percent."

CHAPTER TWENTY-THREE

He sat back in the small metal chair and propped his feet up on the table, imagining himself as the high-powered client he was about to play. It had all come together so easily. A sick mother, an important client, and now Amy would be coming to him. They had thought he was stupid. Growing up, people had looked at him like an imbecile. His mother, his sister, the whole town—they had all underestimated what he was capable of.

He had held Casey's hands in his, he had touched the very scars he had created. And she'd had no idea. She'd sat beside him, her discomfort a sensation he'd created. It was truly artwork. Inside, he'd been boiling with excitement. The feel of her skin, the crooked lines of the scars against his touch, it had almost been too much. But he had contained his emotions. He had played the part masterfully, and now the finale was so close.

One day, when he was a dying man, a renowned surgeon, he would write his memoirs, and confess to his art. From hell, he would watch their horrified faces as they read of his incredible deeds, and he would laugh.

The scene in Golden Gate Park the night before had been perfect. He could still picture the stupid cop, embarrassed as he apologized that he was not in the crowd, searching out the killer. All the cops, in fact, had looked apologetic. He was constantly amazed at the stupidity around him. They hadn't asked him for identification. They had simply told him their plan and then let him walk away.

Then the kid who had agreed to wear the blond wig. He was probably sitting in a jail cell right now. And meanwhile he had transformed from a jogger to an elderly man and walked right out from behind the senior center and met up with an old woman, taking her arm and escorting her to her car. The cops had surrounded the entire area, but no one even glanced at him. It had been too easy.

Once he had Amy, his masterpiece, Casey would rise to the occasion. She would play his game. And it was so close to game time.

Michael and Amy were flying out to California, right into his hands. The housekeeper, Mary, was off to Durham, to see her mother who was sick from the tiny dose of cyanide he had added to a batch of her favorite candy—Almond Rocca—that he'd sent from her cousin almost a month ago. It was amazingly easy to get information these days. When he'd called Michael's home number and Mary had answered, he'd chatted her up like an old family friend of Michael and Casey's. She'd easily told him all about her family, including the details of how her mother loved to hoard candy and the cousin who always made her Almond Rocca. People loved to talk about themselves. He'd timed the poisoned candy perfectly. Just enough that Mary would go down to visit. The dose he'd added hadn't been enough to kill her. She'd probably be better within a few weeks.

The sick old woman served as the perfect decoy for Amy's nanny, though. With Mary going to see her mother on such short notice, Michael was forced to bring Amy to California. They were stopping first in L.A., for some father-daughter time at Disneyland or Universal Studios, he supposed. Their last days together.

Then right into the San Francisco International Airport. He repressed a cackle. There was too much to do to celebrate yet. When he had her in his hands, then he could congratulate himself on his masterpiece. He really was an artist.

Picking up the phone, he cleared his throat and dialed Michael's office line.

"Michael McKinley's office," a woman's voice answered.

"This is Al Washington of StarTechnology in California," he said in a deep, slightly Southern drawl like a Texan who had spent a lot of time out of Texas. He'd read that the head of StarTech, Albert Washington, was originally from somewhere near Houston.

"Oh, yes, Mr. Washington. Mr. McKinley is expecting your call."

"Thank you." The line clicked as McKinley's secretary went to fetch him. Leaning back in his chair, he thought about the incredible plans he had made in preparation for this.

"Hi, Al. How are you?"

"Wonderful, Michael. I think you mentioned in your message that you're leaving tomorrow."

"Yep."

"Coming out for other business first?" he asked,

anxious to hear Michael's plans and knowing he would give them gladly.

"No, we'll be spending a few days in L.A. at Disneyland."

"Bringing out the wife and kids, are you? How many do you have?"

"Just one daughter."

"Me, too. Mine's twelve in May."

"Amy just turned twelve in February," Michael answered.

"Tough age, isn't it?"

"It is. I never would've imagined."

"You know why they're so tough, don't you?"

Michael laughed. "Why?"

"They're basically women. And we know how rough they can be," he prompted, sounding like the men he heard sitting around the lobby of the building where he had worked. They'd unbutton the top buttons of their dress shirts, pull their ties loose, and complain about their wives. It was a ritual he didn't understand at all.

"That's the truth," Michael agreed.

"Is your daughter staying on while you're up here?"

"She is, actually."

"We'll have to get her and Jeanette together," he said, using his mother's name. It seemed wonderfully ironic, since Amy's death would be in her honor.

"That would be nice."

He nodded and felt it was time to get down to business. A little polite talk was good, but Michael billed at seven hundred dollars an hour. No CEO was going to waste too much time chattering with a man that expensive. And he was playing the part too well to screw it up now. "Wanted to discuss a few last-minute details with you. Is now okay?"

"Perfect."

"Have you received my check, then?"

"Got it in today's mail."

"Good, good." He was surprised it had arrived so soon. The check looked legit enough to last a few days through the system—long enough to get Michael and Amy to California, for sure. That was all that mattered to him. "I'm going to be out of town when you arrive. Looking at acquiring a small company in San Diego. It shouldn't take me long to wrap up the deal—I'll be back by Wednesday at the latest."

"That's no problem at all, Al. I'm meeting an investigator to help with some background on Electron. It will help us prepare the case."

He gave a Texan laugh. "Know thine enemy."

"That's what they say," Michael agreed.

The irony was so rich. "My secretary sent all the background, didn't she?"

"Yes. And it was very helpful. But what I need now isn't public information, since Electron is privately held. I want to know how the company is performing, its revenue stream and bottom line. If they're struggling and your technology would save them, it's easier to show motive."

He laughed. "Sounds like you're going to charge them with murder."

Michael chuckled like a smooth businessman. "It's a lot like a criminal case in some respects. Proving how and why they would steal a process or design from StarTech makes it easier to show damage, and sometimes that's all you need—especially in a jury trial.

"And there's a lot more we'll search for as well. For instance, if the company has ever been indicted for theft like this before. Information like that will be very valuable in bringing a case against them. And if we do decide to press them to settle, past infringements will help us get a much heftier settlement."

"Good thinking, Michael. Have that investigator's bill sent directly to me." He paused and made a clicking sound with his tongue. He'd heard more than one businessman do it, though it sounded stupid to him. "Now, remember, I've brought this directly to you. Even my top people don't know about this stealing business.

"Electron is practically a neighbor. A lot of our employees are married to theirs. I need to keep this zipped up. You know what I'm saying?"

"Absolutely," Michael said, his voice confident and reassuring. "My investigator is very trustworthy."

"Good, good. And I don't want you working with anyone other than me. You know how these top managers can be. They say they're discreet, and then they go home and tell their wives while they're screwing." He smiled at himself. God, he was good.

Michael agreed. "I'll wait for your call, then. I faxed my hotel information to you. Did you get it?"

"Got it right here. I'll call you at the Hyatt as soon as I'm back in town, and we can meet for dinner to discuss what you've got."

"I'll need access to some of your records in order to draw up the suit and so on."

"I'd prefer you wait until I get back. It's only three days, and I want to keep this as quiet as possible."

"Fine. I'll wait to hear from you, Al."

"Perfect. And if you need anything, leave me a message at this number. It's my private line, and only I pick up the messages."

"Got it."

"Have a safe trip, and I'll look forward to meeting you and your daughter."

He hung up and looked at the picture of Amy he had pinned to his wall. He had taken the four-by-six photo and had it blown up on a color copier to eleven-by-seventeen. He had spent hours studying her face, separating it into quadrants and committing each characteristic to memory. In honor of his sister, the plastic surgeon, Leonardo planned to operate on Amy's face. Perhaps he'd start around the eyes.

She had her mother's eyes—his mother's eyes—almond-shaped and green, though Amy's were a bit darker than Casey's. The thin patrician nose came from Michael, the high rounded cheekbones from Casey. Her thin blond hair was Casey's color and Michael's texture.

From everything he'd learned about her personality from neighbors and friends when he had posed as a reporter doing a piece on the attack, though, Amy was Casey's daughter—rebellious and strong-willed. The thought of holding her excited him no end. Casey was sidetracked with Billy's illness for the moment, but soon, he would have her full attention back.

He stared back at the picture, rubbing his hand against the bulge in his work pants. The small mole above her right eyebrow was shaped like a tiny star. He closed his eyes, and the image of her face flashed in his mind. He would know her anywhere.

Pulling his hand from his pants, he turned back to the table and his work. The finale was coming so soon he had to stay concentrated.

Yes, this would be the most exciting capture of his life. And he knew he should savor it. After Amy, he would need to leave California. Too many people would be looking for him. It wouldn't be safe to stay.

He'd heard Arizona was nice, or maybe New Mexico. There would be lots of time to think about it later. He would choose somewhere nice and begin the road to medical school again. He was a perfect candidate. Only he would know how much experience he really had.

He looked over the disguises laid out on the far table. The studio makeup class he'd taken had made all the difference. It was amazing how good he'd become. But, for this last kill, he was going to come as himself.

Drawing the small leather kit out of his doctor's bag, he unzipped it and glanced at the shiny scalpels inside. The sight of them created a wave of pulsating excitement in his groin. It was almost more than he could handle just to restrain his hand from rubbing at the aching pressure against his zipper.

With a deep breath, he forced the wave to roll over him and turned his attention back to his tools.

One by one, he pulled them out of the case and laid them on the table to be cleaned and sharpened.

CHAPTER TWENTY-FOUR

Emily squirmed in her arms as Elizabeth Weisman trudged up the cement stairs to the San Francisco Police Department on Bryant off of Fifth. It was out of the way to come to the station, but after seeing that poor little girl's picture in the paper . . . she shuddered. She'd had to come.

"Hush, baby. Mommy has to talk to someone. It will only take a minute, and then we'll go home."

Emily responded by squirming even more.

The station felt cooler than the outside air, and Elizabeth shivered again, holding Emily tight to her chest and trying to suppress the chill that seemed to whip right through her thin cotton sweater.

At the front desk, Elizabeth explained what she'd seen at Nordstrom. A tall man with a mustache and beard listened intently and then excused himself to make a phone call. When he returned, he handed her a visitor badge and directed her through a glass door to an Inspector Jordan Gray.

Passing through the security station, Elizabeth wondered what they knew about the killer. Was hers the first lead? Surely someone else had seen him in that mall. The little girl's face flashed in Elizabeth's mind.

Dead. That girl was dead. She was just about Aaron's age, and he had stolen her and killed her. Elizabeth squeezed her eyes closed, shutting the vision out of her mind.

A tall black man met her in the hallway. "Ms. Weisman?"

She nodded.

"I'm Inspector Gray."

Shifting Emily to her other side, she offered her hand.

"I appreciate you taking the time to come down." He led them to a small office halfway down a long white linoleum hallway. The office walls were bare and though the desk and shelves were piled with books and papers, it was hard to determine who was the rightful occupant of the space.

Through a narrow window in the boxlike office, Elizabeth could see a sliver of the street outside. After offering her a seat, the inspector sat behind the desk, crossing a foot over one knee. "What can I do for you?"

"I was in the Nordstrom Mall last—" What day would it have been? Aaron wasn't in school. No, it was after school. Damn. How could she have forgotten the day? She concentrated a moment. "Monday," she blurted. "No. Monday Aaron had a dentist's appointment. So it was Tuesday. I was getting a present for—" She stopped herself. She didn't want to tell the inspector about her husband's secretary. How ridiculous would that sound? "I was with my son Aaron and Emily."

She motioned to Emily, who seemed to be content for the moment to stare at her new surroundings. Emily's quiet reminded Elizabeth that she needed to talk as fast as possible because Emily wouldn't sit still for long. "There was a man walking with a little girl. We were coming off the escalator and had stopped to look at the long rows of lights hanging from the ceiling. The man bumped into us—" She shook her head. "We probably bumped into him."

The inspector nodded. Elizabeth noticed the ring on his finger. Maybe he had a crazy wife at home, too. That was how she felt right now. Crazy. And overwhelmed. She shook her head. Nothing was as overwhelming as what that poor girl's parents must be feeling.

"He said hello. He was a nice-looking man." She thought about who she was talking about and shuddered. Holding Emily tightly, she shook her head. "I had no idea, of course."

The inspector nodded, and Elizabeth wondered how he could stand his job. "How did you realize it was the same little girl?" he asked.

"It's the strangest thing, actually. My son, Aaron, came home from a friend's house Saturday morning after a sleep over and said he'd seen the girl from the mall on TV. He asked me if she was famous.

"I hardly even remembered who he was talking about. But ten-year-old boys are just starting to notice little girls, and I think Aaron thought she was cute." She paused as she thought again that the little girl was dead. Elizabeth had been the last person to see the girl alive. Smoothing her pant leg, she shook her head.

"Ms. Weisman. Are you all right?"

Blinking hard, she nodded. "I just—I can't believe it. I was standing with that little girl. She didn't cry or scream. I had no idea. I keep thinking back to her face, to try to remember if there were any signs, but she didn't look upset or anything."

"Was it like she knew him?"

Elizabeth frowned, thinking. "No, it wasn't like that. It was like she had gotten in trouble. She looked ashamed."

The inspector wrote something on his notepad.

"I just can't believe I didn't realize anything was wrong. All weekend I've thought about it. Why didn't I ask?" She touched Emily's curls and felt on the edge of tears.

"You couldn't have known, Ms. Weisman."

She looked at the inspector, wondering if he meant it.

"It's not your fault."

"But to think he was right there. So close to my children. He actually touched Emily, told me how beautiful she was." Elizabeth felt herself choking.

The inspector stood and brought her a cup of water from a dispenser outside his door.

"Thank you." With a sip, she set it on the edge of the desk and commanded herself to gain control. She wiped her hand on her pant leg again and then tucked a tiny curly lock of Emily's hair behind her ear. "I've told Aaron a thousand times to scream at the top of his lungs if someone tries to take him, even if it's someone who says they know us."

"It's very important to teach your children safe habits."

Elizabeth nodded, kissing Emily's head. Emily was too young still. She had always wished the children were closer in age, but suddenly, she was glad Aaron would be old enough to watch out for his sister by the time she was five or six.

She blinked and tried to focus. "Aaron said he'd seen her on TV. I told him it was probably just a girl who looked like her, but he insisted. Well, I didn't argue. I didn't know who the girl was, but she looked normal enough to me.

"The next morning, Aaron points to the cover of the paper. 'See, Mom. She's famous.'" Elizabeth pressed her hand to her chest, remembering the way she'd felt when she read the headline. "Child Slayings Terrorize San Francisco Area Malls." "I nearly died when I saw. I must've read the article ten times."

"Can you tell me more about him?"

She nodded. "He was tall with straight sandy-blond hair; pretty nice-looking. He sounded like my cousins."

"Your cousins?"

"My mother was from Indiana. People say Midwesterners don't have accents, but I disagree. I can always tell someone from Indiana."

"And this guy sounded like he was from Indiana?"

She nodded, hesitant. "He sounded like it."

The inspector made a note. "What else?"

"He was wearing a uniform."

The inspector leaned forward and asked, "What kind of uniform?"

She nodded, thinking. "Aaron called him a policeman, but I think it was a security outfit—navy with an emblem—" She squeezed her eyes and tried to picture it. "I want to say it looked like an eagle." What did she know about eagles? "It was some sort of bird, anyway."

The inspector made another note, and Elizabeth glanced at the page. It was much too far away for her to read what he'd written. Maybe she was wasting his time. She shifted Emily's weight to the other side, her arm sore from holding her daughter in place.

"This is very helpful, Ms. Weisman."

She pushed the stray hairs off her face and nodded. "Can you tell me anything more about the uniform?"

Emily started to fuss, and Elizabeth bobbed her up and down, hoping she would settle down again. "I remember his badge said 'Obsgarten.' "

"Can you spell that?"

Emily began to cry. Bucking her head backward, Emily almost smashed Elizabeth in the chin as she fought to break free. Frustrated, Elizabeth let her down. Emily began to crawl around the room, and Elizabeth could sense the inspector watching her daughter as he spoke.

"The spelling of the name?"

"O-B-S-G-A-R-T-E-N." Elizabeth watched as Emily tottered along the edge of a bookshelf and then moved back toward her. "Obsgarten is my maiden name, and it's very uncommon. I remember commenting on it. Now that I think about it, he pronounced the name strangely."

"How so?"

"He said it, *Aub*-sgarten. Everyone in my family says, "*O*-bsgarten. It isn't a big difference, but I hadn't ever heard it pronounced that way."

"If I showed you pictures of some uniforms, do you think you would recognize the one he was wearing?"

"I think so."

One of the officers sat with Emily, encouraging her to draw with a series of highlighters as Elizabeth looked through the third book of uniforms. Emily started to fuss again, and Elizabeth was ready to give up on the uniform search anyway. It had taken a half hour to do the police sketch, and she'd been looking through the books of uniforms for at least another hour. It was already after noon, and she had to get home before Aaron got out of school.

She turned the page, and there it was. "Here," she

said, as relieved to be finished as she was to have found it.

The inspector stood and peered over her shoulder.

"That's an eagle, isn't it?" she asked.

"Looks like an eagle to me."

"Sterling Security," she said. "Never heard of them."

The inspector shook his head. "Me, neither." He took the book from her lap and set it on the desk. "Thank you very much for coming in, Ms. Weisman. I know it's a long way out of your way."

"You think you'll find him?"

The inspector nodded. "I'm set on it."

She exhaled. "Thank goodness." She hadn't slept in two nights, picturing his face. He had been so normal-looking—not at all the monster she wanted to imagine. She had almost thought he was attractive. It made her sick to think about it.

When she was growing up, killers were evil, slobbering monsters. Now they were handsome men in uniforms. She picked up her daughter and looked at her innocent brown eyes. It could have been her in that mall—or Aaron.

How did a mother teach her children to beware of such evil when the man didn't look so different from their own daddy?

CHAPTER TWENTY-FIVE

For the third day in a row, Casey awoke at the foot of Billy's bed. The only time she'd left was to take a cab ride to each of the body dump sites. She'd hoped to learn something more about Leonardo from the location of the bodies. Instead, the evidence of the cases had already been erased by the crime scene team as well as the effects of the weather, animals, and other people. Even when she was in the hospital with Billy, she still couldn't push the case from her mind. She dreamt about it.

In her dreams, she was tied down, flat on her back, and Leonardo stood above her, talking about his crimes, his scalpel poised in the air. Each time she'd tried to get him to reveal a little more about himself, but he grew quickly bored and lowered the knife to her skin. As soon as he made the first incision, she awoke the same way, sweating and close to tears. But each clue, each new idea, made her feel she was further from catching him.

The crick in her neck shot a sharp pain up her spine as she shifted in the small chair in the corner of Billy's hospital room. Standing, she looked at the beeping machinery around him. He lay silent, seemingly in a deep sleep. Casey wondered how she had even been able to doze with the beeps and clicks of the machines in the room. Exhaustion had won, it seemed. She chastised herself for sleeping, though. She should have been awake, watching over Billy.

Sitting on the edge of his bed, she pushed the hair off his face, sweeping it with fingers that worked only because of him. "I'm using my hands," she said, pausing to touch his flushed cheek.

"You always told me that the exercises wouldn't do a thing unless I started trying to do normal things." She paused, waiting, hoping he would respond. "I had no idea you were sick, Billy. All this time you took care of me. I wasn't even paying attention to how you were doing." She paused and kissed his cheek. "I let you down."

"He wouldn't agree."

Casey jumped from the bed and spun around.

"I'm sorry. I didn't mean to startle you." Kevin stood at the door, a beautiful bouquet of sunflowers in his arms. He wore a pair of khaki shorts and a navy polo shirt.

Casey shook her head, her palm pressed to her chest. "I just didn't expect anyone." She felt the same tightness in her belly and forced it away. There would be no palm reading today. She looked at the flowers Kevin had brought and smiled. "Beautiful flowers. Billy loves sunflowers."

"I know. He gave me some when we first met." He paused and looked around the room. "I've been by every day," he said, perhaps to explain or maybe just to fill the empty air. "This is the first day I've gotten the okay to see him." He set the flowers down on the windowsill. "I guess it was family only until he stabilized."

Casey turned her attention back to Billy, thinking of the way she'd been treated the first night. She wasn't family—how ridiculous. Billy refused even to speak about his family. They were from somewhere in Ohio, and that was all she knew. She thought briefly of calling them and then dismissed it. They didn't deserve to hear from him. She glanced back at Kevin but couldn't find anything to say. Instead, her mind drifted back to Leonardo. She glanced at Kevin's feet. She'd become so accustomed to her suspicions that she couldn't shut them off.

"It sounded like he was doing better. Has he been awake at all?" Kevin asked.

She shook her head.

"I remember when my first friend died—out in Arizona. They wouldn't let us in to see him. He'd even asked for us. It was terrible. Things are at least better here."

As he spoke, she recorded his voice in her mind, playing it against her memories. The longer he spoke, the more nervous she felt. She shook her head—the voice was too high, too feminine. She rubbed her eyes. Let it go, she told herself. She'd had too little sleep the past few days. She knew she couldn't function this way. It had started to get to her. Her best friend was in the hospital, and she wasn't even thinking about him. Billy was more important. She turned to Kevin, forcing herself to be polite for Billy. "How long have you been out here?"

"Eight years," Kevin said.

"You grew up in Arizona?"

"Minneapolis actually—just outside. We moved to Arizona when I was seventeen. My folks are still there."

Casey made mental notes, waiting for something to

fall out of place, for some clue that something wasn't right. When she'd found out Billy was in the hospital, she'd wanted to blame Kevin for his illness, to think he was somehow involved. It all came back to Leonardo. Why couldn't she put him aside? When would it end?

When she caught Leonardo. That's when it would end.

She sank down on Billy's bed and stared at the white walls, trying to think of something to say. She took Billy's hand and squeezed it. "Billy told me you're a tax accountant."

Kevin smiled. "I feel like a kid on a first date."

Casey nodded, knowing she was grilling him. "It's more like a second date, but I wasn't very good company the first time." She paused. "I just realized I don't know much about you."

"I'm a tax accountant. I work for a firm called Armstrong in the city."

"You do personal taxes?"

"The firm does some of everything. I do more estate planning, but we have a personal income tax area."

His responses seemed natural, easy. Even knowing it was stupid, she still found herself wanting to push the inquiry one level deeper—was she positive it wasn't his voice? "Do you have a card? I might look at having someone do my taxes this year. I hate all the forms."

Kevin nodded. "Sure." He pulled his wallet out and flipped it open. Instead of seeing his driver's license in the small window, she spotted business cards. He pulled one out and handed it to her. "Give me a call, and I'll put you in touch with someone."

Casey looked at the card. Kevin Wrigley, Estate Tax Planning, CPA, Armstrong & Associates. It was a number in San Francisco—all just like he said. "Thanks." She pocketed the card and turned back to Billy, wishing she could apologize to him for thinking his friend was a killer. She rubbed her face. She was so tired. She really needed to sleep.

"The doctor told me it was an opportunistic infection. Do you know how they're treating it?" Kevin asked.

She shook her head, unable to find a suitable response.

"I've had some experience with this type of disease. It's pretty common with AIDS."

She glanced at Billy and then back to Kevin. "He told you?"

Kevin shook his head. "I sort of guessed. He wouldn't let us get physical. He held me at bay. I should've known."

"Did you see him getting sick?" she asked.

Kevin shook his head. "Nothing more than I've seen with other friends. A little tired, pale, short of breath, that sort of thing." Kevin went back to the window and fiddled with the flowers before turning toward her again. "He called and said he wasn't going to go to the vigil—that he was too tired. He suggested coffee instead. So I met up with him after the show I went to. He seemed tired, but no more than the usual. It didn't seem like anything, and then suddenly he collapsed.

"It happens that way with some people. He's just lucky he wasn't alone. If they don't make it to the hospital fast enough, that's when they're at risk."

Casey took his remark like a shot to the gut. Before Kevin's comment, she hadn't even realized that Billy had never shown up at the vigil. She hadn't thought to ask about him, either. Her mind had been on Leonardo.

"Has the doctor told you what's wrong?" Kevin asked.

"He's got pneumocys—something pneumonia."

"Pneumocystic carinii pneumonia, yeah. How are they treating it?"

Casey tried to remember the name of the drug. "I'm not sure."

"Trimethoprim-sulfa?"

"No. It was something else—something with a *p*."

"Pentamidine?"

"That's it."

Kevin frowned. "That's not a great sign," he said quietly.

"The doctor said they're using it because the fungus is more advanced. He'll be fine," she said, needing to hear it.

"I hope so."

Casey nodded. She looked back at Billy and shook her head. "I should've seen it coming."

Kevin leaned forward and crossed his hands in front of him as though reaching out to her. "You can't blame yourself. It happens really fast sometimes. I had a friend die last year—he got sick and just died in a matter of forty-eight hours. Even his partner didn't know he was sick."

Casey took Billy's hand in hers. "Come on."

From the corner of her eye, she saw Kevin slump back in the chair. His face was distant and pale.

He seemed to be suffering. "Billy talked about you all the time," Kevin said. "He said he'd never met anyone so accepting."

Casey frowned. "Really? Accepting isn't exactly how I would describe myself."

Kevin laughed a tired laugh. "Said you were a pain in the ass, too. But he told me you were his family." Kevin seemed to force himself out of the chair. He stood and picked up the flowers, balancing them upright against the window. "I think he'd be glad to know you were here with him."

Kevin approached the bed and gave Billy a kiss on the cheek and then turned to leave. "I'm going to take a walk. I'll come back later."

Casey nodded. "We'd like that. Both of us."

Kevin smiled and let himself out, and Casey turned her attention back to Billy.

Casey felt her stomach growl again, but she ignored it. She'd seen Billy stir twice in the two hours since Kevin left. She wasn't going to leave and risk missing him when he was awake.

There was a knock, and the door opened. Jordan stepped into the room. "How's he doing?"

She shrugged. "He hasn't woken up yet." She stood and stretched.

"Have you taken a break, Casey?"

She shook her head.

"You look tired. You want me to see if there's an empty room around somewhere so you can rest?"

"No."

"I can watch Billy. If anything happens, I'll come get you."

She shook her head again.

Jordan exhaled, frustrated, but she didn't even glance at him. "I've got some leads on the case I thought you might want to see," he continued.

She shook her head. Although she wanted desperately to know what he'd learned, she found herself remembering his words from after the vigil. "You said it yourself—it's not my case."

He approached the bed. "I'm sorry about the other night. I was a jerk." He paused and shook his head. "I thought we had him and then that kid . . . I got a little heated."

She nodded. "It was frustrating for me, too. I'm as vested in catching him as you are."

"I know you are. And this is your case." He shook his head. "Shit, it's probably more your case than it is mine."

She cracked a smile. "That's more like it. What have you got?"

"I think it's you he's after."

Casey shook her head. "What are you talking about?"

"You saw them on Sunday."

"Saw what?"

"The pictures."

She nodded. "I saw them."

"All of the mothers of these children look just like you. He's fixated on you, Casey. You're what he wants."

She suppressed a shiver and waved him away. She'd already thought about that exact thing. "I know that. He can have me."

"But it doesn't seem like that's his game."

Halting, she focused on Jordan. "What are you saying?"

"I'm trying to predict his next move," Jordan said. "I'm trying to think like you. But I'm no good at it, damn it." He sank into the chair. "I need your help, Casey. I think you're at the center of it. I think you're the game, but I need you to help me figure it out."

Casey rubbed her knuckles against her temples. At

that moment everything hurt. She hadn't been able to figure out Leonardo's game, either. Was he really after her? Then, why hadn't he just taken her while she was in the shower?

The door opened, and the same young doctor they'd spoken with the other day entered the room. She was followed by two nurses—one male and one female. Casey and Jordan stopped and looked at her.

"Hello," Dr. Larson said, though her face lacked any sign of congeniality.

The two nurses paused at the foot of the bed, but the doctor moved up next to the beeping machine by Billy's head. Casey followed her like a puppy.

The doctor ignored her for nearly a minute before turning back and looking at Jordan. "Why don't you take a break? I'm going to check his vitals and run a few tests. The nurses need to bathe him. He won't be alone for a second, I promise."

Casey wanted to argue, but she was hungry and tired and desperately needed a break.

Jordan took her by the shoulder. "Let's go get something to eat."

Her stomach responded to the suggestion by echoing its emptiness. Nodding, she took a last look at Billy and headed into the hallway.

In the cafeteria, Casey looked over the menu, realizing how long it had been since she'd eaten out. Billy had often tried to convince her to go to lunch in Montclair. He'd wanted to try a restaurant called Crogan's that they passed sometimes on the way to the grocery store. He'd heard they had wonderful seafood, and there was also a gourmet burger place he said looked good. She hadn't had a burger in a year.

Each time he'd suggested eating out, she'd refused.

Dealing with her hands in a public restaurant seemed like too much. "No one will even notice," he'd always said. But people would notice. And she couldn't stand even the thought of the pitiful looks she would get.

Ordering Cybelle's pizza for delivery was as close as she'd come to experiencing California dining. And now her first meal out in a year was in a hospital cafeteria. She glanced up and saw cheeseburger on the menu, wishing she'd taken Billy out just once. Suddenly, she would have given anything for just one dinner with him.

"I'm getting a burger. You want one?"

She shook her head. Gripping anything was still extremely difficult and maneuvering finger food seemed impossible. Pizza, at least, she could eat with a fork and knife. The utensils could be tucked nicely between otherwise immobile fingers and then used, albeit awkwardly, to navigate food. But no one cut up a burger. "I'll have the turkey meal."

Jordan made a disgusted face, but ordered what she'd asked for. He carried both trays and arranged them on an empty table in the corner.

"We have a witness who saw our man in the Nordstrom Mall with the Kreiger girl," he said when they were seated.

Casey looked up from her food. "And?"

"At first I thought Leonardo might have sent her, but she was helpful. She was able to ID his uniform, and we traced it back to Sterling Security."

Dropping her fork, Casey sat forward. "You found him?"

"He quit last week."

She exhaled and turned her attention to the strange yellowish mashed potatoes. "What about his employee file?"

"They had him under the name Joe Tharpe there. Tharpe was a police officer out by Sacramento. Somehow he had Tharpe's driver's license."

"Where's Tharpe?"

"Dead. Killed in the line of duty eight months ago. Shot after pulling over a car. Killer was never caught," Jordan said.

"What about home address, rental history, bank account, anything?"

"Everything's closed and emptied out," Jordan said.

Casey exhaled. "He just quit his job and got away clean?"

"But not before stabbing his boss to death and then sticking the corpse in the cafeteria freezer."

Casey looked at the reddish-brown gravy and pushed the plate away. "Thanks." She swallowed a sip of water and thought about it. "You have any witnesses to the murder?"

Jordan shook his head after another big bite of burger.

"Just a guess?"

He nodded.

"What else did the woman say?"

"She said he had a Midwestern accent."

Casey shook her head. "Midwesterners don't have accents—that's why they make good anchorpeople."

Jordan laughed. "Where'd you hear that?"

She shrugged and tried to pick at her food again. She was still starving.

"She did a police composite." He drew a thin stack of papers from his pocket and spread them across the table. Each was a sketch of a man, but other than that, they looked almost nothing alike.

Pushing her meal to the side, Casey studied each one.

"This is Billy's." Jordan pointed to the one on her left. "Then, Officer Jones's from the park. And finally, Ms. Weisman." He showed her the other two, one at a time.

"Same artist?" she asked.

"It's all done on computers, but it's the same guy."

She nodded. "Does your artist go in blind?"

Jordan frowned.

"Does he know what case the witnesses are related to?"

"Never."

She nodded again, ruling out thet the artist might have subconsciously related one drawing to the next. "Give me your napkin."

"You've got one in your hand," Jordan said.

"Give it to me."

Watching her, Jordan handed over the napkin. Folding her napkin and then his into long pieces, Casey covered the bottom half of each picture, leaving only the eyes exposed. Something about the man looked familiar, and it gave her the chills to think she might have been face-to-face with him without knowing it. Still, even the eyes were disguised. Bushy brows in one, glasses in one, fuller eyes in yet another. The sketches weren't good enough to tell what his eyes really looked like.

Covering the eyes, she did the same, leaving only the chins showing.

Jordan moved to her side of the table and looked over the drawings. "Same chin."

She nodded, looking over the drawings. Something about them, though, felt wrong. It was a fat man's chin—fuller jowl. Frowning, she took her knife and fork and pushed them over the edges of the chin, effectively thinning out the face.

"What are you doing?"

She stared at the picture. The new face fit Leonardo's trim physique.

"Casey?"

She looked up. "The chin's a fake."

He stared down at the picture and started to push the silverware aside. "How do you—"

Stopping him, she nudged the silverware back in place, covering the rounded sides of the jaw. "Describe this man in terms of size and stature."

Jordan shook his head. "I'm not in the mood for guessing—"

"Do it," she said.

"He's medium height—five-ten or eleven and trim."

Casey nodded. "Exactly. How about age?"

Jordan rolled his eyes. "Thirty to thirty-five."

"And what doesn't a man with that description have?"

Jordan didn't answer.

Moving the silverware, she motioned to his heavy cheeks and jowls. "He doesn't have face fat. I think our killer wears a face disguise at all times."

Jordan stared at the pictures. "I'll be damned."

"And if he's concerned about being memorable because of his jaw, my guess is he's got a distinctive jawline. That's about all I can tell from these pictures."

A phone rang, and Jordan reached into his pocket and pulled out his cell phone. "Gray here."

Casey looked back down at the food she'd ordered. The burger and fries on Jordan's plate certainly looked a hell of a lot more appetizing.

"Wow," Jordan said.

Picking up her fork, she reached over and stabbed at Jordan's french fries, pausing to dip them in ketchup before stuffing them in her mouth, then repeating the process.

Jordan seemed too enthralled in his conversation to notice. "I'm heading back now." He shut off his phone and jumped up from the table.

"What is it?" she asked with her mouth full.

"I think we've found our guy—grew up in a town of twelve thousand outside Marion, Indiana. Was a suspect in the killings of his mother and sister. They were tied up and cut into pieces with a saw and pruning shears back in '94. I've got to go. I'll call you as soon as I know anything. I'll need your help comparing this '94 murder with what we've got now."

"While you're at the station, will you run a check on Kevin Wrigley?"

Jordan halted and raised an eyebrow. "Why? You find something out?"

She shook her head, feeling a bit of relief just to have asked. "I just want to be sure. I'm wrong, but I need to be sure."

"I'll do it as soon as I get back." He turned and ran from the cafeteria before she could say thanks.

Casey closed her eyes and apologized to Billy for doubting his friend. "I just have to be sure," she whispered. Looking back at the french fry covered in ketchup stuck to the end of her fork, she paused a moment and then put the fork in her mouth. It had taken too much effort getting the fry onto her fork to waste it, especially knowing what they were going to be up against.

CHAPTER TWENTY-SIX

By noon the next day, Jordan had already run a full background check on Kevin Wrigley and come up with nothing. He had grown up outside Minneapolis, then Arizona, went to school at Arizona State, and moved to California eight years before. He'd had a half-dozen parking tickets, but that was the extent of his dangerous past. He had heard the relief in Casey's voice as he told her. Jordan just wished he had some better leads.

At least Renee had been able to locate a sheriff in Indiana who was familiar with the '94 murders.

"Sheriff Douglas?" Jordan Gray said when Renee handed him the line.

"This is Wayne Douglas."

Jordan introduced himself and explained why he was calling.

"I'll be goddamned," the sheriff said. "Haven't thought about that case in a long time. Was a strange one, though, especially in these parts. Awfully quiet neighborhood most the time."

"What can you tell me about the case?"

"The sheriff at the time, Charlie Rickel, is in Kansas

now—working in Lawrence not too far from Kansas City."

Jordan was scribbling notes, but he was also recording the conversation so that Casey could listen and help him with the details. "Do you know how we might reach him?"

"I don't."

"No problem. Do you remember anything about the case?"

"Oh yeah. Be hard to forget that one. I was on the scene—just a deputy back then." The man paused, and Jordan could sense he hadn't had that much exposure to violent deaths. Maybe Indiana was the place for Jordan.

"I remember we got a call from the grade school. Jeanette Allister—that was the mother, was head librarian there. She hadn't come to work three days in a row, and they were worried. Charlie sent me out to take a look. I didn't get past the front porch, and I knew something was wrong. Truth be told, was the smell that tipped me off.

"Course, I was trying to make an impression back then, so I didn't call in right away. I rang the bell, and when no one answered, I tried the door. It was unlocked. I let it open and called out. But I never did go inside—wasn't any need. On the floor at the base of the stairs was Karen Allister's head." The sheriff gave a nervous laugh. "I don't think I'd run that fast since my father chased me out of the house waving his belt."

"Just the head was there?"

The sheriff cleared his throat. "Just the head."

"Who ran the investigation?"

"Now we've got three deputies, me, and a coroner here in town. Back then, we weren't equipped for anything like that. So a couple detectives and a coroner came down from Marion to handle the initial investigation.

"We took over once the crime scene had been searched and the bodies taken care of. The mortician in town took some of the photos, and Charlie and I handled all the inquiries. There wasn't much to handle—no witnesses, no signs of forced entry or robbery. Just a lot of scared folks in town and a lot of speculation. Case is still open."

"What's your theory?" Jordan asked.

"Don't know that I ever settled on just one. Lots of folks think it was just some nut. The Allisters lived off the main highway from town. Would've been a logical place to stop if you were a crazy looking for a couple of unarmed folks to chop up."

"Did you check local authorities for similar crimes?"

"We surely did. Nothing at all like that. In fact, we sent some pictures up to Washington, to the FBI, too. They've got a big database up there now, but I think they were just starting things back then. They couldn't help much, either."

"What about the son?"

"Some folks think the son was involved. Charlie didn't think so. Personally, I sort of favored that theory. They say eighty percent of homicides are someone the victim knew."

Jordan had heard the statistics. He wished they worked on his case.

"But we checked the son out," Douglas continued. "He was at college then and had been real sick. His roommate and a couple others confirmed he hadn't left school during the time the women were killed."

"What else can you tell me about the son?"

"Name's George Allister. Hard to think of him as a killer, to be honest. His older sister Karen was in my class—real smart kid, valedictorian, on the girl's soccer team, a cheerleader, and all that. Got a full ride to Indiana, then on to Ohio State for med school. I think she was practicing in Indianapolis."

"What about George?"

"Don't know much about George. He was quieter than Karen, not as smart, not an athlete at all. He was a year older than my sister, and she always said he got picked on a lot. Kind of scrawny-looking from what I remember. But not the type you'd expect to go chopping people up." He laughed. "I expect people always say that, don't they?"

Jordan nodded. "You'd be surprised."

"Reckon that's true. I don't know how people in cities deal with all the crime. Mostly we get drunks and speeders, some drugs. Mostly kid stuff."

Jordan waited while the sheriff came back around to George.

"George wasn't dumb, though. He went to college on scholarship. I think he wanted to be a doctor like his sister."

Jordan made notes. "Do you know which college?"

"Wooster as I recall."

Jordan had never heard of it.

"It's not too far from here—in the town of Wooster, Ohio."

"Did he graduate?"

"Don't think so. A few months after the incident, we tried to contact George again. We had some more questions for him. But he'd left school. We never could find him. Finished up two years of college and then disappeared."

"What about George's father?"

The sheriff laughed. "There wasn't a father."

"Excuse me?"

"From what I remember, Jeanette Allister was a bit of a man hater. Whoever the father was, he was gone shortly after George was born."

"Any ideas why?"

"None. She wasn't an easy woman. Kids weren't supposed to ask a lot of questions back then, and I don't think I ever knew who he was or when he left. Charlie's a good bit older—he might know more."

"What made you think it was George who killed them?"

"What I saw in that house. I thought it looked like it was done by someone with real strong emotion about those people. There were rumors that Jeanette blamed the husband's leaving on George, which would explain how he might've been affected. He was an angry kid— bitter you might say. My guess is it was mostly because Karen was so successful. Typical second-child stuff. Like I said, you'd never have pinned him for a killer, though."

"But no one followed up on George as the killer after he disappeared?" Jordan asked.

"Charlie was in charge back then, and he didn't think it was possible that it could've been George. Plus, we checked out his alibi, like I told you. That's about where it got left."

"You said the case file was still open. Would it be possible to fax a copy to me?"

"I don't see any harm in it."

Jordan gave Sheriff Douglas his fax number and thanked him for his help.

Renee was standing by Jordan's side, waiting as he hung up the phone. "Good stuff?"

"Great." He told her about the fax she should be

expecting. "Call Kansas City Police, and see if you can't locate Charlie Rickel. He was the sheriff at the time. And call Wooster College in Wooster, Ohio, and find out if George Allister graduated or when he stopped enrolling. Also, get any pictures they have of him."

Renee made notes. "Anything else?"

He shook his head. "Not yet."

"One more thing, Jordan. I got a call from Betty in Quantico." Renee glanced over her shoulder for listeners and then moved closer to Jordan's desk. "She heard the Bureau is sending someone out here."

Jordan stared at her and then looked around. "On this case?"

She nodded.

"They going to let me know about it?"

Renee shrugged. "Betty's working on finding out. She wasn't supposed to tell me. The whole thing's very hush hush."

Jordan digested the news. "Keep on it, would you? And if anyone asks anything about this case, I want them coming to me."

Renee nodded and left.

Jordan wondered what the hell that was about. He'd certainly take any help the FBI wanted to offer, but damn if they were going to start watching over his shoulder without telling him about it first. He wished Casey was there, but he'd call her as soon as he'd digested it all and get her opinion.

Despite a rocky first meeting, Casey had become his unofficial partner on this case. They'd taken to talking at the end of each day to discuss any new leads and for Jordan to get her feedback. People had asked about her presence at the vigil, so he was keeping her out of the station as much as possible. He didn't want

Tapp thinking he'd brought the FBI in on his own. He wondered if she knew anything about the FBI's possible involvement.

Walter Jones knocked on the door. "Got his Indiana license."

Jordan waved him in.

Jones dropped a full-page fax on Jordan's desk and pointed to the picture. "Look like any of the composites?"

Rearranging the clutter on his desk, Jordan spread the police drawings and looked at each of them compared to the picture.

"They look nothing alike," Jones said.

Jordan clenched his jaw. He was right. "When was the license last renewed?"

"Not since '92."

Jordan stared at the information on the one-page application. "Run the same social in every state. Start with the ones close to Ohio, then work your way out."

Jones took the application and left.

Jordan swiveled his chair and stared at the wall. If George Allister had killed his own family, would he have renewed his driver's license after the Indiana one expired? Clearly not in Indiana. Jordan had been hoping for some easy answers. Didn't look like that was going to happen.

"Fax is coming through," Renee called from the hall.

Jordan stood and stretched, and then headed to the media room where three fax machines handled the load of three hundred officers, inspectors, and staff.

"Looks like the good stuff first." Renee handed Jordan a bundle of pages.

Jordan took them and looked at poorly copied crime scene photos. At least the lighting was clear enough to make out the objects. And what he saw was enough to churn any stomach. A woman was sitting upright in bed, her legs jutted out before her. A long Y-cut down her sternum suggested some crude form of autopsy performed by the killer. Her head sat between her legs, facing inward.

Her arms had been cut off at the shoulders, and her fingers were balanced individually along her thigh like bloody sausages. Her feet had been severed and switched, the left on the right leg, the right on the left leg. And her fingerless arms were stretched out separately on the bed. "Damn," he finally said.

Renee refused even to look. Instead, she passed him another page.

Karen Allister's fate had been only slightly less grotesque than her mother's. Her body, also cut into pieces, created a path from her mother's bedroom to the front door. Her feet sat upright by her door as though she'd been walking in when her body was severed from them. Her legs to the knee were balanced on a high stair. Lower, were her thighs. Her body was a legless stump balanced only several stairs up from the foyer where her head had been found. Jordan studied a fuzzy close-up of Karen's face from when she was alive. Her light brown hair and light eyes reminded him of Casey. Jordan turned to Renee. "Call Indiana back and see if you can get more pictures of the mother and daughter before the murders."

Renee nodded.

Jordan took the pictures and walked back toward his desk. He didn't even want to think about the fact that a guy capable of this might be in San Francisco now.

Renee returned with the rest of the fax. "I'm going to get on those calls."

"Thanks, Renee."

Jordan turned past the pictures and started to read the report on the crime. There was no mention of an unusual mark on the victims' thighs. Perhaps Leonardo hadn't started with his signature until later.

"Got something," Jones said as he rushed into Jordan's office.

Jordan looked up.

"George Allister has a Kentucky driver's license last renewed in 1997 under the name Roy McAllister. I called the bureau of motor vehicles there and found out he was in a bad wreck in July of 1998. Totaled the car and nearly went through the windshield. I found the hospital where he was admitted. He was there for more than a month, needed major surgery."

"Surgery?"

Jones grinned, excited. "Facial reconstruction."

Jordan nodded, wishing Allister hadn't survived that crash. The accident was just a few months before the murders started in Cincinnati. "What else?"

"That's all I've got so far."

Jordan handed him a ballpoint and motioned for him to write. "Get the name of the doctor who performed it, how it was paid for, the records. I'm hoping they'll have pictures. Got it?"

"Got it." Jones turned and left.

Jordan could feel the rookie's excitement, and it was contagious. He scooped up the phone and dialed Alta Bates Hospital.

"William Glass's room, please," he said when someone answered.

"Hello," Casey answered, sounding both curious and annoyed at the intrusion.

"How's the patient?"

"He's coming home tomorrow."

"Who's that?" Jordan could hear Billy ask in the background.

"Just the inspector."

Jordan laughed. "Thanks."

"What's going on?" Casey asked.

"It's been an exciting day."

"You going to tell me about it now, or you want to call back when you're in the mood to talk?"

Jordan told Casey about the Allisters and the way Jeanette and Karen had died.

"Fits the profile—very personalized anger. He was already experimenting with dissection, but it was crude. His anger got in the way of doing anything more skilled. Those were probably his first murders. Was the mother's face covered?" she asked.

Jordan shook his head. "What?"

"When she was killed, was the mother's face covered?"

Something niggled at his brain. "No, I told you they found it pressed between her legs."

"That's staging," Casey said. "What about when she was killed. Do you have the file?"

"It's right in front of me."

"Read the part about how they think she was killed and then call me back." With that, she hung up.

Jordan set the phone down with a light curse. At least she could have asked nicely. Focusing on the file, Jordan read the findings. About two and a half pages into it, he found what he was looking for. "How the hell?" he sputtered. Picking up the phone, he dialed Casey back.

"Find it?"

"How did you know?"

"What'd he use?" she asked.

Jordan could tell she was smiling.

"A pillowcase."

"That's how you know it was most likely the son. It would've been hard even for him to kill his own mother. He depersonalizes her by covering her face. Then, she's not his mother. She's just a body."

"So you think it was George? And you think George is Leonardo?"

"I'd bet on it."

"Damn, Casey, you're good."

She laughed. "Don't sound so shocked. Why don't you pick me up at the hospital early tomorrow, and I'll come in and see what you've got. I'd come now if it weren't for Billy."

She was back in profiler mode. Jordan felt a tiny measure of relief. "What about Billy?"

"He's spending the morning with Kevin. You can help me take him home later. See you out front about eight?"

"You're pushy, you know that."

"Yeah, yeah. First great, then pushy. I get no appreciation in this job."

"Do you keep up with anyone at the Bureau?" Jordan asked.

"Not a soul," she said. "See you in the morning."

He nodded, hanging up the phone. She wouldn't know about the FBI's supposed involvement then. He decided to wait to tell her until he knew more. He was looking forward to seeing her the following morning. He could use her insight, and he was starting to like her company. If that wasn't the strangest thing.

Jordan could see the sky darkening and knew they were in for more weather. He was getting sick of the rain.

There was a knock, and he swung back to Jones's unsmiling face.

"What's up?"

"Doctor's name was Joseph Ballari."

"Was?"

"He's dead. Killed in a fire in his office building on September 24, three months after Allister's accident."

Jordan wrote "doctor dead" on his notepad. "No records, either, then?"

"None."

Leonardo was doing a good job covering his tracks. "What about nurses who worked with him at the time?"

"Two were killed in the fire. The last one, a Nina Rodriguez, lived. Quit her job three days before the fire."

"Did you find her?"

"Not yet. She's no longer listed in the area. I haven't called records yet. She could've gotten married, divorced, whatever."

"Try everything, but find her. We need someone who can paint us a picture of the new George Allister."

Jones nodded and left the room, less enthusiastically than he had the last time.

Jordan thought he was beyond disappointment. But he felt the familiar stir himself. He picked up the phone and dialed his in-laws' phone number.

"You've reached the Thomas residence. Please leave a message at the beep." The voice was Ryan's, and Jordan felt a physical pain at the sound of it.

It was almost eight o'clock. Jordan was surprised no one was home. "It's Dad here. Just calling to check on you guys. Angie, give me a call at work when you get in."

He hung up the phone and suddenly felt tired.

Standing, he gathered the notes and files from his desk and packed them in his bag to take home.

"Want to grab a bite?"

Jordan looked up to see Harry McClerkin leaning in his doorway. "Sounds great."

Just then, Renee appeared wearing a solemn face.

"What is it?"

"A call just came in—a missing kid reported at Corte Madera mall."

Jordan sagged, weighted with dread. "Damn."

CHAPTER TWENTY-SEVEN

Casey watched the police car stop in front of the hospital before she realized that the car said San Francisco Police and she was standing in Berkeley.

"Casey McKinley?" the officer asked as he stepped out. He was a tall slender white man with light brown hair and eyes. Everything about his appearance sent off alarms in her mind. She took a step back toward the hospital entrance.

"I'm Officer James West. Inspector Gray asked me to pick you up."

She smiled, then turned and walked back into the hospital.

"Agent McKinley," the officer called after her, sounding puzzled and slightly annoyed. "Inspector Gray said you might be skeptical. Said you should call him."

Once she was safely inside next to the information station with at least a half dozen people staring at her, she glanced over her shoulder at the officer.

He stopped several feet from her and pulled his radio off his shoulder. "We're supposed to call him on the radio."

She folded her arms. "Go ahead."

The officer fumbled with the radio, and after seeming to figure out which button was which, called in.

Nearly a minute later, she heard Jordan's voice. "Officer West? You're at the hospital?"

"Yes, sir."

"Good. Now, McKinley, are you giving my officer a hard time?"

Casey snatched the radio from the officer's hand and pushed the button using the knuckle of her other hand. It seemed easy enough to her. "What the hell were you thinking sending a white guy with size ten shoes over here?" she chastised.

Officer West stared, puzzled, at his feet.

Jordan laughed into the radio. "Do you have to yell?"

Casey could feel the stares, people wondering why she was complaining about the white guy.

Meanwhile, Officer West was staring at his shiny shoes.

"Don't give my rookie a hard time. Just get in the car and go with him."

She frowned. "Why aren't you here?"

"I'm at the scene," Jordan said, his tone suddenly sober.

"Shit," she responded before realizing she was still speaking into the radio.

"Exactly. You coming or what? The whole world is hearing this, you know."

"See you in a few." Casey handed the radio back to the officer. "Sorry," she said to whoever was listening and started for the door again. West was right on her tail. She turned back to him. "I apologize for that."

"Don't worry. Inspector Gray warned me."

She smiled. "He did, did he?"

West cracked an awkward smile. "You know what I mean."

"I certainly do." As soon as he pulled out onto Ashby, Casey began asking questions. "When was Gray called to the scene?"

West stared through the windshield. "I don't know."

"Is this a new victim of the same killer?"

"Couldn't say, ma'am."

"Is this victim black or white?"

West glanced at her before responding. He clearly thought she had an issue with race. "I don't know," he finally said.

"Boy or girl?"

He shrugged.

"What do you know about the most recent victim?"

He didn't even flinch. "Nothing."

"Where are you taking me?"

"I don't know." As soon as the words were out, he looked over, turning red.

"Let me take a guess here. Inspector Gray told you not to answer any of my questions, right?"

The officer nodded without meeting her gaze.

"You mind telling me where we're going?"

"To the scene, ma'am."

Casey rolled her eyes and leaned back against the seat. "Great," she mumbled.

"I'm glad you're here," Jordan said as he met Casey at the officer's car. From his tone, though, she knew it wasn't because he was happy to see her.

She looked around at the sloped hills surrounding Point Reyes. It was different than the other locations, more scenic. It would mean something to Leonardo, and she needed to spend some time to figure out what.

The first was a residential kill—the girl burned in her home, though she hadn't been discovered first. The second girl was dumped in the city—behind an abandoned warehouse. Next, there had been the girl in the alley, also in the city, then the girl in the park. And now this.

This was his first truly suburban kill. This wasn't far from where he was living. Or he had spent some time here. She looked up at the houses that lined the hills, their rear windows facing the sea. "Check and see if any of the places with views of this site are rented."

Jordan glanced up. "You think he's watching?"

"I think he'd love to be if he's not." She turned her attention to the scene. "What've you got?"

Jordan stared at his small spiral notepad as if he hadn't just been looking at the victim in person. "Caucasian male, eleven, somewhat undersized for his age."

"Male?"

Jordan nodded.

"That's odd. This one from a mall?"

Jordan nodded again. "I've got cops casing all the malls, looking out for uniforms. There just aren't enough cops to patrol every place."

"Was he reported missing?"

"I got the call right after I spoke to you yesterday. Couple has twins—a girl and a boy. They were at Corte Madera mall. Parents left the kids to play in a toy store while they ran an errand. Girl went to one end, boy to the other—looking for different toys."

Casey nodded, making mental notes.

"A while later, the boy comes to show his sister a toy she might like." He looked down at his notepad. "Some new game their friends have. Boy finds his sister talking to a police officer. Maybe our guy didn't realize the brother was so close by."

"Wouldn't make sense," Casey argued. "He'd have watched the parents and kids come in. Probably the father and son came in separately, trailing or something."

Jordan nodded. "So, the boy finds his sister talking to a cop. According to the little girl, the officer tells the kids that one of them needs to come with him to meet their mom while the other one waits there."

"And the kids don't question that?"

Jordan glanced at his notebook and shook his head. "Doesn't look like it. All I've got is that the little boy insisted he should be the one to go. Wanted to be a cop when he grew up."

Casey pictured the little boy fighting his sister for the honor of going with the cop. "Guess the girl's lucky she didn't have aspirations for law enforcement," Casey said, trying to lighten the fierce nausea in her gut. "And the mother?"

Jordan nodded without comment.

"How similar?"

"I've got a picture in the car—similar enough. And I figured out why they all look like you."

"What do you mean?"

"Karen and Jeanette Allister."

She remembered Jordan telling her his theory after seeing the crime scene photos. "You got pictures of them?"

He nodded.

"We look alike?"

"There's a resemblance."

Casey digested that and nodded. There was nothing more to say. Leonardo still had her in his sights, and now she knew why. Dismissing the tight knot in her stomach, she returned her attention to the scene. "When did the body turn up?"

"A couple of early joggers stumbled across it this morning at about seven. I got here an hour or so before you."

"A quicker turnaround than the other victims," Casey commented. Leonardo had never seemed like someone who liked to be rushed. Was he getting bored? She knew there was a pattern, a method of some sort. She needed to home in on it to learn where and when the next would happen—to be there before it did. "This makes five?" she asked, starting up toward the body.

"Yep," Jordan said.

Up on the hill, the huddle of people worked like a pack of wolves around the body, taking pictures, dusting for prints, collecting anything they could find. It was one of the more organized scenes she'd seen. A slender Chinese man in a carefully pressed white lab jacket ordered his team around with quick, easy directions.

Standing on the edge of the crowd, Casey took in the sight of the body. She hadn't been on the scene of a child death for over two years. Even when she'd seen one every few months, it had always been the worst type of job. The first thing Casey noticed about this boy was the blue party hat that had been propped on top of his lifeless face. "The hat is the same color as the one you found on your son at the Warriors game?"

Jordan stared back at the hat and shivered. He didn't have an answer.

"Not many more colors in the rainbow," Casey said.

Jordan nodded. "I had Renee check. The hat only comes in six colors."

"It probably won't end when he runs out of colors," she said softly.

Jordan nodded in agreement, but Casey could tell that he had hoped maybe the end of the rainbow would bring the end of the deaths.

"We've got a whole set of those things now," the Chinese man said.

Almost, Casey thought. One left.

Jordan motioned to him. "This is Al Ting, head of the crime scene team."

With her hands shoved in her pockets, Casey said hello. His own hands covered in medical gloves, Ting made no move to shake.

"And Ray Zambotti, our medical examiner," Jordan said, pointing her in the opposite direction.

Casey swung around, and the short balding man practically grabbed her hand right out of her pocket to pump it heavily. "Good to meet you. Great day, isn't it?"

Unlatching her hand, she nodded and replaced the now sore fist in her pocket. Traveling around the country to crime scenes, Casey could safely say she'd met all types. But the medical examiners were often the oddest.

Jordan lifted the sheet that had been draped over the body. "We have the same components as the priors. Duct tape, a standard white sheet, rope. All of it matches."

"Got some nail scrapings this time," Ting said.

Jordan nodded. "Right. Looks like there might be some tissue under the nails."

Casey looked at the paper bags tied over the boy's hands to preserve whatever might be beneath his nails. She suspected it would turn out to be the child's own tissue if anything at all.

"How about cause of death?" Casey asked.

"Looks the same as the others."

"I'll know more when I can get in there," the medical examiner added a bit too enthusiastically.

Casey gave him a strange stare.

He returned a little shrug.

Jordan rolled his eyes and brought the focus back to the victim. "We've got less mutilation than in the prior cases—he's got a couple broken fingers is all."

Casey frowned. It didn't sound right. "You sure it's the same guy and not a copycat?"

Jordan nodded. "Positive."

"How?"

Pointing to the boy's thigh, Jordan explained, "You can see his standard mark—here on the thigh."

Casey glanced at the marks and felt a stabbing pain rip through her fingers. It was agony reborn from memory. She glanced away and then forced her eyes back to the wound. She could feel the knife on her thigh as though it were fresh.

With her hands tucked under her arms, she pushed her arms down until she could feel the pain in her hands from the pressure. Somehow, the physical reminder was a relief from the excruciating pain in her memory.

"Maybe he was rushed," Jordan offered.

Casey looked at the boy and shook her head. "I don't think so. This killer doesn't put himself in a position to be rushed when he takes a child. From what you've said about the circumstances, it's more likely that the boy wasn't the original target."

"He wanted the girl, you mean," Jordan said.

"It seems like it. That, or he's saving himself for the next one. Maybe he even has the next one already." She was thinking out loud, hoping something would fall in place.

"You think he's saving himself for a finale?"

Casey thought about the last color in the rainbow—purple. It was the color of power. Wasn't he exerting his power over all of them? She wondered who he would choose for the rainbow's finale. If all the children's mothers looked like Casey, it only made sense that Casey would be his ultimate victim. Or Casey's child. Amy? Was Amy in danger? She was so far away. But why go from killing adults in Cincinnati to killing children whose mothers looked alike, unless Casey herself was the key? Damn, she couldn't find an answer.

"Casey?" Jordan repeated. "Are you okay?"

Pulling herself back, she nodded and ran her hands over her arms, fighting off the chill. She forced herself to concentrate on the case. She had put the crime scene photos aside before studying all of them. "These marks, they've been on each of the victims?"

Jordan nodded. "We're not sure about the girl from the fire, but the others, yes."

Casey knelt beside the boy and studied the marks. "They're not done freehand."

The medical examiner scurried up behind her. "What do you mean?" he asked, his face only inches from her own.

Jordan, too, leaned in to take a closer look.

"Can I get gloves?" She wanted to touch the boy's skin, but skin was a wonderful surface for fingerprints, and she didn't want to leave hers.

Jordan handed her a pair, and she pulled them on, awkwardly. Kneeling in the grass, she ran her finger across the surface of the cut. "It's an *L* in the center for Leonardo, and the sideways figure eight is the sign for infinity. It's his way of saying Leonardo forever. See how perfect they are. I think he's got an instrument for this."

"No way," Zambotti hollered in her ear.

Casey cringed.

"Settle down, Ray," Jordan said.

"I studied them against an entire file of scalpel cuts I have," Zambotti retorted. "They're nearly a perfect match to a sixteenth-inch scalpel."

"Maybe nearly, but not perfect," Casey said. "If you compare each mark to the others, you'll notice they're too similar to be freehand."

"What are you saying, Casey?" Jordan asked, laying his hand on her shoulder.

"I'm saying it's some sort of cookie cut he does on the victim. He didn't do it on the first three victims in Cincinnati, but it showed up on the fourth. I believe he does it in two parts. The infinity sign first, and then the *L* for Leonardo when he's done with his work. His signature if you will."

"Two parts?" Ray asked.

Casey nodded.

"How do you know?" Jordan continued, ignoring Zambotti.

She turned to Jordan and lowered her voice. "I've seen it before."

"It's impossible to tell from that," Ray muttered.

"Where have you seen it?" Jordan pressed.

Casey looked around. Everyone had stopped what they were doing, and they were all turned toward her, listening.

"Yeah, where have you seen it?" Ray echoed.

Casey stood and touched the fly of her jeans. It was a hell of a lot easier to open them than it would be to get them done up again. Cursing, she pulled the fly free and pushed her jeans to her ankles. Then, turning her leg toward Zambotti and Jordan, she pointed to the sideways figure eight on her thigh.

"Holy shit," Zambotti said, reaching to touch her leg.

She punched his hand away, and he jumped back. "It's only the infinity sign on me." She looked at her audience. "He obviously never got a chance to finish."

CHAPTER TWENTY-EIGHT

Rick Swain felt the rhythm of excitement drum in his stomach. Mueller wanted to see him. He hadn't been excited about the job since Cincinnati. Maybe someone was finally going to tell him what had happened. Maybe they realized the investigator had screwed up, and Swain wasn't at fault after all. Or for all he knew, Mueller was about to fire him.

He couldn't even count how many times in the past year he'd considered quitting the Bureau, but he knew he couldn't leave—not without knowing what had happened in Cincinnati. He knew what people thought of when they saw him. It was like letting his own sister get injured. He had done his job. McKinley's apartment had been carefully wired that night—he'd done it all himself, and he'd checked and double-checked. The question was, what the hell happened after he left?

His worst mistake was not questioning why the apartment had remained quiet even after he'd seen McKinley enter. Shit, how much noise do people make going to bed? But at least he should've heard running water or a toilet flush. They'd wired both Casey's apartment and her partner's as a precaution, but

Swain hadn't been expecting activity. It was going to be a cake job. He'd never imagined the killer would actually show up there. The killer had sent McKinley some strange correspondence. Maybe the Bureau actually expected him to show up there, but they certainly never told Swain that.

Swain took a final drag of his cigarette and headed above ground to Mueller's office. It was 9:07. He was supposed to be there at nine sharp, but Swain knew Mueller liked to keep people waiting. It was a sweating game up at his office. He did it to everyone, and Swain was sick of the fucking games.

As he stepped off the elevator, Swain squinted at the bright natural light that streamed into the building. It was cloudy and raining outside, but even the gray sky seemed impossibly bright compared to his lock-down.

He leaned over to rub a patch of dust off the toe of his black cowboy boot and then walked down the long, quiet corridor. His boots made a clack clack sound as he went that he found reassuring.

In the inner sanctum of Mueller's office, Mueller's secretary glanced up and smiled.

"Hello, Betty," he said, tipping an invisible hat.

"Hi, Rick. Sit down. He should be right out."

With a nod, Swain moved slowly to the small industrial-looking couch and passed it, stopping at the wall. He was too wired to sit. The room had seemed larger the last time he was there. Looking for a comfortable place to rest, he propped one foot against the wall and waited.

Under Hoover, the Bureau had fired people for no reason at all. Hoover was known for his idiosyncrasies when it came to running the FBI. These days it was better, but Swain had still heard stories about agents who'd been asked to resign for reasons that seemed unwarranted in the best of moments. They'd be idiots to fire someone with his talent.

The door clicked, and Swain looked up to see Dan Jamison walk out of Mueller's office.

"Hey," Swain said, pulling his foot off the wall and taking a few steps toward Jamison.

With only the slightest sideways glance, Jamison walked through the room without a pause. His normally pink, fleshy cheeks were a deep red, but his expression was one of cold detachment.

Betty and Swain exchanged glances. Before Swain could gather the nerve to ask her what she thought that was all about, she turned her back to him and began pecking loudly at her keyboard.

Fuck Jamison, Swain thought. He was only holding Swain back. Swain needed to go straight to the big boy. This was his chance to tell Mueller how it was.

"Swain?" Mueller called.

"Yes, sir," he replied, following Mueller into his office. Swain hadn't seen Mueller since his reprimand after the Cincinnati incident. Mueller's dark curls sat short and matted against his head, his dark eyes focused skeptically on Swain. The man seemed shorter than he had back then. Mueller was only five-seven or so and heavyset, all in the belly—like a young version of Santa Claus.

From the rumors Swain had heard, Mueller ate like a horse, but, of course, Swain had never had the pleasure of dining with the assistant director.

For months, Swain had been trying to get an audience with him. He had wanted to plead his case, to ask for another chance.

"Come on in." Mueller waved Swain into the office then turned to his assistant. "Betty, hold my calls."

Betty said something Swain couldn't make out as he was ushered into Mueller's office and the door was closed.

"Sit, sit," Mueller directed, pointing to a comfortable-looking armchair across from his desk.

Unlike the industrial blandness of the outer office, Mueller's office was warm and personal. Frames were huddled in the corners of his large desk as though his family were watching over him. The white walls were covered with awards and letters of commendation. Behind his desk a picture of him and President Bush hung next to one of him and President Reagan. Clinton remained noticeably absent from the wall. A Republican. Well, at least he wouldn't hear Mueller talk to him about the necessity of budget cuts.

"How are things?"

Swain felt a blow coming. Mueller had never been one for small talk. If he was starting it now, it was surely on the road to something unpleasant. But why not have Jamison do the dirty work?

"Agent Swain?" Mueller repeated.

"Fine. Thank you, sir. How are you?" he replied.

Mueller laughed. "I know that tone. Cut the bullshit, right?"

Swain straightened in his chair. "Without disrespect, sir, I don't believe you called me up here to ask how I am."

"You're right, I didn't. I respect straight talk. I'm going to cut the crap, Swain." Mueller shifted in his chair, leaning back and putting his arms behind his head. Studying the ceiling, Mueller was silent.

Swain could feel the cool sweat on his back as he waited.

Mueller put his arms down again and rested his elbows on the table. "You remember Agent McKinley, don't you, Agent Swain?"

"Of course."

"She's out in California now."

Swain nodded.

"You already knew that, didn't you?"

Swain nodded, shifting as sweat pooled at the base of his back.

"Well, the Bureau feels somewhat responsible for what happened to Agent McKinley. She was a damn good profiler. I'm sure you feel badly about it, too."

"Every day, sir. And I've been wanting to discuss the Cincinnati incident. I'd like to know what happened. I think I deserve—"

Mueller held a hand up to stop him. "I know. Are you interested in a chance to make it up to the Bureau?"

Relief rained on Swain harder than the sweat. "I'd love it, sir. Anything." He imagined himself back in the action, another mission. He'd be better this time, he swore. He'd prepare himself as though the Bureau expected a full-on attack—even if they told him it would be a simple surveillance. He'd be ready for anything.

"We're sending you to California, then. You'll leave in the morning. Betty can help you make travel and hotel arrangements."

Swain wondered about the case he'd be working on. "And the briefing will be out there?"

"Nope. The briefing is right now."

Swain frowned. "I don't understand."

"It's quite a simple mission, actually. Surveillance. There's a murder investigation going on in San Francisco that involves Agent McKinley." Mueller shifted in his chair. "We haven't exactly been invited to help on the case, but we'd like to keep an eye on what's going on with it."

Swain frowned but didn't comment.

"I trust you can do your job without letting on that you're there?"

Mueller presented it as a challenge, and part of the game was always accepting the challenges. "Of course."

"Good."

"Who am I surveying?"

"Two people actually. A man named Jordan Gray. He's an inspector with the San Francisco Police Department, handling a case of serial child murders."

"And I'm supposed to watch him?"

"Him and Casey McKinley."

Swain had learned early in the Bureau not to ask why higher-ups made decisions. But this one made no sense. "Is this Inspector Gray a threat to McKinley?"

Mueller shook his head. "Our sources say he's very highly spoken of within the department. And McKinley seems to get along with him quite well."

Then, why track him? "Are they in danger?"

Mueller looked pensive. "You can assume that. We need photographic evidence, video, audio—whatever you can get on everyone they come into contact with. We had audio surveillance on Agent McKinley's house, but unfortunately, it was disrupted."

The FBI had bugged ex-Agent McKinley's house. What the hell for? Swain kept his mouth shut.

"We believe the threat is related to the child murders," Mueller continued. "We're hoping you can find our man. Betty has copies of the newspaper articles, so you can brief yourself."

Swain held himself from smiling outright. He was

on a killer's trail again. And this time he wouldn't make a mistake.

"You are not, however, to go after him on your own. If and when you find him, you will make contact and we will send a task force."

Swain thought about Dan Jamison's reaction in the outer office. "And Jamison thinks this is a bad idea?"

Mueller smiled thinly. "Jamison doesn't have the faith in you that I do."

Holding his composure, Swain asked the logical questions. "Any idea who we're looking for? Male, female? Black, white?"

"White, male."

Swain waited for him to elaborate. When he didn't, Swain nodded and stood, taking the silence as his cue to leave.

"One more thing, Agent Swain," Mueller said.

Swain looked back to meet the concerned stare of the assistant director. "There's a chance we're dealing with the same killer."

"The same killer?" he echoed, trying to remember the last time he'd worked on a murder case.

"The same killer as Cincinnati," Mueller added, his tone and expression solemn.

Swain felt the surprise on his face. "The Cincinnati Butcher?"

Mueller nodded, studying him as though testing Swain's ability to think through a problem before committing him to the assignment.

Swain looked up, the rush of adrenaline that came with a new case stirring his blood. "You think the killer is after McKinley." It wasn't a question. It was a statement.

"And you're there to make sure nothing happens to her."

Swain thought about McKinley's departure from the Bureau. They hadn't wanted to lose her. Was that it? "You want her back."

"If she's ready. But I also expect this killer to go after her again. I want to make sure he doesn't get to her again."

Again, Swain thought. Had the FBI known the killer would go after Casey last time? Had they somehow set her up as bait, and when it failed, blamed him? His mind churned.

"You understand the assignment, Agent Swain?"

"I'll make sure she's safe," Swain promised, and then turned to leave. This time he would.

CHAPTER TWENTY-NINE

Hurrying up the stairs to his office, Jordan couldn't escape the image of the marks on Casey's leg. He had assumed there was more to the case, more to her injuries. But he never would have imagined the killer had carved his signature in her. She was downstairs waiting in the car while he picked up his messages and the latest news before taking her home.

Thankfully, she had been anxious to get away from the crime scene. And after he'd shown her those pictures of Jean and Karen Allister before their murders, she'd been spooked.

Jordan had been anxious to leave the crime scene, too. The blue hat on the last victim had affected him more than he cared to admit. He could still see Ryan, a blue hat strapped to his tiny head. This killer could not be allowed to take another victim. Jordan just didn't know how to stop him yet.

The last clue Jordan had was the doctor who had performed reconstructive surgery on George Allister. With the doctor and two of his nurses dead, and the records burned, there was only one person who could provide him with the information he needed. Jordan needed to find the one remaining nurse—Nina Rodriguez. He only prayed Leonardo hadn't taken care of her, too. So far, he had been very resourceful at cleaning up the loose ends.

Renee nearly barreled into Jordan as he stepped foot in his office. "Oh, thank God."

Jordan felt a new tightness in his jaw. Not again.

But instead of looking grim, Renee smiled, waving a piece of paper in the air. "I found her. I found her right here in Palo Alto!"

Jordan shook his head. "Who?"

"Nina Rodriguez, of course. Only now she goes by Christina Loman. She's married."

"She's here? In Palo Alto?"

"Works for a plastic surgeon named Wharton. I get the feeling Dr. Wharton's a real bigwig. Nina did a great job of covering her tracks when she left Kentucky, too. Police reports show she complained several times about a stalker in August and early September of 1998, two months after Allister's accident.

"Then, she was attacked on September 28—a young man came to her rescue. Two days later, she left town. No forwarding address—didn't tell anyone where she was going. But I found her."

Jordan could tell Renee wanted to tell the story. And even though he would have preferred just the information, he asked, "Okay, so how did you find her?"

Renee smiled, knowingly. "I have to tell you, but I'll keep it short. I figured to be a nurse, you've got to be licensed, right?"

Jordan nodded.

"So, I got her license number from Kentucky and asked if it had been transferred. Anyone who changes states has to renew the nursing license in the new state. Kentucky confirmed that she had moved out here, but that's all they could tell me. I knew she could've been anywhere.

"Well, I have an old friend who works for the California Nursing Board. I called in a huge favor, and she gave me the doctor's name and address."

"That's fantastic."

"There's more. I just called, and she gets off at four-thirty. If you go this second, you can get there before she leaves." Renee gave him a smug grin and handed over the directions.

Jordan took the paper and stared at the address. "You know, Renee, I could kiss you."

Renee blushed. "You can buy me lunch is what you can do."

"You got it." Jordan grabbed his keys and jogged toward the door.

Dropping the third *Sports Illustrated* back on the table, Jordan shifted again and looked around the waiting room. It was well after five o'clock. Casey seemed absorbed in a *Time* magazine that had to be a year old. He had seen a half-dozen patients enter the inner office and never emerge again. They probably shuffled them out some side door. He supposed people didn't want to run into someone they knew right after a nose job.

Standing, he approached the glass window in the corner of the waiting room and rang the bell again. He'd never been in a doctor's office where they locked the window. From the look of the patients he'd seen, it wasn't for security reasons. Confidentiality, more like it.

A blond woman with an obvious boob job opened the window, her open blouse a perfect view for those standing above her. Jordan wondered if the boobs had been a perk of the job.

"Yes?" she asked.

"I'm looking to speak with Christina Loman," he repeated.

The woman glanced at him as though she'd never seen him before, although he had requested the same thing twice already. From her. "And that was regarding what, again?"

"Roy McAllister," Jordan said for the third time. The woman couldn't possibly have forgotten him. From what he'd seen of the clientele, a six-foot-two black man shouldn't have been hard to remember.

"Right," she finally said. "One moment, please." The woman slid the glass closed again.

Jordan remained standing at the window, listening. He heard soft discussion and then silence.

"She's running," Casey called out.

Jordan spun around and saw a woman dressed in nurse's whites cast a nervous glance in his direction as she hurried through the parking lot. "Damn."

Casey right behind him, Jordan ran outside and headed her off before she could lock herself in a blue Honda Accord. "Ms. Loman?"

She shook her head and tried to close the door.

Jordan held it open. "Ms. Rodriguez, I'm Inspector Gray with the San Francisco Police Department. I need to speak with you."

"You've got the wrong person," she insisted.

But from the fear in her eyes, Jordan didn't think so. "You can make this easy and talk to me now, or you can make it rough and we can go to the station."

The woman hesitated, looking around.

"This will only take a few minutes, Ms. Loman. We

really need your help," Casey added, softening Jordan's threats.

The woman shook her head.

"It's a long drive to San Francisco and back. Is there somewhere we could talk?" Jordan pressed.

Her body slumped in the seat, and Jordan recognized the defeat in her shoulders.

"Please," Casey added.

"There's a coffee shop across the street." She pointed to a Starbucks.

"Perfect." He held the door open and waited for her to get out of the car. "We can walk."

Nina Rodriguez got out of the car and locked the door behind her. She remained a careful distance from Jordan and Casey, as though simply by association, someone might assume her guilt. In his peripheral vision, Jordan studied her.

Inside Starbucks, Nina made a beeline for a corner table and sat facing the wall.

"What can I get you?" Jordan asked.

"Decaf, please. Black."

"Grande latte, two sugars," Casey added.

Tossing Casey a stare, Jordan ordered the coffees and brought them to the table, setting one in front of Nina. Casey took hers and pulled off the top, shaking the sugars softly before awkwardly tearing off the tops and dumping them into her drink.

As Jordan sat, his knees knocked the underside of the small table, and he tried to find space to stretch out his long legs.

Her eyes downcast, Nina was fiddling with the coffee Jordan knew she wouldn't drink.

"Do you know why we're here?" Casey asked.

Nina nodded without meeting her gaze.

Her reaction was one he couldn't quite place. As

far as he knew, she had nothing to feel guilty about. But the overwhelming sense he got from her was guilt. "Why don't you tell us about it?"

"What's to tell? I don't know anything about him."

"Nina," Casey cut in. "Let me tell you where we're coming from." She put her hands flat on the table, and Nina looked at them and then away.

"He did that?" she whispered, her voice shaking.

Casey nodded. "I was an FBI agent working his case. He found me alone in an apartment. Now he's here, and he's killing children. We know what he looked like as a kid, but he's had some major surgery from what we understand. You can help us with what he looks like now."

Nina hesitated, stared down at her coffee and then back at Casey's hands. Finally, she nodded. "What do you need to know?"

Jordan opened his notebook and looked at his notes. "Tell us about your employment with Dr. Ballari in Kentucky. When did you start there?"

"January of 1994." The tone of her voice was almost robotic.

"And when did you leave?"

"September 21 of 1998."

"Can I ask why you left?"

Her gaze flickered around the room, and Jordan felt the chill in her eyes. "I felt my life was threatened."

"By whom?"

She met his gaze for the first time, and the fear was as clear in her eyes as the blue. "Roy McAllister."

"Tell us about McAllister."

"What about him?"

"Everything you remember."

"If you promise not to use my name, ever. Not in

a file, not even in your notebook. He'll get it, he'll find me. I've got children to think of, Inspector."

Jordan nodded, knowing there was no way to appease her entirely, though he would speak to Renee. "Your name isn't written here at all." He turned the notebook to face her. "See?"

She scanned the page and then wrapped her sweater protectively across her front and took a tentative sip of the coffee. "He had some surgery," she began. "He'd been in a car accident—not wearing a seat belt. Went through the windshield face first. According to him, he'd been fired from a job and ran his car off the road—rolled it twice. Said it was a rough patch in his life." She shivered. "I'd seen a fair number of car accidents, but nothing like that. His whole face was—" She stopped and shuddered. "He was in terrible shape."

"Was he recognizable?" Casey asked.

She shook her head. "I can't imagine he would have been, but I never saw pictures of him from before. He made it clear that he wasn't interested in looking like himself again."

"Did that strike you as odd?" Jordan asked.

"Not really. You'd be surprised how many people want to look totally different. Before I worked there, I would've thought people might want a new nose or chin, but a whole new face—" She frowned. "How would your family know you?" She paused and stared down in her cup. "But probably one in ten want a whole new look."

Jordan poised his pen. "Tell me what you remember about him."

"He was strange—right from the start. First off, he was nearly healed by the time he came to Dr. Ballari."

"What's strange about that?"

"Usually we get patients right from the hospital's OR. As soon as the patient is stabilized, he would be brought to us. But McAllister waited almost four full weeks before coming."

"Do you know why he waited?"

She nodded and stared at her coffee for a minute. Jordan let her take her time. Leonardo scared him almost as much as he appeared to scare Nina Rodriguez.

When she looked back up, she answered, "Wanted to make sure Dr. Ballari was the best. Which he is—" She caught herself. "Was. McAllister had done his homework. He knew about all of the doctor's clients, where Ballari had studied, his technique, everything. It was almost eerie. McAllister had also checked out most of us, too. Said he wanted to know what he was paying for.

"Ballari was an artist. He could sketch a face and then etch it from flesh and bone the same way a sculptor does from clay. And McAllister knew all of it."

"Was there other stuff?"

She nodded. "It was everything, really. When it came time to decide on his new face, he picked up a magazine, flipped through it for a couple of minutes at the most, and then pointed to a man. The one he chose wasn't anything special. A model with a strong jaw, but nothing spectacular—sort of a generic appearance. All that research to find the right doctor, and he didn't even care what he ended up looking like.

"I was surprised. McAllister seemed very vain, very sure of himself. I couldn't understand why he hadn't taken the time to figure out what he wanted to look like. Everything about it was weird."

Jordan pulled his sketches out and laid them across

the table, setting his coffee on the floor to make room. "Do any of these pictures look familiar?"

Nina looked at each one and then shook her head. She pointed to the one Officer Jones had done. "The face is okay—the eyes and nose. But the chin is all wrong. The chin he chose was really squared, sculpted."

Casey nodded.

Casey had been right about the fake chin. Jordan was amazed at how she figured these things out. He took the napkin from his lap and tore it into long strips, then laid them across the pictures as Casey had done in the hospital cafeteria, leaving only the noses showing. "You're sure about the nose, though."

Pointing to Jones's sketch, she nodded. "It's this nose." She turned to the sketch from Billy. "This one's too wide." She touched Elizabeth Weisman's. "This one's right, too." Picking up the napkin, Nina rearranged them to leave his eyes. "The eyes are definitely right." She looked up as if to explain. "There's not a whole lot you can do with someone's eyes. Ballari always said the windows to someone's soul are difficult to redress." She smiled softly and shook her head.

"I know this is difficult, but can you confirm any of the other features?" Casey asked.

She pointed at the cheeks in one sketch and nodded. "Those look right." Then, pushing the napkin aside, she studied all three again. "The chins are what's wrong, but it's definitely him. I'd know those eyes."

Jordan looked back at Nina. "What about the surgery? Were you there?"

She nodded. "I was there. It was awful. McAllister wanted minimal anesthesia—insisted he didn't need it at all."

"No anesthesia? What did Ballari do?"

"He insisted, of course. But McAllister fought him on it, so Ballari agreed and administered the minimum dose. McAllister hardly seemed affected by it. He was in and out through the entire procedure, mumbling." She shivered. "It was so eerie. Made everyone nervous. Of course, Ballari still did wonderful work.

"Then, when the surgery was done, he wanted to see his face." She shook her head and stared, her gaze that of someone who had encountered evil and realized what it could do. "He'd wanted to wear his contacts—he was meticulous about his sight. He argued, but Ballari refused to do the surgery if McAllister was wearing contacts. Of course, it made perfect sense. But McAllister wanted to see what Ballari was doing.

"So, as soon as the surgery was over, he demanded that I set his glasses over his eyes and show him a mirror so he could look at the work before we bandaged. It was really not a pretty sight, but McAllister actually seemed genuinely pleased. It was so creepy."

"What about after the surgery?"

"We were all so relieved it was over, but he didn't go away. As soon as he was out of the hospital, he started calling the office all the time. Said he wanted his chart and his file. He wouldn't leave us alone."

"Did he follow you outside of work?" Casey asked.

Nina's gaze shot up to meet Casey's, and she blinked hard before nodding.

"We read the police report about the stalker," Jordan said.

She exhaled. "I started getting strange calls and then threats in the mail. They didn't say anything about work, so I didn't make the connection. But I was having trouble concentrating at work. I called the police and asked for help. They told me it was a kid, playing a prank. But I didn't think so."

"And how did you end up leaving your job?"

"I wanted to take a couple of weeks off, go see my sister in Chicago just to get away. Ballari was under a lot of stress, too. He needed me to be there. He said if I had to go, I shouldn't come back." She shook her head and pushed the coffee away. "I went. I figured that I would be able to talk to Dr. Ballari when I got back. I never imagined . . ."

Jordan nodded. "You did the right thing."

Nina looked up with surprise. "I feel like I let them down. Michelle, one of the other nurses, was my best friend."

Casey laid her hand on Nina's. "There's nothing you could've done."

She stared at her for a minute and then exhaled, a long, deep breath. "I know. I just can't help blaming myself for not doing something else—" Nina smoothed her dark hair back. "We were all in danger, and I think I sensed it more than the others."

"What about the fire?" Jordan asked.

"I heard about it from Chicago. I'd tried to call Michelle and reached her mother, who had come from Detroit to deal with her things. I came right home, of course. But as soon as they said arson, I knew what had happened."

"Did you tell the police?"

She met his gaze and looked away.

"It's okay."

"I was too scared. He was already following me. The police weren't helping. I thought if I told them, he'd kill me."

"You think he was the stalker," Casey said.

"I know it was him," she said. Her voice held the edge of someone who had been doubted before.

Jordan knew what the police were facing, though. They got so many phony reports. It was sometimes hard to tell the imagined situations from the real ones. "Did you see him?"

She shook her head, looking upset.

"Then, how did you know it was him?"

"Because when he attacked me from behind, he whispered in my ear."

"You recognized the voice?" Casey asked.

"That was partially it. But it was more what he said."

"What did he say?" Jordan prompted.

"He said, 'If you think that fool Ballari was an artist, wait until you see what I can create.' I was scared, terrified, but I thought it was him. I just had to be sure. So, I asked, 'Who are you?'" Nina looked up and met Jordan's eyes. Her expression showed the strength of someone who had survived.

"What did he say?" Jordan pressed.

"He laughed and said, 'I'm da Vinci.'"

CHAPTER THIRTY

Casey stared down at the plate the waiter had set before her. She thought about the fear she'd seen in Nina Rodriguez's face the day before. It was all fitting together. Officer Jones had discovered the apparent stressor for the killing of George Allister's mother and sister. Three days before their murders, Indiana University had sent a letter of rejection to George Allister for their premed program.

According to a nurse who had worked with Karen Allister, she had been going home to celebrate her birthday with her mother. Casey still didn't quite understand the significance of birthdays, but somehow she was sure it tied in with the party hats.

After disposing of his mother and sister, George Allister became Roy McAllister and worked somewhere successfully for almost five years. Nina had told them he had confessed to driving recklessly because he'd been fired from his job. Again, it made sense. The stressor of losing his job might have spurred him to kill again. Either that, or the freedom the reconstructive surgery had brought him. After unsuccessfully stalking Nina Rodriguez, he'd gone to Cincinnati and hunted easier prey. That was when Casey had been called into the picture. All of it fit. The only missing piece was the present. What the hell was he up to now?

"Are you going to eat that or just stare at it?" Billy asked.

Casey focused on the burger and pushed Leonardo from her mind. "I can't believe I ordered this," she whispered.

"Why? You've been craving a burger for months."

She nodded. "I have, but how the hell am I going to eat it?"

A couple at the next table glanced over at her and began whispering. Casey did her best to ignore them. The popular restaurant hummed with Sunday afternoon traffic. Waiters wore starched white shirts and aprons. Linen dressed the tables, yet the TV blaring a game and the easy banter of the bar gave the restaurant a casual, relaxed feel.

"Pick it up," Billy prompted.

Casey scowled in his direction, then focused on the plate. The hamburger patty sat open-faced, and the smell was killing her. After retrieving the ketchup from the center of the table, Casey fought to open the bottle, using the center of her palm, and poured the red sauce over the fries.

With the fork held awkwardly in her fist, Casey stabbed at the mound of fries.

"Use your fingers."

She ignored him, wishing it were so easy.

"Try it," Billy pushed.

Laying her fork on the table, she glanced around to be sure no one was watching. The couple at the next table seemed to be occupied watching a man and woman make out at the bar.

Like a child eating finger food for the first time,

Casey pushed the fries around on her plate and then caught one between her forefinger and thumb and lifted it to her lips. A french fry had never tasted better.

"Ha! I told you," Billy exclaimed.

"Will you shut up," she hissed. "I feel like a fool as it is."

The couple glanced over at her again. Casey sent them a scalding stare.

"Now try the burger," Billy said.

Casey scowled.

"You've done a lot tougher things than eat a burger."

"Don't push," she warned, smiling.

Billy grinned. "Pushing's my job."

Casey smoothed her hands over her napkin, wiping off the ketchup. With both hands, she reached for the burger, gripping it in an awkward clutch and bringing it to her mouth. A dollop of mustard landed in her lap, missing the napkin by a full inch. "Shit."

"Ignore it," Billy said, watching her. "Half the people here have dripped mustard in their laps."

She brought the cheeseburger to her mouth and took a bite.

"Good?"

She nodded. Setting the burger down, she wiped up the mustard stain, feeling strangely triumphant. As she rubbed at the yellow spot, she noticed her fingers obeyed her.

"It's easy, isn't it?"

"Not easy."

Billy smiled. "You got hungry enough to do it."

Casey rolled her eyes and reached for the burger again. Billy was right about one thing. She was starving. She took another bite and swallowed, setting the burger back down and reaching for her iced tea.

The waiter stopped beside her. "How is everything here?"

"Great," Casey answered, picking up her glass.

"Can I get you anything else?"

The glass slipped, and Casey tried to right it, but her fingers couldn't catch it quickly enough. The glass went over, pouring the full iced tea down the waiter's front.

"She could probably use some more iced tea," Billy said, laughing.

"You should drive us home," Billy said, dangling the keys.

Casey laughed and shook her head. "No way."

"You did a great job—once you put your mind to it."

Casey rolled her eyes to downplay his enthusiasm, though they both knew this was a small triumph.

"We should have ordered cake to celebrate. You could've eaten it with your fingers."

"You're intolerable."

Billy grinned. "You sure you don't want to drive?"

"Positive," she insisted, fighting her hands to pry the passenger side door open and then collapsing on the seat from the effort.

Billy got in and started the engine, the Volvo stirring to life. "I think that waiter thought we were insane."

"Hey, it was your idea. I told you months ago eating out with me would be trouble."

"You were great." He touched her hand.

"Thanks." She pulled the seat belt across her lap and fumbled to get it into place, noticing how Billy watched her from the corner of his eye but made no move to help her.

When she was safely belted in, Billy pulled out of the parking spot. Though he looked better than he had, Casey noticed he was still pale and seemed more than a little lethargic, especially for someone who normally had the energy of a dozen ten-year-olds on M& Ms. "You should lie down when we go home. Take a nap."

Billy waved a finger. "You're not getting out of your exercises that easily."

"I can do them on my own. You look tired."

He nodded. "A little. What I'd really like to do is take some bread to the park and feed the ducks."

Casey smiled. "You're getting transparent, Billy."

"What do you mean?"

"Going to the park means breaking up the bread and that means finger exercise—I know what you're up to."

With a smile, he shrugged. "It was worth a try." His smile, even his shrug, lacked his normal enthusiasm. Rubbing a hand over his eyes, he added, "I am a little tired."

"Maybe we shouldn't have gone out."

"No," Billy said. "It was wonderful. I've heard great things about Crogan's. I appreciate you treating." He glanced over at her. "And it was time for you to get out, Casey. You're ready to get back."

Casey waved the comment off. "Don't be ridiculous."

"I'm serious. You're ready. You don't need me anymore. It's like you said—you can do the exercises yourself."

"Stop talking like that, Billy."

"Casey, it's the truth. I see it in your eyes. Whether

or not you admit it to yourself, you want to get back to work. Inspector Gray's been good for you. As scary as this killer is, the situation has proved that you can do it."

She shook her head. "I still can't do it, Billy. All I can do is sit at a table and think about a killer's M.O., give my suggestions about what he will do, and maybe why." She paused and thought about Cincinnati. There was no way she would ever be that strong again.

As much as she hated to admit it, he had destroyed parts of her she couldn't even remember. She pushed the thought from her mind. "I can't hunt like I used to. It's not the same."

"Because you've convinced yourself it won't be. I've seen you when you're determined. You can do anything you want to. You've started to run on that knee. And look at your boxing."

Casey stared out the window. She wasn't ready to go back. She never would be. How could she be a profiler? She couldn't tie her shoelaces, or drive. Even boxing was nothing like it had been.

And most importantly, she couldn't shoot a gun. The Bureau had shooting requirements she would never pass again. Despite the access Jordan had gotten her to the shooting range, she still couldn't shoot. The three times she'd gone to the range, she'd tucked herself in the far stall and stood, hands shaking while she tried to get her fingers to cooperate. She'd gotten a few shots off, but none had come close to a target. Beyond that, she was just plain weak, and in her job weak meant vulnerable. And vulnerable meant dead. There was no future for her with the Bureau. She still didn't see much of a future at all. Working with Jordan was a distraction from her life over the last year. But it was only that—a distraction.

"I mean it, Casey. The only barrier you have has nothing to do with your hands."

She looked at him and frowned.

"It's between your ears."

She turned away, waving him off.

"You can put it off, but we're going to have to talk about it soon." Billy exhaled hard, and she turned to see him press the palm of his hand to his chest.

Something in his expression scared her. "Are you okay?"

He nodded as he pulled into the driveway. "Looks like we have company."

Casey frowned at the unfamiliar white Ford Taurus sitting in the driveway. "Who the hell's that?"

"Should we stop?"

Hesitating only a second, she nodded. Leonardo wasn't going to park in her driveway and ring the doorbell.

As Billy stopped the car, Casey peered through the windshield. She didn't see anyone. Maybe it was someone visiting one of her neighbors, she thought, noticing the rental-looking car. But then why would they park in her drive?

Casey got out of the car and walked to the front door, pausing to feel the hood of the car. It was still warm. Her shoulders back, she kept her chin high, her gaze hovering over the perimeter. The muscles in her arms and back tightened as if preparing for fight. As she reached the front porch, she stopped and looked around. There was no one.

As she leaned down to put the key in the lock, she felt a light tap on her shoulder. Arms to her face, she whipped around and jabbed twice—hard. Though she couldn't hold her fists correctly, her arm strength was enough to provide some punch.

She heard a male moan before a girl's scream.

Casey blinked hard and looked at the man lying on the ground. Michael!

He moaned again, and Casey couldn't move. What was he doing here?

"Mom!" someone yelled. "You punched out Dad." Casey heard the sound of a young girl laughing, and everything was dreamlike. Prying her gaze off Michael, Casey looked up. Amy stood before her, tall and thin. She seemed nothing like the little girl Casey remembered, and everything about her face made Casey ache from the inside out.

"Mom!" Amy leapt at Casey, throwing herself into her mother's arms and knocking Casey back up against the house.

Casey wrapped her arms around the girl and then closed her eyes, feeling the softness of her daughter's hair, recalling the way Amy had smelled when she was little, remembering what she and Michael had been and how much she had let them down. She thought she might never let her go. After seeing the little boy on the hill, she was so relieved to see Amy in one piece where she could personally watch over her.

"Mom, are you crying?"

Casey shook her head and wiped her sleeves across her eyes. "No. I'm just so surprised." She looked down at her husband, who was now sitting up, a white handkerchief pressed to his bleeding lip. He wore shorts and a polo shirt, his favorite outfit for twenty years. Everything about him was familiar. Keeping hold of Amy's hand, Casey knelt beside him. "Michael, I'm so sorry. You startled me."

Michael smiled softly and shook his head. "She's got her hook back, that's for sure."

"That she does," Billy agreed, standing on the side-lines, smiling.

Michael reached to Amy. "Help your old man up, would you?"

Amy took her father's hand and pulled him up while Casey watched. She would have pinched herself to make sure they were really there, but she still couldn't get her fingers to do it.

"Maybe you should invite them in," Billy whispered as he came up beside Casey.

Casey nodded. "Of course. Come on in." Taking Amy's hand again, she led them inside. Looking back at Michael, Casey pushed her hair off her face and remembered the mustard stain on her jeans. It was the first time in months she'd even thought about what she looked like. "We'll, uh, get some ice for your lip."

Amy laughed. "Wait till I tell the kids at school." She turned back to Michael. "Sorry, Dad, but it's too cool not to tell."

Michael rolled his eyes and smiled at Casey. "No problem. Maybe I can come in for show-and-tell."

Amy laughed. "That would be awesome." She turned to Casey. "Mom, could you come in and give Justin Blake a black eye?"

Casey shook her head. "Who's Justin Blake?"

"He's this total dork in my class."

Nodding, Casey stared back and forth between the two of them. Amy was hardly recognizable, and Michael looked exactly like he had the day they met.

"We had one of those in my school, too," Billy said. "Joey Mazrotti—big guy, used to beat everybody up."

"Bullies don't bother me," Amy said as though not a day had passed since Amy and Michael were living here. "I'm bigger than most of the guys in my class."

"Anyone want lemonade?" Billy asked.

"I do," Amy said.

"That would be great, Billy," Casey agreed. "Thank you."

He headed into the kitchen. "Amy, come help me. I want to hear more about Justin Blake."

Amy followed. "Well, his big problem is that he thinks he's totally cool," she explained, her voice fading as she disappeared into the kitchen.

Casey watched her until the door swung shut, fighting the urge to follow.

"I'm sorry to just drop in like this," Michael said, standing right behind her.

Savoring the sound of his voice, Casey turned slowly. Suddenly she felt like a self-conscious sixteen-year-old. "Really, it's no problem."

"I must've called a dozen times. There's no machine."

Casey looked around. "I haven't gotten around to getting one."

"You look great."

Casey nodded, smoothing her stained jeans. "Thanks."

He motioned to her clothes. "No more sweatpants?"

She shook her head.

There was a brief silence.

"I wouldn't have brought Amy unless it was an emergency," Michael explained.

"I'm glad you brought her. I've been meaning to call," she said, knowing how stupid and worthless it sounded now. "It's been a long time."

Michael nodded. "Since her birthday."

Casey remembered the phone call. It had been almost two months ago.

"We missed yours. I'm sorry."

Casey shook her head. She'd missed her own birthday. Who wanted to count at her age? Gathering her thoughts, Casey motioned to the couch. "What are you out for? Business, I assume."

"A tech firm out here hired me to prosecute an intellectual property case."

Casey was impressed. "Your reputation followed you all the way out here?"

Michael smiled. "I think it was a referral. I guess passing the California bar all those years ago had paid off."

"Yeah. It's not like there aren't plenty of great intellectual property attorneys out here." She paused. "That's great."

"Thanks. I have to go down to the valley for a couple of days. I was hoping Amy could stay here."

Casey started to nod.

"Mary had to go to North Carolina because her mother's sick and I couldn't find a replacement in time. I'm sorry to—"

"Michael—" she interrupted. "I'm glad she's here—I'm glad both of you are here. Amy's welcome to stay." With Amy there, though, Casey didn't want to wait another minute without having someone watch the house. The mothers who looked like Casey, their children—the alarm system no longer seemed like nearly enough. "I need to make a call," she said, wanting to do it before she had to explain it to Michael.

"Go ahead. I'll wait here."

From her bedroom, Casey called Jordan's line and spoke with Renee, explaining what had happened and what she needed. Quick to respond, Renee made arrangements to call the Oakland Police Department and have someone there within five minutes. "Hold on, and I'll get a car number so you know if the right person has arrived."

When Renee returned, she gave Casey a patrol car number and the name of the officer. "He's black," Renee added. "I figured it would be easier to be sure he's not our nutcase."

"Thanks, Renee."

"No problem. Give me your phone number, and I'll have his unit call you and confirm when he's in place. Jordan's out this afternoon, but I'll have him call you as soon as he's back."

When Casey hung up, she felt a hundred times better.

"Everything okay?" Michael asked when she returned to the living room.

"It will be in about four minutes."

Michael frowned. "What do you mean?"

Trying to be as casual as possible, Casey explained about the killer they'd been tracking and about the similarities between this case and Cincinnati.

"Maybe we shouldn't be here," Michael said, looking toward the kitchen door.

"The call I just made was to the police. There will be an officer out here any minute. This is the safest place she could be."

The phone rang, and Casey answered.

"This is the Oakland dispatcher to confirm that the squad is at your residence."

Casey moved to the window and looked outside, noting the numbers on the side of the car—#1742. "He's here."

She waved to the officer, and he waved back.

Michael watched over her shoulder. "How long has it been like this?"

"Just a couple of weeks."

"It's terrible, Casey. I hate it. It's like you're in the Bureau all over again."

Casey could feel the tingle in her belly as Michael looked at her. She wanted to touch him, to kiss him, but it all felt so foreign and strange.

Michael took a step forward and leaned to kiss her. "I worry about you," he whispered as his lips met hers.

Just then, the kitchen door burst open. "Lemonade all around," Amy declared.

Casey straightened and felt herself blush as she looked away from Michael.

"She's never had good timing," he whispered in her ear. "That's from your side."

Casey laughed and felt a giddy excitement that she hadn't remembered feeling in years.

"Amy, do you promise to behave for your mother?"

Her eyes lit up, and Casey saw shades of Michael clearly in their bright gaze. "I get to stay?"

"Absolutely," Casey said.

Billy gave her a smile of approval.

"Can we rent *Men in Black*?" Amy asked.

"You've already seen it five times," Michael said.

"Six," she corrected. "But it's so cool," Amy argued, turning to her mom. "Did you see it, Mom?"

Casey shook her head. She couldn't remember the last time she'd seen a movie.

"You'll love it. There are these aliens, and Tommy Lee Jones is in it. And Will Smith. He's such a fox. They have this awesome machine that makes people forget. I swear, it's the best! Can we see it? Please!"

Casey shrugged, amazed at how her daughter had been able to talk for so long without pausing for a breath. "Sure."

Amy's face lit up. "And can we have microwave popcorn and pizza for dinner?"

"Amy, enough already," Michael scolded.

Casey laughed. "I think pizza and microwave popcorn sounds perfect."

Amy bounded over to Casey and put her arms around her mother. Casey noticed that Amy was only six or seven inches shorter than her now. She was sure Amy had been so much smaller only a few months ago. Her previously long hair was cut in a stylish bob, her clothes showing off her long thin figure. Casey couldn't believe this was her daughter. Looking at Amy, Casey ran her hands over her daughter's head and then pulled her close. Amy didn't seem to hate Casey for being gone, for sending them away. Instead, Amy appeared simply happy to have her mother back. Casey was so thankful that Michael had come.

And as much as she had wanted to argue, Billy was right. It was time to reassemble the strewn pieces of her life. And her family was the perfect place to start. She had pushed them away once. She wasn't going to do it again.

Casey focused on Amy's beautiful, young face. When she blinked, she saw a flash of the faces of the children who had been killed.

The sharp talons of fear clawed at her spine. Amy was too close to the danger. Even with the officer parked out in front, Casey knew she wouldn't stop worrying, no matter what she told Michael.

But the worrying was okay. It would keep her focused. Casey wasn't going to let Leonardo destroy Amy the way he had tried to destroy her.

CHAPTER THIRTY-ONE

Amy was here. He didn't even try to suppress the smile that curled his lips. It had been much too easy to lure Michael out. And he had watched as Casey greeted them. She was happy. He hadn't ever seen her look happy before.

The very idea that he was at the root of that made him glow from the inside out. And the control he would have over her when he had Amy was almost overwhelming. Her every emotion would be in his power, Casey like a puppet for him to play with. And he couldn't wait to pluck the strings and watch her dance.

Taking the keys from his pocket, he found the one with the red plastic cover and unlocked the basement door. He entered quickly, and carefully locked the door behind him as he always did, inhaling the smell of metal and the cleanser he had used to scrub every inch of his workspace. The blood was gone, but memory gave him its sweet aroma.

His tools, the blood, they were the smell of power. It was a smell that intoxicated him. He never allowed himself to drink. It had been his mother's weakness— she had been especially wicked on those nights when the bottles were drained. She'd come at him with a belt that she claimed his father had left her to whip him with. It had a solid brass buckle that weighed easily a pound. He could still feel the weight of it on his arms and back. He rubbed his arm and closed his eyes, pushing the images away.

He didn't need alcohol. His work provided intoxication enough.

At the base of the stairs, he stopped and trained his eyes on the dark room, waiting until his pupils dilated to let in sufficient light to supply the images. He loved the colorlessness of a room without light.

In the darkness, the ones he'd brought there saw shapes and motions that didn't exist in the light. He loved to watch them struggle with their terror. Of course, once he was prepared to operate, the intricacies of his craft demanded light.

He found the long string in the center of the room and pulled it. A lone bulb popped on, shadowing the room with a yellow glare. The room was almost ready for Amy. He had removed all remnants of the last victim. The boy had been very disappointing.

He hadn't seen the boy enter the toy store with his father. He had only noticed the mother and the girl. Only afterward did he remember that the father and son had been only a few steps behind. And he had seen the father come out first and sit on the bench. It was so obvious now that the man must have been waiting for the wife. He hadn't wanted the boy. It was the girl he had chosen. He had felt himself reacting to her even in the short time in the store.

But what choice did he have when the boy insisted on going? And he had known that two children together would be excessive trouble. He still worried what the girl might remember. But worry was a waste of time.

In each step of the game so far, he'd had a carefully defined strategy for his acquisitions. Each had worked well. But Amy was the final test.

Before, he had merely cruised the malls, watching the women and their children, waiting for a mother who looked like Casey. So many women in the malls these days, it hadn't taken long—a few days at the most. Then, he would watch mother and child, waiting until he could separate them.

Sometimes, it was as easy as it had been with the little black girl. The mother left the child to run an errand. More often, though, it had been a matter of following the women until they got sidetracked and then luring the child away. The capture was the most exciting part of the game. Thrilling and terrifying both. One time, he'd even been caught leading a child away.

But instead of looking suspicious, the mother had actually thanked him for bringing the child back. "My pleasure, ma'am."

He smiled to himself now. Yes, it would have been if she hadn't interrupted. But nothing came of it, and no one questioned his presence. He changed his appearance and location often enough that everyone assumed he was a mall security guard. And why not? He had learned to disguise his intelligence, and people instantly accepted the appearance of a uniform as authority. It was time to finish up and move on to new challenges.

Resting in his director's chair, he picked up a scalpel, reflecting the light off the blade as he thought. Tomorrow was Monday. His check to Michael McKinley would surely be at the bank by then, so he only had until Tuesday before it could be cashed. Once the check bounced, his access to Amy would vanish.

He didn't have as much leeway as he would have liked. He had been surprised to hear Michael had already received the check in the mail when they'd spoken on the phone last week. He should have known the postal system would be efficient the one time he required slow service. It was only a minor issue, and certainly not one he couldn't overcome.

But it did tighten his time frame. He looked around the room, ticking off everything he would need. He had checked and replenished his supply of rope and duct tape. His tools were clean and sharp. He set the syringe of anesthesia beside the bag he carried with him. He had pilfered a great deal of the drug from Dr. Ballari's office before the fire, and it worked beautifully to subdue his patients in the initial stages of panic.

He continued his mental checklist. A fresh white sheet lay still wrapped in plastic on the makeshift operating table. One day, someone else would set his tools out for him. He would come and perform his art and let someone else clean up the mess. That was the day he would truly feel his power. Now he was just finishing the last stages of preparation for his official vocation.

The purple hat sat upright on a small table with his tools, waiting to be fit on Amy's lifeless head. The sight of it reminded him that he had control over how long she lived and when she died. The purple was for the last child in his palette of death.

Tomorrow, he would begin watching them. He was positive he would be able to catch Amy alone. Even the rent-a-cop was no match for him. He had paid for a room at a cheap hotel near Casey's house several days ago, the kind of place where people didn't ask questions. He hoped he wouldn't need the room, but it would give him a place to subdue Amy if need be. He had taken every precaution.

He glanced at the floor he had scrubbed and bleached. Everything was ready. He stood and moved to his table, flipping the pages of his uncle's old *Gray's Anatomy* in search of the perfect sketch to use. For Amy, the eyes—her mother's eyes, his mother's eyes—would be his focus. He found a perfect diagram of the eye and studied the muscles surrounding it. He would detach the rectus lateralis from the bottom of the eye and the rectus medialis from the top. He would have to enter from the eye cavity because of the hard bone that surrounded the eye, but he would be cautious to do so without injuring the cornea. Once he was in, he would sever the optic nerve and remove the eye. What a wonderful final gift from daughter to mother—a masterpiece indeed.

And she would be his so soon.

CHAPTER THIRTY-TWO

"Are you up, Mom?" Amy yelled from the hall.

Casey rolled over and looked at the clock. It was only eight-thirty. Of course she wasn't up. With Amy in the house, Casey had stirred at the slightest creak all night. She must have checked on the patrol car a dozen times.

"Mom!" Amy yelled again.

Grunting, Casey forced herself onto her elbows. The sound of her daughter's voice in the morning was so foreign, she had to push off the sense that she was dreaming.

"Come on in, honey," she called back.

"Did I wake you up?" Amy asked, coming in wearing Casey's heavy terry-cloth robe. Her wet hair hung just above her shoulders, her face bright with excitement. She plopped herself on the bed.

Casey put her arm around her daughter and closed her eyes.

"Mom!"

"It's early."

"It's eight-thirty. I'm going to make you breakfast— pancakes, okay?"

Casey pushed herself up in bed. "Now, that's worth getting up for."

"And the phone's for you." Amy pulled the portable phone from the robe pocket.

"Is it your dad?" Casey asked.

"No." She shrugged. "Some man."

Casey glanced at the phone with a tight knot in her chest. "Why don't you go into the kitchen and get started. I'll be right in."

Amy jumped up. "Okay."

"No cooking until I get there," Casey added, all the fears of parenthood washing back over her.

When Amy was safely from the room, Casey put the phone to her ear. "Hello."

"It's Jordan."

Casey exhaled. "You ought to introduce yourself when you call," she scolded.

"Caught me off guard to have a kid answer the phone. Is that Amy?"

"Yeah. Michael came by yesterday. I guess he's in town for business. Amy's staying here for a few days. Didn't Renee tell you?"

"I got a message from her about the Oakland police, but I didn't quite understand it."

Casey looked out her window. The patrol car was still parked in front of the house. "He's still here. Did you call to check up on us?"

"Actually, no," Jordan admitted. "You know someone named Rick Swain?"

Hearing Swain's name brought back a wave of helplessness that Casey despised. "Why? What do you know about Swain?"

"So you *do* know him?"

"Yes, I know him. Jordan, what's going on?"

"Renee has a friend at the Bureau who called to let her know that this guy, Swain, was coming out here."

"Out here?" Casey tried to digest the information and the discomfort it brought. "Why?"

"That's what I want to know. As far as I know, the FBI isn't involved in this case. We haven't notified the Bureau. How did they find out about it?"

Casey studied the far wall of her bedroom, remembering the look on Swain's face as she stared up at him, half-conscious, from the gurney. He had blamed himself for the attack. She had blamed him, too. Swain was supposed to have wired her apartment for sound. To this day, Casey didn't know what had gone wrong.

Maybe Swain had been too lazy and had just skipped the wiring. Or maybe something had been faulty. For all she knew, he'd done it all correctly and then fallen asleep without his headset on. But she did know that when she was carried out by the EMTs, she had seen guilt in his eyes.

"Casey?"

"I'm here."

"Who is he?"

"He was with me in Cincinnati."

"Your partner?"

She shook her head, forcing herself to put her lips together and make sound. "He was our surveillance."

"What happened?"

"I don't know."

"He fucked up?" Jordan pressed.

She nodded, reliving the horror of the sound of Leonardo behind her, wondering when someone would burst in on them, when someone would save her from the terror, from the excruciating pain. Then later, knowing something had gone wrong, that no one was listening, no one was coming for her.

"Casey?"

"Yes. Something went terribly wrong," she blurted. Rubbing her eyes, she added more softly, "I don't know what. I never asked. After the attack, I didn't care."

"So why would he be here?"

There was a long pause.

"Unless the Bureau thinks this killer is their man," Jordan added. "Would they send him out then?"

"I don't know. I haven't had any interaction with the Bureau since the month after the attack."

"They're getting their information from someone in my organization, then."

Casey laughed. "That's not tough to imagine. They've got a field office here. It'd be easy to get information from one of your officers. They've got a million ways to do it." Casey thought a minute. "It's not protocol, though. Unless it becomes a federal jurisdiction case, they normally don't intercede until someone's requested help. Are you sure your captain didn't call them? Or maybe the chief?"

"No way." Jordan was adamant. "The chief detests the Bureau. And Tapp wouldn't do anything against the chief's wishes."

"Well, assuming you didn't contact them about the links with the Cincinnati killings, maybe they were able to link the murders themselves. Then, the crimes cover two states, and the case becomes federal jurisdiction."

"They'd connect the crimes without telling me as head of this investigation?" Jordan sounded furious.

"I'm just guessing, Jordan. I don't have any clue why he's here. I don't even know if he's really here."

"Oh, he's here all right. I called the airport and confirmed it," he continued, without hiding his aggravation. "Traveled under his own name and arrived yesterday. He rented a car from Hertz. A white Mustang."

Casey nodded. "That sounds like Swain. You know where he's staying?"

"No idea. You'll keep an eye out for him?"

"Yes," Casey said, wondering where Amy was. Pushing the covers off, she took the phone into the hallway. Immediately, the sounds of Billy and Amy talking in the kitchen soothed her worries. "He's a bit of a cowboy, actually. Likes to do his own thing. I think what happened in Cincinnati hurt his career pretty badly. He's probably doing mostly desk work."

"So why send him out here?"

"I told you I don't know."

"You worked for the Bureau. Guess," he demanded.

Frustrated, Casey shrugged. She hadn't thought of the way the Bureau worked in six months, maybe more. And she wasn't all that anxious to think about the politics now. "You want a guess? Fine. The Bureau loves to give everyone a chance for vindication. Maybe this is his." She stopped. "But honestly, I don't know."

"Thanks for the info." Jordan paused, changing the subject. "So Amy's there. I'd love to meet her."

"Why don't you come by for dinner? It's just Billy, Amy, and me. I'm sure she'd love to meet you, if you can handle the probing questions of a twelve-year-old."

Jordan laughed. "I'd love it. If she's anything like her mother, it should be an eventful evening. Should I bring anything? Wine?"

"None of those vices allowed around here. How about ice cream? See you around six?"

"Sounds good. Any favorite flavors?"

"If I recall correctly, anything chocolate will do."

"Got it."

Casey turned the phone off and set it on the table. The idea of having Rick Swain in town made everything that had happened seem all the more ominous. Would the Bureau use her to lure Leonardo? Was this all some sort of setup? She'd always wondered if that's what had happened before. Had the Bureau used her to lure a killer? And the fact that Amy was here, so close. The timing couldn't be worse. Tonight, when Jordan was over, she would ask for additional surveillance on the house. Her own safety was something she would gamble, but no one was going to touch Amy.

"Mom, look at the pancakes," Amy said delighted, running toward her carrying a plate. "Billy's making Mickey Mouses."

Pulling herself out of her daze, Casey looked at the creation. "Looks almost too good to eat."

"No way," Amy protested. "I'm starved."

Casey followed her daughter into the kitchen and watched Billy hovering over the stove. He still looked tired, and Casey knew Amy's visit wasn't helping him relax. "Sit, Billy. Let me give it a go." It was an offer she knew he couldn't refuse.

Casey stood at the stove and worked the spatula beneath the brown cakes, prying the sides up until she could loosen them enough to flip them over. It was a sloppy job, and the batter splattered out the side of Mickey's face.

Amy patted Casey's arm in sympathy. "That's okay, Mom. We'll just pretend that's wind or something."

Casey turned and looked at Billy. He sat back and took a sip of his tea.

"Okay, Billy," Casey agreed as she scooped the

pancake off the skillet and onto a plate. "Here's your Mickey in the wind."

"That's just how I like him best," Billy said.

In the rearview mirror, Casey watched the police officer park several car lengths behind them as Billy pulled to the curb in front of Montclair Park. It was a different officer from the one the night before. Also a black man, this officer looked fifteen years older than the first. He'd also appeared half-asleep when Casey had come out of the house, and she checked to make sure he was up to the job. He hadn't been happy about her questioning, but she had to be sure. This was Amy's life at stake.

She was also keeping her eyes open for signs of Swain. She assumed he would surface eventually—if he was actually here on business. Maybe he was on vacation. Somehow she doubted it.

Billy and Amy walked ahead as Casey took one last look around.

"Hurry, Mom! Billy says you're in charge of breaking the bread."

"Oh no, you don't. I made breakfast," Casey said, hurrying after them.

The threesome sat on a bench near the water, and Amy opened up the bag of Wonder bread, handing out slices. She tore her pieces quickly, her hands moving in rapid motions. She was finished in seconds. Jumping up, she said, "Come on. Let's go to the water."

"You go ahead," Casey said. "Billy and I will break up more bread right here."

"Come on, Mom."

"Us old folks need to rest," Casey protested, enjoying the fact that the water was a mere fifteen feet away and Casey could easily watch Amy without getting up. "We'll be down in a minute."

Amy started off.

"Stay on this side of the lake," Casey called after her. She felt Billy's gaze on her, and she looked over. "What?"

"Who you calling old?" Billy teased.

"Sorry. Guilt by association."

Billy's gaze followed Amy toward the water. "She's a great kid."

Casey nodded, regret at missing the past months swarming around her like angry bees.

"You're a great mom, too. I'm glad they came."

"I am, too. It will be weird after they leave."

"You could go with them."

Casey shook her head, watching Amy taunt the birds with the bread. "I don't know. I don't know what I'm going to do."

Billy touched her arm. "You belong with them, Casey."

She turned and looked at him. "Would you come with me?"

He looked away and blinked hard. "I don't know. I don't think—"

Casey took his hand in hers, squeezing with as much pressure as she could, which she figured might be just enough for him to feel her increased strength.

Billy laughed again, his eyes glimmering with emotion.

"I'm not leaving you, Billy. I'm going to take care of you."

He shook his head, pulling his hand away. "I'm not your problem."

"And I wasn't yours."

"That's different. It's my job."

Casey shook her head and stood from the bench. "Maybe in the beginning it was your job, Billy, but it hasn't been for a while. I'm not going to argue about it. You can take all my coffee away—crush my cigarettes, drag me out of bed at six a.m. I don't care."

Billy laughed.

She touched his arm. "I'm staying with you."

The laughing turned to tears, and Casey leaned over and kissed Billy's cheek. "I love you, Billy Glass."

He sniffled. "Me, too."

"Mom!" Amy shouted from the edge of the water. "I need more bread."

Billy handed her the bag and waved her off. "Better go."

"Don't play stubborn with me."

"How could I? I know that's *your* job."

"Damn straight," Casey agreed, carrying the bag toward the water.

Amy ran up to meet her and took the bag from her hand. "You have to see this, Mom. They all rush up to get the bread." She pulled out a handful of bread crumbs and tossed them over the water.

Casey watched as a group of mallards and a couple of swans swam for the food.

"Watch that big one." Amy pointed to the larger of the two swans. Her long neck extended, she swept down over the smaller mallards and grabbed the largest piece of bread for herself.

"Did you see that?"

Casey nodded. "What a pig."

Amy laughed. "Yeah." She stepped toward the water and picked up a twig. "Maybe I can trick her." She tossed the stick into the water, and the big swan swam for it. Then she tossed the bread crumbs to the smaller birds. They ate quickly, as though sensing they didn't have much time before the swan returned. Amy grinned. "She's not very smart, the big bully."

Amy put her arm around Casey and pointed to a play structure on the other side of the park. "I want to go play on the bars."

"Let's go get Billy."

"Okay." Amy turned back, her smile fading.

Casey followed her gaze. Billy was slumped over on the bench, but from his awkward position, Casey didn't think he was sleeping. "Oh, my God."

Amy started to run toward him, but Casey caught her arm.

"Stay here."

"But—"

"Stay here, Amy."

Amy nodded, casting a furtive glance over her shoulder that Casey knew came from understanding her mother had a dangerous job.

Casey ran to Billy, praying he was still breathing. There was no sign of blood. She touched his face. "Billy?" His skin was moist and cool. "Billy!" she said louder, shaking him. He didn't move.

Her own heart pounding, Casey pressed her fingers to his neck, feeling his weak pulse. "Oh, thank God." They had to get him to a hospital.

Casey waved to the police car for help. "Officer!" she screamed when no one emerged from the car. Surveying the park, she couldn't see a sign of him anywhere. Where the hell had he gone?

"Shit!" Casey screamed, furious. "You're fired, you moron," she muttered under her breath, vowing to raise hell with his captain. She looked around the park, but there was no one else to help them.

She turned her attention to Billy. The idea of getting him to the hospital by herself seemed overwhelming, but she had no choice. She couldn't risk leaving Billy or Amy to go call for help.

Amy was at her side, her expression panicked. "What's wrong with him?"

Casey struggled to hoist Billy up. Her hands couldn't manage the weight. "I don't know. Help me get him to the car."

Amy lifted Billy's right arm over Casey's shoulder and then took his other arm, and together they moved slowly toward the car. Casey could hear Amy crying. Tears streamed down her own face as well. "It's going to be okay," Casey said, for all their sakes. "We're going to get Billy to the hospital. He's going to be fine. Amy, honey?"

"Yeah," Amy sobbed.

"You're doing great. I'm so proud of you."

"Are you sure he's going to be okay?"

"Positive," Casey said, turning her gaze to the sky to pray she was right.

They reached the car, and Casey patted her pockets for the keys. She didn't have them. Reaching into Billy's pants pocket, she fished out the keys, fighting to grip them in her clumsy fingers. "Amy, take these keys and unlock the door."

Amy opened the back door and then helped Casey lay Billy across the backseat.

Rivulets of sweat poured down Casey's back as she moved frantically toward the driver's seat. Her hands shaking, she latched onto the handle and fought the door. "Come on," she cursed, unable to grip the handle and get it open.

Amy reached across and opened it from the inside.

"Thanks." Casey sat in the driver's seat and stared at the wheel. "I can't drive." She looked over at Amy.

Amy couldn't drive. "I'm going to need your help, baby."

Wide-eyed and teary, Amy nodded.

Casey handed her the keys. "Put these in the ignition and turn them to the right when I say."

Amy stuck the keys into the ignition as Casey pushed the clutch in.

"Turn," Casey said.

Amy turned the key and then let go. The car rumbled and then died.

"It didn't work, Mom." Amy began to cry harder.

Casey inhaled quickly and touched Amy's leg. "It's okay. Try it again. This time hold it to the right until I say. Okay?"

Amy nodded and put her hand back on the key.

"Turn," Casey said.

The car rumbled to life. "Okay, let go," Casey told her daughter when the engine had safely started.

Casey put her hand on the stick shift and pushed it into first gear. Taking her foot off the clutch, the car eased forward. It was working. Casey put both hands on the steering wheel and thanked God for power steering. She let the clutch out completely and with a glance over her shoulder for oncoming traffic, reved the engine down Mountain Avenue toward the freeway. She didn't want to take her hands off the wheel to shift, afraid she would lose control. "When I say, pull the stick shift straight toward the back of the car. Ready?"

With both hands on the gear, Amy nodded.

"Now."

Amy pulled down, and the car shifted into second.

"Good." Casey paused and touched her daughter's hand. "Put your seat belt on."

Strapped in, Amy looked up at Casey. "Yours isn't on either, Mom."

"Don't worry about me, baby. I'm fine." Casey kept her eyes glued to the road, pulling onto the freeway in second gear. "Look back at Billy. How does he look?"

"He's not moving."

Casey nodded, pressing the gas harder. They weren't far from Alta Bates Hospital. They would be there within a few minutes. *Hang in there, Billy. Please.* "We need to shift again."

Amy put her hands back on the stick shift. "Which way?"

"This time back up to the front of the car, but you need to go a little to the right. Ready?"

Amy shifted and as Casey took her foot off the clutch, the rpms flew up to six thousand.

"We're in first gear now. We need to try it again. Put your hands on the wheel, Amy."

Looking frightened, Amy grabbed the steering wheel.

"Just hold it steady, okay?"

Amy nodded.

Casey took her hands off the wheel and grabbed the stick shift, throwing the car into third and taking her foot off the clutch. "Perfect."

The traffic on Highway Thirteen was sparse, and Casey stayed in the right lane with the pedal to the floor. At the exit, she caught a green light and headed down the hill past the Claremont Hotel and onto Ashby. She caught a yellow light and honked as she sped through the intersection. Someone honked from behind, but Casey ignored it.

A block from the hospital, they hit a red light. Cars moved slowly across in both directions, leaving Casey with no option but to wait. She shoved the car into first gear and gripped the steering wheel, waiting.

"He's still not moving, Mom."

Casey couldn't bear to look back. "It's going to be okay."

The light turned green, and Casey lurched through the intersection, hurrying toward the hospital. The car's engine screamed in first gear, but Casey didn't bother to slow down or try to shift. At the intersection by the hospital, she sped past the backed-up traffic and turned into the hospital, driving straight to the emergency entrance.

Amy was out of the car before her, screaming. "Help us. Please, he's not moving."

An older doctor with thick gray hair came running out, followed by two nurses. "What happened?" the doctor asked.

Casey pulled herself from the car. "He just passed out."

The doctor opened the back door. "He didn't fall or anything?"

"No, nothing like that. He was here last week. He's been sick—an opportunistic infection, the doctor called it. He's HIV positive."

His expression grim, the doctor nodded and directed the male nurse to lift Billy from the car and onto a gurney held by another nurse. While the nurse strapped Billy down, the doctor put a stethoscope to his chest. As they ran into the hospital, pushing Billy, the doctor began shouting directions that Casey didn't understand.

Amy was by her side, and Casey wrapped an arm around her daughter, following them inside. "He's going to be okay, right, Mom?"

Casey couldn't speak for the emotion caught in her

throat. Inside, she and Amy slumped into the same chairs Casey and Jordan had sat in just a week ago when Billy was first admitted. She should have watched him more carefully. He wasn't well yet. She should have taken better care of him.

Casey watched the second hand of the clock tick slowly around the numbers.

"What's wrong with him, Mom?" Amy asked after several minutes.

"I'm not sure, honey. The doctor will let us know as soon as they find out."

Amy's eyes were wide with worry, her cheeks tear-stained. "Was he sick before? You said he was in the hospital before."

Casey nodded. "He's going to be okay. Don't you worry."

"Where's Billy? What's happened?"

Casey looked up to see Kevin, his face flushed.

"How did you know?"

Kevin sank beside Casey and took her hand, breathless. "I was supposed to meet you guys at the park. When I got there, no one was there. I got worried. I called your house and then his, and then I got this terrible premonition, and I called here." He pressed his hand to his chest. "Where is he?"

Casey blinked back her tears. "They took him into the E.R. He just collapsed. I don't know what happened."

"What does the doctor say?"

"He hasn't come out yet." She stood, pacing, wishing she could go back to see what was happening. "Maybe I should go back."

"I can wait here with Amy," Kevin offered, as anxious to know what was happening as she was.

Casey shook her head. She wasn't leaving Amy alone—not even with Kevin.

"Do you want me to talk to the doctor?" he asked.

Shaking her head, Casey caught sight of a uniformed officer standing near the front desk. "Follow me, Amy." Kevin and Amy followed behind as Casey rushed to the front desk. Facing the attendant, she pointed to the security guard. "You know him?"

"Harold?"

Casey pointed again. "The security guard."

The woman stared at her like she was crazy. "Of course I know him."

"How long has he worked here?"

"He started two months after me."

Casey rolled her hand in impatience. "How long ago was that?"

"Sixteen years, four months," the woman responded, hands on hips.

Casey exhaled. "Perfect." Holding on to Amy's arm, she approached the guard. "I'm Agent McKinley of the FBI. This is my daughter. I need you to guard her while I find out about a friend of ours who's been admitted. Can you do that?"

The guard raised an eyebrow and stared at her like she was insane.

"Mom," Amy pleaded. "You're embarrassing me."

Kevin just stood back and watched.

Casey yanked open her purse and told Amy to pull out Casey's ID. Amy retrieved it, and Casey handed it to the guard.

After inspecting it, he nodded slowly. "Wow. You really work for the FBI?"

"I need to know if you can handle guarding this girl. If not, I'm going to have to call the police in."

The guard put his arm on Amy's back. "I'll guard her with my life."

Casey nodded.

"What's going on?" Kevin asked, watching the interaction.

"Will you stay with Amy and the guard? I'm going to find out what's going on."

"Is she okay?"

Casey met Kevin's gaze. "She will be if you don't let her out of your sight."

His expression was worried. "I promise."

She started to turn away when he called after her.

"What about your car?" Kevin said. "It's double-parked."

Casey patted her pockets. "The keys are still in the ignition. Can you move it for me?"

Kevin nodded. "Sure."

"Thanks." Leaving them, Casey rushed down the hall to find out about Billy. She got halfway down when a nurse stopped her.

"You can't be down here," she warned.

Without stopping, Casey flashed her FBI badge and continued. The nurse muttered something but didn't stop her. At the end of the hall, Casey surveyed the rows of small curtained cubes. Where was Billy?

She started to approach one, ready to start pulling back curtains when a voice called out, "Mrs. Glass?"

Startled, Casey looked up to see the same gray-haired doctor staring down at her.

"Oh, good. I'm glad I found you, Mrs. Glass."

"No, I'm not—" But from the look on his face, it didn't matter who she was. She could tell it didn't matter. "No."

Pulling her into the closest seat, the doctor sat beside her and stared at his hands. "I'm so sorry. He's gone."

"No," she repeated, the stabbing ache in her chest overwhelming.

The doctor met her gaze. "He'd had a massive heart attack. There was nothing we could do."

"The pentamidine," she whispered. "The other doctor said it could cause arrhythmia."

The doctor nodded. "It's a chance we take with the drug. I'm sorry."

"Oh, God, not Billy." And Casey sobbed as she hadn't since the attack. She was sure this moment was more painful.

CHAPTER THIRTY-THREE

Michael walked out of Stanford's business school library with enough reading on Electron Industries to last a year. In his shorts and shirt, Michael felt like a law student again. New Haven, unfortunately, wasn't graced with quite the same climate as Palo Alto. On the other hand, if it had been he probably would have failed the bar. He shifted the weight of the reading he had gathered, remembering what it had been like to burrow down in the Yale law library stacks and read all night.

Thankfully, now he could FedEx the reading back to the office and let one of the paralegals wade through it for anything pertinent to the case. His next step was a meeting with a local investigator in a little over an hour. It was the investigator's job to sniff around for the inside scoop on the company, and Michael was glad to have someone else do it. The investigator could walk at the edge of the law, something Michael was not at all comfortable doing.

Michael reached the rented Taurus and got inside, pulling out his cell phone to check messages. He thought about seeing Casey. She had looked good. No, great. He would never have imagined that she could improve so much in only six months. She had been right. He and Amy weren't good for her. They had babied her. Billy, on the other hand, had worked wonders. Michael reminded himself to thank Billy next time he saw him. It was obvious he and Casey had grown quite close.

The phone in his hand rang, and Michael jumped slightly. "Michael McKinley," he answered.

"Mr. McKinley, this is Jack Pearce from accounting. Have I caught you at a bad time?" He spoke with a British accent.

"No, it's fine."

"Carolyn gave me your mobile number. Bouton suggested I call, since you're out there already."

The senior partner had wanted him to call? "What's up, Jack?"

"The check from StarTechnology bounced," he said, sounding rigid and disapproving.

Michael laughed. "Bounced? Ah, you had me scared for a second. I'll give Al Washington a call and get things squared away. I'm sure it's nothing."

"Right," Jack agreed. "I just wanted to let you know since it was such a sizable check."

The seventy-thousand-dollar retainer for Michael's services wasn't actually that much. But Michael was sure there was some simple misunderstanding. "I'll call in as soon as I know what happened. Check with Carolyn before you go home tonight."

"Will do. Thank you, Mr. McKinley."

Michael hung up the phone and opened his Franklin planner to the current week and looked at Sunday. Before his trip, he'd written out all the contacts' names, numbers, and his schedule for the week. It was a habit he'd gotten into early in his practice, and it had saved him on more than one occasion.

Skimming down the page, he found Washington's private number and keyed it into his phone, then pressed send. With the window down, the cool, California coastal breeze floated through the car. The phone rang twice. Then an automated voice said, "The number you have reached has been disconnected. Please check the number and dial again."

Michael sat up in the car and looked down at his phone, shaking his head. He pressed recall and watched the number flash up. He checked it against the one he had written in his book. It was identical. "Damn it."

After clearing the phone, Michael punched the numbers in again more slowly and pushed send. He got the same message.

He looked at his writing again. Had he inverted two of the numbers? He was normally so careful about it. Cursing, he dialed his secretary's number.

"Michael McKinley's office."

"Carolyn, it's Michael. How are you?" He was in no mood for small talk, but he didn't want to come off as rude or flustered. Carolyn had a tendency to read too much into things, and the last thing he wanted floating around the office was that something had gone wrong.

Carolyn gave him a brief update on his cases.

"I just need to check a phone number from my StarTech file."

"Let me get it."

Michael waited on hold, trying to loosen the tenseness in his neck and shoulders.

"I've got it here."

"Will you read me Al Washington's private line? Should be the first number in the file. I've written it down incorrectly."

"Sure. It's right here. Area code 650-425 . . ."

Michael watched the numbers. His were identical to what she was reading. "Those are typed, aren't they, Carolyn?"

"Yep. I've also got your handwritten original here." She paused, and Michael could hear her mind working. "Is everything okay, Michael?"

"Fine. I'd just written it down wrong. I've got a meeting now, but I'll give you a call later." Michael hung up and stared at his phone. He had to be dialing wrong. But he'd been able to call Carolyn. He'd used his phone a million times on business trips. "Damn it all." He dialed again and got the message for the third time. He'd just have to call Washington at his main number.

Michael called information and asked for StarTechnology. "Al Washington, please," he said when the operator put him through.

"May I ask who's calling?" the receptionist asked.

"Michael McKinley." He heard several rings then a click.

"Alfred Washington's office," the next woman answered.

"Yes, this is Michael McKinley calling for Al."

"And what is this regarding, please?"

Michael wanted to respect Al's request for confidentiality. "Please tell him I'm with Bouton, Leventhal, and Lewis."

The secretary didn't seem to appreciate his encrypted message. "One moment, please."

The line went quiet, and Michael closed his eyes, feeling the California sun beat down on his legs.

"I'm sorry, Mr. McKinley, Mr. Washington is not available. If you'll leave your name, I'll give him the message as soon as I can."

Michael sat up. "It's very important that I speak with Mr. Washington." Michael didn't want to embarrass the guy, but this was ridiculous. "I'm afraid my firm had a problem with the check he sent us."

"Your firm?"

"Bouton, Leventhal, and Lewis," he repeated, growing frustrated with Washington.

"One moment."

Back on hold, Michael stood from the car and paced slowly. He wasn't prepared for this glitch in his day, and the whole thing was making him uncomfortable.

"Mr. McKinley," the secretary came back on the line.

Michael straightened, feeling his pulse speed just slightly. What was wrong with him? Why was he so nervous?

"Mr. Washington has never heard of your firm, I'm afraid."

Michael could feel his mouth drop open, but no words came out.

"So, I'm very sorry, but you must have reached the wrong person," she continued.

"That's impossible," Michael spat. "He and I spoke several times on the phone. He signed a contract with my firm. Tell him it's about Electron Industries."

The secretary exhaled into the phone, and Michael felt himself losing his patience, too.

"I need to speak with Al. Please tell him I'm waiting," he said with finality. He'd flown all the way out here, billed sixty hours already on the case, plus the hotel, the car. It was fifty thousand at least. Washington could pick up the goddamned phone.

"This is Alfred Washington," came a booming male voice less than a minute later.

Michael slumped. The voice wasn't the least bit familiar. "Al Washington?"

"It's Alfred. Who is this?"

Michael forced himself to regain his composure. "Mr. Washington, I apologize. There must be some sort of miscommunication. I'm an intellectual property attorney from Virginia. Two weeks ago, I received a call from a man who said he was Al Washington, head of StarTechnology. I gather that person wasn't you."

"Damn right, it wasn't."

Michael looked around in the distance. What was going on? "And you aren't bringing a case against Electron Industries for infringement?"

"Hell, no. They're one of our biggest clients. What the hell's going on here?"

"I don't have any idea, Mr. Washington."

"I think we should call the police," Washington continued. "This is libel, slander . . ."

Michael tuned him out. His thoughts moved to who would do this. Who would drag him all the way out here? He had taken Amy out of school. He thought about Amy and Casey, and suddenly he couldn't get off the phone fast enough.

"I'll take care of this, Mr. Washington. Thank you for your time." Michael ended the call and found Casey's number in his book. He'd had it memorized once, but no longer. Flustered, he dialed. "Please be home," he whispered as the phone rang.

Five rings, then six, seven. "Damn it, Casey. Where the hell are you?"

Throwing the phone on the seat, Michael got in the car and revved the engine. He pulled out in a long screech of burning rubber and headed north, praying he could stop whatever the hell was happening before it was too late.

CHAPTER THIRTY-FOUR

Jordan sped off the freeway toward Alta Bates Hospital. The red light on the top of his Explorer warned people from his path, but they were slow to move. Jordan blasted his horn at an insolent Mercedes and then sped around him. He had an inkling to pull that guy over and give him a ticket, but there wasn't time.

Casey's call had been frantic and almost completely nonsensical. Someone was in the hospital, and it wasn't her. That was all he knew. On the ride over, he'd tried to call twice, but no one named McKinley was there and the nurse hadn't been able to locate Casey. The only thing Jordan could figure was Billy was sick again.

He turned up Ashby and into the hospital entrance, stopping to the side of the emergency area parking. He dropped his police parking pass in the window and rushed from the car.

Inside, all the same sensations about hospitals came rushing back. He hated these places. Scouring the area, Jordan spotted Casey shuffling back toward the waiting room with her head in her hands. She was alone, and Jordan wondered where Billy and Amy were. Casey had said that they were all spending the day together.

He jogged to her. "Casey."

She looked up, her cheeks tearstained, the tough, hard-edge, FBI profiler gone. She looked like a little kid.

Jordan pulled her to him and held her. "What happened?"

"It's—Billy," she choked. "He's—"

She didn't need to finish the sentence. Jordan knew. He closed his eyes and rubbed her back. When Casey told him that Billy had full-blown AIDS, he had wondered how she would deal with his death. She seemed more than a little dependent on him. And, of course, he on her. But at the time, Jordan had reminded himself that Billy could outlive Jordan himself.

Casey looked up and wiped her eyes. "We were at the park. He just slumped over." She sniffled and stared at her hands. "The doctor said he must have had a massive heart attack."

"I'm so sorry, Casey." Jordan looked around the waiting room. It was nearly empty. "Where's Amy?"

Casey looked around. "She's with the security guard and Kevin."

"What happened to the cop who was with you? I didn't see a patrol car outside."

Casey shrugged as she surveyed the room. "That asshole disappeared at the park." She paused and looked around again. "Where did they go? They promised they'd wait right here."

Panic burned like flames in Jordan's chest as he watched Casey's eyes. A flash of the Warriors game rushed back at him. Walking into the men's room and looking for Ryan, wondering where he could have gone. How had the boy gotten past Jordan? But he had been sidetracked, scolding Will. And suddenly, his son had been gone.

As Casey stood and searched the room, the sorrow in her expression was quickly replaced by worry. "They wouldn't have gone anywhere."

Jordan took her arm. "You said she was with Kevin?"

Casey's eyes met Jordan's. The fear reflected deep in the green pools. "You don't think someone—" Casey pressed her fingers to her lips. "Oh, my God." She turned and rushed toward the exit.

Jordan ran to the information desk and flashed his badge. "I need to make an announcement over the P.A. Please page Amy McKinley back to this area."

The woman stood motionless and stared.

"Do it now," he said.

With a scowl, she picked up the phone and dialed.

Jordan heard her voice from above. "Amy McKinley, Amy McKinley, please report to the ER waiting area."

"Is there a speaker outside?" he asked.

She nodded. "People within twenty yards or so can hear it."

Jordan turned back to the room and addressed the few people sitting in the waiting area. "Did anyone see a young white girl leave the premises with an older male and the security guard?"

No one moved.

Casey reentered from the outside, her expression pure alarm. "We need help out here. The security guard's been shot."

Two nurses ran past them to tend to the guard.

"I don't see Kevin." Casey thought about his shoes. They'd been smaller than a size ten. Had he known she would recognize him by his shoe size? Was he that clever?

"What are you thinking?" Jordan asked.

"If Kevin isn't Leonardo, then Kevin should be lying there with the guard. Leonardo wouldn't take any extra hostages."

"Jesus Christ."

Casey felt herself start to shake. "The distinctive jaw Nina Rodriguez mentioned—Kevin had that jaw. Oh, God. It all fits. It's Kevin."

Jordan grabbed her arm. "What was Kevin wearing?"

She shook her head. "I don't know." To the room, she announced, "He's got curly, blond hair, nice-looking. The girl's twelve, about four-seven, has shoulder-length blond hair. Her name is Amy. She was with me earlier."

Jordan scanned the room and saw a few heads shaking. People seemed wrapped up in their own tragedies. The ER was a place where people, worried about the outcome of whatever disaster brought them there, probably didn't notice much.

The nurses wheeled the guard back in, but when Jordan approached, he was waved off. The guard wasn't going to be able to answer any questions in his current state.

"Damn," Jordan said, looking around the room. Amy hadn't surfaced. He wanted to believe that she was somewhere safe, but he didn't believe it. And he didn't want to risk it. He'd seen the look on Ryan's face, the terror. Amy was only a few years older. Had Kevin really taken her? If so, how far could he have gotten? Jordan had to believe Amy would fight once she realized what was happening.

An older woman walked toward them. Her voice

was like a rickety old wheel as she spoke. "I saw that girl."

Casey grabbed her arm. "Where?"

"She walked off with that guy you described. Looked like they were having a fight," the woman said.

"Did you see where they were heading?" Jordan asked.

The woman stopped and frowned. Turning a small circle, she looked around.

The suspense was killing him. "Ma'am," he finally said.

She came back to face him and shook her head. "I can't remember."

Casey let out a low, desperate moan.

Jordan whipped around to the attendant at the desk. "I need to borrow your phone."

She shook her head. "Sorry, it's for—"

"This is police business. Dial 9-1-1, then give me the goddamn phone," he spit back.

The woman turned and dialed, handing the receiver over without another word.

"This is Inspector Jordan Gray from the San Francisco Police Department. I've got a kidnapping from Alta Bates Hospital. Suspect is believed to be the same responsible for the child murders in the San Francisco area. I need as many cars as you've got to search the area."

"You have a description of the suspect?" the dispatcher came back.

Jordan shook his head. "A description? Not much of one." He turned to face Casey. Her eyes were wide with terror, and she looked as though she might fall over.

Casey took the phone, staring down. "This is Agent

Casey McKinley of the FBI. The suspect is in his early to mid-thirties and may change appearances frequently. Currently he is dressed as a trim, five-eleven, blond man. The girl, Amy, is twelve, about four-seven, eighty pounds, shoulder-length straight blondish-brown hair, green eyes." Her voice was strong and professional, and Jordan knew the full reality hadn't sunk in.

"She was wearing a pair of straight black pants and a white T-shirt with 'bebe' written in small letters at the top of the back. She had a chambray shirt tied around her waist. White Steve Purcell's on her feet— no socks. It's possible they are driving a 1982 white Volvo sedan. Plate is X-A-B-5-8-2."

Jordan nodded and took the phone from Casey's hand. "This is Gray."

"I'm sending four cars to the hospital now," the dispatcher said.

Jordan nodded. "I'll be waiting by the emergency entrance." He watched Casey take off through the back entrance and prayed she found Amy and Kevin coming around a corner, but knew that would not be the case.

He handed the phone back to the attendant, who seemed suddenly the epitome of helpfulness.

"Sometimes kids just go off to explore the hospital," she said. "Maybe the two of them went to explore."

Jordan only wished it were true. Within minutes, the whirring of sirens caught Jordan's attention, and he hurried outside. Four Berkeley patrol cars pulled up, lights flashing. The officers emerged, one by one.

"Inspector Gray?" the first one asked.

Jordan nodded.

"You know what we're looking for?" he asked.

Jordan wished he knew more but explained what he had.

"He's got the Volvo," Casey yelled.

Jordan turned around to see Casey running back.

"I saw him drive down Ashby," she gasped, panting. "I think he turned left on Shattuck toward the freeway. I didn't see Amy, but she has to be with him. He's in a 1982 white Volvo sedan. Plate is X-A-B-5-8-2." She waved at the motionless police cars. "Go, damn it!"

"Send your cars out Ashby," Jordan said. "Check both directions. Get on the radio. Anyone you can reach should be looking for that car. This man is very dangerous. Tell your officers to proceed with extreme caution."

"Stress is increased now. He'll be fleeing," Casey said, panting. "Watch the freeways closely. Don't close in on him. He's liable to react. Just find him and keep him in sight." She paused, pressing her hand to her chest. "This is my daughter he's got," she added, and Jordan could feel the tension rise with her words.

The officers returned to their cars, and engines revved as they pulled out. Jordan could see the closest officer lift the radio from the dash and call for additional units.

"Let's go," Casey said.

"We need to stay here in case you were wrong. Maybe some guy just stole your car. Amy could be here."

Casey shook her head. "Kevin is Leonardo and he has Amy."

Jordan knew she wasn't being objective. It was impossible under the circumstances. "How do you know?"

"You can take me, or you can give me the keys to

your goddamn car, Gray. You're wasting time. That lunatic has Amy."

Jordan nodded and headed for the Explorer.

Jordan dialed the Berkeley police station for the fifteenth time. It might have been the sixteenth. He'd lost track. "This is Inspector Gray. Any word?"

"Not yet, Inspector. The officers are still out looking."

"Thanks. You've got my number." Jordan dropped the cell phone to his lap.

Casey sat with her face almost pressed to the window as she surveyed the area for her car.

"We should go back to the hospital—wait there," he suggested.

Casey shook her head.

"We've been out here for almost an hour, Casey. He's probably hiding. I've got officers on the lookout in the four surrounding counties. I don't think he's going to get away in that car."

Casey looked at him for the first time in more than half an hour. He could see the agony etched on her face. "We both know he's not in that car anymore."

Jordan had thought about that. If he was clever, his first move would be to switch cars. "We don't know."

Casey let out a hollow laugh. "I know. I know how he thinks. This was the whole game. It was laid out right in front of me." She kicked the dashboard in a series of quick slams and then crumpled back into silence.

Jordan blamed himself. As soon as he'd heard Amy's voice, he'd been concerned. He should have sent an officer to Casey's house right away. If Jordan had someone tailing them, Amy never would have been lured away.

"Fine," Casey said. "Go back. He's probably in Oregon by now, anyway."

Jordan felt his shoulders sag, wishing somehow he could redo so many things in the last ten hours.

As they pulled up to the hospital's emergency entrance, Jordan noticed no young girl came running out to meet the car. Leonardo had Amy. He'd had her for an hour already. All Jordan could think of was how close Ryan had been. And Jordan had sat by and let it happen to Casey's child.

Jordan parked the car, and Casey got out and walked straight inside. He could tell from her stance that she was hoping, praying that Amy might have turned up.

"Casey," a male voice called.

Jordan turned around to see a man, about forty, approach Casey.

"What's going on?" the man asked. "I called and called you at home, and no one answered. Then I called the inspector's number you gave me, and they told me he had rushed over to the hospital. Is Amy all right? What's happened?"

Casey collapsed onto the ground, her face in her hands as she cried.

Suddenly protective of Casey, Jordan stepped between the two. "I'm Inspector Gray. You must be Mr. McKinley."

The man looked from Casey to Jordan and back again. "I'm Michael McKinley." His gaze met Jordan's. "Has Amy been in an accident?"

"No accident," Jordan answered, instantly identifying with the panic-stricken look on the father's face.

Michael exhaled. "Thank God," he said before Jordan could continue.

Jordan tried to explain. "She—"

"I got this terrible feeling today," Michael interrupted. "This whole case out here was some sort of prank. The president of the company I was supposed to be representing, the one I'd talked to a dozen times, he had never even heard of me. The guy who called was a fake. Then his check bounced. I don't know what the hell happened, but my whole trip out here was a bad joke."

Casey looked up, and Jordan could read the equation in her eyes as she solved it. "He lured you here."

"Who lured me here?" Michael asked.

"The killer, the one we've been tracking," Casey said, crying. "The same one from Cincinnati." She shoved her hands toward him. "The one who did this." She gasped and let out a sob. "He has our baby girl."

CHAPTER THIRTY-FIVE

He looked over at Amy as he pulled the Nissan off Highway 101 in Mill Valley and headed to Highway 1 and the house he had rented. He ran his hand across her cheekbone, where he would soon be working his masterpiece. Everything had gone perfectly. He had hoped Casey would be with them, but he couldn't manage to get her, too. Perhaps she'd find them when he was finishing his work. Otherwise, he'd have to wait until she found her daughter's body to see her reaction.

Amy had put up quite a struggle, and he felt the ooze of warm blood on his face from her nails. It would be well worth it, he knew, though he hadn't met a twelve-year-old with so much fight. Even the knife hadn't quieted her, and he had been forced to strike out several times. He hated when circumstances caused him to lose his temper. Thankfully, the injection had calmed her quite nicely.

In the last few minutes, though, he had sensed she was starting to stir. He had hoped she would be quiet until he reached the house, but he wasn't sure his luck would hold.

He had considered pulling over and using duct tape

to confine her, but there was too much traffic to risk it. Even if she fought, they would most likely look like a father and daughter having a quarrel. He checked his wig in the mirror. The gray was more paternal than his natural blond hair. He'd been able to switch cars, too, dumping Casey's in a local medical building parking lot. He knew the police would be looking for the Volvo.

Amy moved, murmuring something he didn't understand, and he pressed the gas a little harder. He wanted to be there, and his vein of impatience was taking over. "Sloppy," he warned himself. Disappointed with his own behavior, he lifted his foot from the gas and brought the speedometer back down. He knew better than to rush. Better to have to control Amy than to get pulled over.

As he wound down Highway 1 toward Stinson Beach, the traffic thinned out. The beach was too cold and foggy to lure vacationers so early in the spring, and those who commuted would still be at work. Past the Pelican Inn, Leonardo turned onto Seascape Road and began the journey uphill. He restarted his odometer. The house was exactly eight miles from the turnoff.

Within two miles, there would be very little traffic. After the next two, almost none. By the time he reached the dilapidated house he rented, it would feel like they were in a different state. The house sat on three acres of abandoned fields.

According to the guy he'd rented it from, the field had been abandoned for a number of years. With the value of land so high out here, the owner was looking to sell the whole lot to a developer. That was fine with him. He had explained to the owner that after separating from his wife, he only needed someplace to get his head straight for a few months. His lease was up in less than three weeks. The timing was ideal. He'd saved and planned carefully for his time with Casey. What was left of his savings would get him away from California when he was ready for a new canvas.

He reached the four-mile point and turned off Sea Ranch Road onto Cliff Ranch. Unlike on the other streets closer to the city, here the houses became more spread out. With its amazingly large parcels of land, the area reminded him a lot of where he had grown up in Indiana.

He remembered the final day with his mother and sister. He had known they would be together that day—celebrating her birthday as they had never celebrated his. Spilling their blood, avenging all those years of belittling and condescension from them both. He had lived his revenge through the titillation of their screams. The sheer thrill of seeing them die had been almost overwhelming. The reminder would make his time with Amy even more exciting.

He was almost there. The road ran north-south, and he headed north, starting the last stretch to his house. Keeping his speed steady, he studied the rearview mirror. A white Mustang took the same turn. Though a lot of vacationers made the wrong turn off Highway 1, very few of them got this far. He didn't like the feel of it.

Reaching over Amy, he opened the glove compartment. His gun sat on top of some papers. He grabbed it and pulled out the magazine, checking his ammunition. It was half full, which was enough to deal with any problems. He started to tuck the gun in the compartment of his door when he saw motion from the corner of his eye.

"Ah!" Amy screamed, and he felt the impact of her foot in his ribs.

The wheel slipped from his grasp, and the car spun out. He was sure they were running off the road. Amy fell backward and he heard her moan as she hit her head on the dash. Served her right. Moving quickly, he gathered his bearings and pulled the car back onto the road.

As soon as he had straightened the car, he reached for his ribs. But before he could protect them, Amy kicked again.

He moaned and threw his hand out. Missing her, he hit the back of the seat as Amy ducked. He was tempted to pull the car over and smack her, but the white Mustang was gaining on them.

Pulling the gun out, he pointed it at Amy's head and made the deliberate motion of switching off the safety. "One move, and I'll blow your little brains out." He touched his aching ribs, wondering if she'd broken something. "That wasn't very smart of you. It's going to make things tougher on you when we get home."

Amy's face crumpled. "You're just a crazy," she said, trying to sound strong.

He smiled at her. "How cute. Mommy's little girl."

"My mom's going to kill you."

"Don't you worry, I've dealt with your mom before."

"But she got away, and she'll come rescue me."

"She didn't get away. I let her go to save myself. I knew I'd be back, and here I am." He basked in the girl's growing terror. "And maybe she'll try to come save you, and I'll get to enjoy you both."

Amy stared at the gun and then turned to face forward. Her hands were tucked up under her arms, and he grew suspicious of her lack of movement.

"Sit on your hands," he demanded.

She glanced at him, puzzled.

"Put your hands under you, so I know where you've got them." He waved the gun at her. "One false move, and the trigger on this gun might just go off."

Amy put her hands beneath her and began to cry.

With a wry smile, he straightened and let the gun sag a little. At least now she was acting like a normal child. He looked into the rearview mirror and saw the Mustang was still behind him. He was certain he'd never seen that car on this road before. And the driver of a Mustang appeared to be going too slow to be pleasure-driving out here.

But law enforcement didn't drive Mustangs, either—too showy. Maybe he was wrong. Maybe the driver was visiting someone out here. Or maybe it was some old guy who didn't know how to enjoy a fast car. Either way, he wanted to check it out.

Putting his signal on, he slowed and turned into a driveway nearly two miles before his own. He knew this one was nearly a half-mile long, but it would give him a chance to check out the Mustang without letting the driver see his real house.

The car whizzed by, and the driver didn't even glance at him. He waited several minutes, and then pulled out of the driveway and checked the road.

Smiling, he turned to Amy and ran his finger down her cheek. "We're alone after all."

Amy began to sob.

CHAPTER THIRTY-SIX

A mile past where the killer had stopped, Swain turned the Mustang down a sloped driveway and out of sight of the main road. He was confident that the car with Amy McKinley had stopped to make sure he wasn't following. On this road, there had been no way to go unnoticed. Driving past and continuing on the road around the curve was the smartest thing Swain could do.

But he still prayed he wouldn't lose the girl because of it. It had been too dangerous to Amy to risk pulling the car over. And Swain had no way to track the car other than by sight. He had guessed the killer would have stopped short of his house, which meant he would be passing again. If he was wrong, the girl was dead.

He shut the car door and hurried up the hill. The road was quiet. Lying on his stomach in a small patch of grass, Swain made note of the time and waited. Starting to get nervous that he'd been wrong to drive past, he waited impatiently. Several minutes later, he heard the distant rumbling of an engine. The noise grew for ten, maybe fifteen, seconds before the car passed. Swain watched the suspect's gold Maxima fly past, worrying it would get around a corner and he would miss where it turned. But about a mile up the road, the car slowed down and turned into a driveway on the east side.

Swain jumped up, and moved toward his car. He needed to be careful about his next move. This killer could have been the one to disable Swain's surveillance in Cincinnati, which meant he knew something about cameras and sound. Swain needed to do some surveillance of his own before he blew his cover. Right now, Amy McKinley's only chance for survival was him. And damn if he wasn't going to get it right this time.

He opened the car door and hit recall and send on his cell phone.

"Mueller here," came the response.

"It's Swain."

"You were supposed to check in twenty minutes ago." Mueller was clearly on speakerphone, and Swain wondered who else was in the room. "Have you confirmed the identity of the suspect?"

"I'm still on his tail. He's traveled farther out of the city than I had anticipated."

"Where are you?" Mueller barked.

Swain glanced at the mailbox on the road. "My location is 1347 Cliff Ranch Road. I'm north of San Francisco, somewhere past Mill Valley. I'm not exactly sure what city limit this is."

"Why the hell are you out there?" Mueller asked, and Swain could hear murmurs in the background.

"I've tracked the killer," he explained. "He suspected I was following so I passed and pulled off. His location is about a mile farther down the road. He's pulled into a driveway on the east side. He's driving a late model Nissan Maxima—gold color. Plate is 4-

B-D-U-3-5-9. I'm going to need backup here, but it's not an easy place to find. Are you recording?"

"Yes." Swain recognized Jamison's voice.

"Take 101 North to Highway 1. Past a place called the Pelican Inn, take a left on Seascape. Follow that until Sea Ranch, and then Cliff Ranch is about a quarter mile up on the right."

"You should have backup, Swain. What the hell are you doing tracking him way out there alone?" Mueller asked.

"He's got Amy McKinley."

Swain heard silence as everyone in the room digested the information. He hadn't wanted to tell them until he was positive, but he'd gotten a clear view of her on the freeway.

"You're sure?"

It was the same girl he'd seen with Casey earlier that day. "Positive."

"Continue," came Mueller's voice.

"Backup is going to need to be cautious. I believe we're dealing with an especially clever killer. This man may have deactivated my surveillance equipment in Cincinnati. They should expect cameras and sound devices within one hundred yards in each direction."

"Agent Swain, this is Director Purcell."

"Yes, sir." Though they had never spoken in person, Swain recognized the director's voice without the introduction.

"Your reputation proceeds you."

Swain swallowed hard. "Yes, sir."

"And I'm told you're a bit of a cowboy. I want to make sure you're not taking any unnecessary risks—for your sake and for the girl's."

"Director Purcell, with all due respect, sir, the way I see it, I've got two choices. I can go in there and try to prevent this little girl from being hurt. Or I can sit tight and wait for backup to do it for me. I believe I'm making the best decision, sir."

"I'll trust your judgment, Agent Swain," Purcell agreed.

Swain smiled.

"And you don't need to worry about the killer's surveillance capabilities. The backup team will be advised to check this out as standard procedure."

This guy required more than standard caution if he'd disabled the system in Cincinnati. "I think extra precaution is needed here," Swain said.

"It's handled."

Swain thought about his last big case, about the blame he'd been assigned when things had gone wrong. "In Cincinnati, I thought it was all handled—"

"Cincinnati was an agency mistake," a voice cut in, but Swain couldn't tell whose. "We added a second surveillance team on McKinley and something got screwed up."

Swain halted. He heard muffled reactions in the background.

"I can say whatever the hell I want," the same gruff voice insisted.

Agency mistake? "I always thought *I* was at fault for Cincinnati," Swain said.

Someone cleared his throat, and Purcell spoke. "You do good work out there, Swain, and we'll get the other mess cleared up. I'll see to it personally."

His mind reeled. "You used McKinley as bait for the Butcher?"

"Suffice it to say you weren't to blame," Purcell said. "Now that'll stay between us. Right, son?"

"Absolutely." Swain smiled. All he could think was that it wasn't his fault. He had done good work. He thought momentarily to be pissed off—for himself and for Casey, but he was too relieved. Hot damn. He was back.

"We'll get backup to you immediately, and we'll warn them to proceed with caution," Mueller said. "Be careful."

"I'll call as soon as I can." Swain disconnected the call and started the engine with a heavy rev. "Watch out, motherfucker, your day of reckoning awaits."

He pulled his car back onto the road and drove slowly for three-quarters of a mile until the driveway the killer had taken was in sight. Parking his car on the main road to mark his location, he switched his cell phone to vibrator and pocketed it. Then he pulled his second gun from the glove box. After checking the ammunition in the .22, he strapped it into his ankle holster and checked his glock. Everything was in order. He was going in.

The glock in hand, Swain shut the car door quietly and headed down into the woods surrounding the killer's location. Within a few minutes, he could see a shack-like house at the end of a long straight gravel drive. The Maxima sat quietly in front, and Swain assumed the girl and the killer were already inside.

Staying out of view of the house, Swain pushed his way through the thin woods, thankful for the Eucalyptus trees that provided a decent camouflage. He walked for almost ten minutes, trying to hurry but wary of attracting any attention. By the time he was within a hundred yards of the house, his back and neck were drenched with sweat. Even the cool coastal breeze couldn't fight off the heat of his racing heart.

As he approached, the first thing about the house that struck Swain as out of the ordinary were the basement windows. From the blackened glass, Swain as-

sumed the killer's lair was there. He surveyed them
for any change in their tint and wondered if they were
as opaque from the inside as they looked from the
outside. There was no way to tell if the killer would
be able to see him.

Unwilling to risk it, Swain remained in the woods
until he had passed the house. The small woodshed in
the back would provide good cover. Swain wiped his
face against the sleeve of his shirt and prepared to
make his move. He listened carefully for any sounds,
but heard nothing. Amy had to be drugged or gagged.
From what he'd seen of her in the car, he guessed
drugged. He bottled his impatience and moved on.

Swain crept to the edge of the woods and gathered
his breath as he counted to three. On three, he
sprinted across the driveway and ducked behind the
shed. From the new angle, he could see a short set of
stairs leading to the basement on the far side of the
house from the drive. He'd have to make his way
there and see if he couldn't get a look in one of the
windows.

Eyeing his watch, he waited exactly three minutes.
It had been adequate time for someone inside to react
to his presence. No sounds came to indicate that he
had been discovered. Confident he was still safe,
Swain prepared to continue. With his breath even, he
counted again, pushing himself to run faster and more
quietly to the basement stairs.

Pausing, hidden behind the small outcropping of the
stairs, Swain touched the cool cement and listened
again for sounds. It was ominously quiet. On his belly,
he crept around the stairs and peered in the closest
window. Through the dark paint he could barely make
out a workshop below. It appeared empty.

As he started to turn around, he heard a soft whimper and halted.

"If you want her to take another breath, you won't move."

Swain felt fear and adrenaline wash a cold sweat down his spine. His back to the killer, Swain thought about the cell phone in his pocket. It wouldn't help. The Bureau knew where he was, and in the meantime, he had a chance to save both himself and Amy McKinley.

"You missed the camera right above your head," the killer snapped, laughing lightly.

Swain ignored him, his mind flipping for the next move.

"Stop wasting time, or she dies," the killer warned. "Turn around slowly."

The girl cried out, and Swain lifted his hands in the air. He sat slowly and turned around on his knees.

The killer had shed his gray wig, and Swain was surprised by his youthful appearance. Blond curls and a handsome face, he couldn't have been older than thirty-five. "Stand up nice and slow," he said, the barrel of his gun pressed to Amy's head.

Swain could tell the safety was off, and he didn't doubt the guy would shoot.

"Where's your weapon?"

Swain kept his hands in the air, searching for a move. "My back."

The killer nodded, pushing Amy forward, careful to keep her in front of him. "Hands on your head." The killer smiled then, and Swain saw the dementia in his eyes. "So fun to be the one saying that."

The killer's expression leveled. "Turn around and keep your hands where they are."

His back to them, Swain could feel them drawing

closer. With the killer's gun placed at Amy's temple, he didn't dare make a move.

"Take the gun, Amy. Hold it by the barrel. One wrong move, and I'll blow your head off, understand?"

"Uh-huh," the girl said, terrified.

Swain felt her small fingers reach for his gun, and he did nothing to stop her. There was nothing he could do but play it out.

"Good girl." There was a short pause. "Now, turn around and go down the stairs. We'll dispose of you down there."

Swain swallowed hard and stepped down the cement stairs, sensing this might be his last glance at daylight, and knowing he wouldn't go without a fight.

CHAPTER THIRTY-SEVEN

The expression on Jordan's face could only be described as grim. "They found the cop at the park—the one that was supposed to be watching you."

Casey waited for the punch line.

"Shot twice in the head." Before he could continue, his cell phone rang. "Inspector Gray." Without a word, he handed the phone to Casey.

"McKinley," she answered, wishing she could force herself to sound stronger than she felt. Instead she awaited the sound of Leonardo's voice with a tight gut and weak knees.

"Agent McKinley, it's Mueller here."

Though she should have been relieved at the FBI assistant director's voice, Casey detected something familiar about the tone of his voice that prevented her from relaxing. "Why are you calling me?"

Mueller was slow to respond. "I've got some news for you."

Casey was right. She knew the tone. It was the same one he had used when he'd called her in the hospital after her surgeries. Pity. Somehow Mueller knew Leonardo had Amy. Casey didn't have any idea how the hell he knew, but he did. She'd kill him if those bastards at Quantico had watched Amy get taken. "What news, Ken?" No one used Mueller's first name and for what little it was worth, Casey enjoyed uttering it so casually. "Why don't you tell me your news?"

"We've sent Rick Swain out there."

"Thanks, but I'd already heard Swain was here. Why don't you cut to the chase, Mueller? Where the hell is Amy?"

There was a brief silence and the sounds of papers shuffling. Casey knew that was the Bureau's surprised sound. Shock the Bureau, they respond by shuffling papers.

"Jesus Christ, Mueller. You obviously know where she is. Where the fuck is my daughter?"

"Casey, I'll tell you where she is, of course. I was getting to that. Swain is with her."

"What the hell's going on? How are you involved in this?"

"Agent McKinley, this is Director Purcell."

Casey nodded. She was not impressed. "I'd like some answers, Director."

"When we got wind of your situation, we sent Swain out to keep surveillance. We were concerned your life might be in danger. Swain was at the hospital when Amy was abducted. It was lucky he was following her."

"Is she in Swain's custody?"

"Not exactly."

"Where the hell is she?"

"We have agents heading out to her location right now," Purcell said as though he had single-handedly cracked the case and had everything under control.

"Is she safe?"

No one answered.

"Is she safe?" Casey repeated.

Mueller spoke next. "We believe the killer has them both at a secluded house approximately fifteen miles north of San Francisco. We've got agents en route."

"You don't know what the fuck you're doing," Casey cursed. "This is not a Bureau case, and you know it." Casey put her hand over the phone and motioned to Jordan and Michael. "Let's go."

"Where are we going?" Jordan asked.

"I don't know yet, but these assholes are going to tell me."

"Agent McKinley?"

"I'm here," she said into the phone. "I'm with Inspector Jordan Gray of the SFPD. This is his case and my daughter. We're in the car, and you're going to give me directions to find Amy, and then you're going to put me in touch with whichever of your agents arrives at the scene first. We're running this show, not you." She paused and inhaled, her jaw tight, her blood steaming. "Understand?"

"I understand you're upset, Agent McKinley," someone else said.

Casey thought it was Jamison's voice. "You don't understand shit," she said. "And stop calling me Agent McKinley, for God's sake. We need directions—now."

There was more shuffling of paper and then a voice Casey didn't recognize said, "They're north of San Francisco. Take 101 to Highway 1 and I'll give you directions from there."

Casey repeated the directions to Jordan.

"That's not close," he said, pulling out of the hospital and heading toward the freeway. He flipped on the siren and light on his car and began weaving in and out of the traffic toward the city.

Jordan took the phone and connected the power

cord into the cigarette lighter. Pointing to a microphone next to the rearview mirror, he whispered,
"Speaker."

"We're somewhat concerned that the situation may
become volatile," Mueller said, his voice echoing
through the car.

Michael leaned forward from the backseat.

"With this guy it's already volatile." Casey wished
she could say something to comfort Michael, to comfort all of them, but there was no good news to be
given. Instead, the best she could do was to retain her
analytical edge, to try to think of this killer as she had
thought of every other—and to keep her emotional
reaction, her fear, no, her terror under wraps. "Put
me in touch with the agent in charge of the scene."

"Agent McKinley, I don't think—"

"Director Purcell, I don't give a fucking rat's ass
what you think," she spit back.

From the corner of her eye, she could see Jordan
nod.

"Put me in touch with them, or I'll sue the Bureau
for reckless endangerment, unlawful termination—"

"She was never terminated," someone said.

"Hush," Purcell snapped.

"Okay, McKinley," Mueller said. "Give us a minute, and we'll put you in touch with the agent in
charge."

Casey held her hands to her cheek, picturing Leonardo with Amy. Oh, God. Please.

Michael leaned in from the backseat and touched
her shoulders. "It's going to be okay, Casey. She's not
alone, and we know where she is." But even Michael's
soothing voice wasn't convincing.

Casey knew what Leonardo was capable of. She

could only hope that he was distracted by Swain long enough to give her a chance to get there.

"We'll be at Highway 1 in ten minutes." Jordan had taken the northern route instead of cutting through San Francisco and, thankfully, the midday traffic on the Richmond-San Rafael Bridge was light.

Ten minutes passed in silence before Casey heard a series of clicks over the speaker and then a new voice.

"This is Agent Franklin," a woman's voice said.

"Franklin, this is Casey McKinley. Are you in charge there?" Casey asked.

"Yes."

"Okay. I'm familiar with this killer, and I don't want anyone making a move without my consent. The child in the house is my daughter."

"I've been fully briefed on the situation. I think we're prepared to deal with it."

Casey exchanged a look with Jordan, who shook his head.

Michael rubbed his temples. "Jesus Christ," he muttered.

"Franklin, I want to make sure you understand me. Hopefully, your bosses in Quantico are still with us."

A series of responses came from the background, indicating the big guys were still listening.

"Good."

"We're at Highway 1," Jordan interrupted. "Where do we go from here?"

A male voice Casey didn't recognize read out directions. When he finished, Jordan said, "We'll be there in ten minutes."

"What do you propose to do, Franklin?" Casey asked.

"I've been through hostage negotiations before, Ms. McKinley. I think I'm prepared to deal here."

Under other circumstances, Casey would have laughed. This wasn't funny. "What are you going to deal with? This isn't a negotiation. He doesn't want anything from you—any of you. He wants my daughter. He wants to take her apart piece by piece and to hear her screaming while he does it."

"Ms. McKinley, it's my job—"

"Hush, Franklin," Mueller interrupted. "How close are you, McKinley?"

"I'll be there in less than ten minutes."

"Franklin, no one acts until McKinley arrives. When she does, you're under her direction."

"Sir, I think—"

"Franklin, right now, I don't care what you think."

Jordan sped up, taking the corners with screeching tires.

Everyone was silent as they approached the scene. Casey tried to clear her mind and imagine how Leonardo was reacting. He might be pleased that he was gathering so much attention. She was confident he knew who was there. He would have surveillance. She imagined that was how he caught Swain, if that's what happened.

"There's a white Mustang up ahead," Jordan said.

"Turn right at the Mustang. We're positioned about a hundred yards down the driveway," Franklin said.

Jordan turned down the gravel drive, and Casey was out of the car before he had come to a complete stop. Michael was right behind her.

"Franklin?"

A petite black woman stepped forward. "I'm Franklin."

Casey nodded. "Any sign from inside?"

"None so far. We'd like to send some agents to move in closer, but we were waiting for your okay."

Casey shook her head. "No way. The last thing I want to do is to make him feel pressured. If anything, I want you to pull back."

"You think he can see us?" Michael asked.

She met his gaze. "I'd bet on it."

Jordan moved up next to her. "What do you want to do?"

Casey surveyed their surroundings for signs of cameras or microphones. She hated to say too much for fear he might be listening. "I think I need to go in."

There was a rush of negative responses, and Casey could even hear Mueller on the speakerphone, voicing his disapproval.

Michael stepped forward and took her by the shoulders. "No, Casey. That's our daughter in there. We need to let the police handle it. I couldn't lose both of you."

"It's not smart, Casey," Jordan echoed. "You're too involved. Let the Bureau handle it. They've got hostage training."

"This isn't a hostage situation," Casey argued.

"Yes, it is," Franklin said. "Please let us handle it."

Casey shook her head. "I'm going in there alone."

"Casey," Michael and Jordan said at once.

"Stop," she commanded. She had to go in. If she offered herself, at least Amy wouldn't be alone. She wondered whether Swain was still alive. Leonardo would have no purpose for him. Casey pictured Amy having to watch Swain die. She couldn't stay out there and wait. Turning to Jordan, she motioned him to the side. "You have a pocketknife?" she asked in a hushed voice.

"On my key chain."

"I need it."

Jordan watched her. "What are you going to do?"

"I'm going in there."

"With a pocketknife?" Jordan asked.

"That's insane!" Michael said.

"I've got no other choice. You remember the look on Ryan's face when he came back wearing that hat?"

Cringing, Jordan nodded.

"Would you go in after him?"

He paused, then said, "Hell, yes, but I didn't have backup."

"This isn't about backup. Give me your pocket-knife."

Jordan took the knife off his key chain.

"Open it up," she said.

Jordan opened the knife. "What are you going to do with a little pocketknife? You need a gun."

"I can't shoot a gun."

"Then, let someone else go in."

She shook her head. "If anyone else gets close, he'll kill Amy."

Everyone was silent.

"It's true. If I go in, there's a chance I can keep Amy safe." Even if it meant getting herself killed.

Jordan seemed to sink into the ground.

Michael clasped his hands together and stared at the building where his daughter was captive. "Oh, God," he whispered.

"Are you sure?" Jordan said.

Without replying, she nodded.

Jordan handed her the knife.

She pulled her belt out from her pants. "Tuck it flat against my pants under the belt."

"It could stab you," he warned.

"I'll be careful."

Jordan took the knife and placed it flat under the

length of her belt, the blade out to the left. "Can you get it?"

She reached in and felt the blade against her finger. "I'll manage."

"I wish you wouldn't do this," Jordan said.

"I can't let him hurt her."

Michael approached them and took Casey's hands. "For God's sake, Casey. Won't you let them try another way?"

Casey shook her head. "You don't know what he can do."

"Please be careful," Michael said.

Unable to speak, she nodded, wrapping her arms around her husband.

Forcing herself away, Casey turned and headed for the house.

Agent Franklin stepped in her path. "Ms. McKinley, I have to strongly urge that you not go in there. You may jeopardize any ability we have to negotiate for both your daughter and Agent Swain."

Impatient, Casey stepped around Franklin. She remembered being a young agent, too. It was normal to believe there was a chance for negotiation. Only after working with serial offenders did Casey realize that negotiation was not part of the game. "Agent Franklin, consider your advice heard. Thank you."

She turned to Jordan. "If I'm not out in five minutes, send someone in."

He took her shoulder and nodded. "Be careful."

"Ms. McKinley, please."

Casey took a step toward the house, but Franklin caught her arm.

"Do you really think you can do better than a team of hostage negotiators?"

Jordan stepped forward and removed Franklin's arm. "Let her go."

"I just think—"

Casey turned back and stepped into Franklin's face. Trying to stay tough, the young agent didn't step back, though she did appear shocked. "If we waste any more time, it's going to be too late for both of them."

Just then, the sound of a gunshot echoed from inside the house. It was followed by a young girl's scream.

CHAPTER THIRTY-EIGHT

Amy screamed as the FBI agent staggered back and then dropped to the ground. The blood looked like what she'd seen on TV, but Amy knew it wasn't fake. The gun the man had fired was real. The blood that had splattered from the FBI agent's chest was real. She could feel it, sticky and warm on her arms. Oh, God, she couldn't look. She was going to throw up. Someone help her, please.

Amy closed her eyes, trying to fight off her panic. She shifted, struggling against the tape that held her arms to the chair.

"Don't worry," the crazy man said. "You'll be moving soon enough."

The expression on his face made her shiver. She looked at the man groaning on the floor. She was next. He was going to kill her next. "Oh, God." She fought to loosen the tape.

"I'll be moving you to the operating table in just a minute."

Amy fought back her tears, but it was too much. She was so afraid. All the stories her mother had told her about what happened to innocent kids. She didn't want to die. Fight, her mother would have told her. Scream and kick and fight.

The crazy man started to walk toward her, and she was ready to kick him when he was close enough. Just out of her reach, he stopped at the sound of a soft alarm.

"Looks like our company's coming in for a closer look." He moved away and flipped on what looked like an ancient computer monitor. Amy saw her mother on the screen. "Mom!" she screamed. "He can see you!"

The crazy man whipped around. "Silence!"

Amy kicked hard, hitting his knee and knocking him backward. She thought he might fall, but instead he lunged back at her, hitting her hard across the mouth.

Stunned, Amy felt the warm blood drip into her mouth, the copper taste familiar on her tongue. "Please, Mom," she whispered. "Please help me."

"Leonardo," her mother's voice called from outside. "Or is it George Allister, or Roy McAllister?"

Amy started to sob at the sound of her mother's voice. Thank God. Thank God she was there to save her. "Mom," she choked. "Mom, hurry."

Leonardo smiled, and Amy prayed he wouldn't shoot her mother. Her heart racing, she closed her mouth and prayed.

Taking his gun off the table, he pointed it at her head.

Amy whimpered.

"Tell your mom what I'm doing."

Amy shook her head.

Leonardo brought the gun around the back of her head and hit her with it. Knocked forward, Amy felt a rush of heat and then suddenly she was light-headed.

"Do it," he repeated.

"Mom," she said.

"Amy, honey, is that you?"

Nodding, Amy started to cry harder.

"Talk to her," he demanded.

"Mom! Help me."

"Leonardo, why don't you let me in?" her mom called.

"How do I know you're alone, Mac?"

Amy prayed her mother wasn't alone. She wouldn't have come alone. Amy hoped there were a hundred people outside, all waiting to shoot the crazy man.

"You've got Amy, Leonardo. How stupid do you think I am?"

He smiled. "I've got my gun pressed to her head right now. I really don't have time to chat, though. Amy and I have some plans."

Tears ran down Amy's cheeks. She could feel the barrel of the gun press against the spot where he'd hit her. It hurt, and she wanted to rub it.

"Why don't you let her go, and I'll come join you?"

"I don't think so, Mac. This is all about Amy."

"I thought it was about me. You don't want me instead? I'm too big for you? I guess you're not as good as I remember. Getting tired?"

He flashed an angry smile. "You're predictable, Agent McKinley—or should I say ex-Agent. Our last meeting really changed your life, didn't it? You can join us if you like. I always intended to share this final masterpiece with you."

Unable to turn in her chair, Amy could hear the doorknob turn, and a ray of light shone across the room.

"Good to see you. You look surprisingly well. Please stay where you are."

The gun butted up against the bruise on Amy's head, and she winced in pain.

"Close the door behind you and move this way slowly. Move too fast, and I'll have to leave you with your other FBI friend."

Amy struggled to see her mother, but tied to the chair, she couldn't turn around. "Mom."

"I'm here, baby."

Her mom came into her view, and Amy began to sob again.

Casey stood beside her and, hands in the air, gave Amy a kiss on the cheek. "Trust Mommy," she whispered. "You're going to be okay."

Amy sucked in her breath and nodded.

"That's Mommy's girl." Turning back to the man, Casey kept her arms up and walked to the FBI agent.

She knelt beside him.

"McKinley," he whispered, and Amy was surprised he wasn't dead. Maybe he could still help them. "I'm so sorry," he gasped. "I did everything right in Cincy. Purcell told me it wasn't my fault."

"I believe you, Rick," Casey answered, shaken. "I'm sorry, too."

Amy didn't understand what they were talking about.

Swain whispered something else, and then he was quiet.

Casey stood and wiped blood on her pants.

Amy gasped and started to cry again.

Casey gave her a look as if to tell her it was okay, but Amy didn't think it was. It didn't feel okay.

"Where would you like me to sit?" Casey asked.

Stopping her, the man patted down her back and chest, and down her legs.

"No gun, no wires," she said.

He nodded quickly. "So it seems."

Amy didn't understand who was going to save them if her mom didn't even have a gun. Shaking, she just tried to stop crying like a baby.

The man motioned to another chair, and Casey sat. "So, Kevin—shall I call you that? Or is it still the Butcher?"

"It's always been Leonardo, Mac. We both know I'm that good."

Casey shrugged. "Did you arrange to have Billy killed, Leonardo?"

He smiled. "No. That opportunistic infection was convenient, though, wasn't it?" Holding the gun in one hand, he started to tape her down. "I am surprised you found me," he said. "Pleasantly surprised, though. Amy's going to be so good, it would be a shame not to share her."

Amy shivered.

Casey looked at her and gave her the okay sign. Then she turned back to Leonardo. "What about Kevin Wrigley? I ran a background check, and he checked out."

Leonardo smiled. "He would. He's a real person, someone who worked in the building where I did. We looked a bit alike. I just got hold of some of his business cards."

"Did you watch the cops come to the scenes?" Casey asked.

The man laughed. "No, I didn't need to. I could imagine the little circles I had the police running in. But I read the papers and watched the news. It's all very entertaining."

"You thought you'd be allowed to continue, that we wouldn't catch you?"

"I've got you and Amy, don't I? I'm not worried

about your troops out there because it doesn't matter
to me if this is the end." He laughed. "This will make
every newspaper in the country. Everyone will realize
my talent. This may be my last work of art, but it will
also be my masterpiece."

Amy closed her eyes and tried to block out the
sound.

"As long as you feel that way, Leonardo. 'Cause
you're not getting out of here alive."

He finished taping Casey's legs. Standing, he winked
at Amy. "That's okay—neither are the two of you."

Amy panicked. If her mom was taped down, how
would they get away? Why didn't her mother look
worried? Was she crazy now, too?

"You didn't tape her legs, I notice," her mom said,
motioning to Amy. "Getting sloppy."

Leonardo looked back at Amy, and she gasped,
struggling to stay calm. Why did her mom say that?
Amy saw her mother's hands move, but she couldn't
tell what she was doing.

"She's got quite a kick, doesn't she?" Casey said,
smiling at Amy.

Amy tried to smile back, but she was too scared.

Leonardo taped down Casey's arms without saying
anything. Then, turning his attention back to Amy, he
set his gun down and brought the tape over. Starting
from behind her, he taped her legs to the chair.

Amy watched Casey, trying to understand what was
going on. Her mother wasn't acting normally. Maybe
she wanted to die. She'd come with no gun, and now
he was going to kill them both. Amy struggled against
the tape, trying to free a leg so that she could kick.
Where was her dad?

Leonardo stood up and faced her, looking pleased
with his work. He picked up a thin knife from the

table. It was the kind doctors worked with, but she couldn't remember the name. He touched the blade to his thumb and drew blood, lapping it up with a long, disgusting tongue.

Amy closed her eyes and screamed.

He took hold of her face and shook it. "You have to pay attention now. This is important."

She watched, terrified as he brought the knife toward her and then gave her a terrible, scary smile. "This will only hurt a lot."

Amy screamed again. "Mom!"

Her mother cried out.

But the man didn't look at her mother. Instead, he brought the knife down beside her eye, and she could feel the knife pressed to her skin.

Amy pulled away, struggling to work free, to escape.

"We're going to work on your eye today," he explained, sounding calm and reassuring like a normal doctor. "Something new for both of us, I'm sure. There are a series of muscles connecting the eye to the surrounding tissue—rectus muscles above and below the eye. Once we detach those, if you're still with us, we'll hit the optic nerve. We're going to have to be careful, though, lest we hit the central artery of the retina. So, be sure to sit still."

The blade came into Amy's view and approached her eye. She squeezed her eyes shut and felt the stabbing pain as the knife struck the skin at her eyelid. "Mom! Help me!"

CHAPTER THIRTY-NINE

Tears streaming through her line of vision, Casey struggled with the pocketknife she had stashed under her hand when Leonardo looked away. She needed to cut through the tape and then get to Leonardo's gun. She'd known Leonardo used tape from the other crime scenes. Had he switched to rope or something heavier, her plan would have failed. The little knife was her only shot.

She was almost through half of the tape on the first arm, but he was hurting Amy. Her fingers shook as she struggled to push the knife through the tape. The knife slipped and started to fall from her fingers, but she caught it, the blade stabbing into her palm. Ignoring the blood coming from the small wound, she turned the knife back to the tape.

Her mind raced across the events of the past weeks. Why hadn't she recognized Kevin's voice? It was as though the drugs that night had somehow warped her brain and his voice became a deep, haunting whisper. But it was real enough now. And now he was hurting Amy. Her own pain came rushing back at her. People always think you can eventually block it out, but you can't. It was there as clearly as the moment he'd cut open her hand. Focus, she told herself, as she carved through the tape.

Her hands shaking, adrenaline began to take over and she broke her way through the first tie. With one arm free, she maneuvered the knife more easily, working desperately, praying that Leonardo wouldn't turn around.

From the corner of her eye, she saw red soaking into Amy's shirt. Her daughter's blood being spilled by this monster. Amy's screams echoed again and again in her mind. Hadn't five minutes passed? Where the hell was Jordan?

The second tie began to loosen as Casey heard Amy let out another horrible scream. Sobbing, she commanded herself to cut faster. Her hands cramped, but she sawed as fast as she could.

"I've only barely touched you," Leonardo protested. "Not even to anything exciting yet."

With most of the tape cut away, Casey ripped her arm free, then sawed though the tape on her legs until she could tear herself free. Fighting to contain her anger, she waited until Leonardo lifted his scalpel and then lunged at him, stabbing the pocketknife into the fleshy space between his spine and his shoulder bone.

"Bitch," he cursed.

He yanked the knife from his shoulder and clutched at the open wound. "Amy's going to pay for that reckless maneuver first. I think a few severed nerves will teach a mother to behave." He turned to Amy and smiled.

Amy whimpered.

Casey turned and leapt for his gun.

Before she could get there, though, Leonardo pushed her, knocking her out of the way.

She fell hard back against the bookcase and slammed her head against one wall. The pain flashed in her head, and she fought the grogginess that came with it.

She saw Leonardo stoop to the floor. He came up holding the gun, pointing it at her. "You shouldn't have done that, Mac. I would have preferred to keep you alive a while longer."

Casey struggled to get her bearings, searching for a way out. He had the gun. Her only weapon had been the pocketknife, and it was gone. Her one chance spent.

Amy's gaze pleaded at her to do something.

Casey tried to think, to form a plan.

Leonardo aimed the gun at her. "Good-bye, Agent Mac," he said.

Casey held her hand out as she heard the pop pop of two gunshots. She was knocked backward by a heavy weight, and her head slammed into a table behind her. She shook her head and tried to open her eyes. She was dead.

Amy screamed.

Casey felt the warmth of blood and forced her eyes open. Strangely, she didn't feel any pain. As her vision cleared, she saw Rick Swain lying in front of her, two gunshot wounds to his chest. She blinked and touched her chest. She wasn't dead. Swain had saved her.

Leonardo pointed the gun again and pulled the trigger. It was silent. "Damn it." He turned to reload, then moved toward Casey. She felt Swain's ankle holster against her leg and started to reach for the gun.

Amy let out a scream and jabbed an elbow out, knocking the gun from Leonardo's hand. He turned and slapped her in return.

Knowing he would only be distracted a moment,

Casey lifted Swain's pant leg with one hand and felt the gun. It was small, probably a .22, perfect—if only she could shoot it.

"Up, Mac."

Casey bent over, pretending to get to her knees. Pulling the gun out of the holster, she gripped it in her left hand and stood. With a step forward, she pointed it at Leonardo and prayed to heaven that she had the strength to pull the trigger.

Amy started to cry harder, fighting at the tape on her wrists and ankles.

Spotting the gun, Leonardo started to reach for another weapon. "But you can't shoot—"

"Want to bet?" Casey steadied the gun with two hands and fired twice into Leonardo's chest.

Leonardo dropped to the ground with a low thud, and it was all Casey could do to get to Amy and wrap her arms around her as they both cried. She saw the purple birthday hat sitting on the counter, and thanked God it had never made it to Amy's head.

"Oh, God, Mom. I thought he killed you. I thought you were dead," Amy sobbed.

Tears streaked her own cheeks. "I'm okay, baby, everything's okay."

"He was so scary."

"I know, but he's gone now. He can't hurt us ever again." Casey exhaled, holding her daughter tight. "It's over now," she said, as much for her own benefit as for Amy's.

Just then the door burst open, and a hundred people seemed to fill the room. Casey only cried harder. It was finally over.

EPILOGUE

Two months later

Casey put the vase down on the mound of fresh grass and fiddled with the yellow roses until they were spread out in perfect order. She turned her face toward the sky and felt the warm sun on her skin. It was perfect weather. Clear, blue, with the slightest wind that made the sun feel warm rather than hot. Fat cumulus clouds looked down like cherubs as Casey stood over Billy's grave.

She wiped off the top of the gravestone and read the familiar inscription. "William D. Glass, 1962–2000. Loving friend. You will be deeply missed."

She stood and brushed the dirt off her hands. "He always loved yellow roses." She straightened the sleeves on her button-down and smiled. Billy would've been proud. Ten buttons including the sleeves, and she'd done them in under four minutes. She turned and looked up at Jordan.

He gave her a sad smile.

Putting her arm through his, Casey kissed Jordan's cheek as they started to walk back down toward the car. "I talked to Nina Rodriguez."

"Yeah? What'd she say?" Jordan asked.

"She sounded so relieved. You could tell she'd been living in fear since her attack." Casey thought a minute. "I guess I wanted her to know firsthand that it was over. I know how fear can take control of your life."

Jordan pulled her toward him and gave her a hug.

After a moment Casey stepped back and punched his arm playfully. "The newspapers sure did cover it. Did you see that big picture of you on the cover of the *Chronicle*?"

Jordan stopped and crooked an eyebrow. "You mean the one where I'm standing next to you?"

Casey grinned. "Great picture, eh?"

Jordan smiled. "We made a pretty good team."

"True," she agreed. "Let's hope we never have to do it again."

"I'm all for that."

They started walking again. "How are the boys?" Casey asked.

"Settling back in up here. Everyone seems happier so far."

"You really considering the job out in Contra Costa County?"

Jordan looked over at her. "Hard to believe?"

"Smarter than I would've imagined, actually."

Jordan laughed. "I'll have to give Angie the credit for that one. She wants to see more of her husband. And the captain said he'll welcome me back if I change my mind down the road." He paused and looked down at her. "What about you? You going back to the Bureau?"

She shrugged. "Haven't given it much thought yet. I'm going to head back to Virginia for a while, see how that goes. I'm not sure what'll happen with me and Michael, but I'd like to spend some time with Amy."

"She's a great kid. How's she doing?"

Casey nodded. "Better every day, I think. The cuts were fairly superficial. It's the fear that's hardest to repair." She looked up at Jordan. "But I know all about that."

"I'm sure she'd love to spend some time with her mother."

Casey nodded. "I'm looking forward to it. Taking everything one step at a time." She opened the car door and unlocked the opposite side for Jordan. "Where do you want to go for lunch?"

"How about Crogan's for burgers?" he suggested, getting into the car.

She remembered the lunch she'd had with Billy a few days before he died. Sitting in the driver's seat, Casey started the engine and put the car in first gear. "Crogan's it is."